DAVID HOUGHLAND

Vireona Publishing

DEDICATION

To Suzy

FAÇADE

Act I
Captivity

CHAPTER 1

PRESENT DAY

THE BLACK CADILLAC GLIDED along Highway 190, outside D.C. Its wheels whispered over rain-slicked asphalt. Thick woods flanked the winding road, their shadows clawing at the edges of the dim moonlight. Headlights flickered across rusted road signs and mile markers. The engine purred, drowning out the distant hum of another car.

Evelyn Parker's eyes fluttered open to pitch blackness. The stench of gasoline filled her nostrils, mingling with stale air. Pain radiated through her body—sharp, unfamiliar. She tried to move; agony shot through her limbs like lightning. She lay still, her mind a fog. Where am I?

The car lurched, slamming her against the metal walls of the trunk. A wave of panic surged through her, adrenaline cutting through the haze. She pressed her hands against the rough carpet. It was cold, unyielding metal beneath. She pushed hard against the lid, but it didn't budge. Trapped.

The air was thick and stifling, making her chest tighten with every shallow breath. Her heartbeat thundered in her ears, echoing in the oppressive silence. She tried to scream, but her voice was a whisper, lost in the darkness.

She felt the rumble of the engine, the vibration passing through her bones. Each bump sent fresh waves of nausea rolling through her. Absolute darkness pressed in from all sides. Her fingers clawed at the rough lining, searching for a seam, a weakness—anything.

Time seemed endless, each minute dragging on. Evelyn's thoughts tumbled, fear and fractured memories swirling together in a disorienting blur. How did I end up here? She pictured her apartment, her living room. There was a knock at the door—a face she couldn't quite place—and then … nothing.

The car swerved, tossing her to the side. Stay calm, stay calm, she told herself, struggling to control her breathing. Memories flashed through her mind. It was the day of her first promotion. She felt pride. Her friends celebrated with her. Something to anchor her, to hold on to.

Then a sharper thought stabbed through the haze. Max. Her golden retriever. Max, loyal and loving, was with her through every tough moment. He was always by her side, offering silent comfort. He was her constant companion. He warmed her on lonely nights. He always made her smile, even on the worst days. Who will feed him? Who will let him out? The thought of him alone, confused, waiting for her—it was almost unbearable.

1

Irrational as it seemed, the worry gnawed at her, twisting her insides.

The car's movements grew more erratic, each turn more violent than the last. Her body throbbed with pain. The restraints on her wrists and ankles chafed her skin. Her muscles ached from the cramped space. She forced herself to take steady breaths, fighting the panic rising in her chest.

The car jolted as it hit a pothole, her teeth snapping together. The sharpness grounding her in the moment, reminding her she was still alive and had to fight. She clenched her jaw, focusing on the pain, letting it fuel her determination to survive. Focus. She couldn't afford to lose herself to fear. She needed to think, to listen. Somewhere, there had to be a way out.

She strained her ears, trying to pick up any sound beyond the roar of the engine, but there was almost nothing. A distant echo—another vehicle or the wind—and her heartbeat, a drumbeat of terror. The darkness pressed in, squeezing the air from her lungs. She thought of her family—her parents, their reassuring voices, telling her to stay strong. She imagined Max, his big brown eyes, his trust in her. The thought of him alone gave her strength. She had to survive. She had to get back to him.

The car slowed, and her heart skipped a beat. Was this it? The end of the ride? She tensed, muscles coiled, bracing for whatever was to come. The car came to a stop, and Evelyn heard footsteps crunching on gravel. Her breath caught in her throat as the trunk lid opened, blinding her with sudden, searing light. A figure loomed above her, and she tried to scream, but terror had stolen her voice.

Rough hands grabbed her, dragging her from the trunk. The cold night air bit into her skin, a stark contrast to the stifling heat inside. Before she could react, a cloth pressed against her face. The sickly-sweet scent invaded her senses. Her thoughts blurred, the world dissolving into blackness. The last thing she saw was the date circled on her calendar: August 23rd. She had a doctor's appointment that afternoon—after coffee with her friend Alex. Alex would realize something was wrong. Someone would come looking for her. She had to hold onto that hope as everything went dark.

CHAPTER 2

SPRING 1969

THE BOY WAS SEVEN, growing up in a household shaped by two very different parents. His father, 25 years older than his mother, demanded silence with his severe presence. Deep lines etched his face. His cold, calculating eyes and hollowed cheeks gave him a skeletal, forbidding look. His slicked-back, graying hair framed a gaze. It spoke of control over compassion, strength over empathy.

In stark contrast, his mother, Elizabeth, was a gentle force. Her green eyes were warm and strong, a softness that balanced Arthur's cold intensity. Light freckles dotted her cheeks. Her chestnut waves framed a serene expression. It brought calm wherever she went. Where Arthur commanded silence, Elizabeth radiated comfort. With her, the boy was safe and loved. Even at her most vulnerable, her warmth was a steady light. Arthur's hardness never dimmed.

The mother's love wrapped around him like a cocoon, an armor against the world's harshness. In her embrace, he found a rare sanctuary. It sheltered him from all beyond their walls.

"Mom?" One evening, the boy's small voice broke the room's quiet. His eyes, wide with wonder, were those that only children can have. "Do you think there are really dragons out there?"

Elizabeth smiled, her fingers brushing through his hair. "Oh, my love, there are dragons everywhere. But not all are bad," she said, her eyes sparkling. "Some are only misunderstood. And some," she said, leaning closer and whispering, "just need a brave soul to show them kindness."

The boy's eyes grew even wider. "Would you be brave enough?"

"For you, sweetie? I'd face any dragon," Elizabeth replied, her voice filled with warmth. She hugged him closer, her embrace making the monsters in the corners of the room fade away. "But remember, you have that bravery too. One day, you'll see."

Laughter echoed in the hallways, and stories spun. They held back the shadows creeping in. His mother's gentle reassurances made monsters vanish.

Elizabeth had a natural, ethereal grace, moving like she was part of a dream that he never wanted to end. Her voice possessed a kind of magic, gentle and nearly otherworldly. To him, she was not his mother; she was a

3

guardian angel, a fairy straight from the bedtime stories she spun.

"Tell me about the brave knight again," the boy pleaded, his voice muffled as he snuggled closer.

Elizabeth smiled, her eyes softening as she looked down at him. "Ah, the brave knight," she began, her voice taking on that familiar lilting tone. "He was not the biggest or the strongest, but he had the most courage. True bravery isn't about looking strong. It's about doing what's right, even when you're scared."

The boy looked up at her, his small face serious. "Like you?"

Elizabeth's breath caught for a moment, her eyes misting. She kissed the top of his head. "Yes, my love. Just like that."

They would curl up in the worn-out armchair. Her presence wrapped around him like a lullaby. Her voice painted vivid pictures. It created castles, dragons, and heroes who overcame the impossible. In those moments, the world shrank to him and her, safe in that small bubble of warmth. It was as if the universe had folded in on itself. It gave them precious alone time, away from everything else.

One of the boy's favorite memories was baking with his mother. The kitchen, once a place of stern rules under Arthur, softened under her touch. Elizabeth would lift him onto a chair beside her, rolling out cookie dough with a gentle smile. She guided his tiny hands through the motions, her voice warm with encouragement.

The air filled with the scent of vanilla and sugar. For those hours, it was his own little kingdom. Elizabeth let him shape the cookies however he liked. Lopsided stars and odd blobs filled the flour-dusted table. She praised every effort. It was never about perfection; it was about being together. Her laughter rang out like a bell when flour dusted his nose, her hand moving to wipe it away.

In the afternoons, they often went for walks. Elizabeth loved the gardens behind their house. She taught him to see the small things: the petals of a flower, a sunset's colors, and the wind on their faces. They would sit on a weathered bench. She would tell him stories of her childhood, the places she'd seen, and her dreams before she settled down. At times, her voice turned wistful, her gaze distant, as if she longed for another world. But when she looked at him, her smile brightened, and that longing disappeared. To the boy, those moments were magic. He and his mother, bathed in sunlight, seemed untethered from time.

Elizabeth had a way of making him feel more than a child; she made him feel important, capable, and loved. She nurtured his curiosity about the world and his sense of wonder. When he was afraid, she was always there to reassure him, to let him see it was okay to be sad, to feel. When he scraped his knee, she knelt beside him, wiping his tears and whispering that it was all right. Pain was part of growing up, and it would pass. With her, he was safe. She taught him that, even though the world was daunting, it was also full of love.

But in the spring of 1969, the illness came. At first, it seemed like a cold. His mother would cough, then she'd smile and reassure him it was nothing to worry about. But the cough didn't go away, and Elizabeth grew tired. The walks they loved so much became shorter, and her laughter came less often. Some days, she would sit in her chair, pale and worn. She smiled at him, trying to protect him from a truth she couldn't deny.

As weeks went by, her condition worsened. The cough deepened, turning into fits that left her breathless and exhausted. The boy would watch as she struggled to catch her breath, her face growing paler each day. She began spending more time in bed, her once vibrant energy fading. Her hands, which used to be so warm and full of life, became frail and cold, trembling when she tried to hold the boy close. He sensed, even as a child, that something terrible was happening. The strong, nurturing figure he had known seemed to be slipping away.

Elizabeth tried to keep things normal, but her strength was fading. She forced a smile when he entered the room, hiding her pain, though the strain was clear. The baking stopped, the walks ended, even reading stories became too much. Her voice was too weak to carry the words, so he took over. He would sit beside her, reading her favorite books, hoping to comfort her as she had always comforted him. Tears would glisten in her eyes, and she would whisper, "I'm proud of you," her voice still full of love.

Near the end, his mother could no longer leave her bed. She spent her days under heavy blankets. She labored to breathe. Her eyes were often closed, as if opening them required too much energy. The boy would sit by her side, holding her hand, feeling the frailty of her fingers in his small grip. She would whisper to him. She loved him. He must be brave. He must remember the world's beauty, even in the dark. He clung to her few words, filled with a deep, abiding love, even as he watched the life leave her eyes.

Arthur reacted to Elizabeth's illness with frustration and denial. He refused to see how bad things were, insisting she'd recover if she pushed herself harder. He berated her for resting, his voice cold and full of irritation. Her weakened state seemed to infuriate him, as if her illness was a personal affront. He grew distant, spending long hours away from home, leaving Elizabeth and the boy alone. When he was home, the tension was palpable, the air thick with unspoken resentment. The boy sensed his father's anger, though he didn't understand it. To Arthur, sickness was weakness, and he had no patience for it. But Elizabeth's condition only worsened.

After Elizabeth's death, Arthur's behavior grew abusive. The verbal abuse was relentless. Arthur would call him useless, weak, and a burden. He blamed the boy for Elizabeth's death. He said that if he hadn't needed so much care, Elizabeth would have had the strength to fight her illness. These words cut into him, he internalized the blame, the guilt settling in his young heart. Arthur's cruelty was not only about control. It was to break the boy's spirit. He wanted the boy to know he was nothing without his father's

5

approval, which would never come.

Arthur also used isolation to control. He forbade the boy to play with other children. He insisted he had no time for such foolishness. He kept him busy with endless chores, making sure the boy was too exhausted to think about anything else. When the boy tried to cling to his happy memories of his mother, Arthur would sneer. He dismissed Elizabeth's gentleness as weakness. He said love made people soft and vulnerable. He demanded that the boy toughen up, that he learn to face the world without emotion, without weakness.

The house, once filled with Elizabeth's warmth, became a place of cold fear. The boy would tiptoe around his father, trying to avoid being noticed. Any mistake might set Arthur off. The magical stories, the warmth of baking, the garden walks—they were his memories. They sustained him against the darkness that followed. They reminded him of a love that once made the world feel beautiful. But as the months passed, those memories faded. The harsh reality of life with Arthur replaced them. Fear replaced love, and safety existed only in dreams.

The boy felt fear, guilt, and a deep longing for lost love in response to Arthur's abuse. At first, he tried to win Arthur's approval. He thought that if he worked hard enough, his father would soften. His small hands were raw from scrubbing floors and tending the yard. He would spend hours doing the chores Arthur assigned. He would stay silent and suppress his tears whenever Arthur yelled or struck him. He hoped that showing strength might change his father's mind. But no matter how much he tried, nothing was ever good enough.

The constant barrage of insults and physical punishment wore the boy down. The hope of gaining his father's love began to wither. He stopped trying to earn Arthur's approval and instead focused on survival. He learned to be invisible, to blend into the background. He moved and avoided eye contact, anything to prevent Arthur's attention. He spoke less. Fear and exhaustion dulled his once-curious, imaginative spirit. The world his mother had once made beautiful now seemed bleak and unforgiving.

The isolation Arthur imposed on him only deepened the boy's loneliness. Without friends or a supporter, his world became one of silence and obedience. He learned to expect Arthur's moods, to sense the tension in the air, and to respond. His once-bright eyes grew guarded, and his laughter disappeared. A constant state of vigilance replaced the joys of childhood. He always prepared for the next outburst.

Yet, somewhere deep inside, a small part of the boy resisted. It was the part of him that clung to his mother's memory, that refused to let go of the love she had given him. That tiny spark kept him going. It kept him from succumbing to the darkness Arthur tried to impose on him. Though he was battered in spirit, he wasn't broken. A part of the boy remembered that someone loved him. That memory gave him the strength to endure, even when each day was like a losing battle.

CHAPTER 3

NOVEMBER 1969

THE BOY'S WORLD had changed forever after his mother passed. The warmth, light, and love she brought into their home had vanished. Only cold emptiness remained. The house was the same, but it felt different—hollow. The shadows in every corner had swallowed the echoes of laughter. The boy was alone with the quiet and his father, Arthur, who seemed to grow colder with each passing day.

The boy had learned that Arthur's grief turned to rage. It was a rage fueled by a sense of helplessness and loss. He could neither understand nor control it. This rage often found its target in the boy. Arthur needed to blame something for the emptiness that had consumed his life.

"Why can't you stay out of my way?" Arthur would bellow, his voice echoing through the empty halls. The boy would stand there, head down, trying to make himself as small as possible.

"I'm sorry," the boy whispered, his voice trembling.

Arthur would glare at him, his eyes filled with a mixture of pain and anger. "Sorry won't bring her back," he'd mutter, turning away. The boy was even smaller and more powerless. It wasn't the yelling or harsh words. It was his father's look. He reminded him of all that he had lost. As if the boy was the reason his mother had grown sick and faded away. The boy felt the weight of that blame every day, even though he couldn't understand it. He was small, powerless, like a leaf tossed in the wind with no control over where he landed.

But there was one thing the boy could control: himself. He couldn't control Arthur's anger or his father's cold eyes. But he could control his own actions and thoughts. He learned to move in silence, aiming to become completely invisible. He would tiptoe around the house, head down. He avoided anything that might draw his father's attention. If Arthur was in one room, the boy would slip into another. If his father spoke, the boy answered, never raising his voice above a whisper.

He found solace in routine. The chores Arthur assigned became his lifeline, a way to bring order to the chaos his life had become. Scrubbing the floors until they shined was like washing away the grime of his fears. Polishing the furniture let him see his reflection. It was a reminder that he still existed, that he had form and substance. Stacking firewood gave him purpose; the weight of each log was solid, grounding. With nothing else left, he found control in the clean floors, the neat stacks of wood, and the folded laundry. They were the only things that made sense.

At night, after Arthur's anger had faded and the house fell silent, the boy would retreat to his room. He'd pull out his mother's old storybook, its cover faded, its pages worn. She used to read it to him. Now, he couldn't read it aloud; his voice would catch, the words too painful. Instead, he traced the illustrations with his fingers. He remembered her voice and the warmth of her presence. In those quiet moments, he pretended—pretended she was in the other room, waiting to tuck him in.

In these quiet moments, alone in his room, the boy found a new way to cope. He began to imagine himself as someone else—someone brave, someone strong. He became the knight from his mother's stories. He faced dragons and protected the helpless. In his daydreams, he was no longer small or powerless. He was fearless, standing tall against monsters that looked a lot like his father.

He created worlds in his mind, places where he wasn't afraid. He was in control. He was the hero. In one world, he was a knight. He defended a kingdom from a fierce dragon. The villagers cheered as he stood, victorious. In another, he was an explorer, crossing uncharted lands and discovering hidden treasures. These worlds were vivid and alive. In them, he was brave and strong. In them, he rewrote his own story.

The boy found small, secret ways to assert himself. He did tiny acts of rebellion that Arthur would never notice. He would leave a corner of the bedsheet untucked, or hide a toy beneath his pillow, something that was his. They were small things. But they gave him a sense of power. They reminded him that, in a world controlled by others, some parts of himself still belonged to him. It wasn't much, but it was enough to keep that tiny spark of resistance alive.

CHAPTER 4

OCTOBER 1972

IT WAS MID-OCTOBER, the leaves had turned golden and crisp, and the air had a chill that signaled the arrival of fall. The boy, now ten, walked the school halls, hunched. He tried to make himself as small as possible. It was another day of fifth grade. But, for him, it was another day of nursing wounds his father, Arthur, had inflicted.

He adjusted his book strap. It pressed against a fresh bruise on his shoulder. The bruises were constant, hidden beneath long sleeves and careful movements. Arthur had a way of ensuring that his discipline left invisible marks.

One teacher, Ms. Stevens, had noticed. She had seen the boy come to class with injuries. He had bruises, a slight limp, and a hand that ached too much for a ten-year-old. She was a kind woman, with a soft voice and a gentle manner that made her students feel safe. But her concern for the boy grew with each passing day.

After class one afternoon, Ms. Stevens asked him to stay behind. He shifted, his heart pounding in his chest.

"How are you today?" she asked, her eyes searching his face for any signs of distress.

"I'm fine," he replied, avoiding her gaze.

"Are you sure? I notice you often have bruises or seem to be in pain. Is everything okay at home?"

He hesitated, the fear of his father's wrath making it hard to speak. "I'm fine," he mumbled again.

Ms. Stevens wasn't convinced. She persisted, "If you ever need help, you can tell me. I want you to be safe."

The boy's eyes darted around the room, panic rising. He couldn't tell her the truth. Arthur had made sure he understood what would happen if he ever spoke out. But Ms. Stevens's kind words and concern stuck with him, leaving a glimmer of hope that he didn't know he had.

Ms. Stevens gathered enough courage to report her suspicions. She contacted the authorities. She described the injuries and feared that the boy's father might be abusing him.

The police began an investigation, but Arthur's wealth and influence proved formidable. He met with the local detective. They exchanged money and made promises. The case, like so many others involving the powerful,

9

disappeared without a trace.

One day, as school ended, students packed to go home. Arthur then appeared at the school. He was a tall, imposing man, and his presence alone was enough to send a shiver down the boy's spine. As the boy stepped out of Ms. Stevens's classroom, Arthur was there, blocking his way.

"Come with me," Arthur said, his voice low and threatening. He motioned for the boy to go back into the classroom.

Ms. Stevens looked up, startled to see Arthur standing in her doorway. "Can I help you?" she asked, her voice wavering.

Arthur's eyes were cold as he stepped into the room, closing the door behind him. "Yes, you can," he said, his tone icy. "You can mind your own business."

Ms. Stevens's eyes widened, a mixture of fear and confusion crossing her face. "I'm concerned for your son. He seems hurt often."

Arthur stepped closer, his presence menacing. "You don't understand who you're dealing with. I can make your life very difficult if you continue to interfere."

Ms. Stevens stood her ground, her concern for the boy outweighing her fear. "I'm trying to help."

Arthur's lips curled into a sinister smile. "Help? You think you can help? Let me show you what help looks like."

He began to speak, detailing the ways he might ruin her career. "I have friends on the school board. A few well-placed words can get you fired for incompetence. I can fabricate complaints from parents, make it look like you're unfit to teach."

Ms. Stevens's face paled, but Arthur wasn't finished. "I know people in the community, influential people. It would be so easy to spread rumors. Imagine trying to get another teaching job with a reputation for . . . inappropriate behavior with students. People will believe what they're told, especially if it's scandalous."

Her eyes filled with terror, but Arthur's voice grew colder. "And if that doesn't scare you, think about your personal life. I know where you live. I can make sure you never feel safe in your own home. Accidents happen all the time—someone can tamper with cars, and someone can break into houses."

The boy watched in silent horror as Arthur terrorized Ms. Stevens. Every word, every threat was a calculated blow, stripping away her courage piece by piece. He saw her resolve crumble, her hands shaking, eyes welling with tears. Arthur had painted a vivid picture of a nightmare that would leave anyone trembling.

But as terrifying as it was, the boy felt something else stir within him. A twisted sense of pride. This was power. This was what money and influence did. His father was untouchable, and he was learning how far that reach extended. It was a dark, uncomfortable thought. But it also filled him with a twisted admiration for the man who controlled so much with his words.

Ms. Stevens nodded, too terrified to speak. The cold, calculating look in

Arthur's eyes told her everything she needed to understand. She had crossed a line, and now she was paying the price.

The next Monday, Ms. Stevens was gone. A substitute teacher stood in for her. She fumbled with the lesson plan and tried to restore order. The boy had a pang of guilt and loss, knowing that Ms. Stevens had tried to help him and suffered for it. He sat at his desk. A hidden bruise on his shoulder throbbed, a reminder of Arthur's power over him and anyone who cared.

CHAPTER 5

JUNE 1975

IT WAS A WARM summer evening. The boy sat alone on the porch steps of his father's vast estate. His fingers traced the weathered wood, as if searching for answers. He tried to nurse his left ear, which still rang from the blow his father had delivered only fifteen minutes ago. The evening air was thick with the scent of pine and rain. A heavy silence broke only by distant thunder.

It had started as a typical Saturday morning. He had been in the kitchen, pouring himself a bowl of cereal. His father, Arthur, had been reading the newspaper at the table. His eyes flicked up to check his every move. The tension in the room was palpable, a constant undercurrent in their interactions.

He had reached for the milk. His mind wandered to the latest comic he had under his bed. Distracted, he poured the milk into the bowl. His hand wavered, splashing a few drops onto the pristine countertop. He froze, the white droplets stark against the dark granite. He knew, at once, that he had made a mistake.

Arthur's newspaper rustled as he set it down with deliberate slowness. He rose from his chair, the wooden legs scraping against the tile floor, a sound that made his heart race. Arthur's face was a mask of controlled fury, his eyes cold and unyielding.

"What have I told you?" Arthur said, his voice a low growl. "Only the best will do."

That phrase, "only the best will do," was a mantra in their household. Arthur wielded it like a weapon, an ever-present reminder of his unforgiving standards. He used it whenever his son fell short, which was often. A B plus on a math test, a missed spot while mowing the lawn, or a crooked tie always led to punishment. Those five words always preceded it.

His stomach churned with a familiar dread whenever he heard it. It made his world shrink. It trapped him in a bubble of fear and expectation. He knew what would come next: the sting of his father's disapproval, often followed by a beating. No matter how minor the infraction, Arthur's response was the same. It was always swift, harsh, and uncompromising.

"I'm sorry. It was an accident. I'll clean it up," he stammered.

But Arthur was already beside him, the towering figure casting a long shadow over the boy. "An accident," he repeated, his voice dripping with

12

contempt. "There are no accidents in this house. There is only carelessness."

Before he could react, Arthur's hand lashed out, striking his left ear with a sharp crack. The force of the blow sent him staggering, his vision blurring with tears he dared not let fall. The pain was immediate and intense, a ringing that seemed to echo through his entire skull.

Arthur loomed over him, his expression unreadable. "Clean it up," he said, turning back to his newspaper as if nothing had happened.

Now, sitting on the porch steps, he tried to make sense of it all. His ear throbbed, each pulse a reminder of his father's lesson. He pressed his fingers against the side of his head, wincing at the tenderness. It wasn't fair, he thought. It was a few drops of milk. Why did it matter so much?

He stared at the storm clouds. Their dark, roiling masses mirrored his turmoil. He was thirteen that summer of 1975. Most kids were riding BMX bikes or skateboarding with friends. He had long since learned that perfection was the only acceptable standard in his father's eyes. Anything less met with swift and brutal correction.

His mind drifted back to his mother. Her gentle touch was distant now, almost hollow. She would have laughed off the spilled milk, teased him for being a daydreamer—but she wasn't here. She'd left him, vanished into a void, leaving him in Arthur's world of harsh discipline and precision. With each passing day, her absence was more like a betrayal.

A gust of wind rustled the trees outside, carrying a faint scent of rain. He took a deep breath, trying to calm the storm within. He would clean up the milk. He would be more careful next time. He would try to meet his father's impossible standards. Because here, in this house, there was no room for error.

Arthur didn't speak his lessons—they resonated. Each time his voice boomed or his hand hit the boy, it caused more than physical pain. It left a message carved into the boy's soul: power meant making others afraid. You achieved control when those around you cowered and bent to your will. To dominate, you had to be ruthless.

The week before, the boy had knocked over a stack of firewood in the yard. He heard Arthur's heavy footsteps before he even had the chance to begin cleaning up the mess. His heart pounded in his chest, and he scrambled to put the logs back in place, his fingers fumbling. But it was too late.

"What the hell are you doing?" Arthur's voice roared, and the boy froze. He turned, only to see his father's face twisted in fury, his eyes narrowed, and his jaw clenched.

The blow came, sending the boy sprawling to the ground, the hard earth scraping against his hands. He tried to get up, but Arthur was already towering over him, his shadow swallowing the boy whole.

"You can't even stack a few fucking logs," Arthur muttered, his voice dripping with contempt. He kicked one of the logs, sending it flying. The boy flinched, curling into himself, wishing he could disappear.

In that moment, the boy understood something he hadn't before—fear was power. He saw it in his father's eyes. Arthur took satisfaction from seeing him cower and hearing his pleas. Arthur's voice grew quieter, almost calm, after he reduced the boy to a trembling heap on the ground. Breaking the boy made Arthur feel whole, making him feel like he was in control of something.

The boy hated how his father's dominance made him feel small. But a dark realization began to take root deep down. Power was not gentle; power was not kind. Power was the ability to hurt without consequence. It was to make others bend to your will because they were too afraid not to. Power was making someone else smaller so that you were bigger.

The boy began to internalize these lessons, not because he wanted to, but because they were all he had. He learned that his tears brought no sympathy and that he needed to hide his pain, burying it deep. He learned to stay quiet, not out of fear anymore, but out of a twisted sense of strength. If he didn't cry, if he didn't flinch, he was winning—at least in his own mind. He took what Arthur dished out, and that meant he was strong.

He also began to notice the way Arthur acted around other adults. The way he would smile, shake hands, his voice smooth and agreeable. No one else saw the monster that lived in their home. They saw Arthur as a respectable man, someone who worked hard, who provided. It confused the boy at first—how could someone who made him feel so worthless appear so decent to everyone else? But then it made sense: power wasn't about fear; it was about deception. It was about making people see what you wanted them to see.

14

CHAPTER 6

MAY 1977

THE BOY'S NEED for control had grown. It was the only way to keep the fear at bay, the only way to cope with the helplessness that threatened to consume him. He couldn't change that his mother was gone. He couldn't change his father's stormy, angry moods. But he could change himself. He would be quiet. He would be careful. He would ensure the floors were spotless, the laundry folded, and the firewood stacked. He retreated into the worlds he created in his mind, places where he wasn't a frightened boy trying to survive.

He found comfort in organizing his small space. Every item had its place. The books on his shelf formed a straight, satisfying line. His folded clothes had sharp, crisp edges, like soldiers at attention. In this tidy refuge, he was calm. It was his escape from a world spinning out of control. He would spend hours aligning his books and folding his clothes with great care. Here, at least, he had peace. No matter how chaotic the rest of the house was, his room remained a sanctuary of order and quiet. Each arranged item was like a small victory. It was something to hold onto when everything else fell apart.

The boy found solace in tinkering with electronics. In the attic, he found a dusty box. It was full of wires, circuit boards, and broken devices his father had forgotten. He would spend hours in his room. He took apart an old radio or a broken clock. He wanted to see how each piece fit together. The hum of a power supply or a flickering light filled him with a quiet sense of accomplishment. It became his secret world of creation. It was a place to solve problems, bring order to chaos, and make things work. With each project, his confidence grew. Tinkering gave him a sense of power, a chance to control something in a life that often felt beyond his reach.

When Arthur's voice grew too loud or the house was too suffocating, the boy would slip into the garden. His heart pounded—a mix of fear and exhilaration—as he crept through the shadows. Every step was dangerous, the risk of getting caught heightening his senses. But the cool night air and the open sky above gave him a taste of freedom he craved. In those moments, he felt alive, as though he'd escaped the prison his life had become.

He knew the risk. If Arthur caught him, there would be consequences. But the open air, the sky, and the scent of earth were worth it. Crouching by the flowerbeds, he touched the petals his mother had once loved. It made him feel closer to her. It reminded him that, despite everything, beauty still

15

existed—he only had to search for it in secret. The garden became his refuge, a place where, for a brief moment, he breathed.

The boy also found solace in coding. One day, in an unexpected moment, Arthur handed him a new Apple II computer.

"Here," Arthur grunted, thrusting the bulky machine into the boy's hands. "See if you can make something of it."

The boy stared at the computer, eyes wide with surprise. "Thank you," he whispered, questioning the gesture.

"Don't thank me. Just keep yourself busy," Arthur muttered, turning away before the boy replied. The boy spent hours tinkering with the computer. The blinking lights and endless possibilities fascinated him. By flipping switches and typing commands, he figured out how it worked. Soon, he began teaching himself basic programming. Coding became his way to channel thoughts and emotions, to create something of his own. Simple programs and lines of code brought order to the screen. They reflected the control he craved in life.

In each successful script, each small victory, he found a quiet rebellion. It was a way to build something meaningful in a world that often felt empty. The logic of coding made sense; it was predictable, unlike the chaos around him. With every line, he had a spark of hope, a glimpse of a future he might one day shape.

And so, the boy held onto those small, fragile pieces of control. He survived by finding strength in small things. He refused to be completely broken. The world outside was harsh; the house was cold. But, deep inside, the boy kept a spark alive. It was a tiny ember of his mother's love. It was enough to keep him going and to survive.

CHAPTER 7

PRESENT DAY

EVELYN AWOKE in a dim room, her mind foggy and her body aching. She struggled to make sense of her surroundings, drifting in and out of consciousness. Her hands and feet tied to the bed. She realized with a jolt that she was half clothed, vulnerable, and terrified.

As she lay there exposed, the door creaked open, casting an ominous shadow across the room. A figure stepped inside, and Evelyn's breath caught in her throat. He was of average height. His face was in the shadows. But his cold, calculating eyes pierced the gloom.

Her thoughts scrambled, and she found herself thinking of Max. The irrational worry for her dog's well-being gnawed at her, even in her dire situation. She also thought about her missed coffee date with Alex. Is Alex worried? Is anyone looking for me?

"Hello Evelyn," he said, his voice carrying a sinister edge. "I trust you're enjoying your little slumber party."

Evelyn's mind raced, her fear intensifying with each passing moment. She tried to speak, to plead for her freedom, but her throat trapped her voice, turning it into a mere whisper of a scream.

"Oh, don't worry, I won't keep you long," he continued, his tone dripping with mockery. "Just a little game we're going to play. A little dance, if you will."

With a swift movement, he approached the bed, his presence looming over her. Evelyn's body tensed, her eyes darting around, searching for an escape, a way out of this nightmare. But the man, with a cruel smile, laughed at her futile attempts.

"You see… Evelyn, I've been waiting for this moment for a long time. A chance to play with a toy like you."

The man, sensing her vulnerability, moved closer, his breath hot and foul against her skin. He ran his fingers along her cheek, a gesture that sent chills down her body. "I know your secrets, Evelyn. I know what haunts you. And now, I will be your new nightmare."

With a sudden force, he tore off her remaining clothes, exposing her trembling body to the cold air. A sadistic smile met Evelyn's cries of protest. He grabbed her roughly, his hands leaving imprints on her delicate skin. His touch was like fire, burning through her very being.

"You're mine now," he growled, his eyes fixed on her with an intense hunger. "Mine to break, mine to control."

As he assaulted her, Evelyn's mind raced. She tried to escape the present horror by delving into the past. She remembered her family's love and support. Their warm embrace made her feel safe. She clung to those memories. They were her only hope against the brutality unfolding before her.

He moved violently, pressing his body against hers with great force. Evelyn's cries turned to sobs. The pain was excruciating, a constant reminder of her powerlessness.

As the assault continued, Evelyn's mind wandered to happier times. She remembered a summer day at the beach with her friends. It was a time of laughter and joy that had once filled her life. She clung to these memories, a desperate attempt to escape the reality of her situation.

But the man, with a cruel satisfaction, continued his brutal assault, showing no signs of mercy. Evelyn's battered, bruised body cried for release. But her mind was strong, determined to survive this nightmare.

The oppressive darkness of the room swallowed Evelyn's screams and cries. Her mind tried to retreat, to find a place where the pain couldn't reach her, but it was relentless. As the pain grew unbearable, she felt herself slipping away. The darkness consumed her mind again. But the man, with a final cruel twist, leaned in and whispered, "This is the beginning, my dear. A taste of what's to come." Evelyn gave one loud scream and blacked out.

CHAPTER 8

TOMMY HAYES WAS a typical 12-year-old boy. He had short brown hair and friendly, curious brown eyes. He was an active, adventurous boy. He loved the outdoors, exploring, and playing sports with his best friend, Austin. One day in late August, they met up to play catch at their favorite spot, Windmill Park, in Old Town Alexandria.

The setting sun cast long shadows on the grassy field. Tommy and Austin were playing catch. Laughter filled the air, along with the thud of a baseball hitting a glove. Tommy and Austin had been best friends since kindergarten. They were inseparable. They shared a love of baseball, especially the Nats. They also had a secret stash of comic books hidden under Austin's bed. They had a bond that only childhood friends had. They understood each other without needing words. Today, they were making the most of the last days of summer before school started again.

"You throw like my grandma!" Austin yelled.

"Yeah? Well, your grandma's got a killer fastball. You ready?" Tommy replied, winding up for a pitch.

"Whoa! You almost took my head off!" Austin replied as he ducked from the wild pitch.

"Nah, you just weren't paying attention. Gotta be quicker than that."

"Quicker, huh? Alright, I'll show you quick." Austin replied, putting his glove up to his face, with the other hand hiding the ball. He wound up and threw it, but the ball hit the ground well before reaching Tommy.

"Geez! You trying to bury it in the ground?" Tommy said chuckling.

"That's my special move. The moleball. Hard to hit." Austin replied without missing a beat.

"Yeah, if I had a shovel." Tommy yelled, walking over to pick up the ball.

As the sky turned from orange to deep purple, Austin caught the ball one last time. He glanced at the darkening horizon. "It's getting late, Tommy. I should head home," he said, hopping onto his bike.

"Yeah, me too," Tommy replied, picking up his backpack. "See you tomorrow?"

"Definitely!" Austin called out, pedaling away with a wave.

Tommy waved back and turned west, heading towards the Wilkes Street Tunnel. The tunnel loomed ahead, an ancient relic from the early 1900s. Its brick-lined walls scarred and worn down by time. The dark mouth of the tunnel swallowed the dim light, daring him to step inside. The ceiling lights failed to reach the dark. They cast a sickly yellow glow that flickered and buzzed, like a dying heartbeat.

As he stepped inside, the temperature dropped, the chill wrapping around him like a cold hand. Tommy's footsteps echoed in the tunnel. Their hollow rhythm bounced back at him in uneven patterns. It was as if another presence was mirroring him. The sound began to twist in his ears, almost taunting, a disjointed chorus that unsettled him. He took a deep breath, but the air was stale, carrying with it the damp musk of rot and decay.

The tunnel was always still this time of night—silent. Most people had long since gone home, leaving Tommy alone with the suffocating quiet. He enjoyed the solitude, but tonight it was different. The darkness pressed in on him, thick and almost alive. With every step, he felt an unease, as if unseen eyes were watching, waiting.

Halfway through the tunnel, a movement caught his eye. A figure was ahead, emerging from the shadows. Tommy's breath hitched. The man looked to be in his early 60s. The dim light made his features hard to see. But what little Tommy saw unsettled him. The man's eyes seemed unnatural. They reflected the flickering light. His hunched posture made him look predatory. As Tommy approached, the man's lips twisted into a crooked grin, a smile that didn't reach his eyes. It was the kind of smile that seemed to hide something sinister beneath its surface.

Tommy forced a quick, awkward smile back. He hoped it made him seem unbothered. But as they passed, the man's gaze lingered too long. It chilled him, like ice seeping into his veins. The air grew colder. A primal sense of danger made the hair on the back of Tommy's neck stand on end.

He quickened his pace, heart pounding. The darkness was heavier, almost tangible. He had not made it a few more steps when he heard it—footsteps behind him. They were slow, deliberate steps. They belonged to someone who was following, not in a hurry to leave. Someone who was savoring the pursuit. Tommy's stomach twisted. His instincts screamed to run. But his legs were heavy. It was as if the darkness was clutching them, pulling him back.

Without warning, a hand clamped over his mouth—strong and unyielding. Tommy's eyes went wide, terror exploding within him as he struggled. The tunnel's emptiness swallowed his muffled screams. A cloth pressed against his face. The sickly-sweet odor filled his nostrils. It blurred his vision and sapped his strength. Panic surged, but his body refused to obey; his muscles went limp as the world spun around him. A flickering streetlight above cast long, twitching shadows on the tunnel walls. The shapes seemed to dance, mocking him as his mind faded. Then, everything went black.

CHAPTER 9

EVELYN'S FIRST SENSATION was cold. Not only from the air around her but from the icy ache in her bones, the numbness spreading through her limbs. She returned to consciousness in fragments. First, she felt the tightness around her wrists. Then, the ropes burned her ankles. They bit into her skin. Her body was a map of pain, a nightmare she couldn't comprehend.

The blindfold was rough. The darkness it caused was suffocating, more than the silence. Her chest rose and fell. Her shallow breaths broke the stillness.

Then, the memories slipped back in, like shards of glass. They cut into her fragile mind. The footsteps. The door creaked open. The voice—calm, almost casual—knew her name. The pain.

Her mind rebelled, trying to pull her back to sleep. But a distant creak forced her to stay alert. He was coming again.

Her heart pounded, her pulse echoing in her ears. Her body tensed in response, though she knew it was futile. The ropes held her tight, her body naked and vulnerable. She tried to scream, but her voice failed her. Fear had strangled it.

Then, as before, the faintest sound of footsteps. Deliberate. Measured. Each step closer sent a fresh surge of panic coursing through her veins, but there was nothing she could do. Nothing except wait.

Light—dim and weak—flooded the room as the door opened. Through the tiny sliver beneath her blindfold, she saw it. The familiar shadow stretched across the floor as the man entered. She could hear his breathing now. It was slow and steady. It was as if this were part of some routine, something ordinary for him.

He said nothing at first. His presence alone was enough to fill the room with dread. The bed creaked as he sat down next to her, the pressure of his weight pressing her down into the mattress. She felt the cold air shift as he leaned closer.

Then, his voice, so close to her ear that it made her skin crawl: "You've been waiting for me, haven't you?"

She didn't respond—couldn't respond. Her body froze, paralyzed by the sheer terror of what was to come.

"Only the best will do," he whispered, the words sliding into her mind

21

like a toxin. There it was again—that phrase. It rang with a personal cruelty. He believed those words to his core.

He didn't waste time this time. His hands, cold and clinical, moved over her body with precision, as if testing her limits. Every touch was calculated, designed to draw out the most pain with the least effort. Her body reacted, convulsing against the restraints, though there was no escape.

But the worst part wasn't the pain. It was the silence between his touches. The waiting. The knowing that the next wave of agony was coming, but never knowing when. It was in those moments of quiet, when his fingers weren't digging into her skin, that her mind began to unravel.

"Does it hurt?" His voice was a mockery of concern, laced with amusement.

She bit down hard, fighting the urge to cry out, not wanting to give him the satisfaction. Her breath came in ragged, shallow bursts as her body shuddered with each new wave of torment.

He laughed, the sound more chilling than anything else. "You're strong. But that's not why you're here. You're here because you're perfect. And only the best will do."

The words rattled inside her head, and she realized with horror that there was no escaping him. His voice filled her mind. His hands controlled her body. No willpower could free her from his control. He had designed a mental labyrinth for her. Each twist of his words pulled her deeper into his pain. It also dug into her very core—her memories, her relationships. They were all that had once made her feel safe. He knew things about her. The details were so specific that they made her wonder if he had been watching her for months or longer.

"Do you think Max misses you?" he said, his hands still moving over her skin. "That dog always follows you around, doesn't he? I can picture him now, waiting by the door. His tail is wagging like an idiot. He thinks you'll walk in any minute and everything will be normal again."

Evelyn's chest tightened, a sob rising in her throat, but she forced it down. How does he know about Max? She had never mentioned him to anyone, not anyone who would have led her to this. She clenched her teeth, biting down against the terror rising inside her. How does he know this?

"And then there's Alex," he continued, his tone casual, as if they were discussing something mundane. "You were supposed to meet her for coffee, weren't you? On the twenty-third, right? Or was it the day before?" He chuckled. "Time must be getting away from you now. But I've seen the two of you. Always sitting at the same little café, always talking about the same dull things."

Evelyn's breath caught in her throat. How does he know that? The coffee shop, their routine—it was sacred, private. It was where she was safe, where she unwound. Her mind raced, trying to find any rational explanation, but none came. He must have been watching. He must have been stalking me.

For months.

His hand brushed a sensitive part of her arm, making her flinch, but it wasn't the physical pain that hurt the most. He stripped away her security, one small piece at a time, with every detail he revealed about her life.

"Alex doesn't know where you are, does she?" His voice dropped to a near whisper, intimate and cold. "But maybe she will. Maybe I'll find her, too. You think she'd cry? Or do you think she's stronger than that?"

Evelyn's body convulsed in the ropes, panic flaring like fire under her skin. The thought of him finding Alex, hurting her the same way, sent a new wave of terror coursing through her. No, please, no.

"And your parents…" he continued, his voice trailing off as if savoring the effect his words were having. "I saw them, you know. They were at your place last month, weren't they? Your mom, what's her name? Linda? She brought you that ridiculous scarf she knitted. You didn't like it, but you smiled anyway, didn't you?"

Her mother. How did he know something so trivial, so intimate? The scarf—she had only worn it to make her mom happy. Her father, quiet and polite, had been there too.

"They didn't stay long though, did they?" He laughed again, cruel and amused. "I wonder what they'd think if they knew where you were right now? Maybe I'll pay them a visit next. Wouldn't that be something? Your dear mother, sitting there knitting while I explain exactly what you've been through."

Evelyn's body trembled. He can't. He can't know all this. Her mind reeled, trying to grasp how someone could have such deep, invasive knowledge of her life. It was as if he had been lurking in the shadows, watching every mundane moment and quiet interaction. She was exposed, more so than she already was in the physical sense. He was hurting her body and destroying her identity, her life.

"Your father," he continued, his voice dropping to a near hiss, "he wouldn't take it well. He'd probably try to stop me. But you and I both understand how that would end. Maybe I'll let him watch."

The words crawled over her skin like spiders. They filled her with a revulsion so deep it felt as if her soul were being carved apart. She wanted to scream, to beg, but her voice refused to come. All she could do was listen as he tore down everything she had ever cared about.

He leaned in closer, his breath hot against her ear. "You see, Evelyn, you think this is just about you. But it's not. I know everything about you. Every. Little. Thing." His words were slow, deliberate, each syllable a dagger.

"And if I wanted to, I would bring them here. Max. Alex. Your parents." He lingered on each name, as if tasting the power it gave him. "I'd make them suffer, just like you are. Maybe worse."

The weight of his threat settled over her, suffocating. She couldn't think. Panic spiraled in her mind. The images of her loved ones, dragged into this nightmare, played over and over. It was too much. Her body convulsed, as if

23

it were rejecting the horror, but the ropes held her fast, allowing no escape.

"And you know what I'd say to them?" he whispered, his voice dripping with sadistic glee. "Only the best will do."

That phrase again. It slithered into her consciousness, an echo from a place she couldn't quite reach. Why did he use those words?

But before she grasped it, the darkness began to close in again. Her body, mind, and soul were crumbling under his cruelty. Her only escape was the void. As she slipped into unconsciousness, his words lingered, like a curse. They branded themselves into her broken mind.

"Only the best will do."

CHAPTER 10

APRIL 1978

THE DAYS GREW LONGER and the sharp chill of winter had finally given way to the first breaths of spring. For most sixteen-year-olds, this time of year meant warm, sunny afternoons outside. A time for youth and freedom. But for him, the boy, spring was another season under the suffocating shadow of his father, Arthur.

His father was a disciplinarian—omnipresent, dominating, always watching. The boy could never forget when he appeared behind him, his shadow falling over his work. He would stand there, waiting, his gaze fixed, ready to catch a mistake. The creak of floorboards at night chilled the boy. His father might be near, watching him.

The boy had learned to read his father's moods. To avoid the back of his hand, he stayed silent, disappeared, or nodded in agreement. But even in his submission, something else grew within him—a twisted pride, a simmering anger. It was no longer fear that held him to his father's commands. He had begun to admire Arthur's power, his absolute control over everyone and everything.

Arthur's world revolved around himself. Anyone who stepped out of line, especially his son, paid the price. His lessons were always brutal. They had an unspoken message: Weakness is failure. Power is control. The boy began to absorb this. He internalized his father's ways, molding himself into a reflection of the man who hurt him.

The boy no longer flinched when Arthur spoke down to him or called him worthless. Instead, he mirrored his father's coldness. He learned to hide his feelings. He suppressed his fear and anger until they surfaced in darker ways. It started small—crushing ants under his shoe, pulling the wings off flies trapped in jars. Each time, he felt a flicker of control, unsettling yet addictive. He told himself it was curiosity, but deep down, he knew better. It was the thrill of power over something weaker. It made him feel less helpless in a world ruled by his father's iron will. With each act, he found something dark yet satisfying—anger mixed with the thrill of control, a taste of power.

But the insects weren't enough. One afternoon, in the warm spring, the boy saw the neighbor's cat in the yard. The cat was a fat, lazy thing, always lounging in the sun and making a mess of the flower beds. The boy had watched it many times, its movements slow and unbothered. Its carefree, consequence-free existence filled him with seething resentment.

He approached it, calling to it with an outstretched hand. The cat, familiar with people and trusting, walked toward him, purring as it brushed up against his leg. For a moment, the boy hesitated, feeling the softness of its fur against his skin. But then, his father's voice echoed in his mind: Weakness is failure. Power is control.

Without thinking, the boy grabbed the cat by the scruff of its neck, lifting it off the ground. The animal hissed and flailed, its claws scratching at him, but the boy's grip tightened. His heart pounded in his chest as adrenaline surged through him. He began to swing the cat, slow at first, then faster and faster, the animal yowling in terror. In a final act of rage, he flung the cat into a nearby tree. The sickening thud of its body against the bark echoed in his ears.

The cat lay motionless, its body crumpled beneath the tree. For a brief moment, the boy felt a twisted surge of satisfaction. His pants grew tight with an erection as he realized the consequences of his actions. But exhilaration quickly gave way to a hollow ache in his stomach, an unsettling thrill that left him trembling. Staring down at the cat, his mind went blank, struggling to process what he had done. Panic crept in as the reality hit him—he had killed it. His hands shook as he knelt beside the body, breath coming in short, shallow bursts. Glancing around the yard, he half-expected to see someone watching, but there was only silence.

In a frantic daze, he dug a shallow grave in the field behind the house, his hands caked with dirt as he buried the cat. He piled the soil over its body, patting it down with trembling hands. Then, he stood there, staring at the ground, as if waiting for it to rise again. But it didn't. The cat was gone.

That evening, as he sat at the kitchen table, his mind still racing, there was a knock at the door. It was the neighbor. She was polite but concerned, asking if the boy had seen her cat. "It's been missing since this afternoon," she said, her voice tinged with worry.

The boy's heart pounded in his chest, but he kept his face blank, as his father had taught him. "No, ma'am. I haven't seen it," he lied, his voice steady.

Arthur stood behind him, arms crossed. He watched, eyes sharp, as they exchanged glances. His lips pressed into a thin line, and his jaw clenched, the tension radiating from him in waves. His posture was rigid, every muscle taut, as if ready to pounce should the boy slip up. When she finally left, Arthur turned to him, his expression unreadable.

"You better be honest with me, boy," Arthur said, his voice low and dangerous. "Where's the cat?"

The boy felt his stomach churn. He had always feared this moment. A mistake would bring punishment. He hesitated for a moment, then whispered, "I buried it... out in the field."

He braced himself, expecting the usual slap or worse. But it didn't come.

26

Instead, Arthur smirked, his lips curling in approval.

"Good," Arthur said, his voice calm. "That cat was a menace."

The boy blinked, confused. He had expected rage, punishment, something. But instead, his father turned and walked away. He stood there, stunned and silent. It was the first time the boy had a sense of accomplishment in his father's presence, as twisted as that was.

CHAPTER 11

THE BOY WAS NOTHING like the carefree teenagers he saw around town. They laughed, gathering in groups at the diner or racing their bikes down the street. He envied how they floated through life, untouched by the shadows that weighed him down. He had grown taller, his frame filling out, his eyes cold and calculating. Arthur's lessons had changed him; he now understood power and the thrill of control. He had learned to mask the darkness within. He hid behind an indifferent expression and a quiet, unnoticed demeanor. But inside, that darkness twisted and grew, taking deeper root with each passing day.

It was early summer when the new family moved in next door. The house had been empty for months. Its windows were dark and lifeless. But now, it was alive again. Noises from moving vans and strangers filled it. The boy watched them from his window, his gaze lingering on the girl. She was his age—sixteen—with bright eyes and a soft smile that made something stir within him. She moved with a carefree grace. Her laughter floated on the breeze. She fascinated the boy.

He learned her name was Laura. He watched her from a distance, hiding behind curtains, observing the way she moved. Her voice, her laughter, and her hair toss captivated him. Each time he saw her, he found something deeper pulling him in—a fascination that soon began to fester. She was beautiful in a way that made his chest ache, but his feelings were far from innocent. Something darker brewed beneath the surface. It twisted a fascination into an obsession. Her beauty made his chest ache. It was a dark, obsessive longing.

At first, it was fantasies. He imagined what it would be like to touch her, to have her look at him with those bright eyes, to have her smile for him. But the fantasies didn't stay innocent for long. His thoughts turned darker, fueled by the lessons Arthur had drilled into him. Weakness is failure. Power is control. He imagined her scared, imagined the fear in her eyes, the way she would tremble under his gaze. The thought made his heart pound, a rush of adrenaline that left him breathless.

Soon, watching from afar wasn't enough. He wanted more—to be closer, to feel part of her world, all while she remained unaware. He told himself it was curiosity, a desire to know her better, but he knew it was more. He craved the power of being unseen, of controlling something she didn't see she was

28

losing.

One afternoon, after Laura and her family left, he made his move. Their car vanished down the street. He slipped out of his house, crossed the yard, and approached her house. His heart pounded—not from fear, but from excitement. His fingers trembled as he tried the back door. Locked. But the kitchen window was open enough. He pushed it wider and climbed inside, his feet landing on the wooden floor.

He moved through the house, senses heightened, taking in everything. The floor creaked beneath his feet. The silence amplified each sound, making his breath catch. The air was heavy, charged. A faint rustle of curtains stirred as a breeze slipped through the open window. Her perfume lingered. A sweet, floral scent mixed with the metallic taste of adrenaline on his tongue. His pulse pounded in his ears, his skin prickling with each step.

He found her room, the door ajar, and stepped inside. It was neat, tidy, the bed made, a few posters on the walls. He stood there, absorbing it—her space, her life, her world, all laid out before him.

He moved to her dresser. His fingers trailed over the smooth surface. Then, he opened the top drawer. Inside, he found her folded underwear in delicate fabrics and soft colors. He picked up a pair, feeling the fabric between his fingers, his heart pounding in his ears. The thrill was intoxicating. He was in her space, touching something intimate. She had no idea he was even near. He stayed a while, rummaging through her things. His eyes darted to the door, listening for any sound that meant he was no longer alone.

That day was the beginning. He went back again and again, each time pushing his boundaries a bit further. He would touch her clothes, run his fingers along her jewelry, and sit on her bed. He imagined her there—scared, vulnerable. He wanted her to feel the fear he'd known so many times, the way his father had made him feel. Making her afraid, he thought, would erase his own helplessness. If he made someone else small and vulnerable, he wouldn't feel so powerless.

He began leaving small clues—a drawer left ajar, an earring out of place, the edge of her blanket pulled aside. Subtle things, but enough to make her uneasy. Enough for her to sense that something was off.

One day, he found her diary tucked under her mattress. He opened it. His eyes scanned the pages. Her neat handwriting detailed her thoughts, dreams, and fears. He read about her friends, her crushes, her worries about school. He read about her suspicions after hearing something one night. She had woken up feeling as if someone had been in her room. The boy smiled, a slow, twisted smile. She was starting to feel it—the fear, the uncertainty. He closed the diary and put it back, making sure it was exactly as he had found it.

He kept going back, the thrill of it growing each time. He wanted more. He wanted to see her face when she realized she wasn't alone. He wanted to watch her fear. He wanted to see the power he held over her. It wasn't enough

29

to imagine it anymore. He wanted to make it real, to feel that rush of control, to see her eyes widen, to see her tremble.

The boy had learned well from Arthur. Power wasn't about kindness; it wasn't about love. It was about control, about making others weaker, about instilling fear. And as he stood in Laura's room, his fingers brushing over her things, he was powerful. He was alive.

CHAPTER 12

JULY 1978

THE BOY SAT on the porch, eyes drifting over the yard when he saw her walking by—Laura. Her hair shone in the afternoon sun, her steps light and carefree. He watched her, his mind slipping into a fantasy before he could stop it. His pulse quickened. He imagined her smile, warm and for him. Her hand brushing his. The fantasies grew bolder—she leaned in and whispered his name. Her vulnerability stirred something in him. It was a mix of desire and a need for control. It left him breathless. She caught his gaze, and for a moment, he thought she might look away. Instead, she gave him a shy wave.

He hesitated. Then, he lifted his hand in response. His wave, tentative and uncertain, mirrored hers. She smiled—a small, genuine smile that seemed to light up her face—and took a step closer to the porch.

"Hi," she said, her voice soft but friendly. "I'm Laura. We moved in next door about a month ago. I didn't know who lived here; I always saw a man."

The boy swallowed, his throat dry. "That's my father," he said, his voice quieter than he intended. A mix of emotions surged within him. Fear, resentment, and a longing for something different. Talking about his father was like walking on broken glass. Each word threatened to cut deeper. He shifted on the porch step, unsure of what else to say.

Laura nodded, her eyes curious but kind. "I see. I haven't seen you around," she added, her gaze lingering on him. "Do you go to school around here?"

He nodded. "Yeah. I just . . . keep to myself," he said, glancing away for a moment. He wasn't used to this kind of chat. It was normal and casual. The other person didn't look at him like he was wrong.

"I get that," Laura replied, a hint of understanding in her voice. She leaned against the railing, her fingers brushing the wood. She looked at him, her eyes curious and a bit interested. Her lips parted, as if waiting for him to say more. "Moving here has been kind of weird for me. I don't really know anyone yet. It's nice to finally meet someone my age."

The boy forced a small smile, his heart pounding in his chest. "Yeah, I guess it is." He paused, then added, "I'm Billy." The name felt strange coming out of his mouth—it was his name, but it was like something distant, almost foreign. It reminded him of the times his father used it, each time with a cold detachment or harsh reprimand. People had rarely spoken his name with warmth. So, it was like a label that didn't fit. It reminded him of all he

31

had endured.

Laura smiled again. "Nice to meet you." She shifted her weight, her eyes still on him. "So, what do you like to do around here?"

The boy blinked, surprised. No one had asked him anything like that before—not like this. He hesitated, glancing back at the door, knowing Arthur was inside. But Laura was looking at him, her eyes bright. For a moment, the shadows that always loomed over him were less heavy.

"I don't know," he said. "I guess I just . . . stay home a lot."

Laura nodded, her expression thoughtful. "Yeah. Sometimes it's easier to stay in. But it's nice to get out sometimes too, right?"

Billy shrugged, unsure of what to say. "Maybe," he admitted.

Laura smiled. "Well, maybe I'll see you around more. It was nice talking to you, Billy."

He nodded, a small smile tugging at his lips. "Yeah, it was." He couldn't quite believe how normal it had been, how easy it was to talk to her. It was strange, almost unsettling, to have a pleasant interaction. It was so different from what he usually experienced. A part of him wondered if he trusted it, if he could let himself hope for more moments like this.

Laura gave a final wave before turning away, her steps light as she walked down the street. He watched until she disappeared, his heart still pounding. But as the warmth of the moment faded, darker thoughts crept in. His mind wandered back to his fantasies, imagining the next time he'd be in her house. The idea of leaving clues, of watching her realize someone had been there, thrilled him. It was a twisted thrill. The thought of power, of control, made his pulse quicken again. Maybe life offered more, but maybe the shadows were where he belonged.

CHAPTER 13

THE NEXT TIME he found himself in Laura's house, it was different. He moved with calm, calculated purpose. Excitement mixed with something darker pulsed within him. His fingers brushed her things as he moved through her room. Each touch fed his growing obsession. Being here, in her space, filled him with a sense of power he craved.

He opened her dresser drawer, his eyes settling on the soft colors of her underwear. The thrill was there, that rush quickening his heart, but this time he wanted more. He wanted something to take with him, a piece of her to keep. He picked a few pairs, fingers lingering on the fabric before tucking them into his pocket. A surge of possession washed over him. It wasn't the thrill of sneaking into her space—it was about owning a piece of her. She would never see it was missing until it was too late. The thought of her confusion, her fear, made his pulse race with a twisted excitement.

His gaze then shifted to her desk, where a Commodore personal computer sat. He moved towards it, tapping the keyboard and watching the screen light up. The password was simple—her birthdate, something he had learned from her diary. He typed it in, and the desktop opened before him. His fingers hovered over the keyboard for a moment before he began to type. He wanted to unsettle her. He wanted her to feel vulnerable and watched. A simple message, but it would leave a mark. It would echo in her mind, reminding her that her space was no longer her own.

"I see you."

He saved the message as a text document and left the file open. Then he stepped back feeling satisfaction with his note. The power he had was intoxicating. The thought of her finding it, and the fear it would bring, sent a shiver down his spine.

He left the house as he had come in. He slipped out the back door, the stolen pieces of her still in his pocket. As he walked back home, he had a sense of triumph, a twisted satisfaction in what he had done.

The next day, as he sat on the porch, he saw her again. Laura walked by. Her steps slowed. Her eyes darted around, as if looking for something—or someone. She saw him and hesitated, then walked closer, her face pale, her expression uncertain.

"Hey, Billy," she said, her voice shaky. "Can I . . . can I talk to you for a second?"

He nodded, his face a mask of concern. "Sure. What's wrong?"

Laura bit her lip, her eyes glancing back towards her house before meeting his. "It's just . . . something weird happened. I think . . . I think someone was in my room." Her voice dropped to a whisper, and he saw the fear in her eyes, the way her hands trembled as she spoke.

Billy frowned, leaning forward, his brow furrowing in what looked like genuine worry. "In your room? What happened?"

She took a deep breath, her gaze dropping to the ground. "I found a message on my computer. It said 'I see you.' And . . . I don't know, I didn't write it . . . someone had been there... in my room." Her voice broke, and she looked up at him, her eyes wide, searching his face for answers.

He reached out, his hand resting on her arm. "That sounds scary, Laura. I'm so sorry you're dealing with this." As he spoke, a thrill bubbled beneath the surface. It was the satisfaction of seeing her so vulnerable. He masked it well, keeping his expression soft and caring, but inside, he relished her fear. It was exactly what he wanted—to be the one she turned to, all the while knowing he was the cause of her terror. His voice was soft and comforting. He saw her relax a little, her shoulders loosening under his touch. "Do you think you should tell your parents? Maybe they can help."

Laura shook her head, her eyes watering. "I don't know. I don't want them to freak out. Things have been tense since we moved here, and I've been arguing with them a lot. I don't want to give them another reason to worry or think I'm acting out. It might be nothing . . . maybe I'm just imagining things."

He shook his head, his expression serious. "You're not imagining it. If you feel like something is wrong, you should trust that. I can help if you need me to."

She looked at him, her lips parting as if she wanted to say something, then closed them again, nodding instead. "Thanks, you're sweet. It just . . . it helps to talk about it."

He gave her a small smile, his eyes soft, though deep down, he had a rush of satisfaction. She felt scared, like he wanted her to feel. The fear in her eyes, the way she clung to his words, seeking comfort—it made him feel powerful. It was all he had ever wanted: control. And now, he had it.

"Anytime," he said. "I'm here if you need someone." She gave him a weak smile. Then, she walked away, her steps hesitant. She turned her head to check her surroundings.

He watched her go, the smile fading as she disappeared down the street. A dark thrill lingered, curling in his chest—a secret that gave him power. The tremble in her voice, the widening of her eyes, that raw fear he had caused— that was what thrilled him the most. Knowing he had created that fear made him feel invincible. He was the source of her vulnerability. Each small sign of her distress fed his twisted need for control. It reinforced his belief that he could bend her emotions to his will. She was exactly where he wanted her— unsure, afraid, and turning to him for comfort. As he turned back to the house, darkness settled over him. It reminded him of who he was and what he craved.

CHAPTER 14

AUGUST 1978

BY LATE SUMMER, the boy's urges grew stronger, darker. Watching Laura from afar was no longer enough. Sneaking into her house while she was away had lost its thrill. He wanted more. He wanted to be near her, to watch her when she was unaware and vulnerable. Part of him hesitated, a faint whisper warning him he was crossing a line he might never return from. But he silenced it. He craved control, something his father had always denied him. The thought of being in her room while she slept filled him with a twisted excitement. She was completely oblivious.

One night, when the lights in Laura's house went out and the neighborhood grew quiet, he decided to act. He moved with precision, slipping on his gloves and a dark mask that covered his face. He had spent days observing her. He learned her routine. He knew when her parents would be asleep and when Laura's light would go off. He approached the side of her house, his heart pounding. A rush of adrenaline fueled him as he opened the window he had unlocked before.

He climbed inside, his feet landing on the creaking floorboards. The dark mask hid his face; the gloves would leave no fingerprints. Lavender lingered in the air, mixing with the musty scent of old wood. The cool night air clung to his skin, sharpening his senses to every sound and shadow.

A faint glow from the moon slipped through the curtains, casting a dim light over the room. Laura lay on her side, her breathing slow and steady, her chest rising and falling. The sight of her—unaware, completely vulnerable—made his pulse quicken.

He moved closer, each step deliberate, silent. Her soft breaths filled the room, steady in sleep. He leaned in, listening, his own breaths growing shallow. How easy it would be to disturb her, to shatter her sense of safety. The thrill of control washed over him as he realized she was completely in his power, unaware.

Her hair splayed across the pillow, her face peaceful. His gloved hand hovered inches from her skin, tempted to feel her warmth. But he held back. He couldn't risk waking her—not yet.

Instead, he knelt down beside her bed, his eyes fixated on her. He continued to watch the slow rise and fall of her chest, the way her fingers twitched in her sleep. He felt powerful, knowing that he was there, so close, and she had no idea. He was in control, and that control made him feel alive in a way that nothing else did.

After a moment, he reached into his pocket. He pulled out a small, nondescript object—a single button from an old coat. He'd chosen it for its ordinariness, something easy to overlook at first glance. But later, it would seem out of place, unsettling. He set it on her nightstand, a subtle clue to stir unease, a reminder that she wasn't alone. He wanted her to feel it—the fear, the uncertainty—that he was there whenever he wanted, that she was never safe.

He stood up, his eyes lingering on her for a moment longer before he turned away. He retraced his steps to the window, his movements fluid and practiced. He slipped into the night. The cool air hit his face as he closed the window. It left no trace of his presence but for the button on her nightstand.

As he walked away from her house, a thrill coursed through him, a dark satisfaction settling in his chest. He had been so close, and she had no idea. The power over her was intoxicating, and he knew this was the beginning. He would keep pushing, testing the limits, until he had her completely. He was untouchable. The shadows would always hide him. So, he never feared getting caught. The thrill of control blinded him to any risks, leaving only the desire for more. The shadows were his domain, and from there, he would watch her, control her, and make her his.

CHAPTER 15

THE CROWDED GROCERY STORE hummed with voices and the clatter of carts filled the aisles. The boy moved through the store. His eyes were on the shelves. He picked up the items on his list. He preferred being alone, slipping in and out of places unnoticed, but today was different. As he reached for a carton of milk, he felt a sudden tap on his shoulder.

"Hey, Billy," Laura's voice called out, her tone more subdued, almost hesitant. There was a hint of nervousness in her voice, as if she were looking for reassurance. He turned, his heart giving a jolt, his face betraying a flicker of surprise before he masked it.

"Hey," he responded, his voice even, a small smile tugging at the corners of his lips. Laura's bright eyes watched him. Her familiar presence disarmed him. But she was unaware of what lurked beneath his facade.

"I didn't know you shopped here," she said, her smile wide, her eyes crinkling at the corners. She shifted her weight, her basket dangling from one arm. "I was just grabbing some stuff for dinner."

He nodded, his eyes flicking to her basket and then back to her face. "Yeah, I come here sometimes," he said. He forced himself to sound casual, to act as if nothing had changed since their last encounter. Inside, tension rose. He had to keep his mask in place. It might all unravel if he wasn't careful. They chatted for a few minutes—small talk about school, about the weather, about how boring the neighborhood was. He nodded and smiled at the right times. But inside, he had a growing tension and anticipation for her next words.

Laura's smile faded a little, her expression turning serious. She glanced around, making sure no one was within earshot before leaning in closer. "Hey, can I tell you something?" she asked, her voice dropping to a whisper.

He nodded, his brow furrowing, his face the picture of concern. "Yeah, what's up?"

She took a deep breath, her eyes flicking away for a moment before meeting his again. Her hands fidgeted. Her gaze darted to the floor and back up. She was unsure whether to continue. "It's about . . . what I told you before. About someone being in my room." She hesitated. Her voice trembled. Her lips pressed together as she searched for the right words. "I think it happened again. I woke up the other night, and I felt like . . . like someone had been there. And I found this." She reached into her pocket and pulled out a small button, holding it out for him to see.

His stomach flipped. A rush of exhilaration flooded him as he stared at the button. It was the same one he'd left on her nightstand. It was a subtle clue, meant to unsettle her and make her question her safety. The thought of her lying awake at night, afraid, sent a twisted satisfaction through him. Her vulnerability was his power, and seeing her shaken only fed his desire for control. It had worked; he saw the fear in her eyes, the tremor in her voice. Inside, he was dizzy with the thrill, her fear pounding through him. But he kept a neutral expression, his eyes widening as he took the button from her hand.

"This was in your room?" he asked, his voice laced with concern. He examined the button, turning it over in his fingers as if he were trying to make sense of it. He looked back at her, his brow furrowed. "That's . . . really strange. Are you sure it wasn't there before? Maybe it fell off something?"

She shook her head, her lips pressed into a thin line. "No, it wasn't there before. I know it wasn't." She paused, her eyes searching his face, as if hoping he had an answer that might make it all make sense. "I don't know what to do. I feel like I'm losing my mind."

He reached out, his hand resting on her arm. "Hey, you're not losing your mind," he said, his voice steady. Inside, he was thrilled, an almost giddy excitement at her vulnerability. He had to keep his composure, to hide the satisfaction he had knowing he was the cause of her fear. "Maybe . . . maybe you should tell your parents. Or the police. This sounds serious."

She looked down, her shoulders slumping. "I don't know. I don't want to scare my parents. And what if they think I'm making it up?"

He nodded, his face thoughtful, his hand still resting on her arm. "I get it. But you shouldn't have to deal with this alone. If you ever need to talk, or if anything else happens, you can tell me, okay? I'll help if I can."

Laura looked up at him, her eyes glistening with unshed tears. "Thanks, Billy. It really helps to know you're here."

He gave her a small smile, his heart pounding with the rush of power he felt in that moment. Her misplaced trust in him filled him with a dark, euphoric power. He relished the control he held, the way her fear fed into his dominance, making him feel invincible. "Anytime, Laura," he said, his voice warm, his eyes betraying nothing of the darkness within. He watched as she gave him a shaky smile and turned to leave, the button still clutched in her hand.

As she walked away, he stood there. A thrill coursed through him. A dark satisfaction settled in his chest. He had her where he wanted her—unsure, afraid, and looking to him for support. And he knew he wasn't done. Not yet.

CHAPTER 16

THE BOY WAITED for the right time, the perfect opportunity to act without risk. He had spent days watching Laura's house. He studied her parents' schedules. He learned when the lights went off and the world around her went quiet. The fantasies had grown darker, more intense. He wanted to be in her room again while she slept, but this time, he wanted to take it further. He imagined her bound, gagged, completely at his mercy. The image of her terrified and helpless was intoxicating.

Late at night, alone in his room, he filled his thoughts with fantasies of control. He imagined her bound, wrists and ankles tied, her muffled cries as she struggled. A small voice sometimes questioned if this was too far, if there was a line he shouldn't cross. But he silenced it, letting his desire for power drown out any hesitation. Her vulnerability excited him. It fueled a need he couldn't contain. He needed to make it real, to experience the exhilaration of having her within his grasp.

Finally, one night, he decided to make his move. He waited until the house was dark, the neighborhood silent, then slipped on his gloves and mask. As he neared Laura's house, his heart pounded. Adrenaline surged through him. He reached the window he had used before, but his heart sank when he found it locked. The cold metal handle was unyielding in his grip. His breathing grew louder in his ears. The faint rustle of leaves and the damp scent of earth pressed in around him. They amplified the stillness. Panic clawed at the edges of his mind, the realization sinking in that his plans were slipping away.

He paused, his mind racing. He couldn't leave, not after all the planning, the waiting. He moved around the house, heading for the back door. As he neared the back door, a security light above him blazed to life. The sudden burst of light blinded him, and panic shot through his chest. He couldn't risk it—not now, not with the possibility of someone seeing him.

He turned, retreating into the shadows, his breath coming in quick, shallow bursts. He slipped away from her yard, his heart still pounding, the fear of getting caught gnawing at him. He would have to wait for a better day, a better opportunity. He made his way back home, his body tense with frustration.

As he entered his yard, he froze. A shadow moved—Arthur stepped out of the darkness, his face cold and unforgiving. Before he could react, Arthur lunged, gripping him by the throat and slamming him against a tree. The rough bark bit into his back as he gasped, his hands instinctively clawing at Arthur's. Fear flooded him, shock and confusion coursing through his body. A wave of shame washed over him—his fantasies of power were worthless in the face of his father's wrath. He was terrified, vulnerable, and completely at his mercy.

"You foolish boy," he muttered, his voice low and filled with venom. "Are you trying to destroy your life and our family name?" His hand tightened around the boy's throat, cutting off his air. Then, with a swift motion, Arthur punched him in the ear. Pain exploded in the boy's head, leaving him disoriented and terrified.

The power he had over Laura vanished in an instant, replaced by the cold, familiar fear of Arthur. All the fantasies of control, all the delusions of power, crumbled in the presence of his father. He was no longer in control. He was nothing, a scared child under his father's grip. He knew that the illusion of his imagined power was fragile. In front of Arthur, he felt his true place: weak, powerless, and insignificant. Arthur's face twisted in disgust as he slapped him across the face, the blow sending him to the ground.

"Get up," Arthur barked, dragging him by the collar towards the house. The boy stumbled, his vision blurred, his head ringing. Arthur pushed him inside, slamming the door shut behind them. He continued his tirade, his voice a harsh whisper. "You think I don't know what you're up to? You think I don't see the twisted desires festering inside you?"

The boy tried to speak, tried to explain, but Arthur's hand came down again, striking him across the face. "Control yourself, and your filthy urges," Arthur spat, his voice full of contempt. "You think this won't come back to ruin everything? You think I won't be dragged down with you?"

The blows kept coming. Each one was harder than the last. Arthur's rage was unrelenting. The boy tried to curl in on himself. He tried to protect his head, but it was no use. The pain was overwhelming, each strike driving him further into darkness. He felt his body give in, his consciousness slipping away as Arthur's voice became a distant echo.

Finally, the boy's world went black, the pain fading as he lost consciousness, his body limp on the cold floor. Arthur's voice, still angry, was the last thing he heard. It reminded him of his father's control. Of a power that would never be his.

CHAPTER 17

SEVERAL WEEKS HAD PASSED since Arthur's rage had left the boy battered and broken. In that time, Arthur hadn't spoken a word to him. The silence was heavy, oppressive—almost worse than the blows. It was a silence that made him feel invisible, as if he didn't exist. It weighed more than any bruise. It reminded him of Arthur's power. It made him feel small and worthless.

This time, he bore a black eye—a mark Arthur usually took care to avoid. But that night, Arthur's rage had slipped, leaving evidence of his fury. He'd called in, saying the boy was too sick for school. He kept him hidden until the bruises faded and the swelling went down.

Now, his face was almost healed, the purples and blues fading into a dull yellow. He sat on the porch, staring at the yard, his mind numb. The weight of the past few weeks still lingered, a dull ache deep within him. He heard the rumble of an engine, the sound of doors slamming, and looked up to see a moving van next door. His heart skipped a beat when he spotted Laura.

She stood by the moving truck, hair in a loose ponytail, dark circles under her eyes. Her shoulders slumped, yet her gaze held a forced determination. When she caught sight of him, she hesitated, then gave a shy wave. He raised his hand in return, but it was hollow. He tried to escape into his familiar fantasies, to summon the thrill he once had. Instead, a dull throb of fear and anger rose up. He remembered his father's hands wrapped around his throat.

Conflicting emotions swirled within him. He wanted to escape, but a painful memory of his vulnerability held him back. The fear overshadowed everything. It made it impossible to find solace in the fantasies that had once given him control. Those once-consuming thoughts now felt distant. A haunting reminder of that night's terror replaced them.

Laura walked over, her steps hesitant as she approached the porch. "Hey, Billy," she said, her eyes searching his face. He saw the concern in her gaze, her brow furrowing as she looked at the fading bruise around his eye.

"Hey," he responded, his voice above a whisper. He forced a smile, though it didn't reach his eyes. Laura looked down, biting her lip before speaking again.

"I . . . I wanted to tell you something." She glanced back at the moving truck, her parents busy loading boxes. "I told my parents about the button. And the message on my computer." She paused, her eyes flicking back to his. "The cops came over, dusted for prints, but they didn't find anything." She

41

let out a sigh. "My parents freaked out. They decided it was best for us to move."

The boy's stomach twisted at her words, a strange mix of emotions swirling inside him. Relief, fear, anger—it all tangled together, leaving him feeling hollow. He nodded, trying to process what she was saying. "You're . . . you're moving?" he asked, his voice cracking.

Laura nodded, her eyes glistening. "Yeah. They think it's safer. I guess they don't want to take any chances." She looked away, her voice trembling. "I don't know if this will really help, but they're scared. I'm scared too. I just . . . I wish I could feel safe again." She gave a small, sad smile. "I didn't want to leave without saying goodbye. You've been really nice to me. I wish things were different."

He swallowed, his throat feeling tight. He didn't know what to say, didn't know how to respond. The power he had over her, the twisted thrill—it was gone. In its place was an emptiness he couldn't quite understand. He nodded again, forcing himself to meet her eyes. "Yeah, same here. I wish things were different too."

She reached out, her hand resting on his arm. "Take care of yourself, okay?" she said, her voice filled with sincerity. He nodded, watching as she turned and walked back to the moving truck, her steps slow, her head bowed.

He sat there, staring after her, the weight of everything pressing down on him. Laura was leaving, and with her, the fantasies that had once consumed him. He was alone with only memories of Arthur's rage, the silence in their house, and an endless emptiness. He wondered about his future. Might he regain control? Or was he doomed to remain, powerless and hollow, under Arthur's shadow? It filled him with hopelessness. A void threatened to swallow him whole.

CHAPTER 18

DECEMBER 1980

THE COLD CREPT into every corner of the Drake household. But it was nothing compared to the chill that often radiated from Arthur Drake. By the winter of 1980, the boy was now eighteen, a senior in high school. He had grown into a colder, sharper version of himself. His father's physical abuse had waned, replaced by more precise mental torment. Arthur didn't need to strike the boy often anymore. He had learned to manipulate and degrade with a glance or a word.

The boy had grown used to the gnawing comments. The constant jabs said he wasn't good enough. They warned he might one day destroy all his father had built. Still, something inside him had shifted. He didn't like Arthur—not at all. But he admired some traits: the raw power, the unflinching control, and the ability to bend others to his will. The boy saw those traits as valuable, even if others had used them against him for most of his life.

The boy, a top student, was on track to be valedictorian. Arthur had made it clear that this was the only acceptable outcome. From a young age, Arthur had drilled into him the need for perfection, especially in school. "Only the best will do," Arthur often said. His voice dripped with disdain if the boy brought home anything less than an A.

"You screw this up," Arthur said at a tense dinner. "I'd rather burn my company than leave it to an incompetent, lazy cog."

The boy was no cog. He had never been lazy, and he wasn't going to fail, not when so much was at stake. But there was one person standing in his way: Scott Hall.

Scott Hall was everything the boy wasn't, and the boy despised him for it. Scott was not only smart. He was a natural athlete, the school's star quarterback. He charmed everyone around him. Scott was handsome, charismatic, and well-liked. He had what the boy lacked: admiration, talent, and the attention of the prettiest girls. To make matters worse, Scott was kind. He was an "every person's person." He was always ready to help. He treated everyone, including the boy, with respect.

In fact, Scott had once helped him. In their sophomore year, some upperclassmen began to mock the boy. It was Scott who stepped in, telling them to stop. He hadn't had to do it, but Scott, with his good nature, couldn't help but stand up for people.

The boy had thanked him, of course—he had smiled and said all the right things. But deep down, he had loathed Scott from that moment forward. The animosity had only grown, festering beneath the surface. It didn't matter that Scott had been kind to him on many occasions. What mattered was that Scott Hall was everything the boy wanted to be. Worse, Scott was better than him at the one thing Arthur cared about most: academics.

Sophomore year, the boy had fallen to number two in his class. When Arthur found out, the boy endured a verbal tirade that was worse than any beating he had ever received. Arthur's face turned red with fury. He ranted about his son, a lazy idiot, a worthless cog who couldn't stay at the top of his class.

"And who is this number one?" Arthur had demanded.

"Scott Hall," the boy had replied, bracing himself.

"Scott Hall?" Arthur sneered, as though the name itself disgusted him. "You mean that pretty-boy quarterback? Son of that worthless attorney? You lost to him?"

The boy had only gotten out a word before Arthur had smacked him hard across the ear. The pain was not only physical. He felt shame when his father told him he was inferior to Scott Hall. For weeks, Arthur wouldn't let it go. He berated him for being lazy and not good enough.

The boy never made that mistake again. Junior year, he reclaimed his spot at number one, and Arthur's tirades ceased—at least on that front. But now, in his senior year, the race was tighter than ever. The boy and Scott were neck and neck for valedictorian. Finishing second to Scott Hall in their final year was unbearable.

Arthur had taught him that the world was not fair. Only control and manipulation can bring power. Scott was better, but that didn't mean he deserved to win.

So the boy came up with a plan. A scheme to take Scott out of the running once and for all. He had learned from Arthur that you don't need to beat your opponent if you can sabotage them. Precision and planning were everything, and the boy's plan was flawless.

He spent weeks watching Scott, noting every detail of his routine and habits. The boy waited for the right moment. It was a quiet December day before winter break. He hoped Scott would leave his locker open for a minute while he chatted with friends. The boy seized his chance. He slipped a cheat sheet into Scott's backpack, tucking it between his notes.

When the time came for the midterm exam, the boy knew exactly what would happen. A teacher, alerted by a tip-off, "discovered" the cheat sheet in Scott's backpack during the test. Scott, bewildered and humiliated, had no explanation. Episcopal High School had a strict honor code. Scott swore he hadn't cheated, but the evidence was undeniable.

The scandal spread through the school. Scott Hall lost his valedictorian status due to disqualification. Once untouchable, his reputation now tarnished. The boy had done it. He had destroyed his only competition.

Arthur found out about the incident through his connections at the school.

He cornered his son that evening, a strange look on his face—a mixture of suspicion and, beneath it, a flicker of pride.

"You had something to do with this, didn't you?" Arthur asked, his voice low and probing.

The boy hesitated for a moment, unsure if he should admit the truth. But when he saw the glint of approval in his father's eyes, he gave a small nod.

Arthur smirked, his lips curling upward. "Good," he said, placing a hand on his son's shoulder. "That boy was nothing but a nuisance. And remember—only the best will do."

For the first time in his life, the boy felt a strange kind of warmth from his father, not love, but approval. Arthur was proud of him. The boy had learned the most important lesson of all: people did not give power; people took it.

As winter deepened, the boy knew he had won. Not only valedictorian, but also the game that Arthur had set in motion years ago. He had embraced his father's worldview completely. He had become the kind of person Arthur respected. He was ruthless, calculating, and willing to destroy anyone in his way.

The boy, though he despised his father, was starting to become like him.

CHAPTER 19

SUMMER 1981

THE BOY GRADUATED as valedictorian from Episcopal High School, as he had planned. Scott Hall, now disgraced, was long gone from his thoughts. The boy had secured his spot at the top. Amid the flood of congrats, one piece of news mattered: he got a full scholarship to MIT.

It wasn't that he needed the money. His father had a vast fortune. He made it through decades of ruthless business practices. It was enough to pay for any school or program. But the boy didn't care. He had earned that scholarship—he was the best. If it meant some less deserving kid had to scrape by without it, then so be it. Screw them.

The summer stretched out before him like a blank slate. It was the last chapter of his childhood. He would head to MIT in the fall to study electrical and computer engineering. He felt a growing sense of superiority, a confidence that this was the beginning. The boy loved electronics. He loved circuits and machines that obeyed commands. They were better than the messy unpredictability of people.

It surprised him when Arthur approached him one afternoon. Arthur insisted the boy join him for a tour of his business. The boy had never been inside Helix Industries, his father's empire. He'd always imagined Arthur didn't think him capable. Arthur raged about the "lazy, dumb cogs." He treated him like one of them. But today was different. Arthur wanted to show him the place that had built his fortune.

The boy followed his father to the sleek, black Cadillac parked in the driveway. They left before dawn. It was a 45-minute drive to a sprawling industrial complex near Dulles. The ride was as he expected: cold, silent, and uncomfortable. Arthur wasn't one for chit-chat, and the boy had long learned not to bother trying. They moved through the world like two strangers. They were bound only by blood and a heavy, unspoken expectation.

They arrived at headquarters after 6:30 a.m. It was a gleaming glass-and-steel building. It was modern and imposing, a reflection of Arthur himself. The boy noticed the parking lot was already half full. People had been working for hours, something that didn't surprise him. Arthur expected nothing less than dedication from his employees.

They walked into the lobby, where Arthur's secretary greeted them with a crisp "Good morning, Mr. Drake." Arthur mumbled a response, not even slowing his pace as they moved toward the elevators. The boy took it all in, feeling an unfamiliar mix of curiosity and trepidation. He had never seen this side of his father's life—the place where he ruled over his empire.

Arthur's office was expansive, austere, and filled with top-notch furniture. It screamed power. As the boy entered, he was immediately drawn to the cold precision of the space. Everything had its place, as Arthur had always demanded. There was no room for clutter, no space for anything less than perfect. This was what power looked like.

Arthur wasted no time. He walked across the room to a large west wall. He pressed a button. A panel slid open. It revealed a huge window overlooking the manufacturing floor below. The boy stepped closer, his eyes widening as he saw the scale of the operation. Hundreds of workers moved along the assembly lines. They assembled parts, tested electronics, and performed various tasks with precision.

Arthur stood beside him, watching the floor with a look of mild disdain. "Those cogs down there cost me millions of dollars each year," he said, his voice cold and matter-of-fact. "They're slow, they make mistakes, and they're inefficient."

The boy nodded, though he wasn't sure what to say. He had always known his father valued efficiency above all. But seeing it firsthand was different. The workers below were now numbers on a spreadsheet.

"They're necessary for now," Arthur continued, "but in the future, they'll be obsolete. Replaced by something more efficient, more reliable."

Arthur's words carried no remorse, no concern for the lives of the people he employed. The boy wasn't surprised. His father cared only for his growing fortune, not for others. The boy had learned that sentimentality was a weakness. Power was all that mattered.

Arthur turned to him, his face stern but with a flicker of approval that the boy rarely saw. "This is the future, boy. Precision. Efficiency. Results. Don't waste your time worrying about anyone who can't keep up. Only the best survive in this world."

The boy felt a chill run through him, not of fear, but of realization. Arthur had built this empire on control—over people, over systems, over outcomes. The boy still despised his father in many ways. But the father's control and power resonated with him.

"Come," Arthur said, motioning toward the door. "I want to show you the rest."

They moved through the facility. They walked past assembly lines, labs, and the engineers' and project managers' offices. The scale of it all impressed the boy. Arthur controlled every detail, every decision, every outcome. The boy saw how this power had shaped his father. It had made him ruthless and calculating. He was now indifferent to anything that didn't serve his bottom line.

As they made their way back to the car, the boy sensed a strange sense of pride, not in his father, but in what he had seen. The precision. The control. The ability to command so many people, to shape the world around you to

47

your will. Arthur was a cruel, distant father. But the lesson was clear: power is reshaping the world to suit your needs, without hesitation.

On the drive home, a cold silence filled the car. The boy's thoughts shifted to MIT. He didn't only want to understand the mechanics of electronics and computers. He wanted to learn to control them. To bend them to his will, like his father had bent this empire to his. Arthur had shown him what it meant to hold power. Now, it was up to the boy to decide how far he was willing to go to seize it for himself.

CHAPTER 20

AUGUST 1984

IT WAS NOW THE LATE SUMMER. Graduating with honors in computer and electrical engineering from MIT took years of hard work. It was the moment he finally proved himself, the point where all the sacrifices made sense. But the boy, now preferring his given name William, faced yet another obstacle. He was still far from where his father, Arthur, wanted him to be. As eager as he was to join Helix Industries, Arthur had other plans. He wanted to use his skills and carve out his own identity. But his dreams were pushed aside, his aspirations insignificant.

"It's not only about circuits and machines," Arthur had said, with his usual cold detachment, at one of their rare dinners. "Running a business means knowing how to manipulate markets, people, and money. You need to understand how to take control. You'll be going to Wharton for your MBA."

He wanted to protest. "I haven't applied," he countered, but Arthur only offered a dismissive wave of his hand.

"Applications are for those who do not already belong. I've made it happen. You start next month."

There was no disagreement after that. Arthur's word was final, and it wasn't worth the fight.

By September, he had settled in at the Wharton School of Business. The coursework was too easy, almost simplistic, compared to MIT's rigor. It gave him a false sense of superiority. He coasted through, often irritated by the uninspired discussions and classmates. Yet beneath the ease of excelling, he had a hollow ache. No matter how well he did, something was missing. He couldn't shake the feeling that he was being groomed for a future he didn't want. His father's expectations loomed, making his own desires feel small, even irrelevant.

Socially, little had changed. He remained a loner, shaped by a life focused on being the best. Friendships were distractions. At MIT, he had isolated himself. He poured all his energy into machines and problem-solving. It was lonely, but he told himself it was necessary—the price of greatness. Girls, too, were a mystery he couldn't solve. His few attempts at relationships were fleeting and awkward. They were always marked by an inability to connect. A divide separated him from others, and he didn't recognize how to bridge it.

He told himself emotions were unnecessary. Yet at night, the silence was

49

heavy. He was missing something important—something human.

And then he met Sarah.

Sarah was unlike anyone he'd met before—brilliant, ambitious, and independent. She didn't back down from his sharp wit or his probing challenges, and that drew him in. She had an energy and charisma that made her stand out. Sarah was passionate and determined. She chased her dreams, despite others' expectations. She studied finance. But, she was curious about more than business. So, she moved from deep discussions on economics to debates about literature.

Sarah connected with people. He had always struggled with this. She was empathetic. She sensed when someone was hurting or needed support. She wasn't afraid to reach out. She balanced her intelligence with warmth, something he found both alluring and disconcerting. Unlike him, she wasn't driven by a need to prove herself to anyone. She was confident in her abilities, but she didn't flaunt them. Her strength was quiet but undeniable. She seemed to see through his defenses, recognizing both his brilliance and his flaws.

They spent long nights debating and studying. They pushed each other in ways that thrilled him. For once, he didn't feel alone in his thoughts; for once, someone matched his intensity. Yet, as much as he admired Sarah, a part of him feared her. She represented something he'd never known—an equal. It was both exhilarating and terrifying. She saw through his facades, challenged his ideas, and called out his flaws. With her, he felt a vulnerability he'd always avoided, and it made him uncomfortable. That discomfort shifted into something else. As much as he wanted her, he also craved control.

It began with subtle suggestions about her clothes and where they'd go. He framed them as casual preferences, but he knew they were tests. He enjoyed watching her agree, feeling a surge of power with each small concession. "Why don't you wear the blue dress tonight? It looks good on you," he'd say, and when she smiled and agreed, something primal stirred. Every time she followed his lead, a thrill ran through him—a confirmation of his control. It soothed the insecurity beneath his confidence, yet fed a growing darkness. As their relationship deepened, he wanted more. Her compliance wasn't enough; he wanted total submission. He wanted to own her, to erase any trace of independence.

"Let's stay in tonight," he suggested gently. When she agreed, canceling her plans with friends, a surge of power washed over him. It was as if he were reshaping her world to revolve around him alone. Soon, he began dictating every detail of their time together, and though a part of him knew it was wrong, he couldn't stop. Her occasional resistance only fueled his urge to assert control. Fear drove him—the fear of losing her, of not being enough. To him, control was the only way to keep her close.

He reveled in her changes, her adjustments to his demands. Each act of obedience tightened his hold on her, filling him with a sense of power and invincibility. The thrill of domination drowned out any trace of guilt.

But Sarah didn't allow anyone to control her. She pushed back, asserting

50

herself, and he hated it. The more she resisted, the stronger his need to dominate became. His possessiveness darkened, driven by a relentless urge to prove his power. He knew, at some level, he was crossing lines. But he rationalized it. He convinced himself she needed his guidance. Her once-bright eyes grew clouded with fear and sadness. But that didn't bother him. It only confirmed his power over her. The thought of losing that control made him push even harder.

It all came to a head one rainy evening in late November. He had driven to her house, which was at the end of a quiet block near a forested, undeveloped area. They had argued, the details already blurred in his memory. She said she needed space, that his suffocating control was too much. Those words had hit him like a blow. The idea of losing control over her filled him with rage. But beneath that rage, there was something else—a fear that he couldn't bear to confront. The fear of someone leaving again, of being unlovable.

In that moment, everything boiled over.

"I can't do this anymore!" Sarah shouted, her voice breaking. "You can't keep controlling everything! I need space, I need…"

"Space? From me?" His face twisted in anger. "After everything I've done for you, do you think you can just walk away?"

"You haven't done anything for me! You've taken everything! My friends, my independence—"

His fury flared. He grabbed her by the arm, pulling her close, his voice low and dangerous. "You're not going anywhere," he snarled.

"Let go of me!" she yelled, her eyes wide with fear, struggling to pull away. But that fear only fueled the fire inside him. Without thinking, he shoved her—an instinctive, desperate move to assert his power.

Sarah stumbled, her foot catching on the coffee table, and before he reacted, she fell. In the silence, her head hit the table's edge. It made a dull, sickening thud that seemed to last forever. He watched, paralyzed, as she lay motionless on the floor. The room was colder now, an icy chill seeping into his bones, and the metallic taste of fear coated his tongue.

"Sarah?" he whispered, his voice cracking. He knelt beside her, his hands trembling. "Sarah . . . wake up." He reached out, shaking her shoulder at first, then with increasing desperation. "Come on, Sarah. Please. I'm sorry. Just open your eyes." His voice broke, a sob escaping his lips. "Please . . . don't do this."

But she remained still, her face pale and lifeless. The reality of what he had done settled in, a weight pressing down on his chest, suffocating him.

Panic set in. He couldn't think, couldn't move. The silence was deafening, pressing in on him from all sides. He only knew one thing: he needed help. He called Arthur, his fingers trembling as he pressed the buttons. The seconds were like hours as he waited, the reality of what he had done sinking in. He knelt beside her. His hand hovered over her still form. He wanted to help but terrified himself of touching her, fearing that he would

51

make things worse. Tears welled in his eyes, blurring his vision. He had never felt so powerless, so broken.

When Arthur finally answered, his voice was sharp. "What is it?"

"I . . . I need you," he stammered, his voice a whisper. "It's Sarah . . . she . . . I messed up. I need your help."

There was a pause, a heavy silence that made his stomach drop. "Stay where you are," Arthur said, his tone devoid of emotion. "I'll be there soon." Then the line went dead.

He stared at the phone, his breath hitching. He knew his father would come, but the coldness in Arthur's voice was like a knife twisting in his gut. There would be no comfort, no reassurances—only consequences.

Arthur arrived within the hour. He parked far away to avoid detection and showed up at the back door. Arthur's face was a mask of cold indifference. He asked no questions, his eyes narrowing as he assessed the room. His lips pressed into a thin line, a hint of irritation flickering across his face. He took in the scene, his eyes scanning every detail, the mess, the stillness, before turning to his son. He felt a chill from his father. It was a disappointment that cut deeper than words.

"We'll fix this," Arthur said, his voice devoid of emotion. "You stay out of the way."

Minutes later, Arthur's fixer, Vincent, arrived at the back door. Solving problems like this was his life. Tall and gaunt, he had sharp features and keen eyes. He moved with calm, detached efficiency, as if he had seen worse and felt nothing. He surveyed the scene with a practiced eye, noting every detail. He inspected the coffee table, where Sarah had fallen. Then, he repositioned a nearby rug to make it look like she had tripped. With precision, he adjusted small details, crafting a story of a tragic accident. Each change served to make the scene appear seamless and natural.

"She tripped. Hit her head," Vincent said, glancing at William. "A tragic accident." He set to work, erasing any sign of struggle, wiping surfaces clean. He arranged Sarah's things to fit the story. Her coat draped over the chair. The book she'd been reading lay as if she'd meant to leave. He adjusted the coffee table, angling it to suggest her foot caught. A tipped glass of water on the side table hinted that she'd lost her balance reaching for it. He even placed her shoes near the rug, one overturned, implying she'd slipped while putting them on. Every detail was deliberate. The scene had to look like a tragic, plausible accident—no room for doubt.

He watched in a daze, his body numb as the fixer worked, as Arthur stood by, silent and unwavering. William's future and Arthur's empire were both protected. Sarah's life was now a convenient narrative. The weight of losing control over her crushed him. Everything was spiraling beyond his grasp. She had been his, someone he molded, and now that power was gone. He wanted to scream, to cry out—not for her, but for the loss of the control he so needed. His throat was tight, as if the words were being strangled before they could escape.

Before leaving, the fixer turned to him, his eyes colder than anything he had seen before. He stepped closer, his gaze boring into William's soul, each word dripping with contempt. "Next time, keep your temper in check," he said. His voice was a sharp blade, cutting through the tension. The words were a final, unforgiving rebuke that left him trembling.

Arthur said nothing as they left the apartment. His silence spoke louder than words—there was no room for error, no space for weakness. His only concern was the family's reputation, ensuring the story stayed intact.

As they drove, William began to grasp the full weight of what had happened. His father's love—if one could call it that—was conditional and transactional. It was never about love or care. It was about power, about erasing mistakes and rewriting reality. Arthur's coldness drove home the price of family. People sacrificed feelings for reputation.

Arthur glanced over at him, his eyes devoid of any warmth. "This is your life now," he said, his voice a cold reminder. "Mistakes can happen, but only if they can be cleaned up."

That night, William called Sarah's voicemail. He left a message in which he expressed his worry and asked her to call him back. He kept leaving messages for the next few days. Each time, he sounded more desperate. He wanted to prove he was a concerned boyfriend. Later that week, he even called Sarah's parents and one of her friends, feigning worry and asking if they had seen her. By then, the police had already gone to her house and found her body. The investigation concluded. It pointed to an accident.

Sitting in silence, William realized the truth. Power wasn't only about controlling people. It was about rewriting reality, erasing anything that didn't fit his narrative. The inconvenient parts had to vanish without a trace. And he knew, from that moment on, that control was everything. That realization settled deep inside him, like a dark seed. It would grow, shaping him into someone who would never be vulnerable again. As the car sped through the darkened streets, the lights blurred outside. A single tear slid down his cheek. It was a bitter, silent farewell to his old self and to the illusion of love he had shattered forever.

CHAPTER 21

THE HOUSE WAS QUIET, a silence that was unsettling. Shadows stretched across the walls of the dim room. The man moved through the space with methodical purpose. Each step measured, each breath a steady rhythm, as he gathered his thoughts. It was almost time. Time to see the boy.

The man paused in front of a small mirror that hung on the wall. His reflection stared back at him, cold eyes that showed little sign of life. He raised his hand and smoothed back a strand of graying hair. His lips twisted into a pained, hollow semblance of a smile. This was what he had been waiting for. The day when he might mold Tommy into the perfect being—a son crafted in his own image.

He was thrilled with the power he held when he'd forced Evelyn to her knees, breaking her spirit bit by bit. She'd fought, of course. At first, her defiance was amusing. It was a rebellion that only made his dominance sweeter. But now, it was Tommy's turn. The boy needed to learn. The boy needed someone to mold him, reshaping him into something... pure.

The man approached the basement door. He let his fingers linger on the rough wood for a moment. He heard nothing from beyond. A heavy silence wrapped around the house, tightening like a noose. He liked it that way. Silence was his ally, his canvas upon which he painted his own world. A world where no one questioned his authority, where no one disobeyed him.

He pulled the door open. The old hinges creaked in the hallway. He began to descend the stairs.

***

Tommy woke up, disoriented, his body heavy with sleep and confusion. His eyes blinked open to a dim room—bare walls, a single small window high above, covered by thick metal bars. The bed he lay on was stiff and cold, the thin blanket doing little to offer comfort. As his senses returned, so did the fear. He sat up, scanning the room, trying to piece together where he was.

The last thing he remembered was walking through the Wilkes Street Tunnel. He had been heading home after playing catch with Austin, and then—that man. The man with the dark features, the unsettling grin. Tommy's pulse quickened as the memories rushed back—the cloth, the sudden darkness.

Now, here he was. A locked room, with no clue how long he had been here or why. His mind raced, trying to process what had happened. He swung his legs over the edge of the bed and stood, his knees wobbling. He was free to move, but he found the door locked, and the handle was useless against his tugging. He checked the small window, but it was far too high, and even if he had reached it, the bars would have kept him inside.

He paced the room, heart pounding in his chest. Where am I? How long have I been here? His thoughts went to his parents—they must be looking for him. The panic began to rise, but he fought to keep it under control. Tommy had always prided himself on being level-headed, but this—this was different. He didn't know what day it was, what time it was. He might have been here for hours or days, and the not knowing clawed at his insides.

He heard it with unexpected clarity. Footsteps.

Faint at first, then louder, heavier, approaching the door. His breath hitched as he froze, his eyes darting to the sliver of shadow under the door. Someone was there—someone fumbled with the lock. Tommy's heart raced in his chest, and he backed up instinctively, pressing his back against the cold wall. The footsteps stopped, and for a brief second, there was silence.

Then the door opened.

The man who entered was the same one Tommy had seen in the tunnel—the man with the graying hair and the unsettling grin. His eyes were cold, sharp, and calculating. Tommy stared, speechless, too afraid to speak, too afraid to move.

The man closed the door behind him, his gaze never leaving Tommy. His smile was small but unnerving, the kind of smile that didn't reach his eyes. He took a step closer, hands clasped behind his back as if he had all the time in the world.

"You're awake," the man said, his voice calm and controlled. He spoke as if nothing unusual had happened. As if someone hadn't abducted Tommy and locked him in this strange room. "Good."

Tommy swallowed, his throat dry. He wanted to ask a thousand questions, but fear held him still, frozen in place. What does he want? What is he going to do to me?

The man stepped closer. His eyes studied Tommy, as if to inspect him. "You're wondering why you're here," the man continued, his tone soft, almost conversational. "Why I brought you here."

Tommy remained silent, but his mind was screaming. Yes—why? Why am I here? What do you want from me?

The man's smile widened a fraction, as if he heard the questions Tommy wasn't asking. "I'm not going to hurt you, Tommy, if you do as I ask," the man said, his voice steady.

But Tommy was afraid. Every fiber of his being was screaming for him to run, to fight, to do something. But there was nowhere to go, no way out. His legs were like lead; his mind was still struggling to catch up with the situation.

The man stepped closer, standing a few feet away now. He tilted his head, observing Tommy with a strange intensity. "You're special," he said, almost to himself. "I knew it the moment I saw you. You have potential."

Tommy's brow furrowed, confusion flickering through the fear.

Potential? What was this man talking about?

"I'm going to teach you," the man continued, his voice low, as if he were sharing a secret. "There are things you need to learn. Things about the world, about power, about control." His eyes glinted, and Tommy felt a shiver run down his spine. "You'll understand soon enough."

Teach him? Control? None of this made sense. Tommy wanted to scream, to demand answers, but his throat was tight, the words caught in his fear.

The man circled him, never breaking eye contact. "You'll stay here for now," he said. "Until you're ready. You have much to learn, and I'll make sure you learn it well."

Tommy's heart was pounding so hard he thought it might burst out of his chest. What does he mean? What does he want with me? The questions swirled in his mind, but none of them made it to his lips.

The man stopped in front of him again, his smile fading, replaced by a look of cold determination. "You'll thank me one day, Tommy," he said, his voice calm. "Everything I do is for you. To make you stronger, smarter. To make you better."

Tommy didn't respond; he couldn't respond. His mind was racing, trying to make sense of it all. The man's words were chilling. But his calmness was more terrifying. It was as if this were normal, and Tommy should be grateful to be here.

"I'll leave you now," the man said, stepping back toward the door. "But I'll be back. We have much to do."

Tommy's limbs were frozen in place as he watched the man reach for the door. He wanted to shout, to scream, to beg for help, but nothing came out. He watched as the door clicked shut, the man disappearing once more, leaving him alone in the room.

Tommy sank to the floor, his legs no longer able to hold him. His heart pounded in his chest, and his thoughts raced, trying to make sense of what had happened. Why had this man taken him? What did he mean by teaching him? And what would happen next?

Fear gnawed at him, but it was the uncertainty that cut deeper. He didn't know how long he had been here. He didn't know what day it was, or if anyone even knew he was missing. His parents... Are they looking for me? Do they think I'm dead?

The room was silent again, save for Tommy's ragged breathing. He sat there, staring at the door, his mind racing with a thousand unanswered questions. He knew one thing for certain now—whatever this man wanted, it wasn't good.

CHAPTER 22

TOMMY SAT on the cold, hard floor, knees pulled to his chest. The room was dim, lit only by a flickering bulb that barely pushed back the shadows. The walls were bare, cracked concrete, stained and damp. A heavy silence pressed in from all sides. Time had lost meaning—he had no idea how long he'd been trapped or what day it was. All he knew was the fear. It clung to him like a second skin, a suffocating weight around his heart, tightening with each passing second.

The first time the man had entered, he hadn't hurt him. He had spoken in a calm, almost casual tone. He told Tommy he was special, with potential. It was in the way Tommy observed his surroundings and the quiet determination in his eyes. But those words had chilled Tommy to his core. They weren't comforting. They weren't meant to be. They were a warning, a threat wrapped in a promise that made Tommy's stomach churn.

And now, he heard those footsteps again. The steps were slow and deliberate. It sent a jolt of terror through him. His chest tightened, and his breathing grew shallow. The shadow under the door grew larger, and Tommy's breath caught in his throat. He squeezed his eyes shut for a second, wishing he could vanish, disappear into the walls. The lock clicked, the door creaked open, and the man stepped inside.

The man's face was unreadable, but his eyes were sharp and cold, watching Tommy. His presence filled the room. It was oppressive, suffocating, like a heavy fog that blotted out all hope. Tommy pressed his back against the wall. His heart raced. His body trembled with dread.

"Get up, Tommy," the man said.

Tommy hesitated, torn between resisting and obeying. His legs were heavy, his heart pounding with dread. But fear of the consequences finally propelled him to his feet—he didn't dare disobey. He had learned from the man's last visit that compliance was safer for now.

The man set an unmarked box on the table at the center of the room. Tommy's stomach churned; he knew it meant trouble. His legs were weak, as if they might give out at any moment.

The man motioned for Tommy to sit down. "It's time for your first lesson."

Tommy's legs were weak as he moved to the chair, his body stiff with fear. His eyes flicked to the box, then back to the man, who stood over him, his gaze never wavering.

"I told you before," the man said, his voice calm, but with an edge that made Tommy's skin crawl. "You have potential. But potential means nothing without training. You're here to learn, Tommy. To become better. Stronger."

Tommy swallowed hard, his mouth dry as sandpaper. He still didn't understand why this man had taken him, what he wanted, or what "training" meant. But none of that mattered right now. All that mattered was surviving whatever came next.

The man opened the box, pulling out a tangle of small wires, a worn battery, a switch, and a dull, cloudy light bulb. Tommy stared, confusion mixing with fear as he tried to make sense of it. What am I supposed to do with these? Panic rose inside him, swirling like a storm. He didn't know what this was, but he knew it wouldn't be easy. A lump formed in his throat as he looked at the pieces, his mind scrambling, dread building with each second.

The man pushed the box closer to Tommy. "Your task is simple. Build a working circuit that lights the bulb. You will have fifteen minutes."

Tommy blinked, his mind reeling. He had never done anything like this before. The wires looked like a tangled mess, and the components were foreign to him. His hands trembled as he reached for the first wire, trying to make sense of what he was to do. He felt his stomach twist, a sense of hopelessness settling over him like a dark cloud.

"Go ahead," the man said, setting a cooking timer for fifteen minutes. The ticking sound filled the room, each tick amplifying Tommy's fear and urgency. "Start."

Tommy's fingers fumbled with the wires, his mind racing. He didn't know where to begin. He had seen something like this in a school textbook once, but that felt like a lifetime ago. His vision blurred. Fear, confusion, and pressure mixed, almost too much to bear. The timer's ticking grew louder, a reminder of his dwindling time. Each tick made his heart pound faster. He felt the man's eyes on him, felt the weight of his expectations, the unspoken threat. Don't make a mistake.

Seconds ticked by, each one feeling like an eternity. Tommy's breathing grew shallow as he tried to connect the wires to the battery, his hands shaking. Why isn't this working? Why can't I do this?

"That's not how it fits," the man said, his voice slicing through Tommy's growing panic. "Think, Tommy. The circuit needs to be complete. Positive to negative."

Tommy swallowed hard, his pulse thundering in his ears. He tried again. He rearranged the wires. He tried to remember anything about circuits. His fingers fumbled, sweat slicking his palms as the pressure bore down on him. He felt like he was drowning, the air thick and suffocating. Why couldn't he get it right?

"Ten minutes," the man said, his voice calm but laced with warning. The timer's ticking grew louder, echoing in Tommy's head. It heightened his anxiety and made it harder to focus.

Tommy felt the panic rising in his chest. His mind scrambled, but every solution he tried seemed wrong. Nothing fit, nothing made sense. The frustration bubbled up, mixing with the fear.

"Stop rushing," the man said. "Focus." Tick, tick, tick. The timer sounded. Each second grated on Tommy's nerves and made his heart pound.

But Tommy couldn't focus. He couldn't breathe. His heart was racing, his hands trembling so much that he barely held the wires. He kept trying, his frustration and fear growing with every failed attempt. His vision blurred, his thoughts a chaotic mess. He was slipping, losing control.

"Five minutes."

Tommy felt his throat tighten. His chest heaved as he tried to concentrate, but his thoughts were spinning out of control. The wires blurred. All he heard was the ticking of time slipping away. The relentless pressure was crushing him. He wanted to scream, to cry, to make it stop, but he couldn't. He had to keep trying. He had to.

"Two minutes, Tommy."

His hands froze. He stared at the table, at the mess of wires in front of him, and he knew. He had failed. The timer made its last tick and let out a loud ring, the sound cutting through the silence like a knife. The hopelessness hit him like a wave, a deep ache in his chest. He had tried, and it hadn't been enough.

The man stood up, his chair scraping against the floor. Tommy had little time to brace himself. The man's hand shot out, gripping his collar. Then, he yanked him out of the chair. The sudden movement left Tommy breathless, his heart pounding with terror.

"Look at me," the man snarled, his calm façade cracking. The rage in his eyes made Tommy's blood run cold. "What did I tell you about precision? What did I say about focus?"

Tommy's body trembled as the man dragged him across the room, his fingers digging into Tommy's skin. He tried to speak, to explain, but no words came out. Fear had paralyzed him. He wanted to tell the man he had tried, that he had done his best, but he couldn't find his voice.

"You had one task," the man growled, his voice low and dangerous. "One simple task. And you failed."

With a violent shove, the man threw Tommy to the floor. Tommy gasped, pain shooting through his body as his head struck the cold concrete. He scrambled to his knees. But the man was already there, looming over him. His shadow stretched long across the floor, swallowing Tommy in darkness.

"Failure has consequences," the man said, his voice cold and steady again. He crouched down, grabbing Tommy's chin, forcing him to meet his gaze. Tommy's breath hitched. "You will learn that."

Tommy's heart pounded in his chest. He wanted to scream, to beg, but the words caught in his throat. The man's eyes bored into his, cold and unfeeling, and Tommy's last hope drained away.

The man's hand tightened on Tommy's jaw. "If you can't handle something simple like this," the man said, his voice full of disdain, "you're not worth my time."

With that, the man's hand released Tommy, and he stood up, walking to the door. Tommy's body ached, his head spinning from the sharp impact against the ground. He wanted to curl into himself, to disappear, to escape this nightmare.

The man paused at the door, turning back to glance at Tommy one more time. "You will not fail again," he said, his voice a soft threat. "Next time, the consequences will be far worse."

He left without a word. The door slammed shut behind him. Tommy was alone in the cold, silent room.

Tommy lay on the floor, his breath ragged, pain throbbing in his chest and head. Defeat crushed him. No matter how hard he tried, it was never enough. A deep worthlessness washed over him. Would he ever meet the man's expectations, or was he doomed to fail again? He closed his eyes, trying to block out the fear, the shame, the gnawing sense of failure. He hadn't even understood the task, and now he had paid for it. He was sinking, the weight of his failure dragging him down.

He curled up on the floor, the cold seeping into his bones, as the truth settled over him like a weight he couldn't shake.

CHAPTER 23

SPECIAL AGENT JAMES LAWSON stepped out of his car into the downpour. The rain was relentless, soaking him to the bone as he approached the apartment building. Authorities had called the FBI to investigate a potential human trafficking circuit. D.C. police responded to a domestic violence call. They contacted the FBI after finding a larger group of women in the home. D.C.P.D. had secured the scene inside. He knew it wasn't only a domestic violence case—it was far more sinister.

Upon arrival, the first agents found signs of human trafficking, not domestic violence. And that the assailant had fled, leaving behind a group of women who were being sold, beaten, and abused.

James entered the apartment. He saw several women sitting. Their eyes were hollow with fear and trauma. His gaze moved to the woman, Angel Ramirez, she was bruised and beaten. She claimed her boyfriend attacked her. He got jealous, accused her of cheating, and it was all her fault. But James had seen this before. The story wasn't lining up.

He glanced at her forearm. He spotted the telltale mark—a brand. Someone had carved it into her skin, not inked it like a tattoo, but etched it. It was a sickening symbol of ownership. Pimps used it to control their victims through brutality. This wasn't jealousy or a lover's quarrel. This was something far darker.

James knelt in front of her, his voice calm but probing. "I know this isn't easy, but I need to hear the truth. This wasn't a boyfriend getting jealous, was it?"

The woman kept her gaze low, sticking to her story. "It was. He thought I was cheating… that's why he hit me; it was my fault. You should all just leave, it's none of your business."

James didn't push too hard. He knew victims clung to these stories, often out of fear or loyalty to their abusers. But the evidence was clear.

Before he continued, another agent approached him. "Agent Lawson, one of the other women is talking. She says she knows what's really going on."

James nodded and stood. He walked to a corner of the apartment. A woman sat there, her arms folded across her chest. She looked up as he approached, her face a mixture of anger and fear. Her Spanish accent was thick as she began to speak.

"I'm from Venezuela," she said, her voice shaking. "I paid a man everything I had to come to America. But when I got here, he put me on the

61

street, made me... made me do things."

Her words came faster, the fear and rage bubbling over. "The other girls, they're the same. We're not here because we want to be. He forces us. He's a gorilla, not her boyfriend. He beat her because she no make quota."

Her eyes met his, desperation written all over her face. "Please help us. I don't want to do this anymore."

James had the familiar burn of anger rise in his chest. He had seen it too many times. The manipulation, the violence. The women trapped, believing they had no way out. But he was here to give them that way out.

"That's why we're here," he said, his voice steady but full of conviction. "Agent Foster is going to take your statement. We're going to do everything we can to make sure you're safe."

He signaled to Foster, who moved in to take the woman's testimony. James then instructed the other agents to secure the scene. They had to collect every piece of evidence. This was the start of a bigger investigation. It would uncover the full extent of this trafficking ring.

As James left the apartment, the rain continued to pour, drenching him as he walked back to his car. He sat behind the wheel for a moment, staring through the rain-soaked windshield. The weight of the world pressed down on him, the familiar heaviness that came with these cases. No matter how often he faced this evil, the horror and frustration never lessened.

In his car, James let out a primal yell. It was a release of his rage at the traffickers, the abusers, and the system that enabled these atrocities. His scream echoed in the small space, but even that didn't offer much relief.

As his yell faded, James's mind drifted back. He tried not to think about it—the night his father came home drunk. He was ten, hiding in his room, listening to his parents argue. The shouting escalated into violence. He remembered it all too well. The crash of objects. His mother's screams. The sickening thud of a body hitting the floor.

His father had been a monster. A towering figure of rage, drunk and filled with fury, tearing their home apart in a fit of anger. James had cowered in the shadows, powerless. He listened to his mother's desperate cries as his father beat her.

"Stop! Please, stop!" she had screamed.

But his father hadn't stopped. He'd kept going, his fury unchecked, until James's mother lay motionless on the floor. It wasn't until the police arrived, their sirens wailing in the night, that the violence ended. But by then, it was too late.

They arrested his father, but the damage was already done.

They had found James hours later, still under that table, still trembling, eyes wide and vacant. His father had worn handcuffs while they took him away. His face was blank, as if he'd done something mundane, like taking out the trash. For years, his father's cold, unfeeling face haunted James. It was a stark reminder of the darkness a person carries.

After that night, his mother's parents—his grandmother and

grandfather—took James in. They were loving and kind, wrapping him in warmth he hadn't known was possible after the trauma. They gave him a home. It was not filled with shouts and violence. Laughter filled the air. Gentle hugs and the scent of cooling, homemade pies followed.

His grandparents never spoke ill of his father, never let their own grief taint the way they raised him. Instead, they taught James about goodness and justice. They showed him the world's beauty, the kindness of strangers, and life's joyful moments. These made life worth living. They taught him that the world was not evil. Darkness was not part of the human condition.

"It's just people, James," his grandmother used to say as she stroked his hair on sleepless nights. "There are good people and bad people. But the world, my dear, the world is full of good. You must never forget that."

James clung to those words, letting them heal the broken parts of him bit by bit. He knew, deep down, that without their love, he would be quite different. Their patience and belief in goodness saved him. The anger could have consumed him, as it had consumed his father. But instead, James grew up with compassion and justice as his guide. His grandparents showed him the way, reminding him he had a choice and that he could help others.

His mother was gone, and James had only scars—both physical and emotional. It was that night that shaped him, driving him into law enforcement. He had dedicated his life to putting men like his father behind bars. He wanted to spare others from enduring what he had.

Now, as he stared through the rain-soaked windshield, his past mixed with his heavy present. He had dedicated himself to fighting for justice, but some days it was like the fight would never end.

He gripped the steering wheel, the anger simmering beneath the surface. But he couldn't let it consume him. He had a job to do, and there were people depending on him. With a deep breath, James started the car. His urge to put this pimp behind bars burned brighter than ever.

As he pulled away, the rain fell, washing the city. James drove into the night, determined to bring justice to those in need.

CHAPTER 24

WEEKS HAD PASSED since the man took Tommy. The days blurred together, filled with fear and the constant struggle to survive. Tracking time no longer mattered; all that mattered was enduring each moment. His life had settled into a grim rhythm: lessons, punishments, and brief solitude. At first, the lessons seemed impossible. The time limits were absurd. The tasks were too complex for someone his age. They included assembling electrical boards and learning to write Python code. Each task demanded something different. Electrical boards required precision. Mechanical gears needed an understanding of movement. Code challenged his logic.

The man sometimes left reference materials. They were manuals, diagrams, and programming books on electrical engineering. Tommy pored over them, deepening his understanding. But failure was inevitable. The man never hesitated to retaliate with brutal precision. A blow to the ear left his head ringing; a slap burned his skin. Some punishments were more creative. They left Tommy in no doubt. The man took pleasure in his suffering.

But lately, things had changed. The lessons hadn't grown easier—Tommy had grown better. He began to comprehend things, surprising even himself. He didn't understand how he was picking it all up. Perhaps it was the abuse. The punishment forced him to learn, adapt, and survive. The realization unsettled him. Was this who he was? Someone who thrived in a nightmare?

But he pushed the thought aside. He had no choice but to keep going. He met each challenge with precision. The more he succeeded, the less punishment he received. Soon, he predicted the man's expectations. He saw through the absurdity and executed tasks with cold efficiency.

He learned how to survive.

Today, Tommy sat in his usual spot on the floor, the familiar sound of footsteps approaching. The lock turned, the door creaked open, and the man appeared, framed in the doorway. Tommy tensed, his body conditioned to expect the worst, though his mind remained sharp.

The man entered, his expression unreadable, holding a metal box. It was like the others Tommy had seen. It had a mix of delicate parts. Each required precise assembly under strict time limits and tough constraints. But today was different.

The man set the box on the table and gestured for Tommy to sit. He obeyed, his movements smooth and practiced. There was no hesitation, no questioning. He knew what hesitation brought.

"Today's lesson is about precision and efficiency," the man said, his voice cool. "Every piece must fit perfectly. No room for error. No wasted time." The man brought out the timer, his eyes never leaving Tommy. He set it for fifteen minutes. The steady tick echoed through the room. Each tick tightened the knot of anxiety in Tommy's chest. The ticking was relentless, a reminder of the pressure, of the consequences of failure.

Tommy nodded. He'd heard it before. No mistakes. No failure. But his mind was already working. Over the weeks, he had noticed something— something that gave him hope. These lessons weren't only about obedience. They were teaching him skills. Skills that, if he were smart, he would use to his advantage.

The man opened the box. It held delicate components: copper wires, steel rods, interlocking gears, and tiny screws. There was also a small circuit board and a set of schematics. A faint metallic smell filled the air. Tommy felt the cold, smooth components as he reached out to touch them. It was another intricate mechanism, like those he had assembled before. But this time, as he began to work, Tommy's thoughts were elsewhere. He had learned a lot from these challenges.

He had learned to be precise. To observe. To think beyond the task.

As the man watched, Tommy's fingers moved, each movement quick and efficient. The man loomed over him, inspecting his progress, but Tommy's thoughts were miles away.

I've been learning, Tommy thought. He thinks he's training me to be obedient, to be perfect. But he's also teaching me how to escape.

The thought had first come a week ago, during a lesson involving a complex lock mechanism. The man had focused on precision and the cost of failure, but Tommy had learned more than that. He learned how locks worked—how they were manipulated.

Now, as he assembled the challenge, his mind worked in the background. Every lesson, every piece of training—it was all forming a larger picture.

The key to his escape.

The man leaned closer, his presence cold, but Tommy didn't flinch. His fingers moved, snapping pieces into place.

"Faster," the man said, his voice low and commanding. "You're running out of time." The timer continued ticking, but Tommy felt his emotions shift. Instead of panic, a calmness settled over him. He became focused, cool, and collected. His movements were precise as he worked against the clock.

Tommy's heart quickened, but he didn't let it show. He increased his pace, fitting the final pieces with practiced ease. The last gear clicked into position.

The man sat in silence, staring at Tommy for almost a minute. The silence was heavy, uncomfortable, and Tommy felt the tension growing. Then, the timer bell went off, startling Tommy. The man smirked, his lips curling into a faint smile. "Good," he said.

Tommy sat back, heart pounding, face expressionless. No punishment today.

The man inspected the puzzle, eyes flicking over every detail. Finally, he nodded. "You're improving," he said, an undercurrent of satisfaction in his voice. "Keep this up, and you might prove useful."

Tommy said nothing. He knew better. But inside, his mind raced.

Useful. The man thought he was molding Tommy into something useful. But Tommy knew the truth. He was learning—faster than the man realized. He was learning to outthink him.

As the man turned to leave, Tommy allowed himself a small, fleeting thought of hope.

Soon. Not yet. But soon.

He wasn't ready to escape. Not yet. There were still things he needed to understand. Still lessons to learn. But each day, each task, brought him closer. The man had no idea that the very skills he was drilling into Tommy were giving him the tools to break free.

All Tommy had to do was hold out a little longer.

The door clicked shut, leaving Tommy alone. He stared at the completed puzzle, his mind already working on the next steps. Locks. Mechanisms. Systems. Everything was starting to come together, piece by piece.

He needed to be patient.

CHAPTER 25

IT HAD BEEN WEEKS. Evelyn wasn't sure. Time had become a blur. Each day bled into the next. Her world was a dim room and the man who visited her daily. There was no sunlight, no way to measure the passing of time. Only the man's footsteps down the stairs, the creak of the door, and the darkness he brought with him.

Every visit was the same. His voice, calm and controlled, mocked her. His hands, cold and clinical, inflicted both physical and emotional pain. He would whisper things—things that made her feel small, worthless, broken. It wasn't only the physical abuse. It was the mental erosion, the way he stripped her of her sense of self, piece by piece.

Each time he left, Evelyn would lie there, trembling. She was hollow. Not only because of what he did to her body, but because of what he did to her mind. He was in her head now, more than she could bear. "You're nothing," he'd say. "You belong to me."

At first, she had fought back. She had screamed, cursed him, sworn he would never break her. But now, those fights seemed distant. They felt like someone else's past. A version of herself she couldn't reach anymore. She was too tired to resist. Too broken.

The blindfold had become her world, her shield against the darkness. In the moments after the man left, she lay in the quiet, forcing her mind to drift elsewhere. Anywhere but here.

Today, her thoughts floated back to her parents.

A small, distant smile formed on her lips as she let herself remember them. A time, not so long ago, when life was full of laughter. She heard her mother's voice, warm and filled with joy, calling her to the kitchen. She remembered the smell of baked bread wafting through the house. Her father cracked jokes that never made sense. But, they always laughed anyway.

"You know why I love camping, right? Because it's in-tents!" her dad had said once, grinning as if he had told the greatest joke in the world. Evelyn and her mom had groaned in unison, but deep down, they loved it. They had all doubled over in laughter, their sides hurting. It was the way families do when everything feels simple and right.

A favorite memory surfaced: a weekend trip to the mountains when she was twelve. The sun had been warm, the air fresh and crisp. They'd hiked for hours, stopping at the top of a hill to look over the valley below. Standing arm in arm, they'd gazed out at the endless green and sky. Her mom had kissed her head, her dad pulling them both into a bear hug. In that moment, they had been the happiest family in the world.

She clung to that memory now, as if it were a lifeline. That was real. That was hers.

But the memory soon faded, and the pain returned. Her parents didn't know where she was. They thought she was dead. How long had it been? They were searching for her, hoping for some miracle that would never come.

Her thoughts shifted again, this time to Alex. Her best friend, her soul sister. Alex, who had been there for her through everything—the good times and the bad. She pictured Alex's bright smile, her eyes always filled with mischief and adventure.

They had many great memories. But their last vacation together was the most special: Spain. They had walked the Camino de Santiago together. It was a wild, life-changing adventure.

Evelyn felt the Spanish sun on her skin. She felt the weight of her backpack as she walked the ancient pilgrimage route. They had spent weeks on the road, walking through vineyards, villages, and fields of wheat. At night, they stayed in simple hostels. They shared meals with fellow travelers from around the world. It had been the adventure of a lifetime, a journey of self-discovery.

She remembered the moment they reached the cathedral in Santiago de Compostela. It was the end of their journey. They stood together, exhausted but exhilarated, in front of the grand, ancient structure. Alex had thrown her arms around Evelyn, laughing through tears. "We did it!" she had shouted, her voice echoing off the cathedral walls. "We actually did it!"

They spent the last night celebrating with their new friends. They shared wine and stories, toasting to their adventure and the bond they had forged on the trail.

Evelyn's heart ached at the thought of Alex. Does she realize something is wrong? Is she looking for me?

The memories brought her a small sense of peace, but they couldn't last. Not here. Not in this place. The sound of footsteps echoed once again from the stairs, dragging her back to the present. Her chest tightened, her pulse quickened as the all-too-familiar fear crept back in.

The door creaked open, and she heard the man's voice, low and mocking. "Did you miss me, Evelyn?"

She bit her lip, the words she wanted to scream caught in her throat. The air seemed to thicken with his presence, every breath she took feeling heavier. She felt the blindfold tighten as he approached her, his hands rough and possessive. The torment was about to begin again. He would whisper more of his lies, his taunts, the twisted words that gnawed at her mind.

"You're mine. You're nothing without me."

Evelyn clenched her fists. She wanted to hold onto the memories. She wanted to remember that there was a world outside this hell. But the pain was overwhelming. It consumed her, pulling her back into the darkness.

The memories of her parents, of Alex, were all she had left. But even they were starting to feel distant.

Please, she thought. Please let this end.

CHAPTER 26

TOMMY FIGURED it had been near a month since the man had taken him. Each day was the same. Relentless tests of his endurance, patience, and obedience. But something had changed yesterday.

The man was pleased with Tommy's progress. For the first time in what was like forever, he experienced no punishment or pain. Instead, the man had handed him a gift—a Washington Nationals baseball jersey. The gesture was bizarre and unsettling. Tommy wasn't sure how to react. Was this supposed to be a reward?

The man had smiled, a cold, calculated smile. Then he said something that made Tommy's heart race with both curiosity and fear.

"Tomorrow, I want to introduce you to somebody."

That was all he had said before leaving the room. Now, Tommy was alone with the jersey and his swirling thoughts. Somebody? What did that mean? Was it a person? Was it another test? A dog—a pit bull? Some new form of torment? Tommy's mind raced through possibilities, each one more unsettling than the last.

His fingers traced the smooth fabric of the jersey. Its bright red color contrasted with the dim, lifeless room. He didn't know why, but the jersey had triggered something deep inside him. It was something he hadn't thought about in a long time.

It reminded him of Christmas.

Not any Christmas—the last one with his parents, the best he remembered. He closed his eyes. He let the memory wash over him. He hoped to escape his reality, if only for a moment.

That year, it snowed. The kind of snow that piled on the window ledges. It turned the world outside into a quiet, white wonderland. Inside, the house had been warm, filled with the smell of roasting turkey and baked cookies. His mom had been in the kitchen all day, preparing the big family dinner. His dad had been sitting by the fire, teasing Tommy about the gifts under the tree.

But the best part had been the jersey.

Tommy had unwrapped it with shaky hands, his heart racing as he tore through the paper. There it was. A brand-new Washington Nationals jersey. His favorite player's name stitched on the back. He had screamed in joy, throwing his arms around his dad. It had been the best gift he had ever received.

His grandparents had been there, too, smiling as they watched him from their seats on the couch. His grandpa leaned over and whispered to Tommy, "You're destined to be a baseball star, just like your dad was."

After dinner, Tommy had rushed out of the house, eager to meet up with Austin. They had spent the evening showing each other their gifts. They ran through the snow and talked about the games they would play in spring.

It had been perfect. A perfect day. The last perfect day.

Tommy opened his eyes, the cold, dark reality of the room settling back in around him. The memories were so vivid, so real. It was like he had the warmth of that day, the love of his parents, the joy of his best friend. But now, it was distant, like something from another life.

The jersey still sat in his lap, but now it felt heavier somehow. The man's words echoed in his mind again. "Tomorrow, I want to introduce you to somebody." Who might it be?

The sound of footsteps outside the door interrupted his thoughts. Tommy's body tensed; his pulse quickened. The handle of the door jiggled, and the familiar creak of the door echoed through the room.

This is it, Tommy thought, his heart pounding in his chest. Who is it? What's next?

CHAPTER 27

THE DOOR CREAKED OPEN, and the man stepped inside. He never knocked, never gave warning. His presence filled the room, cold and commanding as always. Tommy sat up, his body instinctively tensing.

"Come with me," the man said, his voice as flat as ever.

Tommy stood without hesitation. The man turned and walked out. Tommy followed, his pulse quickening with each step.

They walked through the narrow, dim hallways. The air was thick and stale. A damp scent clung to the walls. Tommy kept his eyes forward, trying to suppress the growing knot of anxiety in his chest. Something was different today. There was a tension in the man's movements, a purpose that wasn't there before.

After what felt like an eternity, they stopped in front of a door. The man pulled a key from his pocket, sliding it into the lock with a soft click.

The door swung open, and the man stepped inside, motioning for Tommy to follow. Tommy hesitated for a second, his eyes adjusting to the dim light of the room.

In the center, at a small table, sat a woman. Her hair tangled, and her skin looked pale and worn, as if she hadn't slept in days. She wore a faded green shirt, wrinkled and loose. Her hands rested on her lap, her eyes downcast. She looked... empty. Drained. Like someone had siphoned the life from her.

"This is Evelyn," the man said, his voice low but firm. "You'll be spending time with her from now on."

Tommy's breath caught in his throat. Another person. He hadn't seen anyone else since the man had taken him. The sight of Evelyn, broken as she seemed, stirred something inside him. She wasn't like the man.

The man stepped closer to Evelyn, his gaze cold and detached. "She's fragile," he said. "But she's still useful." He turned to Tommy, his eyes narrowing. "Learn from her."

Tommy frowned, unsure of what that meant. Learn from her? What did that involve? The man wasn't one to explain himself, and Tommy knew better than to ask for clarity.

He glanced at Evelyn again. Her eyes were on the table. But her shoulders were tense. It was a subtle sign she knew of their presence. She seemed fragile, but something about her made Tommy want to be gentle and kind. She was the first person he had seen in weeks who didn't treat him with cruelty.

Tommy stepped forward, unsure of what to say or do. "Hi," he said, his voice quiet and tentative.

Evelyn didn't respond at first. She kept twisting the edge of her shirt. Then she raised her head. Her eyes met his—dull, yes, but there was still a flicker of something there. Recognition. A spark of life that hadn't completely faded away.

"I'm... Tommy," he said, feeling awkward but determined to make some kind of connection.

For a moment, Evelyn stared at him, her expression unreadable. Her lips parted, as if she were trying to speak but couldn't find the words.

The man's presence loomed behind them, cold and indifferent. Tommy felt his gaze on them, watching, waiting. He had an odd pressure to act, to do something, though he didn't know what. This wasn't like the other tasks the man had given him. This wasn't about solving puzzles or enduring pain. This was different.

"You'll come here every day," the man said, his voice breaking the silence. "Spend time with her. Learn what you can. But remember, she's not your equal. She's another part of the task."

Tommy swallowed hard, glancing between the man and Evelyn. Another part of the task? But she didn't feel like a task. She felt like... someone. Someone who had suffered, like him.

The man didn't wait for a response. He turned and walked back toward the door, his footsteps heavy against the concrete floor. Tommy's heart raced as the door clicked shut behind him, leaving the room quiet.

For a moment, neither Tommy nor Evelyn moved. The silence between them was thick, heavy with unspoken things. Then Evelyn's eyes softened, and her lips trembled as if she were about to cry but was too tired to make the effort.

"I'm... Evelyn," she whispered, her voice hoarse and broken.

Tommy nodded, his throat tight. He didn't know what to say, but for the first time since the man had taken him, he didn't feel completely alone.

They sat there in silence for what felt like hours, both of them too tired to speak, but somehow that was enough. In this place, in this moment, it was like something had shifted. There was another person now—another soul who had suffered. Somehow, being there together, even in silence, made the darkness a bit less unbearable.

CHAPTER 28

SPECIAL AGENT ISABELLE STONE cruised the George Washington Parkway. Her eyes were on the road, but her thoughts drifted to South Beach. The Miami heat still lingered in her mind. South Beach had been exactly what she needed—a getaway, a break from the grind. But now, as she headed back to work, she was trying to forget about her three-day fling with Tiffany and get into work mode. South Beach drew her into short-lived affairs. The passion was real, but she knew better than to get attached. She never did. Tiffany was fun, but nothing more.

At thirty-four, Isabelle knew herself well enough to recognize her patterns. She was a striking figure. Attractive and confident, she had deep brown skin, a piercing gaze, and a thin athletic build. It showed her years of rigorous training and discipline. Today, she wore her natural curls loose. They framed her face as she navigated the familiar route. There was an edge to her that never softened. It was a mix of determination and a tough past that had made her strong. She was always in control, always ready for the next challenge.

Isabelle's background was as layered as her demeanor. Her mother was English, her father American. They'd met while he was stationed at Royal Air Force Base Lakenheath, where Isabelle was born. She was American by nationality, but a part of her clung to her British roots. When her parents divorced at seven, she found herself caught between two worlds. Her mother stayed in England; her father, a maintenance chief in the U.S. Air Force, returned to the States. Isabelle spent her childhood shuttling between them. She enjoyed summers in Yorkshire's green and winters with her father's crisp, American drawl. Though she split her time, her mother's accent stayed with her. It was a soft lilt that made her voice stand out among her colleagues.

It gave her an aura of mystery, one that worked both for and against her in her line of work. She was meticulous and perceptive. She had an elegant, yet steely, resolve. Her colleagues had learned not to underestimate her. Behind her charm was a fierce loyalty and a commitment to her job. She was proud of her roots and her parents' sacrifices. She channeled that pride into her work with the Bureau. People knew her for her sharp instincts. She stayed calm under pressure. And she had a relentless pursuit of justice.

Despite her walls, there were times—like her recent Miami escape—when she felt something more. Something fleeting, perhaps, but real in its own way. It was her outlet, a way to let go of the weight she carried daily.

Isabelle had no illusions about her life or her choices. The work always came first, and she liked it that way. Love and attachment complicated her purpose. For now, she was content with passion without strings.

Staying distant from people made things easier. It was especially true after her last long-term relationship with Kelly. That had ended, thanks to the long hours she worked at the Bureau. The shift work hadn't helped, either. Kelly had always been jealous. She accused her of sleeping with every partner, male or female, that she worked with. Every late-night shift sparked another argument. In the end, it became too much to handle.

Shaking off the thought of Kelly, Isabelle focused on the road ahead. Three years ago, she was new to the Bureau. It had been a childhood dream of hers to become a special agent, one that came with its own set of challenges. Chief among them had been her first partner, Agent James Lawson. She'd heard about him around the office, but they'd never met.

The day they met, James greeted her with a cocky grin and a casual, "Hey, rook." Isabelle had bristled at the nickname. She may have been new but, she had been a cop for three years before the Bureau. The last thing she considered herself was a rookie.

With a calm but firm tone, she introduced herself. "It's Isabelle," she said, keeping her gaze level. "Most people call me Izzie."

James, smirking in that way that only he did, responded, "I think I'll call ya Belle. Has a better ring to it."

He enjoyed the pun. Despite her best efforts, Isabelle half-smirked back. An annoying intro had become a trusted partnership.

Over time, Jimbo—as she had taken to calling him in retaliation— became more than her partner. He became the brother she never had. They collaborated with humor and respect, balancing each other's strengths and weaknesses. Their banter kept things light, even in the heaviest of cases. Now, Jimbo was one of the few people she trusted, both on and off the clock.

As Isabelle pulled into the parking lot, she took a deep breath. Vacation was over, and it was time to dive back in.

Inside the office, Jack, another agent, greeted her. He nodded in her direction as she made her way to her desk.

"Welcome back," Jack said with a grin. "How was South Beach?"

"Too short," Isabelle replied, tossing her bag onto her desk. "You seen Jimbo?"

Jack nodded. "Yeah, he's over in the briefing room, working on a case."

"Figures," she said, shaking her head with a small smile. "Thanks, Jack."

She settled into her office, the familiar hum of agents at work filling the air around her. Papers and case files stacked on her desk, and she lost herself in the rhythm of catching up on work. Her vacation was fading as she dove back into her life as a special agent. It meant late nights, tough cases, and, of course, Jimbo. She picked up her mug of coffee and headed to the briefing room.

CHAPTER 29

"WELL, WELL, look who's hard at work." Isabelle teased as she barged into the briefing room.

James shot her a playful glare. "You still remember how to do your job, or should I get you a manual?"

"Oh, is that how you wanna play? I'm certain I can do your job with my eyes closed," Isabelle chuckled, shaking her head.

"I figured you needed time to find those brain cells you left in Miami," he said, smiling. He paused and added, "welcome back, Belle."

"Thanks, Jimbo. It's good to be back," she said giving him a hug.

James grinned. "Alright. Enough with the pleasantries . . . Anyway, I got a new case. Care to join me, or are you too busy catching up on your beauty sleep?"

"Give me what ya got," she said, taking a seat.

James filled Isabelle in on the details. He sat across from her, papers scattered across the table between them. The weight of the human trafficking case hung in the air. James saw concern in Isabelle's eyes as he began to update her.

"We've got all the women from the other night in protective custody," James said, his voice steady but grim. "It looks like this trafficking circuit is much bigger than we initially thought. It spans all the way from Baltimore down to Norfolk and reaches as far west as Erie. Over 200 women are being moved through it."

"This is the shit bag that beat Angel. His name is Victor Blackwell. He's a violent guy with several priors." James said, sliding a photo and file across the table. "The books we found on scene, indicate, this guy has a deeper position in the circuit. Data forensics is also trying to break the code on the laptop we confiscated."

Isabelle leaned back in her chair, absorbing the scope of the situation. "So Blackwell's more than just some low-level thug?"

James nodded. "Yeah, it looks like he's pretty informed on how the network operates. If we can catch him, he might be our best chance at getting intel on the people running this operation. He's likely a key player, but not the brains behind it."

"Any word from the women you picked up the other night?" Isabelle asked, shifting in her seat.

"Some of them told us that D.C. was their third or even fourth city in the circuit. These women have been moved around like products, and most of them are too scared to talk," he said, tossing a folder toward Isabelle.

"I'm Assuming this is the woman he beat up? She provide anything helpful?" Isabelle pressed, looking at the file. "Angel Ramirez, right?"

James sighed, rubbing the back of his neck. "Yeah, Angel. She's with the others in protective custody, but she's been the least helpful. She keeps asking to leave. Honestly, I think she's dealing with some serious PTSD. It's hard to wrap my head around why she'd want to go back there after what that prick did to her. He really beat the shit out of her."

Isabelle gave him a knowing look. "It's what victims do, Jimbo. It's counterintuitive, I know. But trauma does strange things to people. She probably doesn't even realize what's happening to her."

James frowned, his frustration evident. "Yeah, I get it. Just fucking pisses me off when they want to go back to the shitbags that only want to harm them."

A moment later, an agent walked into the room, a sense of urgency in his step. "We think we've got a lead on Blackwell. We received intel he's been laying low at his mother's place in Takoma Park."

James immediately stood up, his expression sharpening. "Let's see if we can grab this guy before he goes off grid again."
She raised an eyebrow. "No rest for the weary, huh?"

"Weary?" James scoffed. "You've been living it up in Miami for the past week. You've had nothing but rest."

Isabelle's smile widened as she grabbed her jacket. "Alright, fine. Let's go so I can remind you how to actually make an arrest."

The two of them moved toward the door, their focus laser-sharp. This was the break they'd been waiting for. Blackwell was the key to the larger operation. They wouldn't let him slip away.

CHAPTER 30

ISABELLE SLID into the driver's seat. James took shotgun. The case weighed on his shoulders. As they drove to Takoma Park, James stared out the window, deep in thought. The deeper they dug into this case, the more he realized how volatile the situation was. Blackwell wasn't some common criminal; he was manipulative, methodical, and unpredictable. The type that doesn't let go until it's too late.

They pulled up to a small 1930s house on Boyd Avenue in Takoma Park. The home's peeling paint and worn shingles hinted at better days long gone. The air was thick, the cool late afternoon breeze doing little to shake the tension. James led the way, pressing the doorbell. They waited in silence, the minutes ticking by, each second a reminder of how little time they had. He pressed the bell again. Finally, the shuffle of footsteps inside broke the quiet.

An elderly woman appeared, pulling the curtain aside before unlocking the door. She cracked it open enough to see them.

"Good afternoon Ma'am. I'm special agent Lawson and this is my partner agent Stone. We're looking for Victor Blackwell," James said, showing his badge. "We have a warrant for his arrest."

Her eyes widened, her face pale. She stammered, "Why? He's been working hard, trying to turn his life around since he got out."

James remained calm, but the pressure behind his words was undeniable. "I understand, ma'am. But we need to speak with him. Can you get him to the door, please?"

The woman wrung her hands, hesitating. "He's... not here."

James's patience thinned, but he kept his tone even. "Where is he?"

"He said he was going to a movie," she replied, her voice wavering.

James shot a glance at Isabelle, a silent exchange passing between them—this isn't adding up. He turned back to the woman. "Do you know which theater?"

Her response was firmer this time, her eyes narrowing. "No, he didn't tell me."

James wasn't buying it. "He's a good boy. He stays out of trouble now," she mumbled.

James clenched his jaw, forcing back the words he wanted to say. Instead, he handed her his business card, his tone tight. "Thank you, ma'am. If your son returns, please call. It would be in his best interest to turn himself in."

She snatched the card from his hand with a huff, her voice icy. "You're wrong about him."

James and Isabelle turned to leave. As they made their way back to the car, James muttered under his breath, "That'll never happen."

Once they were back inside, Isabelle shot him a sideways glance. "Think she's covering for him?"

James stared out the window, his gut twisted with unease. "I don't know. But he's definitely not at the movies, and he's not coming back here anytime soon."

As Isabelle started the car, James's phone rang, the tension in the air tightening. "Agent Lawson," he answered, his voice clipped. He listened for a moment, then his face darkened. "What do you mean she's gone? Who the hell was watching her, Simons? That idiot!"

He slammed the phone down in frustration. "Angel bailed."

"Shit," Isabelle hissed, her grip tightening on the wheel. "I had a feeling. She kept talking about wanting to go back."

James nodded, anger bubbling below the surface. "I knew it was coming. She's probably gone back to Blackwell. That bastard's got his hooks in deep."

"Do you think she's at the apartment?" Isabelle asked, already turning the car around, her voice tense with urgency.

"If she's out and Blackwell's not here, I'd bet on it. Let's get over there, now."

"You might want to step on it," James muttered, his voice low, eyes dark with worry. "I've got a bad feeling about this."

Isabelle's foot pressed harder on the gas, the car picking up speed as they raced through the city streets. The fading light of day gave way to shadowy twilight, the city blurring around them. James clutched his phone, his thumb hovering over the screen. He was desperate for it to ring with good news, but the silence was suffocating.

The knot in his gut twisted tighter with every passing second. Angel was walking into a nightmare. If she contacted Blackwell, it would be too late.

They needed to get there. Now.

CHAPTER 31

JAMES AND ISABELLE ARRIVED at the apartment complex. It was an old, worn-down building, a relic from another era. It looked like a forgotten budget motel. As the city gentrified, few of these remained. The fading dusk light cast long shadows on the cracked pavement. As they got out of the car, a young woman came rushing out of a ground-floor apartment, her face pale with panic.

"I was just calling you!" she cried, breathless. "There's something happening in 2B! I heard a woman screaming, and then a bunch of banging."

James felt his pulse quicken and began running up the stairs. He and Isabelle rushed up, taking the stairs two at a time. Their shoes echoed against the metal steps. They reached 2B in seconds, pounding on the door.

"FBI!" James shouted, his fist pounding against the wood.

No answer.

James kicked the door in, splintering the lock. It slammed open. The sight inside made his blood run cold.

Angel lay in the living room, a pool of blood surrounding her body, her throat slashed open. The gash was deep and jagged, her face frozen in a grimace of terror. But before James grasped the horror, he heard a commotion from the bedroom.

He sprinted down the hall, kicking in the bedroom door with a forceful crack. The window was wide open, curtains flapping in the breeze. James rushed to the window. He saw Blackwell hit the ground below. He was limping as he scrambled to his feet.

Without thinking, James yelled to Isabelle, "Call for backup! We need a chopper out here with a spotlight!" Then he bolted from the apartment, Isabelle's voice trailing after him. "Wait for backup, James!"

James didn't wait. There wasn't time. He tore down the stairs, chasing after the limping man. His heart pounded in his chest, his mind racing with thoughts of the woman lying dead on the floor. He can't get away. Not after what he did.

A helicopter's rotors soon cut through the air. The chopper arrived, its bright spotlight tracking Blackwell. James pushed himself harder, his legs burning as he closed in. Blackwell was slowing, his limp growing worse with each passing second. He hurt from the jump, but he wasn't giving up.

The rage boiled inside James. He had to get this guy. He had to make him pay.

Finally, after what felt like an eternity, James was close enough. He lunged and tackled the assailant to the ground. They crashed hard against the pavement. The man grunted in pain, his hands flailing as he tried to get up, but James was on him, pinning him down with all his weight.

"You fucking piece of shit!" James growled, his voice low and filled with fury.

Without thinking, without hesitation, James swung his fist. Once. Twice. Again. Each punch landed with brutal precision, the man's face snapping back with the force of the blows. Blood began to pour from Blackwell's nose, mixing with the sweat and grime on his skin. But James didn't stop. He couldn't stop.

All the anger and frustration James had bottled up surged out in a violent torrent. His fists slammed into the man's face over and over, the sound of bone meeting flesh echoing in the empty street.

Blackwell gasped for air. He tried to protect himself, but James pinned him down harder. His fists moved like a blur. He lost himself in the rage, consumed by the need to make this man pay for what he had done. At that moment, a patrol car skidded to a stop near the two, and an officer got out, leaving the door ajar.

"Agent Lawson… stop!" It was the officer's voice cutting through the fog of anger. James heard a sound. Then, the officer grabbed his shoulders. He pulled James off the bloodied man.

"Get off him, man. That's enough!" the officer shouted, struggling to restrain James.

Breathing hard, James finally relented. He stepped back, his chest heaving, his fists covered in the man's blood. The officer held James back as Blackwell coughed on the ground, blood dripping from his mouth.

And then, in one quick motion, he moved.

Before anyone could react, Blackwell pulled a knife from his waistband. It was the same knife he used to kill Angel. Then, he lunged at James, a wild, desperate look in his eyes.

It all happened in an instant. Blackwell surged forward. The blade glinted in the faint light as he swung it at James's chest.

But before the knife reached its target, a deafening gunshot rang out. The sound echoed off the buildings. Blackwell staggered as the bullet hit him square in the chest.

Isabelle had arrived on the scene, her gun still raised, her eyes wide with adrenaline. Blackwell dropped to the ground, the knife clattering to the pavement beside him. He lay there, gasping for breath, the life draining from his eyes.

James stood frozen, his breath coming in ragged gasps, the shock of the moment washing over him. He stared at the dead body of the man who had tried to kill him. The reality of what had almost happened sank in.

The officer let out a long breath. "Jesus Christ. You almost got yourself killed."

James didn't respond; his mind was still reeling from the chaos. He glanced down at his bloodied fists, then at the body on the ground, and a strange, unsettling calm washed over him.

Blackwell was dead. And there was a good chance the case was too.

CHAPTER 32

THE DAYS HAD BECOME a blur of routine for Tommy, but one thing had changed: Evelyn. Each morning, the man would unlock Tommy's door and escort him down the long, dim corridors to Evelyn's room. The first few visits were tense, with awkward silences and glances. But over the weeks, something had shifted.

Evelyn had started to open up, little by little. At first, it was small things—comments about the weather, stories from her past. But soon, their conversations began to take on a life of their own. Tommy would sit across from her. They would talk for hours. They shared memories, fears, and hopes. But hope was like a distant dream.

One day, Evelyn had a surprise waiting for him. As Tommy entered her room, he noticed a board game set up on the small table where they usually sat.

"Checkers," she said with a soft smile, her eyes lighter than they had been before. "It was always my favorite game as a kid."

Tommy hesitated, staring at the board. It had been so long since he'd seen anything familiar, anything that reminded him of a normal life. The sight of the simple red and black pieces brought a strange warmth to his chest.

"You ever play?" Evelyn asked, setting up the pieces.

"A long time ago," Tommy said, sitting down across from her.

"Well," she said with a playful smirk, "I should warn you—I'm pretty good."

Tommy felt a flicker of something he hadn't had in weeks—laughter. It bubbled up inside him, soft and unfamiliar, but there. Evelyn's mood was contagious. For the first time in forever, the weight of their captivity lifted, if only for a moment.

They played for hours; the conversation flowed as naturally as the game. Evelyn told him about her childhood. She used to play checkers with her dad on rainy Sunday afternoons. Tommy shared stories about his best friend, Austin. They would stay up late playing video games.

As the days passed, the bond between them grew stronger. Evelyn became a mother figure, advising and encouraging Tommy. She became the comfort he had longed for. She seemed to understand his fears and uncertainties.

After another long game of checkers, Evelyn surprised Tommy. As she stood up to stretch, she reached over and ruffled his hair, the gesture small yet filled with warmth.

"You remind me of a boy I used to babysit," she said, her eyes far away, lost in a memory. "He used to look at me the same way you do, like he needed someone to tell him everything would be okay."

Tommy had a lump form in his throat. He hadn't realized how much he had come to rely on Evelyn, how much her presence meant to him in this dark, lonely place. She wasn't only a fellow captive anymore. She had become something more—a protector, a friend, almost like family.

Their time together became a lifeline. They would talk about anything and everything. From Evelyn's favorite book to Tommy's dream of becoming a baseball player. But every time, the man cut their moments short.

The door would swing open, with no warning. The man's cold presence would fill the room, and their time would be over. The man never said much, a simple, "It's time," before escorting Tommy back to his room.

The abrupt endings felt like a rude awakening from a warm dream. They were thrust back into the cold, harsh reality of their situation. But even after Tommy left, the warmth from those moments with Evelyn lingered. It gave him a small hope to hold onto in the darkness.

One afternoon, after a checkers game, Evelyn leaned forward. Her eyes were serious for the first time in days.

"Tommy," she said, her voice low, "you know we're going to get out of here, right?"

Tommy looked at her, the weight of her words settling over him. He wanted to believe it—wanted to believe there was a way out. But the man's shadow loomed large over everything. It was hard to imagine freedom when the walls were so permanent, so unyielding.

"I don't know how," Evelyn continued, "but we will. You're smart, Tommy. You'll figure it out. And when you do... I'll be right there with you."

Tommy didn't know what to say. He felt the same pull, the same need to escape, but there was something about the way Evelyn said it. She sounded so certain, so confident, like she believed in him more than he believed in himself.

But as always, the man cut their conversation short. The door swung open, and the man stood there, his expression as unreadable as ever.

"Time's up!" He said, his voice cold and final.

Tommy stood, his heart heavy as he glanced back at Evelyn. She gave him a small, reassuring smile, as if to remind him of her words.

CHAPTER 33

SEVERAL DAYS HAD PASSED. In the room where time stretched and blurred, a bond formed between Tommy and Evelyn. It was profound. Evelyn had changed in subtle ways. She smiled more now, her eyes carrying a light that hadn't been there before. But it wasn't only her smile. It was the small things. Tiny habits and gestures tugged at something deep within Tommy.

Her ruffling his hair after a game of checkers. The soft hum of a tune she sang as a kid. Even her little sayings in conversations. Everything reminded Tommy of his mother. It filled him with a bittersweet warmth. It made his chest tighten with both comfort and longing. Sometimes, Evelyn would say something. It would hit him like a wave of homesickness, pulling up memories of his mom.

"You'll catch more flies with honey than vinegar, you know," Evelyn said one afternoon. It made Tommy laugh. His mother had said the same thing whenever he struggled with his homework. The familiar phrase made his heart ache for home.

One evening, as they sat together after another game of checkers, Tommy couldn't hold it in any longer. The overwhelming sense of homesickness had gnawed at him for days.

"I miss home," Tommy said, his voice above a whisper. He stared at the board, his fingers shifting the pieces. "I miss my mom and dad. It's been so long..."

Evelyn, sitting across from him, softened immediately. Her face went from playful to worried. She took his hand. The touch was gentle, warm—a quiet, steady comfort.

"I know, Tommy," she whispered. "I know."

A silence settled between them, but it wasn't empty. Understanding filled it. Tommy didn't pull his hand away. For the first time in a long time, he didn't feel so alone.

One day, after another round of small talk and quiet reflection, Evelyn's demeanor shifted. She grew quiet. Her eyes no longer met his. Her answers became short and distracted, as if her mind were far away. Finally, she spoke, her voice low and secretive.

"Tommy," she began, leaning forward across the table, her eyes flicking to the door to make sure they were alone. "I've found a way out."

A way out? He thought.

Evelyn's eyes locked onto his, the seriousness in her gaze unmistakable.

85

She had spoken about escape, but never with conviction. But now, as she leaned closer, her words filled with urgency.

"I've been watching... listening," she whispered. "I've found a pattern. If we're careful... if we plan this right... we can get out."

Tommy's heart raced. He wanted to believe her. He leaned in, eyes wide, hanging on her every word.

"How?" he asked, his voice trembling.

Evelyn laid out the plan in meticulous detail. She had been paying attention for weeks, memorizing the man's habits. He had a routine—one that was strict, almost mechanical. Every few days, he would leave for hours. He'd leave the house early and not return until nightfall. During these stretches, the house was quiet, and Evelyn saw an opportunity.

"He thinks we're broken," Evelyn said, her voice hardening. "He thinks he has full control over us, that we won't even try to escape. That's why he doesn't bother watching us as much anymore."

"One day, he was careless and left my door unlocked," Evelyn said, her voice low but urgent. "I slipped out and looked around the area. I found a small service door, hidden in a corner of this level. It led to an overgrown path into the woods."

Evelyn told Tommy that she had found a blind spot in the security system. A place where they could slip out without the man seeing them. She had figured this out by watching the man adjust the cameras. She noted where they pointed and where their coverage overlapped.

"I've checked it more than once," Evelyn whispered. "The cameras don't cover certain areas. If we time it right... we can get out. But we need to be careful. We can't rush this."

Tommy's mind raced; the possibilities overwhelmed him. Might it work? He had dreamed of escape for so long that the idea seemed almost impossible. But Evelyn's calm, calculated manner filled him with a flicker of hope.

"I'll help," Tommy said, sitting up straighter. "Whatever you need, I'll help."

Evelyn smiled, a small, tired smile. It carried the weight of everything they had been through. "I knew you would," she said.

They spent the rest of the day refining the plan, making sure every detail was perfect. Evelyn's confidence gave Tommy strength. For the first time since his captivity began, he believed there might be a future beyond these walls.

***

As they planned, the man watched from another room. The closed-circuit monitors bathed him in a blue glow. The flickering light cast an eerie hue over his face. He leaned back in his worn leather chair, eyes darting from screen to screen. Each camera captured Evelyn and Tommy in their small, cell-like space, whispering. They were close enough to touch. They exchanged guarded looks. They forged bonds over weeks of shared hardship. They knew that trust came at a price.

He watched Evelyn's eyes light up as she leaned into Tommy, her voice a mere breath outlining the start of their plan. Determination sharpened her features; Tommy nodded, his jaw tight.

The man's thin lips curled into an almost-smile as he twisted a dial, zooming in on Evelyn's expression. They thought they were in control. They thought they had outsmarted him, but this was his game. They were only pieces on his board. They followed paths he'd mapped out long before they thought of escaping. He had been pulling their strings for weeks. He nudged them together, watching as hope bloomed where he had once planted despair.

But hope was a funny thing. It made people vulnerable. It cracked their self-preservation. It made them reckless. He knew that too well, and that was exactly why he had allowed it. Evelyn and Tommy were desperate, and desperation bred betrayal.

"Which one will it be?" he murmured to himself, his gaze steady on the screen. Evelyn's hand lingered on Tommy's, her fingers curling around his for a brief moment. Tommy squeezed back, and they shared a look—a promise, a secret pact.

He leaned closer, his breath fogging the glass of his whiskey tumbler. Would it be Evelyn, the fierce one with fire in her eyes and vengeance etched into her every movement? Or Tommy, the one who craved freedom so much he would do anything, say anything, to feel the sun on his face one more time? They were both broken in their own ways. Each was so manipulated that they couldn't see how completely they were being played.

He had planted the seeds. He had set the trap, and now it was only a matter of time. They would trust, plan, and dream of freedom. One of them—he was sure—would crack under the weight of it all.

He watched as Tommy turned from Evelyn. He had dark eyes, and he furrowed his brow. Doubt crept into his gaze. The man smiled, a thin, humorless line. Yes, which one would it be? He almost couldn't wait to find out.

***

As the day ended, the man's footsteps echoed down the hallway, signaling the end of their time together. Tommy looked at Evelyn with renewed purpose. They had a plan. They had each other.
All they needed now was the right moment.

87

CHAPTER 34

ALEX GRAYSON SAT by the window of her favorite coffee shop. The soft buzz of conversation around her blended into the background. She sipped her cappuccino, savoring the rich foam and the warmth of the cup in her hands. The novel she had brought with her was open in front of her, but she hadn't turned a page in several minutes. Instead, her thoughts began to drift, pulled back to memories of her best friend, Jessica.

A small smile tugged at the corners of her mouth as she remembered the first day they met. It was move-in day at college. Alex stood at her dorm room's doorway, staring at the bare, institutional walls inside. Then, Jessica appeared in the hallway.

"Hi, I'm Jessica," she had said with an infectious grin, walking right in as though they'd known each other forever. "Looks like we're roomies. Need help unpacking?"

Alex hadn't even had time to respond before Jessica started grabbing boxes and pulling them open. Alex remembered feeling a little overwhelmed but relieved at Jessica's easygoing nature. They worked, chatting as they arranged the room. Clothes, books, and photos found their places. It didn't take long for the two to start laughing about the mishmash of items they each owned.

"I can't believe you brought a stuffed penguin," Jessica teased, holding up Alex's childhood toy.

"I can't sleep without it," Alex had said, pretending to defend herself. "He's been with me through thick and thin."

Jessica had laughed. "Looks like he'll be with us through this year, too."

They were almost done setting up when the door to the room opened, and a girl with dark, goth-styled hair walked in. She looked around the room, her brow furrowed in confusion.

"What are you doing in my room?" the girl asked, her voice edged with irritation.

Alex blinked, startled, but Jessica, as calm as ever, pulled Alex's room assignment information that was sitting on the desk and scanned it.

"Oh no," she said, glancing between Alex and the girl, "I think you're supposed to be in the room across the hall."

The girl, Linda, said, "Well, this is definitely my room."

Jessica gave her an easy grin, completely unfazed by Linda's attitude. "No problem! Let's get this stuff moved across the hall. Alex, I'll help you pack it all up again."

As they moved Alex's things out, her frustration grew. But Jessica's lightheartedness made it impossible to stay mad for long.

"Guess we're getting some extra exercise today," Jessica said, hoisting one of Alex's boxes. "Not bad for a move-in day."

Alex laughed. "Yeah, just what I wanted. More heavy lifting."

They moved everything into the correct room, both giggling at the absurdity of the mix-up. As they finished setting down the last of Alex's things, Linda appeared. She held up a small photo frame that Alex had left behind. She tossed it onto the bed without much ceremony.

"You forgot this," she said, her tone still clipped before turning on her heel and marching back out.

Alex exchanged a glance with Jessica. "She sure is a charm," Alex deadpanned. "Seems like you'll have a peachy roommate."

Jessica burst out laughing. She wrapped Alex in a quick, dramatic hug, fake sobbing into her shoulder. "I wish you were my roommate!" She pulled back, still grinning. With her head hung low in mock disappointment, she added, "Guess I'll just have to live across the hall with Cruella."

"Don't worry," Alex said, smiling back. "You're not getting rid of me that easily."

From that moment on, they were inseparable. Even with rooms across the hall from each other, they spent more time together than apart. Their friendship became a constant in Alex's life, one she never questioned.

Alex sipped her cappuccino. Her eyes glazed over the busy street outside the window. Her mind jumped to graduation day, a snapshot of pure joy. Both she and Jessica had finished their computer engineering graduate programs. They were ready to tackle the world. She remembered the sheer elation they had, arms linked as they tossed their caps into the air.

"We did it!" Jessica had shouted, pulling Alex into a bear hug. "We're going to change the world!"

Alex had laughed; the energy between them was electric. "Yeah, after we figure out how to pay off these student loans!"

"Details," Jessica had said, waving her hand. "We're geniuses. We'll figure it out."

Soon after graduation, they flew to Spain. They began a 30-day trek along the Camino de Santiago. It had been a dream trip. It was full of laughter, deep talks, and awe as they wandered through ancient lands.

"I can't believe we're doing this," Jessica had said one night as they sat on a hillside, looking out at the sunset. "It feels like we're on top of the world."

"Because we are," Alex had replied. The world was at their feet. Endless possibilities for their futures stretched out before them.

But that feeling hadn't lasted. Only a month after they returned, Alex started to notice subtle changes in Jessica. It began with small things—her reflexes seemed off, her hands shaking more than usual. Then her speech

89

became slurred at times, her words not flowing as they once had. At first, Alex brushed it off. She thought Jessica was tired or stressed from their job hunts after graduation.

But the signs grew worse. One morning, over coffee, Jessica had broken the news.

"Alex," she had said, her voice trembling enough for Alex to notice, "the doctor... he diagnosed me with ALS."

Alex remembered the way her stomach had dropped, the air in the room turning heavy and thick. She had stared at Jessica, hoping for a sign that this was a cruel joke. But Jessica's eyes held a quiet, resigned fear. It was the fear of someone facing an impossible truth.

"What?" Alex said in a whisper. "How... how can that be?"

"They gave me two years," Jessica had continued. Her voice was steady, but her hands trembled as she lifted her coffee cup.

Tears had welled in Alex's eyes, but she had blinked them back, trying to stay strong for her friend. Jessica had always been the strong one, the fearless one. Alex didn't know how to be anything but helpless in that moment.

In the end, Jessica didn't have two years. She died eleven months later, her body giving out far sooner than anyone expected. Alex had been there through it all: the hospital visits, the doctors, and the decline. She watched her best friend, the person who had once been so full of life, fade away in front of her eyes.

Back in the coffee shop, Alex's vision blurred as her eyes filled with tears. She blinked, cleared her throat, and looked out the window. The bustling street beyond offered no comfort. She raised her cappuccino to her lips and took a sip, trying to swallow the lump in her throat. The coffee's warmth spread through her. But it did little to chase away the chill of loss that settled deep in her chest.

She missed Jessica every day, the pain dulling only with time but never fading. There were moments—like now—when the grief caught her off guard, crashing over her in waves. Alex closed her eyes for a moment, letting herself feel it.

Then, with a soft sigh, she opened her eyes, wiped away the stray tear on her cheek, and looked back down at her book. But her thoughts lingered on Jessica, her dearest friend. She was the one person who had understood her better than anyone else.

CHAPTER 35

ANOTHER WEEK HAD PASSED, and today was the day. The day Evelyn and Tommy planned to escape. Every detail they discussed, every opportunity calculated. Tommy had gone over the steps in his mind a thousand times, rehearsing how it would play out. The plan had become his lifeline, his only hope.

But as the hours dragged on, something was wrong. The man hadn't followed his usual routine. Instead of leaving as he usually did, the door to Tommy's room opened, revealing him standing there.

The man stepped in, his cold eyes fixed on Tommy. There was a shift in the air, something ominous, as if he knew something Tommy didn't.

"I've trained you well," the man said, his voice low, almost reflective. "To manipulate. To be precise. To be efficient. And to not care about anyone who stands in your way."

He moved closer, his hand resting on Tommy's shoulder, a twisted sense of pride in his expression. "Only the best will do, after all."

Tommy stood frozen, every fiber of his being on edge. His heart raced, but his face remained neutral, as the man had trained him. Any sign of fear or hesitation—those were weaknesses, things the man had beaten out of him long ago.

"Come with me," the man whispered.

They left the room and walked down the narrow hallways in silence. The tension was suffocating. As they neared the door to Evelyn's room, the man leaned down and whispered in Tommy's ear, his words laced with venom.

"I know what you two are planning," he hissed. "And I'm certain you'll tell me everything Evelyn has told you to do, won't you?"

Tommy's stomach twisted, his mind racing. How does he know? He had no time to think, no time to process. The door to Evelyn's room was already open.

They stepped inside. Evelyn sat at the small table, her face lighting up with hope when she saw Tommy. "Hi, Tommy," she said, her voice soft, as if she had no idea of the nightmare that was about to unfold.

The man turned to her, his expression shifting into something darker, more dangerous. "Boyyyy," he said, drawing out the word with a sinister tone.

Tommy's mind went blank, the command searing through him like a jolt of electricity. Without even thinking, without hesitation, he began to speak.

The words spilled from his mouth, cold and calculated, almost robotic.

"She's planning to escape," Tommy said, his voice hollow. "She told me everything. She found the service entrance and knows which cameras to avoid." He continued to detail everything that Evelyn had come up with and confided in him. The strange thing was, as he spoke, he seemed accusatory. It was as if the man forced him to tell.

The shock on Evelyn's face was immediate. Her eyes widened, her lips parted as if she couldn't believe what she was hearing. Betrayal. Her face displayed it all. The hope that had been in her eyes moments ago had vanished, replaced by devastation.

"Tommy..." she whispered, her voice breaking.

The man smirked, his hand resting on Tommy's shoulder, a silent affirmation of approval. Tommy had done what his training had prepared him to do—betray, survive, and eliminate anyone in his way. He had learned the lesson well.

"Good Tommy, good," the man said, his voice dripping with satisfaction. "You see, Evelyn? He was never truly yours. He was mine. Every bond you thought you made, every ounce of trust—just a tool to be used against you."

Evelyn's eyes filled with sorrow, her body trembling with a mixture of helplessness and shame. She had believed in Tommy, had trusted him, and cared for him. And now, she had nothing.

"Thank you, Tommy," the man said, patting him on the back. "Now, go back to your room. Evelyn and I have some unfinished business."

Tommy turned toward the door, glancing at Evelyn. She looked so small, so fragile. Her face in pain—not only from fear, but from the betrayal, the knife he had driven straight through her heart. For a moment, something flickered in Tommy's chest, something that felt like guilt.

The door closed behind him. As he walked down the hall, a hard slap echoed, followed by Evelyn's scream. The sound sent a shiver down his spine, but he kept walking, his steps slow and deliberate.

He reached his room, closed the door behind him, and sat down on the bed, his hands trembling. The walls felt like they were closing in, suffocating him. He pressed his palms to his ears. He tried to block out the sounds from the other room—the sharp crack of blows, the muffled cries of pain.

But he couldn't stop hearing it. Evelyn's screams echoed in his mind, louder and louder, until they became unbearable.

The man had trained him not to care. To be precise. To betray anyone if it meant his survival. But now, alone in his room, a boulder of guilt crushed him.

Why did I do it?

He thought of the bond he and Evelyn had shared, how she had comforted him, how she had become like a mother to him. And now, he had destroyed it. Destroyed her. All because the man had whispered a command, and

Tommy had obeyed like a well-trained machine.

But Tommy knew he was no machine.

He clenched his fists, the shame flooding through him, suffocating him. I have to make this right. He couldn't leave her in there. He couldn't leave her to suffer because of him.

He stood up, his heart pounding in his chest. He had to get them out of here. Both of them.

Before it was too late.

CHAPTER 36

THE TV'S SOFT GLOW FLICKERED in the dark living room. Shadows danced on the walls as Cynthia Hayes sat on the couch, cross-stitching. It was a pattern of two wild horses running through a field. Their manes flowed in the wind. Her hands moved with practiced precision. The needle slipped in and out of the fabric. The rhythm was a welcome distraction. It was an escape. It was a chance to focus on something small and controllable, unlike the grief that lived inside her.

Across from her, Robert sat in his usual spot, sunk deep into his worn-out Lazy Boy recliner, staring at the TV. They were watching a baseball movie. But neither was paying attention to the dialogue. The screen showed a father and son playing catch in the backyard. But, for Cynthia and Robert, it was only noise. It stirred painful memories.

It had been three years since their son, Lucas, died in the accident. But time had not healed the wounds—it had only made their routine more numb, more predictable. The days blurred together. Each night ended the same. They sat in front of the TV, not speaking or watching. They only existed in the same space, the silence carrying their grief.

Cynthia's mind wandered as her hands worked the needle through the fabric. She couldn't help but think of Lucas, of the last time she saw him alive. He had been so full of energy that day, as always. She remembered him running out the front door, the screen door slamming behind him.

"Going over to the park to meet Aus!" he had yelled. She reached the door to remind him to be back before dinner. By then, he was on his bike, pedaling down the driveway.

"Be home before—" Her voice trailed off. She knew Lucas wouldn't hear her. But she also knew he'd be back on time, like always. Lucas was a good boy. He listened, did well in school, and was well-liked by everyone, except for one neighbor kid, Brian. A chubby boy with a mean streak, Brian loved to tease and taunt Lucas at every opportunity. But Lucas never let it bother him. He was always so composed, unwilling to let Brian's jabs get under his skin.

As Cynthia cross-stitched, a memory of Lucas flashed in her mind. It was of him at the park, laughing with his friends, his hair catching the sunlight. But the image shattered. Her thoughts shifted to a moment that had changed everything. Two police officers stood at their door.

She remembered opening the door, puzzled. Then, dread grew as they told her there had been an accident. She still heard their voices. They told her that a car full of teenagers had sped down the street while Lucas was riding his bike. They hadn't seen him. They hit him. He was gone.

Her knees had buckled. The world had gone silent, her body too weak to stand, too numb to understand. She crumbled to the floor, unable to comprehend how everything could vanish from her in the blink of an eye.

A single tear slid down Cynthia's cheek, splashing onto the fabric in her hands. She wiped it away, her fingers tightening around the needle. She tried to steady herself and focus on the cross-stitch. It was her refuge in moments like these, when the memories became too heavy to bear.

Robert sat in his chair, lost in his own thoughts. A scene on the screen showed a father teaching his son to play catch. It took Robert back to a warm afternoon, years ago, when he had first bought Lucas a glove.

He saw it with clarity now, Lucas in the backyard, struggling to catch. They had laughed as Lucas kept dropping the ball. His young hands were clumsy but determined. Robert remembered telling him, "Every time you catch one, you get a point. But if you miss, we start over again. Deal?"

"Okay," Lucas had said, eyes wide with concentration.

They had only started over a couple of times before. Then, Lucas caught twenty-five in a row. His face lit up with each catch. Robert had been so proud, watching his son grow more confident with every catch.

"I think you've got it," Robert had said, calling it a day even though Lucas wanted to keep playing.

Now, sitting in his chair, Robert wished he had kept playing that day, had thrown just one more ball. Maybe then it wouldn't feel like the game had ended too soon.

The TV flickered. The movie's sounds continued. But Robert's mind drifted. He was still thinking about that afternoon. How many balls might Lucas have caught by now if things had been different?

This was their nightly routine now. Cynthia and Robert sat in front of the TV, their minds drifting to the past, haunted by unshareable memories. An unspoken sadness filled the house, with each of them living in their own separate worlds of grief.

Cynthia stitched her landscape. Her thoughts were on her son, who had run out the door for the last time. Robert stared at the screen, but in his mind, he was back in the backyard, throwing to his son, who would never grow up.

CHAPTER 37

IT HAD BEEN A WEEK since Tommy had seen Evelyn. The absence gnawed at him, a constant weight pressing on his chest. Every day that passed without her made the shame inside him grow larger, more unbearable. The guilt of what he had done—the betrayal, the lies—clung to him like a shadow. He had to make things right. He had to get them both out.

Over the months, the man had tested Tommy in countless ways. Each challenge aimed to sharpen his skill in using and controlling both things and people. But in those tasks, in those twisted games, the man had given Tommy the tools he needed, without realizing it. Gears, tweezers, small instruments— the kind used in delicate electronics. The kind that picked a lock with the right technique.

And Tommy had handled them with great skill.

For the past week, he had practiced picking the lock on his door. He would turn off the light, ensuring that the hidden cameras did not see his movements. He would unlock the door, then re-lock it. Each time, it became easier, faster, until it was second nature. But now, the moment had arrived. He wasn't going to lock himself back in. He wasn't going to return to his prison.

That evening, Tommy heard the man yelling into the phone, his voice sharp and angry. "I'll be over in 30 minutes," the man said. He slammed the phone down. Then, footsteps and the jingle of keys followed.

He then heard footsteps across the floor. The door opening. The slam echoing through the house. And then, the engine. Tommy had listened as the man's car pulled away, the crunch of gravel beneath the tires growing distant.

This was it. His chance.

Tommy sprang into action, his heart pounding in his chest. He grabbed the small tool he had fashioned from the pieces the man had left him over the months. With practiced precision, he picked the lock on his door. It clicked open with ease, as it had the twenty times before.

But this time, there was no turning back.

He ran down the hallway, his breath coming in short, panicked bursts. Please let her be alive. Please let her be okay. He repeated the words like a prayer, his legs carrying him faster toward Evelyn's room. He reached her door, hands shaking as he worked the lock.

It gave way. The door swung open, revealing Evelyn lying on the bed, her face turned away from him.

"Evelyn," he said, hoping she was okay.

"Tommy?" she whispered, her voice weak and fragile.

He ran to her, his heart aching as he saw the exhaustion etched into her skin. She looked broken, but she was alive. And that was all that mattered.

"I'm sorry," Tommy blurted, his voice cracking. He knelt beside her, grabbing her hand. "It's my fault. He hurt you because of me. I'm so sorry."

Evelyn turned to him, her eyes soft but filled with pain. "Tommy… it's not your fault."

He hugged her, his voice urgent. "We have to go. I found a way out. I promise. I picked all the locks."

Evelyn stared at him, blinking through her pain, but then she nodded. Tommy helped her to her feet, her body trembling as she stood. She winced, but she moved with him.

They ran together down the hallway, the air thick with tension. Tommy led the way, heart pounding, to the service entrance they had planned to use. His hands worked on the lock, and the door clicked open. But when he pushed, it wouldn't budge.

"It's… it's stuck," Tommy muttered, pushing harder, his panic rising. The door was nailed shut from the outside.

Evelyn's breath quickened, fear flashing in her eyes. "We're trapped," she whispered.

"No," Tommy said, shaking his head. "We'll go through the house. He's gone. I heard him leave. We have to be quick."

Evelyn hesitated, fear radiating off her in waves. She was terrified that the man would be waiting for them, believing that this was all some twisted game. But Tommy's determination anchored her.

"Okay," she whispered, steeling herself.

They ran back through the hallway, their footsteps echoing through the house. Tommy reached the basement stairs. They led to a locked door on the main floor. His fingers flew to the lock, his hands steady despite the panic coursing through him.

They ran up the stairs, reaching the door, and Tommy once again picked the lock. The door opened, which led into the living room. The house was quiet, the air heavy with silence. As they rushed through the large room, Tommy noticed the sterile atmosphere. The furniture was expensive and the floors were polished. Everything looked so perfect, so well-kept, as if it belonged to a different world.

But there was no time to linger. They had to keep moving. They bolted for the front door, the cool night breeze hitting them like a wave of freedom as they burst outside. The stars twinkled above, and for the first time in what felt like an eternity, Tommy breathed in the fresh air.

They were out.

But they weren't safe yet.

They sprinted across the yard. The grass was soft underfoot. Their hearts pounded with the weight of what they had done. Tommy's mind raced as they ran, his thoughts split between relief and fear. They had escaped the house, but what if the man came back? What if he caught them before they got far enough away?

But for now, they had one thing: hope.

And that was enough to keep them running.

CHAPTER 38

IT WAS MIDNIGHT before the man returned to the house, his steps heavy with frustration. The problems at work had piled up, and the phone call earlier had pushed him over the edge. He dropped his keys on the hallway table with a clatter that echoed through the silent house.

Without bothering to turn on the lights, he made his way to the living room. The familiar bourbon bottle stood on the bar cart like an old friend. He poured a neat glass, then turned on some jazz. Miles Davis filled the air with soft, sad notes. He sank into the leather armchair. The bourbon slid down his throat, cool and smooth. He tried to let the jazz take over, to drown out the fury building inside him.

But the call—that damned call—echoed in his mind. It gnawed at him, every word replaying over and over, fueling his anger. His knuckles whitened around the glass, and in a flash of rage, he threw it across the room. The glass shattered against the wall. A constellation of fragments rained down, leaving an empty, quiet space.

He stood there, breathing heavily, with anger simmering beneath the surface. His gaze drifted to the door at the end of the hall. Downstairs. Evelyn. It was time to work off some of this frustration. That thought brought a twisted calm over him. But as his eyes lingered on the door, something was… wrong. The door to the basement was ajar.

His heart skipped. He rushed over, thinking it was his imagination. It wasn't. He grabbed the handle, throwing the door open with a force that sent it slamming into the wall. His shoes thudded on the wooden stairs as he descended. With each step, his alarm grew, and his pace quickened.

He reached the bottom and saw Evelyn's door. Wide open. Empty. The room was a hollow shell, cold and empty.

"Evelyn," he muttered under his breath, but there was no one there. Panic surged through him. He spun around, eyes darting down the hallway to the other door. Tommy. That door was still closed. Locked.

"Tommy, my boy, you better be in there," he muttered, his hands shaking as he fumbled with the keys. The lock clicked open. He yanked the door, believing Tommy was still inside.

The room was empty. His breath caught in his throat. Tommy was gone.

A wave of red-hot rage overtook him. He started tearing through the room. He turned over the bed, kicked the table aside, and threw anything he lifted. He destroyed everything in sight, but it did nothing to quell the storm inside him. He stopped, panting, staring at the wreckage he had created. He picked up a fallen chair and sat, pressing his hands to his temples, trying to gather his thoughts.

After a long moment, he reached into his pocket, pulling out his cell phone. His fingers hovered over the keypad before dialing the number.

On the third ring, someone picked up.

"We have a problem," the man growled, his voice cold and controlled.

CHAPTER 39

SILAS WARD SAT in his quiet, small apartment. The dim light from the TV cast faint shadows across the room. His face, hardened by years of military service, looked older than his actual age. His once sharp, clean features were now softened by rough stubble. His hair, longer than the Marine regulation cut he used to keep, fell over his forehead. His dark, brooding eyes fixed on the flickering screen. But he wasn't paying attention to what was playing. The room around him was sparse—a couch, a small table, and the faint glow of the city outside the windows.

The glass of whiskey in his hand was almost empty, while the bottle next to him was already half-drained. He took another slow sip, savoring the burn as it went down, grounding him in the moment. His military days were distant, yet the man he was now—a fixer, a problem solver—didn't feel that different. The skills he'd honed overseas had shifted to a different battlefield.

The soft buzz of his phone cut through the stillness. Silas didn't jump or rush. He reached over, taking his time. He knew who it would be before he glanced at the screen.

"We have a problem," the voice said without preamble.

Silas leaned back, silent. He never interrupted when he called. He waited for the details, as always.

"Two are on the loose. We need to find them before the authorities do. Do whatever it takes."

The line went dead as quick as it connected. Silas put the phone down, his expression unchanged. He finished his drink in one last swallow, setting the glass down on the table next to the bottle. No hesitation, no moral quandaries—this was just another job.

Standing, he moved across the room, his movements steady and deliberate. There was work to do.

CHAPTER 40

SILAS PARKED HIS CAR down the road from the house, stepping out into the cool night air. His mind was sharp and focused. Anticipation and determination fueled him as he prepared for the chase. The scent of pine filled his lungs as he scanned the area, his senses on high alert. The forest loomed ahead, dark and quiet, but he knew his targets had passed through here. He had done this enough times to recognize the signs. The moon, half-hidden by clouds, cast enough light to see faint footprints in the damp earth.

He crouched, examining the indentations. Two sets, one much smaller than the other. The direction of their steps was clear—they were heading deeper into the woods. He rose and started to follow the trail, his movements quiet and deliberate.

* * *

Evelyn stumbled over a root. Her legs trembled with exhaustion. She caught herself before she fell. Her breath came in desperate gasps, each step feeling heavier than the last. Tommy's hand clenched in hers, his small legs struggling to keep pace. She pulled him along, her heart pounding in her chest. They needed to stay ahead, keep moving, keep hiding. She glanced back, her eyes wide, searching for any sign of the man. The shadows behind them seemed to shift, and she felt he was close. Too close.

"I'm tired," Tommy whispered.

"I know," Evelyn replied, her breath ragged. "Just a little further, okay? We have to keep going."

She tried to focus on the path ahead, her eyes darting between the trees. The woods were thick, but she spotted a break in the distance—maybe a way out. She pulled Tommy along, her steps urgent, her ears straining for the sounds of pursuit.

* * *

Silas moved through the trees. His steps were light. Each footfall whispered against the forest floor. He spotted clues that confirmed their path: a broken branch and a disturbed patch of moss. The trail was recent—hours rather than minutes—but he was gaining on them. He sensed it. The moonlight helped. It lit the ground enough to spot vital clues.

He paused, noticing something odd. The branches ahead were freshly snapped, their pattern confused. The footprints here crossed over each other, erratic and overlapping. They were circling, doubling back, trying to throw him off.

He smirked. They were panicking, and he knew exactly what that meant. Panic made people careless, made them stumble, made them predictable. He could almost see their frantic faces. He could hear their rushed breathing as they struggled to choose a direction. That's when people made mistakes.

He picked up his pace, his eyes narrowing as he moved faster now, weaving through the trees with purpose. He felt their fear, smelled their desperation in the air. He knew he was getting close.

* * *

Evelyn's chest burned, her legs heavy as she struggled forward. She heard something behind them—maybe the wind, maybe not. Her instincts screamed that they were running out of time. She spotted a glimmer through the branches—a road. Relief surged through her. Her body ached from exhaustion. Her heart pounded with hope and fear. She pulled Tommy faster, almost lifting him as they broke through the tree line.

The road was empty, save for a distant light. Evelyn's heart leapt as she recognized the outline of a patrol car. She waved, her voice hoarse as she called out, "Help! Please!"

* * *

Silas burst through the trees, his eyes immediately locking onto the scene ahead. The road. The woman and the boy. His heart pounded, a growl of frustration building in his throat as he saw them waving down the patrol car. He picked up speed, the ground blurring beneath his feet, but it was too late.

103

CHAPTER 41

OFFICER FRANKS CRUISED down Highway 190 outside Potomac, Maryland. The dark night wrapped around the road ahead. It was after 1:30 a.m., and the rhythmic hum of the tires on the asphalt was the only sound in the quiet Maryland countryside. His headlights cut through the night, illuminating the road and trees beyond.

The beam caught two figures walking ahead—a woman in her thirties and a boy of about twelve. They appeared disheveled, their clothes rumpled, their hair wild. The woman's head snapped around as the lights hit them. They both waved their arms, trying to stop the patrol car.

Officer Franks hit his lights. The familiar red and blue flashed across the empty road. He then pulled the car to the shoulder. He stepped out, his boots crunching on the gravel as he approached the two. They were moving toward him, the woman yelling, but he couldn't make out what she was saying yet.

As he drew closer, her voice finally reached him. "Thank God," she gasped, her face pale and strained. "We've been walking for hours. He's coming after us. I know it." Her words came out in panicked bursts, her chest heaving with each breath.

Franks saw the tension radiating off her. Who's coming after you? he wondered, but his focus shifted to the boy standing beside her. The kid's head was down, staring at the ground, not making any eye contact. He looked stunned, almost as if he were in a daze.

"Who's after you?" Franks asked, keeping his tone steady, professional.

"A man... he... he kidnapped us," the woman replied, breathless, her words tumbling out one after another. Panic gripped her. Her body trembled. She glanced behind her, expecting someone to leap from the darkness.

The boy remained silent, his shoulders hunched, his eyes fixed on the pavement.

Franks took a deep breath, trying to steady the situation. The woman's words were becoming more jumbled, almost incoherent, as her panic grew. He took a step forward, his hands raised in a calming gesture.

"Hey, it's okay," Franks said, trying to get her to focus. "You're safe now. Let's get you off the highway, away from here."

The woman nodded, though her eyes were still wide with fear. The boy showed little reaction, remaining lost in whatever trauma had overtaken him.

"Come on," Franks said. "Let's get you both somewhere safe."

They both nodded this time, and Franks led them to the patrol car. The woman climbed into the back seat first, followed by the boy, who seemed to move on autopilot, his face blank. Once settled, Franks got back into the driver's seat and reached for the radio.

"Dispatch," he said, his voice calm but urgent. "I have two possible victims, might be a 134," he reported, using the code for kidnapping. "En route to the station now, ETA twenty minutes."

"Copy," the voice on the other end crackled.

He put the car in drive and glanced into the rearview mirror. The woman sat closest to the window. Her eyes darted, still alert. Her hands gripped her lap. The boy sat beside her, silent, his eyes glazed over, lost in his own world.

For a brief moment, Franks locked eyes with the woman in the mirror. She gazed with fear and relief tangled together, as the two emotions battled for control.

The cruiser's lights flashed, and the door slammed shut. The engine roared to life. The tires kicked up dust as the car pulled away. Its lights switched off as it vanished down the road.

* * *

As the cruiser moved forward, Silas stopped at the forest's edge. He breathed raggedly. The moonlight cast a long silhouette of him on the pavement. Frustration boiled within him, his hands clenching into fists. He needed a new plan, and quick. He couldn't afford to let them slip away—not when he was this close. But he also knew he'd lost them.

He clenched his jaw, watching the cruiser vanish into the distance. He was so close. So damn close.

He's not gonna like this, Silas thought to himself, the taste of failure bitter on his tongue.

Act II
Deception

CHAPTER 42

THE PATROL CAR EXITED Montrose Road and entered the Maryland State Police parking lot. Officer Franks slowed to a stop near the entrance. He glanced at the two in the back seat—the woman and the boy. The woman's face showed a flicker of relief as the headlights swept across the building.

Franks put the car in park and turned to them. "Let's go inside and get you something warm," he said.

The woman smiled. But she darted her eyes around as if she expected someone to snatch her up at any moment. Her cautious, almost paranoid look hadn't wavered since he picked them up. The boy remained silent, his head down, refusing to make eye contact.

Franks stepped out of the car, opening the back door for them. They climbed out. The woman glanced back, as if checking for something. They walked to the station, the fluorescent lights casting a pale glow over the lot.

As they stepped inside, the desk officer looked up from his paperwork. "Hey, Franks. What do ya got?"

"Possible 134," Franks responded, referring to a kidnapping. "Can you take them back to 122? I'll grab her a coffee and a hot chocolate for the kid." He glanced at the boy, hoping for some reaction, but there was nothing. The boy still stared at the floor, his silence becoming unnerving.

The desk officer gave a short nod, leading the two down the hall while Franks headed for the vending machine. As he fumbled for change, another officer—Jonesy—approached, smirking as usual.

"What's up with those two?" Jonesy asked, leaning against the machine.

"Looks like a 134, but I don't know much yet. She's pretty confused, and the boy hasn't said much."

Jonesy glanced back down the hall, grinning. "Well, she's a looker. Let me know if you need help."

Franks shot him a glare, his jaw tightening. "Keep it in your pants, Jonesy. Shitty time to act like an asshole. Looks like she's been through hell."

Jonesy raised his hands in mock surrender. "Hey, I was just kidding. You take shit too seriously, man."

Ignoring him, Franks grabbed the coffee and hot chocolate from the vending machine. The smell of cheap powdered mix filled the air. He turned and walked away in silence, thinking to himself, why did they hire that idiot?

He walked down the hall to room 122. He opened the door. The woman and the boy were at the table, lost in thought.

"Here you go, ma'am," Franks said, placing the cup of coffee in front of her. "And for you, chief," he added, sliding the hot chocolate toward the boy.

The woman smiled. "Thank you," she said. The boy glanced up at the hot chocolate, but his face remained blank, offering no reaction.

"Can I get you some cream or sugar?" Franks asked.

The woman shook her head. "No, but thank you."

Officer Franks leaned forward, pen in hand, ready to jot down details. "Let's start with your name and address," he said.

"Evelyn Parker," the woman replied, her voice steadying a bit. "I live in Alexandria. In Old Town."

"Old Town, huh?" Franks said, raising his eyebrows. "That's a nice area."

She managed a small smile in response, her hands trembling as she gripped the cup of coffee.

Franks nodded, writing down the details. "Okay, and you, chief?" he said, turning his attention to the boy. "Can you tell me your name?"

The boy stared at the floor, silent. His small hands clutched the hot chocolate cup, but he didn't drink from it.

Evelyn stepped in, her voice shaky but firm. "His name is Tommy... I don't know what his last name is."

Franks paused, his pen hovering over the notepad. "You two aren't related?" he asked.

Evelyn shook her head. "No... we were just in that prison together," she said, the words less than audible.

Franks put his pen down, unsure of what to say. He'd seen his share of victims, but something about the way she broke down hit him in the gut. "Hey, it's okay. You're safe now. You're both safe," he said, trying to offer comfort.

A few moments passed as Evelyn ran her hand through her hair, trying to pull herself together. The room fell into an uneasy silence until Tommy spoke.

"Hayes."

Franks leaned forward, confused. "Hayes?" he asked.

Tommy raised his eyes from the floor, meeting Franks's gaze for the first time. "Hayes is my last name," Tommy said. "I live in Old Town too."

Franks nodded, jotting down the name. "Do you have an address, Tommy?"

The boy hesitated for a moment, then provided the address. "It's near Wilkes Tunnel. That's where... that's where the man grabbed me."

Franks's stomach tightened at the mention of the tunnel. The kid's ordeal hit him hard. He asked a few more questions, trying to learn what had happened. But, it was clear that this was beyond his department's jurisdiction, and he'd need to get the Feds involved.

"Alright," Franks said, winding up the interview. "Ma'am, I have to

110

check into a few things, just hold tight, try to relax, you're safe here."

Evelyn nodded, exhausted, but managed a small "Thank you."

Franks stood up and walked out of the room, heading for the front desk. He gave the desk officer a quick nod. "Can you call the Feds? Tell them we have two potential kidnapping victims. Can you also check if there are any missing person reports for Evelyn Parker or Tommy Hayes."

"On it," the desk officer replied, picking up the phone and dialing.

Franks headed back down the hall to room 122. He opened the door and gave the pair a reassuring smile. "Alright, we're waiting to hear back from another agency. It may take a while. Let's move you to a more comfortable location. That room has a TV, some books, and games."

Both Evelyn and Tommy stood up, the weight of their ordeal still heavy in the air. As they began to walk to the other room, Franks turned back. "Wait, let me get your drinks. You can take them with you."

He walked over to the table and grabbed the cups, assuming they were only half full. But as he jerked them off the table, the contents splashed all over him. Both cups were full, untouched.

"Shit," he muttered under his breath, grabbing a handful of nearby paper towels to mop up the mess. He tossed the soggy cups in the trash and looked up, sheepish. "Sorry about that. I'll grab you two more."

"That's okay," Evelyn said, shaking her head. "I'm not much of a coffee drinker."

Franks grinned, a rare moment of lightness in an otherwise heavy night. "Got it. And what about you, chief?" he asked, turning to Tommy.

The boy shook his head from side to side, indicating no.

"Alright then," Franks said, wiping the last of the coffee from his uniform. "Let's get you down the hall."

CHAPTER 43

IT HAD BEEN A LONG MONTH of administrative leave for both James and Isabelle. The investigation into the shooting of Blackwell had been grueling. Internal Affairs had combed through every detail. They scrutinized their actions, words, and treatment of the assailant. Authorities justified the shooting. But James's actions afterward raised concerns. In the end, the FBI's brotherhood proved reliable. The investigation exonerated both agents.

James had learned to mask his emotions in the aftermath. He had done what he had to do, but the weight of the situation still lingered. The relief of having one last shit bag off the streets brought little comfort. Today was the first day he and Isabelle were back in the office.

The sun was rising as they parked in the lot. They both parked under the dim glow of the streetlights. James glanced out of his window to see Isabelle stepping out of her car, her expression hard but familiar.

"Well, well, if it isn't Belle back from her month-long vacation," James called out, grinning. He threw the door shut behind him as he walked over. "What wasteful things did you spend your time on during your 30 days of penance? Did you sit on your couch binge-watching reality TV?"

Isabelle's eyes narrowed, but she didn't miss a beat. "Oh, you know, the usual. Burned through my savings on useless home network purchases. Now I have a heated blanket that can cook a steak in three minutes. You?"

James smirked. "I slept in and gained ten pounds. But hey, welcome back to the grind."

"Yeah, yeah. Welcome back, Jimbo." Isabelle's tone was flippant, but there was an unmistakable edge of camaraderie there. She gave him a light punch on the arm, and the two walked inside together.

The front receptionist, Betty, gave them a nod as they entered the office. "Welcome back, you two."

"Good to be back, Betty," James said, flashing a half-smile.

They moved down the hallway. The office's familiar sounds filled the space around them. Conversations hummed, phones rang, and keyboards clattered. It was as if they had never left.

At their desks, they had little time to sit. Then, Agent Jackson sauntered over and dropped a folder in front of James.

"A Maryland trooper is bringing in two kidnapping victims for an interview. You two lucky ducks get to handle it," Jackson said with a grin.

James raised an eyebrow. "Kidnapping victims? Since when does Maryland bring its cases to us? Can't they handle their own shit?"

Jackson shrugged. "Looks like the abductions happened a few months ago in Old Town, Alexandria. But authorities picked up the victims in Maryland. Looks like a state-to-state crime, so hello, FBI. And since Poole and Alvarez are on leave, congratulations, you two are it."

Isabelle groaned. "Welcome back. Can we at least get a fucking cup of coffee before they dump this shit on us?"

James chuckled and stood up from his desk. "I'm on it."

He headed to the vending machine and grabbed two cups of coffee, one black for him and one with cream for Belle. By the time he returned, a few minutes later, he saw Isabelle talking to a police officer, a woman in her early thirties and a boy, about twelve stood by. The woman looked disheveled. Her clothes looked wrinkled, and her hair appeared unkempt. But there was something striking about her. A warmth shone in her eyes, despite all she had been through.

Isabelle glanced at him as he approached. "James, this is Officer Franks, Ms. Evelyn Parker, and this young man is Tommy Hayes."

James felt a pang of sympathy as he took in the sight of the two. Evelyn seemed calmer than expected. The drive from Maryland had given her some distance, from her physical and mental captivity. Tommy looked more nervous. But, to James's surprise, he made eye contact before looking down again.

James stepped forward and offered his hand to the boy. "Hi, Tommy. It's good to meet you."

Tommy hesitated for a second, then gave James a small smile and shook his hand.

James turned to Evelyn, "Ms. Parker, I'm sorry to meet you under these circumstances, but we'll do everything we can to help."

Evelyn gave a small nod, her eyes still haunted, but there was a flicker of gratitude in them.

Officer Franks briefed James and Isabelle on the facts. Then, he excused himself and left. As he walked away, he turned and said, "Hey, one last thing. We couldn't find any missing person's report for either of them."

James looked at Isabelle with a curious look. Isabelle gave the same look back, turned to Evelyn and Tommy, and smiled, her voice gentle but steady. "Let's get you somewhere a little more comfortable so we can talk. Does that sound okay?"

Evelyn and Tommy both nodded.

"All right," Isabelle said, standing up. "Follow us."

James handed Isabelle her coffee. They led Evelyn and Tommy down the hall to the interview room. A familiar but unwelcome weight settled around them as they returned to duty. James glanced at Isabelle as they walked—this was going to be one hell of a first night back.

113

CHAPTER 44

JAMES SAT ACROSS FROM EVELYN in the bright interview room. The air was thick with tension, her fragile state almost palpable. Isabelle had taken Tommy to the room next door, leaving him alone with Evelyn. She sat, her hands folded in her lap, her eyes flitting around the room. She met his gaze.

"Can I get you something to eat or drink?" James asked, trying to ease her discomfort.

Evelyn shook her head, almost as if the offer itself had startled her. "No, thank you," she whispered.

James nodded, leaning forward. "I know this is hard, but I need you to tell me what happened. We're here to help you, but we need to understand what you've been through."

At first, there was nothing but silence. She stared at her hands, wringing them together. Her shoulders were tense and hunched, as if trying to fold in on herself. James saw the fear radiating off her, the reluctance to relive what she had endured. But he stayed patient, his voice gentle as he encouraged her.

"It's okay," he said. "You're safe now. No one's going to hurt you."

Evelyn raised her head, her eyes filled with sorrow. She took a deep, shaky breath before she finally began.

"I... I don't even know how it started," she said. "I remember going to the front door, and then... it's like I blacked out. The next thing I knew, I was in the trunk of a car. I woke up in the dark, and the car was moving. I tried to scream, but no one heard me."

Her voice wavered, and she paused to collect herself. James stayed silent, giving her the space to continue at her own pace.

"I don't know how long I was in there," she continued, her voice above a whisper. "It felt like hours. Every time I started to panic, I'd lose consciousness again, like he... like he knew when I was awake and would knock me out."

James clenched his jaw. He hid his anger with a neutral look. The idea of this woman, trapped in a car trunk, terrified and alone, made his blood boil. But he couldn't let that show.

"Where did he take you?" James asked.

Evelyn's eyes shifted as she searched her memory. "I woke up in a basement," she said, her words tentative. "The room was small, with a concrete floor and a single lightbulb hanging from the ceiling. There was a bed… if you could call it that. A thin mattress on a metal frame. The walls were bare, and there was a door with a lock on the outside."

She swallowed hard, her gaze dropping back to her hands. "I was locked in there for weeks. Maybe months; I don't know. He would come down. Sometimes, he wore a suit. Other times, he was just without his jacket. But he always looked put-together. Like he wasn't doing anything wrong."

"Do you know who he was?" James asked, keeping his voice low and even.

Evelyn shook her head again. "No. I never knew his name. He was older, in his sixties maybe. He… he was so cold. Like he wasn't even human."

James had a tight knot of rage forming in his chest, but he pressed on. "Did he hurt you? Physically? Or threaten you in any way?"

She hesitated, her lips trembling as if the memories were too painful to put into words. James leaned forward a little more, his voice a steady reassurance.

"It's okay, Evelyn. You can tell me."

Finally, she spoke, her voice cracking under the weight of her words. "He… he hurt me. In ways I didn't think were possible. He… used me, over and over, until I felt like I wasn't even a person anymore."

James gritted his teeth, feeling the familiar burn of anger coursing through him. He wanted to reach across the table, to tell her that the man who had done this to her would pay, but he knew he had to stay composed. This was about her now, not him.

Evelyn continued, her voice growing more pained. "It wasn't just physical… it was everything. He would get inside my head, make me think I deserved it. That no one would ever come looking for me. He'd say things, horrible things, and I started to believe him."

James let her words hang in the air for a moment, then shifted the conversation. "And Tommy? How did you meet him?"

A faint glimmer of relief crossed her face. "Tommy showed up a few weeks after I did," she said, her voice softening. "He was so scared, but… I was relieved, in a way. I wasn't alone anymore. I tried to protect him… he was just a boy."

James nodded, understanding. "Do you think the man hurt Tommy, too? Did he ever mention being touched inappropriately?"

Evelyn's face darkened. "Tommy said he had been hit by the man countless times. But I don't think he hurt him the same way he hurt me. The man… he was different with Tommy. It was like he was trying to be… a father to him. But not in a good way. He was cruel and demanding. He expected Tommy to be perfect, like he was molding him into something."

James's stomach churned at the thought. "Did Tommy ever mention being hurt?"

"No," Evelyn said, shaking her head. "I don't think he was… I don't think he was sexually abused. The man took everything out on me." Her voice faltered, and her eyes grew distant. "But Tommy… he was always so afraid of disappointing him. It was like the man had him under his thumb."

James took a deep breath, trying to focus. "How did you get out?"

Her gaze flickered, and for the first time, there was a spark of hope in her eyes. "Tommy. He learned how to pick the locks. He came to my room last night after the man had left the house. He unlocked my door, and we just... ran. The house was huge, surrounded by trees. It felt like we were walking in circles for hours, but we kept going. We had to stop every time we heard a noise, thinking it was him coming after us."

James listened, his heart pounding. "How long did it take you to get to the road?"

"I don't know," she said, shaking her head. "It felt like forever. But we finally made it, and then Officer Franks... he found us. I don't know what we would have done if he hadn't picked us up."

James paused, taking in the gravity of her story. "Can you remember anything about the house? An address? Any details?"

"It was big," she said, frowning as she tried to remember. "Two stories. It looked expensive... everything was so clean, almost perfect. The living room was pristine, like no one had ever lived there."

James nodded, scribbling a few notes. "Do you have an address I can reach your family at? Is there anyone I can call for you?"

Evelyn's face brightened, a brief moment of panic flashing across her eyes. "My parents—Linda and Allen... they must be going crazy not knowing where I've been." She rattled off their phone number, her voice trembling. "Please... please tell them I'm okay."

"I'll give them a call," James assured her as he stood up, ready to leave the room.

"And Max," she blurted out, her voice desperate. "Please, check on Max."

James turned, confused. "Who is Max?"

"He's... he's my dog. I hope someone picked him up and took care of him."

A small, genuine smile crept onto James's face. "I'll check on Max, too."

Evelyn let out a shaky breath, the first hint of relief crossing her face since they had started talking. It was small, but it was there. James felt a wave of protectiveness wash over him—he was going to make sure this woman and Tommy got justice.

116

CHAPTER 45

ISABELLE SAT across from Tommy in the small interview room. She scrutinized him with great attention. The boy sat hunched over, his eyes fixed on the floor, his body language radiating tension. He withdrew, and Isabelle knew this wouldn't be easy. She needed to break through that barrier without pushing him too hard.

After a few moments of silence, she leaned back in her chair, her tone casual. "Hey, Tommy, do you like baseball?"

Tommy's head lifted, but he didn't say anything right away. Isabelle pressed on, her voice light. "I'm a big Nats fan. I can't get enough of them."

That got Tommy's attention. He glanced up at her, eyes widening a little. "The Nats? They're my favorite team."

Isabelle smiled. "No way. Who is your favorite player?"

Tommy thought for a second, and Isabelle saw a spark of life in his expression. "I like Josiah Gordon. He's got the best arm."

"Gordon's pretty great," Isabelle agreed. "But I'm more of a J.R. Lassiter fan myself. That guy can run."

Tommy scoffed, shaking his head. "Lassiter is good, but he's not better than Gordon. Did you see that first game of the season? Gordon's pitching was on fire."

Isabelle chuckled, happy to see him opening up. "Alright, alright, I'll give you that. Gordon was impressive. But Lassiter is still my guy."

They bantered about baseball for a moment. The tension eased. Tommy became more animated, like a typical boy talking about his favorite team. Isabelle knew she had him now. She shifted the conversation.

"Tommy," she began, "I really want to help you. But I need to know what happened. Can you tell me about the night you were taken?"

Tommy's face darkened, his small hands twisting together in his lap. He took a deep breath and stared at the table. "It was in the Wilkes Street Tunnel. I was playing catch with Austin at the park by the tunnel. We had been there for a few hours, but it was getting late, and we both had to get home."

"Austin?" Isabelle asked. "Can you tell me more about him?"

Tommy nodded. "Yeah, he lives down the street from me. He's my best friend. We always play catch. That day, we were just hanging out, and then... I don't remember much. I just remember waking up somewhere else."

"Where did you wake up?" Isabelle's voice was calm and patient.

"In a basement," Tommy said. "It was just a small room with a bed, a table, and a couple of chairs. I was scared. I didn't know where I was."

Isabelle leaned forward, keeping her tone soothing. "Did anyone come to see you?"

Tommy's expression hardened as he nodded. "A man. He would come

117

and make me do these weird puzzles and challenges. I didn't know how to do them. And when I got them wrong… he'd scream at me. He hit me a lot in the beginning, mostly across the ears and head."

Isabelle's heart tightened, but she kept her voice steady. "Did he ever… touch you inappropriately, Tommy? Or hurt you in your private areas?"

Tommy shook his head, his voice firm. "No, he didn't do that. He yelled a lot and hit me. Sometimes he made me hold my hand over a candle when I messed up on a puzzle. I didn't understand why. It hurt a lot."

Isabelle clenched her jaw, trying to control the anger bubbling up inside her. This poor boy had been through so much. She forced herself to stay calm for his sake. "You didn't deserve that, Tommy. None of it. How did you get out?"

Tommy's eyes brightened, a hint of pride in his voice. "I learned how to pick locks. One of the puzzles he made me do was all about locks. I picked the lock on my door one night after he left. He was mad earlier, yelling at someone on the phone, so I knew it was my chance. I got out of my room and then went to Evelyn's. I picked her lock, too."

Isabelle smiled at him, admiration in her eyes. "That was smart, Tommy. You did a good thing. You saved Evelyn."

Tommy shifted but didn't hide the small, proud smile that tugged at the corner of his mouth.

"Can you tell me more about the man?" Isabelle asked, keeping her tone light. "Is there anything you remember?"

Tommy shrugged. "He was old, like a grandpa. He wore suits most of the time, but sometimes he didn't wear the jacket. His house was big, like a rich person's house. The living room looked fancy, like the ones you see on TV."

Isabelle nodded, jotting down notes. "You've been helpful, Tommy. Can I ask you for one more thing? I need your parents' names and phone numbers."

Tommy thought for a moment, his brow furrowed in concentration. "Cynthia and Robert Hayes," he said, then gave her their phone number.

Isabelle smiled. "Thank you, Tommy. I'm going to call your parents and talk to Agent Lawson for a moment, okay? I'll be back soon. Can I get you a soda, a candy bar, or anything else?"

Tommy's eyes darted to the door, a flicker of concern crossing his face. "I don't need anything…but…can I see Evelyn?"

Isabelle's smile widened. "I can make that happen."

Tommy nodded; his expression softened.

Isabelle stood up, her heart aching for the boy. But she managed to smile and reassure him as she closed the door behind her. She had a job to do, but she also knew that Tommy and Evelyn had been each other's lifelines through this nightmare. And she wasn't going to take that away from them.

CHAPTER 46

JAMES SAT AT HIS DESK, staring at the computer screen, Evelyn's voice still playing in his head. She had given him her parents' names and phone numbers, believing they were waiting for her. He had dialed the number without hesitation, and then faced an unexpected obstacle.

"The number you have dialed is no longer in service."

James frowned, feeling a wave of concern wash over him. That's strange. He checked the number again, confirming it was the one Evelyn had provided. Something didn't add up.

He opened a new browser tab and began searching for information on Linda and Walter Parker. His gut churned as he searched the records for any recent activity linked to them. Then, as he clicked on a news article, the grim reality hit him. Last month, "Local Couple Killed in Tragic Car Accident."

James sat back in his chair, his mind racing. Evelyn had spent over two months in captivity—there was no way she could have known her parents were gone. How the hell am I going to tell her?

Shaking off the dread that had settled over him, James returned to his search. If her parents were gone, who had been taking care of their affairs? He needed answers. After a few more clicks, he found a real estate listing for the Parkers' house. It was for sale, and the listing mentioned an estate sale and that the property had been recently vacated.

He jotted down the realtor's contact information but decided to skip calling for now. Something told him he'd learn more by heading over to the neighborhood himself, talking to a neighbor or two. If there was an open house, he might even walk around without drawing too much attention.

James stood up from his desk, grabbed his jacket, and checked the time. It wasn't late. With luck, he might catch someone at the house or find a helpful neighbor. It would at least let him see where Evelyn had grown up.

As he headed for the door, his mind was already turning over how to approach this. He had a lead, but it was delicate. He didn't want to give Evelyn more bad news. But, he needed the full picture to help her. That meant going to the Parkers' house.

CHAPTER 47

AS JAMES WALKED into the hallway, Isabelle walked around the corner. "I was just coming to talk to you," he said.

"What's up?" she responded with a quizzical look.

James leaned against the wall, running a hand through his hair. "So, I called Evelyn's parents. The number she gave me? It was disconnected."

Isabelle's brow furrowed. "Disconnected? That's odd."

"Yeah," James said, his voice tight. "So, I dug deeper. Turns out her parents were killed in a car accident a month ago. That might be the reason that there is no missing persons report."

Isabelle stared at him, the shock evident on her face. "What? She was kidnapped over two months ago. She doesn't know."

James nodded. "Exactly. I found out the house is up for sale. I'm gonna head over there, see if I can talk to any neighbors. Maybe they can fill in some gaps."

Isabelle crossed her arms, her expression hardening. "Are you sure she doesn't know?"

"Yeah, she couldn't have," James said. "And I don't want her to know yet. She's been through too much already. She's barely holding it together as it is. We need more information before we drop that bomb on her."

Isabelle let out a sigh, nodding in agreement. "You're right. She's dealing with way too much shit."

James's gaze softened, appreciating her understanding. "Thanks. I'll handle it when I get back, but I want to know everything before we break it to her."

"Good call," Isabelle said, rubbing the back of her neck. "I'll keep an eye on her. In the meantime, I'll try calling Tommy's parents. Hopefully, that goes smoother than your call did."

James let out a half-smile, though there was no humor behind it. "Yeah, I hope so. Can't imagine yours going any worse."

Isabelle chuckled, though the gravity of the situation wasn't lost on either of them. "Let's hope we get some answers soon."

With that, James pushed off the wall, straightening his jacket. "I'll head over to Evelyn's parents' neighborhood, see what I can find. Keep me posted on Tommy's end."

"You got it," Isabelle said as she headed down the hall.

CHAPTER 48

ISABELLE SAT AT HER DESK, staring at the phone, her brow furrowed in thought. No missing persons report on Evelyn; that part made some sense given her parents' recent death. But the real confusion gnawed at her—no report on a twelve-year-old boy? That didn't sit right.

She picked up the phone, her fingers hovering over the dial pad for a moment before pressing the numbers. The phone rang. Once, twice, three times. Isabelle's patience was slipping. She might end up like James—another dead end. When she was about to hang up, a voice crackled through the line.

"Hello?" A woman's voice, cautious but polite.

"Hi, I'm looking for Cynthia or Robert Hayes, please," Isabelle said, her tone professional but soft.

"This is Cynthia," the woman replied.

Isabelle hesitated, swallowing. "Ms. Hayes, this is Special Agent Isabelle Stone from the FBI."

There was a pause on the other end, the tension building. "Yes?" Cynthia's voice was uncertain. "How can I help you, Agent Stone?"

"Ma'am," Isabelle began, selecting her words with caution. "We… we have your son here at the station. He's all right, but he's a little confused and frightened."

The silence on the other end was deafening. Isabelle's heart rate picked up. Then Cynthia's voice came through, shaky and strained, as though each word was a battle. "Is this… is this some kind of joke?" Her tone shifted, breaking. "This is cruel… How can you say such a thing? You're a cruel person for calling me with something like this."

Isabelle's stomach twisted. "No, Mrs. Hayes, I—"

"Don't you ever call here again!" Cynthia shouted, her voice full of tears. Isabelle heard the phone slam down on the other end. Then, a sharp click signaled the end of the call.

Isabelle sat there, stunned, the dead silence of the line buzzing in her ear. What the hell happened? She redialed, her fingers trembling. The phone rang once before going to voicemail. Isabelle left a message, her voice firm but apologetic. "Mrs. Hayes, I'm so sorry if I upset you, but we do need to talk. Please call me back. This is important."

She hung up, feeling a pit form in her stomach. Could Tommy have been mistaken? The pieces weren't fitting together. A twelve-year-old boy wouldn't slip through the cracks—someone would have been looking for him. She leaned back in her chair, the phone resting in her lap, mind racing. Something about this didn't add up. They seemed to be missing a crucial part of the story.

With a frustrated sigh, Isabelle glanced down at the file in front of her.

Cynthia Hayes's reaction had been so visceral, so absolute. But why? Isabelle drummed her fingers on the desk, her mind turning over the possibilities.

Whatever the truth is, it's not going to be easy to find. She sat back, letting out a sigh and whispers, "I guess my call topped yours, Jimbo."

CHAPTER 49

JAMES PULLED UP to the Parker house, nestled about six blocks south of King Street in Old Town, Alexandria. The neighborhood was quiet. Well-kept colonial homes and row houses lined the streets. His eyes caught the real estate sign in the front yard. A smaller sign read, "Open House." He glanced around, his mind racing. I can take a quick walk through.

As he neared the front door, a scent of fresh paint and cleaning supplies wafted through the air. The door was open, and a sign-in sheet sat on a small table inside. He hesitated for a moment, adjusting his jacket before stepping in.

"Well hello there," came a voice from around the corner. A woman, wearing a professional suit, likely in her fifties, rounded the corner. She had a bright smile. "Welcome! I'm Kathryn O'Brien, and you are?"

"Hi, Kathryn. I'm John Smith," James said, offering a handshake.

Kathryn's eyes lit up with recognition. "Oh, just like Captain John Smith from Jamestown! How exciting."

James forced a smile, nodding. "Yes… exactly."

Kathryn beamed. "Well, how can I help you today, Mr. Smith?"

"My wife and I are looking to move into the area," James said, keeping his tone light and conversational. "I saw the open house sign and thought I'd pop in for a look while she's at work."

Kathryn wagged a playful finger at him. "Shame, shame, Mr. Smith. You should always bring the missus to these things."

"You're absolutely right, Kathryn," James replied with a chuckle. "She's been wanting to move for the longest time, but I've been the one holding out. Today, I finally thought, 'What the heck.' I wanted to scope out a few places first… then surprise her with some options."

Kathryn's face lit up again. "That's wonderful! Well, feel free to take a look around. Let me know if you have any questions."

"Thanks, Kathryn. Actually, I do have one question," James said, his tone casual. "I noticed the estate sale sign outside. Do you know what happened to the owners?"

Kathryn's face fell, the brightness in her voice dimming. "Yes… it's tragic, really. They were killed in a car accident last month. A drunk driver hit them head-on. It was a horrible accident."

James nodded, feeling the familiar weight of sympathy settle over him.

"That's awful. Any relatives?"

"I believe they had a daughter," Kathryn said, "but I'm not really sure about the legal details. I was hired by the attorney handling the estate to sell the house."

"I see," James said, glancing around the room. "Well, I'll take a look around, see what great features I can report back to the missus."

"Absolutely! Take your time," Kathryn replied, her bright demeanor returning. "And again, feel free to ask me anything. I can also look for other listings if this one doesn't interest you."

James offered a polite smile and made his way through the house. The living room was cozy but old. The furniture was well-used. The fireplace had warmed many winter evenings. Photos on the walls hinted at a life once lived here.

He spotted a portrait on the far wall, three people smiling by a large oak tree. The older couple, a man and woman, were familiar. He recognized them as Linda and Allen Parker from the obituary he found. But it was the girl standing between them that caught his attention. She couldn't have been more than fourteen in the photo. Though it was a few years old, James squinted at the features. Was it Evelyn?

The girl's face was harder to place. She looked happy, carefree, her smile broad as she leaned into her parents. James studied her, trying to compare her to the terrified woman he had interviewed hours ago. It might be Evelyn, but it was hard to say with certainty. Time and trauma change people.

James walked out of the living room. He smiled at Kathryn, who stood nearby, still beaming. "I think I'll check out what upstairs has to offer," he said, keeping his tone casual.

"Oh yes, you must! It's quite lovely," Kathryn replied, her eyes shining as she gestured toward the staircase.

James nodded and made his way up the steps, his mind spinning with questions. At the top, he found himself facing three doors—two open, one closed. He headed toward the first room, a master suite. The room was immaculate, staged for the open house. It had pristine linens and furniture arranged with taste. A few pieces of artwork dotted the walls, but nothing of significance. He moved on.

The second room appeared to be an office, also staged. Yet, this room caught his attention immediately. Photos hung on the walls. James's gaze locked onto one: a photo of Linda and Allen Parker with their daughter in a graduation gown. He moved closer, studying the picture. The daughter appeared to be in her late twenties, but there was no obvious resemblance to Evelyn.

James narrowed his eyes, trying to find some connection. Maybe the eyes, he thought, but even that was a stretch. He shifted his focus to another picture of the daughter. Once again, there was no real resemblance to Evelyn. Confusion gnawed at him.

Curious, he approached the desk and opened one of the drawers without

124

making a sound. Inside, he found a letter addressed to Linda and Allen Parker, bearing the logo of the ALS Network. His heart quickened as he unfolded the letter. It read:

Dear Mr. and Mrs. Parker,

Thank you for your generous contribution in memory of your daughter, Jessica Parker. We are confident that your donation of $10,000 will go far in helping us find a cure for ALS. Your support funds vital research to end this disease.

Sincerely,
Betty Schnieder

James's mind raced. Jessica Parker? He folded the letter and placed it back in the drawer, closing it. The name didn't make sense. Who is Jessica?

He walked toward the closed door at the end of the hallway. He opened it, revealing what appeared to be the daughter's bedroom. The room froze in time. Framed memories of a life that had once thrived there filled it. Sports photos, silly snapshots, and class pictures lined the walls. Her diplomas hung in a prominent place. One was for her graduate degree in computer engineering.

One photo on the far wall caught his eye—a young Jessica hugging a golden retriever puppy. James took the picture off the wall, turning it over. Scribbled on the back was a note: *Day 1 with Max.*

Max. The name Evelyn had mentioned. James's pulse quickened as he glanced around the room again. Then, another photo grabbed his attention. It showed Jessica and another girl, both jumping in the air, wearing caps and gowns. He turned the photo over. *Alex and Jessica, Graduation Day*, the writing read.

His thoughts spiraled. Who is Alex? And what is Evelyn's connection to this family?

Before he thought further, Kathryn's voice echoed up the stairs, startling him. "Are there any questions I can answer for you, Mr. Smith?"

James returned the photo to its place and called back, "Oh, no, Kathryn. It's a beautiful house. I can't wait to talk to my wife this evening. I've seen several homes, but I think she'll like this one."

Kathryn's heels clicked on the stairs as she appeared, smiling. "Be sure to hurry! I've already had several interested parties."

"Oh, I will," James said, offering a polite smile as he followed her downstairs. At the door, he thanked her again and left.

In his car, James sat in silence for a moment. He stared at the Parker house through the rain-splattered windshield. Jessica Parker. Alex. The dog, Max. None of it made sense. Evelyn's connection to this family was becoming more and more convoluted. How did she fit into this puzzle? Was she lying? If so, why?

He started the car, but his mind remained on the tangled web of questions. Something was off.

CHAPTER 50

IT HAD BEGUN RAINING; James sat in his car, the engine idling as he stared at the rain dropping on the windshield. He dialed Belle's number, his thoughts still racing from what he had uncovered at the Parker house. She picked up after the second ring.

"Special Agent Stone," she answered.

"It's me," James said, his voice steady despite the turmoil in his head. "I just left the Parker house. I was able to get in and walk around. The realtor thought I was a prospective buyer."

"Anything unusual?" Isabelle asked, her voice calm but with a hint of curiosity.

"Yeah, you're not gonna believe this."

"What?" she asked, drawing the word out.

"The daughter… she doesn't look anything like Evelyn. And her name isn't Evelyn either. It's Jessica."

There was a beat of silence on the other end. "Wait, what?" Isabelle finally responded. "Jessica? That doesn't make any sense."

"Hold on, it gets even stranger," James continued, gripping the steering wheel. "I found a letter from an ALS charity. They were thanking the Parkers for a donation. It was in memory of their daughter, Jessica, who died from ALS three years ago."

Isabelle exhaled, processing. "So, Evelyn is… not their daughter? Or is she?"

"That's what I need you to figure out," James said. "Can you check into that? Check for any records on Jessica Parker and her death. Also, find any links between the Parkers and Evelyn."

"Of course," Isabelle replied. "Anything else?"

James rubbed his temple, trying to make sense of what he'd seen. "Yeah, I found another picture. It was of their daughter, Jessica, and another woman at graduation—looked like it was from MIT. I checked the photo's back. Someone scribbled, *Jessica Parker and Alex Grayson, graduation.* Evelyn mentioned a friend named Alex. The day she was kidnapped, she was supposed to meet her for coffee."

"Got it," Isabelle said, her tone focused. "I'll look into Alex Grayson too."

"I'm gonna head over to Evelyn's apartment," James said, putting the car into gear. "See if I can find out more."

"Rog," Isabelle responded. "Oh, and to make things more complicated, I called Tommy's parents. You're not gonna believe this, but Cynthia—the mom—answered. I told her we had her son at the station, and she… well, she went off. She said I was cruel for even suggesting such a thing and then hung up on me."

James gripped the steering wheel tighter. "What? Are you serious?"

"Dead serious," Isabelle replied. "I tried calling back, but she didn't answer. I left a voicemail with my contact info, stressing how urgent this was, but no response yet."

"You've gotta be shitting me," James muttered, shaking his head. "What the hell is going on here? I'm starting to think we're being played."

"I checked every database for missing persons," Isabelle added. "No Evelyn Parker and no Tommy Hayes. Nothing. No one matching their descriptions."

"This is insane," James said, the frustration creeping into his voice. "Evelyn gave me a lot of information about her that checks out—but it checks out for Jessica, not for her."

"Could they be grifters?" Isabelle suggested. "I mean, they seem so believable, but… I don't know."

James paused, considering the possibility. "Maybe. But the boy… Tommy, the way he's just in this shell—it feels too real. If they're acting, they're Oscar performances."

Isabelle sighed. "I'll keep digging, see if anything new comes up. Keep me posted on what you find at the apartment."

"Roger that," James said, glancing out at the rainy street ahead. "We'll get to the bottom of this."

"I hope so," Isabelle said, her voice tinged with concern.

James hung up the phone. He sat for a moment in the quiet of the car. Nothing was adding up. And the deeper they dug, the more twisted it became. With one last look at the Parker house, James drove off.

CHAPTER 51

ISABELLE HUNG UP THE PHONE. Her mind spun as she tried to process everything she and James had learned. Nothing seemed to fit together. She leaned forward at her desk and opened her laptop, starting her search for Alex Grayson. Within moments, a detailed profile appeared on the screen.

Isabelle scanned through it, impressed. No criminal background. She had a master's in computer engineering from MIT and a bachelor's from Pitt. Smart girl. She noted Alex's address, work history, and some personal details: her parents and siblings. Everything seemed normal.

She couldn't shake the connection to Jessica Parker, though. The photo of them together. And, that Evelyn had mentioned Alex the day of the kidnapping. But why Jessica? Why the impersonation? Isabelle printed out Alex's profile and tucked it into a folder on her desk.

Next, she typed in Cynthia and Robert Hayes, eager to dig deeper into Tommy's background. They lived in Old Town—close to where James had been earlier. She scanned through their information, and it seemed simple enough. No criminal history, typical residents. But then something caught her eye.

"What's this?" Isabelle whispered to herself, leaning closer to the screen.

A small newspaper article, dated three years ago, popped up in her search results. "Boy Killed in Old Town by Passing Car."

Her heart raced as she read on. A driver killed Lucas Hayes, son of Cynthia and Robert, at a south Old Town intersection.

"Lucas Hayes?" Isabelle whispered the name to herself. Her pulse quickened. What the hell? The boy they had in custody—Tommy—he couldn't be Lucas… could he? But there was something about this that didn't sit right.

Might Tommy have had a brother? she thought, her mind racing. But no, that didn't explain why Cynthia had reacted the way she did on the phone. Is Tommy pretending to be Lucas? Or worse, has someone put him up to it?

The situation was becoming more complex than she had imagined. She leaned back in her chair, her eyes drifting to the ceiling as she tried to process. None of this makes sense.

She continued to stare, her thoughts spinning in every direction. The parallels were too strange—Evelyn wasn't who she said she was, and now Tommy seemed to be an imposter, too. Were they caught in a scheme bigger

129

than either of them realized? Or were they both victims of something darker?

As she was about to dive back into her research, her phone rang, pulling her out of her thoughts. The sharp ring echoed in the quiet office, startling her.

She reached for it, her heart still pounding. This better be good, she thought, picking up the receiver.

CHAPTER 52

JAMES PULLED UP to the apartment building. His mind raced as he replayed the details Evelyn had given him about her supposed home. This case was starting to feel confusing and contradictory. The rain had subsided into a light drizzle as he stepped out of his car and made his way to the front entrance.

The buzz of the intercom echoed in the empty lobby as he pressed the button for the leasing office. After a few moments, a voice crackled through the speaker. "Yes?"

"Good morning, I'm Special Agent Lawson, with the FBI," he said, pulling his badge out of habit even though no one saw him. "I'd like to ask a few questions about one of your tenants."

A pause. Then the door buzzed open. James stepped inside. He wiped the rain from his jacket. Then, he walked to the front desk, where a woman sat with a clipboard.

"How can I help you, Agent Lawson?" she asked, her tone polite but wary.

"I need to ask about apartment 41," James said, his voice calm. "I've been told Evelyn Parker lives there."

The leasing agent looked up from her clipboard, her brow furrowed. "Apartment 41? That's occupied. You'd need a warrant to get in."

"I understand," James replied, keeping his tone easy. "Can you at least tell me who's living there?"

The agent checked her system, her fingers clicking against the keyboard. "Let's see… that apartment is leased to a student named Anna Fillman."

"Anna Fillman?" James repeated. "How long has she lived there?"

"Over two years," the leasing agent replied, glancing up at him with a puzzled look. "Is there an issue?"

James's mind raced. Over two years? That didn't align with Evelyn's story at all. He pressed on. "Has anyone named Evelyn Parker ever lived there?"

The agent tapped at her keyboard again, scanning through the records. She shook her head. "No Evelyn Parker, I'm afraid. Wait a minute… there was a Jessica Parker who lived there."

James's stomach dropped. He couldn't believe what he was hearing. "Jessica Parker?"

The agent nodded. "Yes, but it looks like her lease ended four months early."

"Why did it end early?" James asked, his voice taking on a sharper edge.

The agent leaned in closer to her screen. "It says here that she passed away. Her parents came to collect her belongings. The apartment was in good condition overall, just a few minor scratches. Looks like she had a large dog, a golden retriever named Max."

Max, James thought, the name echoing in his mind. He tried to keep his voice steady as he asked his next question. "Were there any other emergency contacts listed on her lease?"

The agent clicked through the files. "Let's see... Yes, she listed Linda and Allen Parker as contacts. There's also an Alex Grayson."

James felt a twinge of excitement. Evelyn claimed she was supposed to meet her friend Alex Grayson on the day she was kidnapped. "Is there a phone number or address for Ms. Grayson?"

The agent nodded, scribbling the information on a yellow sticky note. "Here you go," she said, handing it to him.

"Thank you," James said, taking the note and glancing at the phone number and address. "You've been really helpful."

"Anytime," she replied with a smile.

"Please let me know if anyone contacts you about Jessica Parker," James added, handing her his card.

"Sure thing," she said, still smiling as she took his card.

James nodded and headed back out into the now-empty lobby. The light drizzle had picked up again, and he made his way to his car, staring at the note in his hand. Jessica Parker, not Evelyn. And now Alex Grayson was in the picture.

He tucked the note into his jacket pocket and started the engine, his mind already racing to his next move.

CHAPTER 53

ISABELLE ANSWERED the phone, her voice steady and professional. "Special Agent Stone."

There was silence on the other end, a hesitation that made Isabelle's pulse quicken. After a moment, a man's voice finally spoke, low and unsure. "Agent Stone, this is Robert Hayes. You left a message… and… you talked to my wife."

"Yes, Mr. Hayes," Isabelle said, recognizing the unease in his tone. "I'm sorry for any confusion with your wife. We're working on a case involving a missing boy. He claims you and your wife are his parents."

There was a pause. Her words sank in. Then, Robert Hayes spoke again, his voice heavy with disbelief. "That's not possible, Agent Stone. Our son, Lucas, died three years ago."

Isabelle nodded, even though he couldn't see her. It confirmed what she had already uncovered. "I understand, Mr. Hayes. But this boy's name is Tommy Hayes. I have to ask, did you have another son?"

"No… no, Lucas was our only son," Robert replied, his voice trembling. "Agent Stone, I… I don't understand what's going on, but this whole situation has upset my wife and me too, for that matter. I don't know how I can help you."

Isabelle took a deep breath, her tone softening further. "I completely understand, Mr. Hayes, and again, I'm so sorry for bringing this up. But can I trouble you for some details? The boy has told us about his family, friends, school, and other memories. It might help us find out who he is and where his real parents are."

There was a long pause on the line. Robert seemed to weigh whether he could handle the conversation. Finally, he sighed. "Well… if you think it will help."

Isabelle felt a flicker of relief. She then listed everything she had gathered from Tommy during their interview. It included the names of his friends and his favorite activities, movies, and sports teams. She also included some sentimental memories he had shared. She had coaxed these details from him while trying to bond with the boy.

When she finished, she asked, "Does any of that sound familiar to you?"

Another long silence followed, and Isabelle braced herself for his response. Finally, Robert's voice came back, strained and above a whisper. "I don't know what's going on, Agent Stone, but… those are all things that

133

only Lucas would know. It's not possible." His voice cracked, the pain evident in every word. "I remember that Christmas, playing catch with him in the backyard. How does this boy know all of this? It's not possible."

Isabelle heard him tearing up on the other end. "And how does he know about Austin?" Robert asked, his voice almost pleading for an explanation.

"Do you know Austin's last name?" Isabelle asked, her pulse quickening.

"Stanage," Robert answered after a moment. "Austin Stanage. He was Lucas's best friend."

Isabelle's heart sank. Tommy—or whoever this boy was—knew intimate details that only Lucas Hayes should have known.

"Agent Stone," Robert said, his voice trembling. "I'm sorry, but this is all very upsetting. I have to go."

"Of course, Mr. Hayes," Isabelle said. She understood the toll the talk had taken on him. "You've been very helpful, and I appreciate your time."

"You're welcome," he said before hanging up.

Isabelle sat back in her chair, the weight of the conversation settling over her. The case had taken another dark and complicated turn. How did Tommy know these things? And if he wasn't Lucas, then who the hell was he?

CHAPTER 54

ISABELLE LEANED BACK in her chair, phone pressed to her ear. The conversation with Robert Hayes had left her more unsettled than before, but there was no time to dwell on it. She had more questions than answers.

"I got a lead on Alex Grayson," Isabelle said as soon as James picked up.

"Me too," James replied, his voice tight. "I just left Evelyn's apartment—well, I should say Jessica's apartment. No Evelyn ever lived there, but Jessica did. The leasing agent confirmed it. She also had a dog named Max, just like Evelyn mentioned. Her parents collected her belongings after she died."

Isabelle's pulse quickened. "Any emergency contacts?"

"Yeah, turns out there was one. You'll never guess who—."

"Alex Grayson," they both said in unison.

"Right," James muttered. "I'm heading over there now to talk to her."

"Good call," Isabelle said, flipping through her notes. "Anything else on your end?"

"Not on my end, you?"

"I got a call from Robert Hayes. He's sure Tommy isn't his son. But he's freaked out. He can't figure out how someone knows so many personal details about Lucas. Needless to say, he's upset," Isabelle said, shaking her head.

She flipped through her notes. "I need you to head over to Tommy's neighborhood, ask around, see if anyone knew Tommy or heard anything about the kidnapping. Also, see if you can track down Austin—Stanage is his last name according to Mr. Hayes."

"Got it. I'm on it." James said. "Anything else?"

"That's it for now," Isabelle confirmed.

"Copy," James said. "Keep me posted."

She hung up, staring at her phone for a moment. The pieces of the puzzle were there, but they weren't fitting together.

***

James parked his car on Union Street, across from Windmill Hill Park. The quiet, tree-lined streets of South Old Town Alexandria seemed tranquil. James stepped out of the car, scanning the surroundings. The historic neighborhood had brick row houses. The park, sloping up to a hill, lay in its center. At its base, the path to the Wilkes Street Tunnel awaited—a narrow, stone-clad passageway dating back to 1856. In 1975, it was repurposed as a

135

walkway. Damp walls and dim lighting fueled rumors that it was haunted.

James approached the houses on the tunnel's northeast side. He knocked on the first door, holding a photograph of Tommy. A woman in her forties answered, her brow furrowed as he explained his investigation.

"Sorry," she said. "I don't recall anything unusual on August 23rd, and I've never seen that boy before."

The second house yielded similar results. A polite but unhelpful elderly man hadn't heard of a kidnapping. By the third house, James expected another dead end. But the resident, an older man named Roy Simmons, surprised him.

"Don't recognize this boy," Simmons said, studying Tommy's photo. But when James showed him a photo, an old newspaper clipping of Lucas Hayes, Simmons's expression changed.

"Lucas? I remember him," Simmons said. "I used to see him and the Stanage kid playing catch in the park. That was a while ago, though. At least three years. I heard Lucas died... hit by a car, wasn't he?"

James nodded. "Yes. That's correct. Thank you for your time."

As James left the house, he mulled over Simmons's comment. He walked down to the tunnel, the Union Street entrance looming like an open mouth. The cool, damp air inside was a stark contrast to the crisp October chill outside. James moved slowly, taking in the worn, age-stained bricks and the echoes of his own footsteps. The tunnel felt like it had secrets of its own, holding whispers of decades past.

Emerging on Royal Street, James turned left. He then climbed the hill on Wilkes Street before turning right at Lee Street. He overlooked Windmill Hill Park. He spotted two boys on a bench, talking and glancing at their phones. One appeared to be around 14 or 15, with a dark complexion and a confident posture.

James approached them. "Excuse me, boys. Are you from around here?"

The darker-skinned boy looked up, puzzled. "Yeah. Why?"

James flashed his badge. "I'm Special Agent Lawson with the FBI. I'm investigating a kidnapping. Do either of you recognize this boy?" He held up Tommy's photo.

Both boys shook their heads. James then showed them the picture of Lucas. The darker-skinned boy froze, recognition dawning in his eyes.

"That's Lucas Hayes," he said. "But he died three years ago."

"What's your name?" James asked, his tone sharpening.

"Austin Stanage," the boy replied, taken aback.

The name hit James like a shockwave. It was the same Austin Tommy had mentioned. James pressed on, describing details that only Austin would know. The more James spoke, the more confused Austin became.

"I don't know a Tommy," Austin insisted. "How does he know all this about me and Lucas?"

James didn't have an answer. "When was the last time you saw Lucas?" he asked.

Austin stared into the distance, as though recalling a distant memory. "It

136

was late summer, three years ago. We were playing catch at the park, right over there." He gestured toward the field. "The sun was going down, and I had to get home for dinner. We said goodbye, and I never saw him again."

James's breath caught. Everything Austin described matched Tommy's story—except it was three years later. How could Tommy know what happened that day?

James stared at Austin, the weight of the mystery bearing down on him. In this quiet, historic neighborhood, he couldn't yet grasp how the past and present tangled. He thanked Austin, handing him his card. "Please call if you remember anything else," James said. His voice was steady despite the confusion in his mind.

CHAPTER 55

JAMES PULLED UP to the curb in front of a charming 1940s cottage house in nearby Del Ray. It was quiet and comfortable. Quaint yet dignified, it had flowers lining the walkway. He sat in the car for a moment, going over his notes, mentally preparing for the conversation ahead. Alex Grayson, he thought, any chance she might help unravel this whole mess?

Stepping out of the car, James walked toward the house. As he neared, he noticed the front door open and the screen door closed. At the door, a golden retriever appeared. It jumped at the screen and barked. The bark wasn't aggressive—more of a friendly, someone's here kind of excitement.

James instinctively stepped back, giving the dog some space. Max, he thought.

"Max, down! Get down!" came a woman's voice from inside the house. The retriever obeyed, hopping down from the door, still wagging its tail.

A moment later, the woman appeared. She was wiping her hands on a dish towel as she approached, surprised to see him. "Oh, hi," she said, her voice warm but curious. "Can I help you?"

For a split second, James felt his thoughts falter. She's beautiful, he thought. Her striking features caught him off guard. She carried herself with confidence, but her expression was soft.

He snapped back to focus, clearing his throat. "Uh, yes, I'm sorry to intrude," he began, fumbling before finding his composure. "I'm Special Agent James Lawson with the FBI." He flashed his credentials, holding them up for her to see.

"The FBI?" Alex asked, her brow furrowing with confusion. "What's going on?"

James offered a small, reassuring smile. "Yes, I'm sorry to alarm you, but we're working on a kidnapping case. Your name came up as an emergency contact for Ms. Jessica Parker."

Alex's expression softened immediately at the mention of Jessica's name. For a brief moment, she seemed to be somewhere else—her mind drifting to memories of her friend. "Jessica?" she repeated, her voice quieter. She hadn't thought about Jessica today. Now, a flood of emotions rushed back, bringing the rawness of loss. She took a breath and composed herself. "That's… that's not possible… Jessica died three years ago."

James nodded, understanding the weight of her words. "Yes, Ms. Grayson, I'm aware. But here's where it gets complicated—our victim claims to know you. She also knew Jessica's parents and… she also knows Max."

Alex blinked, her hand tightening around the dish towel. "She knows Max?"

"Yes," James replied, his eyes searching hers. "This woman, she says her name is Evelyn Parker, and she's given us specific details about family and friends. But we can't make sense of it because everything she's told us matches your friend Jessica's life."

Alex stood there, processing the information, her eyes growing more concerned. "I don't understand. How can someone know those things? And why claim to be Jessica?"

"That's what we're trying to figure out," James said, taking a step closer, his voice low and calm. "We're hoping you can help us. Do you know anyone connected to Jessica's past? Someone who might be pretending to be her, or someone close to the family after her death?"

Alex's mind raced. "I don't know," she admitted, frustration evident in her voice. "Jessica didn't have any enemies. She was one of the kindest people I knew. This is… I don't know what to think."

James glanced down at Max, the dog now sitting at his feet. "Does the name Evelyn mean anything to you?" he asked.

Alex shook her head. "No, not that I can recall. I've never heard that name before."

James sighed, the knot of confusion tightening. "This woman—Evelyn—she knew details that no one else knew. But the more we dig, the more it seems like she's living someone else's life."

Alex's expression shifted, concern turning into determination. "I want to help, Agent Lawson. If there's anything I can do, anything at all… I want to get to the bottom of this."

James nodded, appreciating her resolve. "Thank you. I may have more questions later. For now, if you can think of anything—any connection—it might help us make sense of what's going on. Please give me a call. Day or night," he said, handing her his card. She took the card, then looked up. "Wait, let me grab my card. It'd be a shame if you had to come all this way again when a call is easiest.""

James smiled, knowing what she meant was how do I explain to my neighbors why an FBI agent came to my door. She returned, handing him her card. He looked at it, then looked up at her, "Helix Industries, isn't that out by Dulles?"

"Yes," she responded. "I've been a computer engineer with them since graduation; it's fascinating work."

"Sounds interesting," James responded with a smile. "Again, let me know if anything else comes to mind that might be helpful."

"I'll keep thinking… wait, I don't know if this is important or not. But you mentioned that she told you she was supposed to meet me for coffee about two months ago."

"Yes, that's what she said," James responded.

"I wasn't meeting her for coffee two months ago. But three years ago, I was waiting at a coffee shop for Jessica. Then, her mother called and said she had passed in the night." Alex's gaze lingered on the picture frames in her living room. They were old photos of her and Jessica together. She couldn't grasp what James was saying. But she knew one thing. If someone was using Jessica's name and life, she'd find out why.

"I'll let you know if I can remember anything or anyone," she added, her voice firm.

James nodded, sensing that she meant it. "I appreciate it, Ms. Grayson."

"Please call me Alex."

He smiled. "Alex, then."

Alex gave him a small nod as he turned to leave, walking back toward his car. Max barked once, as if to say goodbye. James glanced back at Alex one last time before pulling away.

CHAPTER 56

JAMES PUSHED open the door to the office, feeling the weight of the day pressing down on him. The sun had long since set, and the quiet hum of the empty office added to the exhaustion pulling at his body. It had been a long day—too long—and the case was spinning more out of control with every passing hour.

Isabelle was still at her desk, her face illuminated by the soft glow of her computer screen. She looked up when James entered, a tired smile crossing her lips. "Rough day?"

James let out a weary chuckle as he dropped his coat over the back of a chair and sat down. "You have no idea," he sighed. "I went to Alex Grayson's place."

Isabelle straightened in her seat, her interest piqued. "Did you get anything?"

James rubbed his temples, trying to gather his thoughts. "I don't even know where to begin. Everything checks out with her. The connections with Jessica, the memories… it all fits. And Evelyn—she knows details, Isabelle. Specific things about Alex and Jessica that only those two knew."

Isabelle frowned, leaning in. "But she's not Jessica."

"I know," James said, shaking his head in frustration. "She swears she's Evelyn Parker, but every answer she gives—every piece of information—is spot on. It's like she has Jessica's memories. It's insane. I don't know what to make of it."

Isabelle ran a hand through her hair, exhaling. "So, where does that leave us?"

"We're gonna have to confront them," James said, his voice firm but tired. "None of this is adding up, and we need to get real answers. There's no other way forward."

Isabelle nodded in agreement but glanced at the clock on the wall. It was well past eight o'clock. "It'll have to wait until morning. I had Victim's Services come pick them up a few hours ago."

James leaned back in his chair. He was relieved. Someone else had taken that responsibility for the night. "Good. They need the rest, too."

"Yeah," Isabelle said, standing up and stretching, her muscles tight from sitting for so long. "Can you call VS tonight and have them bring them over first thing in the morning? I want to get this over with."

"Will do," James replied, rubbing his eyes. "First thing tomorrow. We'll sit them down and see if we can finally get some clarity."

Isabelle gathered her things and shot him a tired but supportive glance. "We'll figure it out, Jimbo. Tomorrow, we'll get the truth."

James nodded, but the weight of the case sat on his shoulders. "Yeah. Let's hope so."

With that, Isabelle gave him a small wave and headed out, leaving James alone in the quiet office. He stared at his notes, his mind still racing with questions. Tomorrow would bring more answers—or more confusion.

CHAPTER 57

THE NEXT MORNING, Evelyn sat in the interrogation room. She was calm and trusting as James and Isabelle entered. She offered them a small, hesitant smile while still placing her faith in the agents to help her.

James sat across from her, his expression softer than usual. He knew they were about to push her in ways that might break her trust, but they had no choice. Too many inconsistencies had surfaced, and they needed answers.

"Evelyn, we need to talk about something important," James began, his tone gentle but serious. He watched her, gauging her reaction. "I want you to prepare yourself for some difficult news."

Evelyn frowned, her eyes narrowing with concern. "What is it?"

James paused, his next words heavy with meaning. "Your parents… Linda and Allen … they were killed in a car accident about a month ago."

Evelyn stared at him, her face going pale. The words seemed to hang in the air, and for a moment, there was nothing but silence between them.

"No… no, that can't be true," she whispered, shaking her head. "That's not possible." Her voice wavered, her hands gripping the edge of the table as if to steady herself.

"I'm so sorry," James said, his voice still soft, watching her.

Evelyn's face crumpled with the weight of the news, her eyes wide with disbelief. "No, you're wrong," she said, her tone rising, her confusion palpable. "I spoke to them. Right before I was taken. It… it all happened while I was gone."

Her face showed deep sadness, a profound loss in every feature. But James noticed something off. There were no tears. Her voice cracked; her expression was one of grief, but her eyes remained dry.

Isabelle watched her, perplexed, but James pressed on. He needed to see how far this went.

"Evelyn," James continued, "we've been digging into your background—into what you told us. I visited your parents' home yesterday and the apartment complex you lived in, and I learned some things. Things that don't make sense."

Evelyn's confusion deepened. "What do you mean?" she asked, her voice trembling.

"There were photos on the wall in your parents' living room," James said, handing her several photos. None of them contained Evelyn.

"That's not possible; someone replaced me for the woman in these pictures. I can remember every day when these pictures were taken," she pleads. She tells James the date, time, and event of each photo.

"Evelyn, the woman in this picture, is Jessica Parker, Linda and Allen Parker's only daughter. She died three years ago of ALS."

"It's not possible," she whispers.

"I also went to the apartment you said was yours—there's no record of you living there. But there is a record of Jessica Parker: Jessica, the daughter of Linda and Allen. She had a dog, Max, the same one you mentioned."

Evelyn blinked, her brow furrowing. "No... that's not right. I'm their daughter. I'm telling you the truth." Her voice was still steady, but now there was a trace of doubt, as if the world around her were unraveling.

James leaned in, his voice lowering. "I spoke to Alex Grayson. She remembers things—details—about Jessica's life, but she doesn't know an Evelyn Parker."

Evelyn's mind raced. What are they saying? she thought, the confusion turning into a knot of panic. Do they think I'm lying? The room seemed to shrink around her, the pressure building. She looked at James, and then at Isabelle, her face flushed with anxiety.

"Do you think I'm lying?" she asked, almost to herself, the disbelief creeping into her voice.

James exchanged a glance with Isabelle, then nodded. "We don't know what to believe, Evelyn. That's why we need you to help us understand."

Evelyn's heart raced. "I... I am who I say I am. I swear it. I'm Evelyn Parker. They're my parents. Alex is my best friend. Max . . . Max is my dog," she replied, putting her head in her hands.

James sighed, steeling himself for the next step. "Alright, Evelyn. I'm going to ask you some questions. Things Alex told me that only she and Jessica would know. I need you to be completely honest."

Evelyn nodded, her hands trembling now. She looked desperate to prove herself.

James leaned forward, locking eyes with her. "Where did Jessica and Alex meet?"

Evelyn's eyes darted up, as if searching within herself. Then she answered, "MIT . . . we were roommates...well almost, she lived across the hall from me at MIT."

James nodded, taking a breath. "What was Alex's favorite class?"

Evelyn didn't hesitate. "Quantum computing. We both loved it—it was our passion."

Isabelle raised her eyebrows, her gaze flicking to James. So far, she was nailing every answer.

James pressed on. "Who was Alex dating in her junior year?"

"Greg Thompson," Evelyn replied, her voice steady. "He was in her robotics class, but they broke up before graduation."

James's brow furrowed. Evelyn wasn't stumbling—she wasn't even hesitating. He continued to ask questions and Evelyn continued to answer every question with perfection.

"What did you and Alex do on their graduation day?" James asked, as he crossed off the last question on his list.

"We went to the Charles River," Evelyn said in a gentle tone. "We sat on the bank, just the two of us. Alex said she didn't want to be around the crowd."

James leaned back, stunned. Everything Evelyn had said aligned with what Alex had told him had happened between Alex and Jessica. Isabelle shifted in her seat, her face a mask of disbelief. None of this made any sense.

Evelyn's eyes pleaded with them. "I am who I say I am. I'm not lying. These are my memories, my life. I don't know what's happening, but I'm telling you the truth."

Isabelle shook her head, perplexed. "Evelyn, we're not saying you're lying… but this information, it's not possible. These aren't things you should know."

Evelyn's face was a mix of sadness and panic; her voice was a whisper. "I don't know how I know them… but I do."

James and Isabelle exchanged another glance. They were now more confused than before. Evelyn had all the right answers. She couldn't know them unless she was Jessica Parker.

But how could that be?

"Evelyn," James said, "something is going on here. And we're going to figure it out. But for now, we're going to keep looking into this. Do you understand?"

Evelyn nodded. Her hands trembled. Her eyes showed desperation. "Please… find out what's happening. I just want this nightmare to end."

James stood, Isabelle following suit. As they left the room, both agents left with the same haunting question: Who is Evelyn Parker?

145

CHAPTER 58

JAMES AND ISABELLE WALKED out of the interrogation room. The door closed behind them as they stepped into the dim hallway. The tension was palpable. The weight of their shared past sat heavily on them.

"This is impossible," Isabelle muttered under her breath, her frustration clear.

James rubbed the back of his neck, nodding in agreement. "I feel like I'm being brain-fucked. None of this makes sense."

Isabelle opened her mouth to respond. But before she did, another agent rounded the corner. His face was serious, and he walked toward them with purpose.

"I've been looking for you," the agent said. "Cynthia and Robert Hayes are in the lobby. They said they wanted to speak with you, Agent Stone."

Isabelle's expression immediately shifted, confusion flickering across her face. She turned to James, her eyes narrowing.

James raised an eyebrow, his mind already racing. "They told you that Tommy wasn't their son, and that their son Lucas was dead. So why are they here?"

Isabelle shook her head, the strange feeling crawling up her spine. "I have no idea."

Without wasting time, they turned and walked down the hallway to the lobby. Their footsteps echoed in the empty corridors, and a sense of unease settled between them. Neither spoke, but the questions in their minds were clear: Why had they shown up? And what did they want?

At the end of the hallway, the office sounds grew louder. Phones rang and voices murmured in the background. The lobby was ahead. Isabelle's heart raced. She braced for the conversation ahead.

They stepped into the lobby, and there, sitting side by side, were Cynthia and Robert Hayes. Both looked uneasy, Cynthia's hands clasped in her lap, while Robert sat rigid, his face drawn with worry. The moment they saw Isabelle and James, Cynthia stood up, her eyes locking onto Isabelle's.

"Agent Stone," she said, her voice trembling. "I want to see the boy... Tommy."

CHAPTER 59

JAMES AND ISABELLE LED Cynthia and Robert down the quiet hallway. Their footsteps were the only sound in the stillness. Neither agent spoke. Tension hung thick in the air as they approached the room where Tommy was waiting. Isabelle glanced over at James, her mind racing with questions. How is this going to play out? she wondered, unsure of what the next few moments would bring.

When they reached the door, Isabelle paused, placing a hand on the knob before looking back at Cynthia and Robert. Cynthia's face was a mixture of anxiety and confusion, while Robert remained stoic, his gaze distant.

Isabelle opened the door, sticking her head inside. "Good morning, Tommy," she said. "I have some visitors for you."

She pushed the door open wider, revealing Cynthia and Robert standing in the doorway. The reaction was immediate. Tommy's eyes lit up with astonishment. His mouth dropped open in disbelief. His face shifted into an expression of pure joy, as if a floodgate of long-buried hope had burst open.

"Mom! Dad!" he shouted, his voice trembling with excitement. He ran toward them, his arms outstretched, his small frame moving as he tried to embrace them.

Robert hesitated, stepping back instinctively, a look of confusion crossing his face. But Cynthia… she knelt down to Tommy's level, her heart pulling her toward him, even though she knew this wasn't her son. Tommy's eyes held something that made her heart ache. It was as if she had to comfort this boy.

Tommy crashed into her arms, hugging her, and Cynthia wrapped her arms around him in return. She knew this couldn't be her Lucas. But the boy's raw, desperate emotions overwhelmed her. Her heart broke for him, for the pain he'd endured, and for the confusion of whatever had brought him to this moment.

Robert stood behind her, his face a mask of bewilderment as he watched his wife hug the boy who was a stranger to him. He shifted his weight, not knowing what to say or what to feel.

Isabelle and James exchanged a glance, confused by what was happening. Neither made sense of it. Tommy's behavior and his intense connection to Cynthia and Robert puzzled them. It was as if he believed they were his parents, as if he remembered a life that didn't exist.

Tommy, still clinging to Cynthia, began to speak, his words tumbling out

147

as if he'd been holding them in for years. "It's been so long," he whispered, his voice thick with emotion. "I remember telling you I was going to the park to meet Aus. I took off and you yelled back, 'Be home for dinner.' That's what you always say, Mom. But... I'm sorry I didn't make it back."

Cynthia's breath hitched as she listened, her heart twisting. Tommy's voice shook as he continued. "A man took me... He locked me in a room. Sometimes he hit me and made me do weird puzzles and things..."

Cynthia's eyes filled with tears. She felt the weight of his pain, the terrible things he'd been through. She knew, deep down, this wasn't her son. But her instincts kicked in. She couldn't bring herself to tell him the truth. Not now. Not when he'd already been through so much. She tightened her grip on him, unable to push him away.

Isabelle, watching the scene unfold, saw the helplessness in Cynthia's eyes. She realized Cynthia didn't know what to do—how to handle the boy's belief that she was his mother.

I can't do this, Cynthia's eyes seemed to say as they locked onto Isabelle's, begging for help. Isabelle saw the moment for what it was. It was a fragile, emotional point that needed careful handling.

Isabelle stepped forward, her voice soft but firm. "Tommy," she said, "I need to talk to your parents for a moment outside. Is that okay?"

Tommy looked up, his face clouding with concern for a second, but he nodded. "Sure... that's okay," he said, his voice small.

Isabelle gave him a warm smile, trying to ease the tension in the room. "We'll be right back, okay?"

Tommy nodded again. He stepped back from Cynthia, but his eyes lingered on her, afraid she might disappear.

Isabelle ushered Cynthia and Robert out of the room, closing the door behind them. As they stood in the hallway, Cynthia wiped at her eyes, overwhelmed. Robert remained silent. His face showed confusion, now mixed with unease.

"Agent Stone," Cynthia began, her voice trembling, "I... I don't know what to say. He's not Lucas, but... he believes he is. How does he know these things?"

Isabelle nodded, her face showing understanding. "I know this is hard, Mrs. Hayes. But we don't have all the answers yet. Tommy—whoever he is—has been through something traumatic. We need to be careful in how we approach this, for his sake."

Robert finally spoke, his voice low. "What's going on here? Who is that boy?"

Isabelle glanced at James, who stood in silence beside her. "That's what we're trying to figure out," she said. "We're getting closer, but right now, we need to proceed carefully. He's been through a lot, and we don't want to cause him any more harm."

Cynthia nodded, still wiping her eyes. Robert was tense, his fists clenched.

"We'll figure this out," James said finally, his voice steady. "But for now, let's take it one step at a time."

"It's going to be difficult to tell Tommy you're leaving and not taking him," Isabelle said, breaking the silence. "He thinks you're his parent. It's going to crush him."

Cynthia looked at the floor, struggling to find her words. She was still reeling from the emotions of the moment, from Tommy's belief that she was his mother. After a long pause, she nodded and whispered, "I'll talk to him."

Robert's face tightened, and he spoke up, his voice firm but laced with frustration. "Cynthia, he's not Lucas. You can't do this. You're making it harder for him."

Cynthia turned to her husband, her eyes filled with a mixture of grief and determination. "I know that, Robert," she said in a soft yet resolute tone. "But he's a scared boy. A boy who has been through hell and believes he's found his family. Right now, he needs comfort, not cold logic. I can't just leave him without trying to make it easier for him."

Robert's jaw clenched, his reluctance clear. He looked like he wanted to argue, but he saw the sadness in Cynthia's eyes and stopped himself. Isabelle and James exchanged a glance, both understanding the gravity of what Cynthia was about to do.

"I think you're right," Isabelle said. "He's vulnerable, and this is already difficult enough for him. It's important to handle this carefully."

James nodded in agreement, though his expression was heavy. "Just… take it slow," he added.

Cynthia gave them a weak smile and took a deep breath. "I'll do my best."

Isabelle opened the door and walked back into the room with Cynthia. Tommy sat on the chair, his legs swinging, looking at them. When he saw Cynthia, his eyes lit up with the same excitement he had shown when she first entered. He immediately stood up, a look of hope in his eyes.

Cynthia knelt down beside him, her heart breaking a little more with every moment. She felt his need for reassurance, for love. He sought meaning in his chaotic world.

"Tommy," she began, reaching out to hold his hand. "We have to go right now."

Tommy's face fell, his eyes darting between Cynthia and Isabelle. "Go?" he asked, confusion lacing his voice. "But… when will I see you again?"

Cynthia's heart clenched. She had to find the right words, something that would ease the pain. "You'll be home soon, okay?" she said, squeezing his hand. "You'll be home soon." She pulled him into a hug, holding him, her voice breaking as she repeated the words again. "You'll be home soon."

Tommy hugged her back, his small arms wrapped around her as if she were the anchor he needed to feel secure. "Promise?" he whispered.

Cynthia couldn't bring herself to say anything more. She nodded, holding him close for a few more seconds, feeling the warmth of his fragile hope clinging to her. Over his shoulder, her eyes met Isabelle's, a helpless look on her face as tears threatened to spill.

Isabelle felt the weight of the situation, knowing there was no easy way out of this. She watched as Cynthia pulled away from Tommy, her face pale and pained.

"Okay," Tommy said, as if trying to convince himself. "I'll wait. I'll be good."

Cynthia smiled, though her heart shattered inside. She stood up, her eyes never leaving Tommy's as she made her way toward the door.

"We'll see each other soon," she whispered, even though she wasn't sure what the future held.

She glanced at Tommy, then left with Isabelle. The boy was alone with his hope and the truth they all dreaded.

As they walked down the hallway, Cynthia turned to Isabelle, "Promise me you'll find that boy's real parents… promise me."

"I promise," said Isabelle with a look of encouragement.

CHAPTER 60

CYNTHIA AND ROBERT LEFT and the room seemed emptier without their tension filling the air. Isabelle and James stood in silence for a moment. They both digested the strange interaction they had seen.

James rubbed the back of his neck, his mind racing. "Would it help if we brought in a shrink?" he asked, breaking the silence.

Isabelle glanced at him, raising an eyebrow.

"What about Dr. Patel?" James said as his face tightened.

"Are you sure about that? I'm not sure she cured your crazy," Isabelle teased, smirking. She referred to James's mandatory counseling after the Blackwell incident.

James rolled his eyes. "You're a really funny person," he said, his voice dripping with sarcasm. "No need to spend money at the comedy club when I've got a stand-up comedian as a partner." He slow-clapped, with his hands making only a faint sound.

Isabelle grinned, pleased with herself. "Maybe Patel can shed some light on both of them," she added. "But I'll let you give her a call, since you're the crazy one." With that, she turned and started walking down the hallway.

"Ah, that's how you want to play it, huh? Just walk away," James called after her as she turned the corner and disappeared from view. He let out a deep sigh.

"Shit," James muttered under his breath. He hated talking to Dr. Patel. All the psycho babble. Still, he knew he had to do it. What the hell, whatever, he thought.

He walked up to the second floor, the familiar dread creeping in as he turned down the first hallway and took a left. As he neared Dr. Asha Patel's office, a wave of PTSD hit him. It reminded him of his mandatory visits here three times a week after the Blackwell incident.

In fairness, though, he admitted to himself that it had helped. He was better at controlling his rage now, more deliberate in where he directed it. Still, he couldn't help but cringe at the memories of those sessions.

He peered into Dr. Patel's office. She engrossed herself in her computer, unaware of him. He tapped the side of the door and said, "knock, knock. Hey, Doc," he added, forcing a small smile.

Dr. Patel turned in her chair, her sharp eyes immediately recognizing him. "Agent Lawson," she said, her tone warm but laced with amusement. "To what do I owe this pleasure? I'm certain you didn't miss our riveting conversations. What brings you back to purgatory?" She smiled, enjoying the playful banter.

James smiled back, though his smile was a little strained. "Relax, Doc. Not my mind this time." He took a step closer, the seriousness of his situation wiping away the last remnants of humor. "I've got two kidnapping victims. A woman in her early thirties and a twelve-year-old boy. They were both held captive for two months—physically and mentally abused. The woman also suffered significant sexual trauma."

Dr. Patel's expression grew more focused as James continued.

"Here's the kicker," James added, lowering his voice. "Both of them believe they are someone who died three years ago. The woman claims she's Evelyn Parker—but there is no Evelyn Parker. All her memories tie to a Jessica Parker, who died from ALS three years ago. The boy, Tommy? Same story. His memories perfectly align with Lucas Hayes, who was killed three years ago."

Dr. Patel's eyebrows shot up in surprise, though she remained composed. "You're saying they've adopted these identities, down to exact memories?"

James nodded. "We've interviewed many people connected to Jessica and Lucas. Both Evelyn and Tommy can recall, verbatim, facts only Jessica and Lucas would have known. It's the craziest thing I've ever seen. It's almost as if they are those people, but that's impossible."

Dr. Patel sat back in her chair, her fingers tapping her lips as she processed everything James had told her. After a moment of silence, she offered a few tentative thoughts. "There are several possibilities. Confabulation is when they create false memories to fill gaps. Or, it can be Capgras syndrome. It's a delusion where someone believes people, or even themselves, have been replaced. Delusional disorder might also explain this behavior, but I'd need to see them to be sure."

"Are they here now?" she asked.

"They are," James confirmed. "Do you have time to talk to them?"

Dr. Patel smiled. "For you, Agent Lawson, my favorite patient. Anything," she teased, a glint of humor returning to her eyes.

James smirked, shaking his head. "Always gotta remind me of that, huh?"

"Always," she replied with a wink.

"Let me introduce you to them," James said. He led her to the hallway, bracing for what might come next.

CHAPTER 61

DOCTOR PATEL SAT across from Evelyn. The room's quiet intensity matched the delicate situation. Evelyn sat with her hands in her lap. Her eyes shifted between trust and confusion, unsure of what to expect from the doctor. Patel had been in this room countless times, faced with countless cases. But this one was different.

"Evelyn," Patel began, her voice soft but steady, "I want to talk to you about your memories and experiences. My goal is to help you understand what's happening. Is that okay?"

Evelyn nodded, her eyes searching for reassurance. "I just want to understand what's going on."

"Good," Patel replied, leaning forward. "Let's start with some questions about your memories. Sometimes, when people go through trauma, their memories can get... mixed up. Have you ever remembered something, then realized it didn't happen as you thought?"

Evelyn's brow furrowed as she thought. "No... not really. Everything I remember feels real, like it happened just the way I recall it."

"That's helpful," Patel said, making a note. "Can you tell me about a specific memory from your childhood? Something that stands out to you, maybe with your parents?"

Evelyn's expression softened. "I remember going to a fair with my dad. I must have been seven or eight. There was this Ferris wheel, and I was scared to go on it. But my dad convinced me. He held my hand the whole time, and it was fine. I was safe."

Patel smiled. "That sounds like a nice memory. Was your mom there too?"

Evelyn paused, her face showing the briefest flicker of confusion. "No... I don't think she was. It was just my dad and me."

Patel jots down something in her notebook. "Do you ever talk about these memories with family? Sometimes talking about them can help clarify details."

Evelyn shook her head. "No, it's just something I've always remembered. It happened. I'm sure of it."

Patel made another note, her face neutral. "And what about more recent memories—like the day you were kidnapped? Do you remember what you were doing before it happened?"

Evelyn nodded. "I was supposed to meet my friend Alex for coffee. We had plans. I remember getting ready, but I never made it to meet her. That's when... it happened."

"How long had you known Alex?" Patel asked.

Evelyn thought for a moment. "Since college. We are really close."

Patel's probing questions began to chip away at the certainty of Evelyn's memories. The more Patel pushed, the more Evelyn seemed to dig her heels in. Evelyn had built a story in her mind. It was real to her. Dr. Patel continued to explore possible diagnoses by asking subtle questions.

"Evelyn," Patel said, leaning in again. "Sometimes, after trauma, our brains can mix up events or create memories to help us cope. Have you ever felt like there are parts of your life that don't quite fit together? Moments where things are missing?"

Evelyn looked troubled, her fingers fidgeting with the edge of her sleeve. "No... I mean, everything fits. But sometimes it feels like there's something... missing. But I don't know what."

Patel nodded, her suspicions growing. This was the behavior of someone whose mind was protecting itself. It was creating false memories.

After an hour of careful questioning, Patel asked her last question. She had probed Evelyn's identity and the gaps in her memories. Evelyn had answered everything with conviction, her belief in her identity unshakable. But it didn't align with the facts that James and Isabelle had uncovered.

Patel finished with Evelyn, her mind spinning with possibilities, but her day wasn't done yet. She moved on to Tommy, the twelve-year-old boy who appeared trapped in a similar mental paradox.

When Patel entered the room, Tommy was sitting on a chair, fiddling with his hands. He looked up at her, wide-eyed and cautious.

"Hi, Tommy," Patel said, sitting down across from him. "I'm Dr. Patel, and I'm here to help you. Is it okay if I ask you some questions?"

Tommy nodded, looking down at the floor.

Patel began, asking him about his life before his abduction. "What do you remember about your family and friends, Tommy? Can you tell me about them?"

Tommy's eyes brightened, and he sat up. "I remember my mom and dad. They were just here. I also have a friend named Austin."

Patel nodded. "Austin. He's your best friend?"

Tommy smiled for the first time. "Yeah. We played catch at the park all the time."

Patel leaned in. "Tommy, do you ever feel confused? Like, memories don't always fit together?"

Tommy shrugged, his face showing uncertainty. "Sometimes. I remember some things... but then other stuff, it's like it's blurry. But I know my mom and dad. I know them."

Patel's questions shifted, probing for signs of cognitive distortions. Tommy's memories were as firm as Evelyn's, and he mirrored her conviction in who he was. Despite the overwhelming evidence to the contrary, Tommy believed he was Lucas Hayes.

After an hour with Tommy, Patel left the room. Her mind pieced together the fragments of both Evelyn's and Tommy's stories.

James was waiting in the hallway, his arms crossed, his face tense. "So?" he asked, his voice heavy with anticipation.

Patel sighed, leaning against the wall. "I've spoken with both of them. I don't think it's Capgras syndrome, and it's likely not a delusional disorder either. Good chance it's confabulation—for both of them. Their minds have filled in the gaps from the trauma they've experienced. It's a defense mechanism. Evelyn believes she's Jessica Parker because her mind can't process the trauma of what happened. The same goes for Tommy—he's created a false identity to protect himself from the abuse he endured."

James frowned, rubbing his temples. "So, they think they're these people? Even though they're not?"

Patel nodded. "Exactly. They are not doing it on purpose. Their minds have created these false memories to cope with the trauma. I'd recommend more psychiatric care for both."

James sighed, the weight of the situation pressing down on him. "What about Tommy? Could he have remembered details about Lucas's life?"

"It's possible," Patel replied. "He may have learned those details in captivity—through conversations or overhearing something. His mind took those fragments and built an entire identity around them."

"Why the different names? Why Evelyn instead of Jessica, why Tommy instead of Lucas?" he questioned.

"I don't know," Patel shrugged.

James nodded. "Alright. So, what's next?"

Patel stood straight, her expression thoughtful. "I'll need to continue working with them. But for now, we need to handle them with care. Their worlds are built on false memories. If we confront them too aggressively, it might do more harm than good."

James exhaled, his exhaustion evident. "Thanks, Doc. I'll bring them back in tomorrow."

Patel gave a small, understanding smile. "I'll be here."

CHAPTER 62

CHARLIE ROSE SAT AT HER DESK at the Washington Post. Her fingers danced across the keyboard as she finished her latest article. At 52, Charlie was a seasoned investigative journalist. Her years of exposing corruption gave her a serious weight. She had uncovered scandals that led to high-profile arrests. She had her dark brown hair, streaked with silver at the temples, cut into a sharp bob that framed her face. Her piercing hazel eyes, always hunting for a scoop, had earned her a reputation. She missed nothing.

Charlie wasn't one to chase flashy headlines. She dug deeper—thorough, methodical, relentless. These traits helped her break the big stories, making her a force of nature in the newsroom. With her sharp, witty curiosity, she would corner the truth, even if it was sprinting away.

For the past decade, she'd been on the tech beat, her reputation as solid as the company she kept. She called things as she saw them. This was especially true for Silicon Valley and the D.C. beltway types. They had big promises and bigger secrets.

Recently, Charlie was deep in a story. It had everything—power, secrecy, and a dizzying promise of the future. The headline seemed to form on its own: "William Drake, CEO of Helix: New Breakthrough in AGI." Drake was the enigma at the center of it all—a billionaire tech genius. His company, Helix, had allegedly made a quantum leap in developing Artificial General Intelligence. It was a kind of intelligence that twisted her stomach. This wasn't the next gadget or the latest buzzword. This was the holy grail of Artificial Intelligence. It was a type that thought, reasoned, and surpassed human cognition.

Her research spanned months and included more than a few dead ends. There were the usual suspects. White papers from MIT. Confidential interviews with former employees who spoke in hushed tones. And, venture capital insiders with much to say off the record but little to offer on it. Charlie had even secured an exclusive sit-down with a former R&D engineer at Helix. He painted a grim picture of a company on the brink of something monumental. It was a situation full of uncertainty.

Drake's statements were not forthcoming. His PR team ran circles around her attempts to get a comment. But she'd pieced together enough. Rumors said this system was already operational.

She sifted through interview notes late into the night. The blue glow of her laptop was the only light in her apartment. She had emailed anonymous sources. She cross-referenced patent applications. She reviewed white papers that highlighted the technology. None of it painted a complete picture, but what she had was enough to run with. There was a story here—a story that the public needed to hear. It was about the future of intelligence, of consciousness even. The more she uncovered, the more she realized. Drake's work wasn't about making something smarter than humanity. It was about playing God.

She hit "Send," and the story was gone. Out of her hands, out into the world. Whatever storm followed, Charlie was ready for it. She closed her laptop, leaned back in her chair, and took a deep breath. She lived for this moment. All the pieces fell into place. The truth, raw and unfiltered, was ready for someone to unleash.

CHAPTER 63

JAMES AND ISABELLE ARRIVED at the Victim's Services house where Tommy was staying. It was a quiet neighborhood. It had seen better days. But it kept a sense of community. In the front yard, they saw Tommy near the steps. A chubby kid taunted him, and he hunched his shoulders.

"You're so weird," the kid jeered, circling Tommy like a predator, sensing weakness. "You don't eat, you don't drink, you probably don't piss or shit either, huh? Freak!"

Tommy stood there, his eyes fixed on the ground, ignoring the boy. The wind messed up his short dark hair. His small frame shrank under the weight of the teasing. He didn't flinch; didn't give the kid any reaction.

Isabelle stormed over to the chubby kid, cutting him off mid-taunt. "Hey!" she called, her voice dripping with a mix of amusement and menace. The kid stopped, blinking in surprise.

She leaned down, getting close enough to make him uncomfortable. "Let me explain something to you," she said with a slow smile. "If I ever catch you messing with him again, you're going to have two problems. First, you'll be learning what it feels like to eat through a straw. And second, I'll make sure your new nickname is 'Chicken Nugget' for the rest of the school year. You get me?"

The kid's face turned pale as he stammered, "I … I was just kidding."

Isabelle's smile widened, all teeth. "Good. Now, go find something productive to do, like running laps. Lots of them."

The kid tripped over himself as he turned and bolted, glancing back as Isabelle stood there, watching him go.

Isabelle shook her head in irritation. James looked at her with a smile, "You'll be a fantastic mom one day."

She smirked and turned back to Tommy, her expression softening as she approached. "Who was that kid?" she asked, her voice gentle now.

Tommy shrugged, looking back up at her, his face calm. "His name's Kyle. He's easy to ignore. More talk than action."

Isabelle smiled, impressed by Tommy's resilience. "Smart kid," she said.

James, Isabelle, and Tommy entered the house. The afternoon sun cast long shadows on the worn porch. The living room was cozy but cluttered. It had mismatched furniture and toys on the floor. A television was blaring in the corner, playing some daytime talk show. Tommy flopped onto a worn armchair, facing the TV, while James and Isabelle sat opposite him on the couch.

The TV was loud—too loud for any real conversation—so James reached for the remote and turned the volume down. The sudden quiet was almost jarring.

Isabelle leaned forward. "Tommy, we want to talk to you about—"

Before she finished her sentence, Tommy's face shifted. His eyes went wide with fear, and he stiffened in his seat. His small hand shot up, pointing at the television screen. His whole body was trembling now; his voice was a whisper.

"That's him," Tommy said, his voice shaky but unmistakable. "That's the man who took me.

CHAPTER 64

ISABELLE AND JAMES immediately turned to the screen. In high definition, a man in his mid-60s appeared. He was clean-cut, in an expensive suit, and spoke with confidence. The caption below him read: "William Drake, CEO of Helix. New Breakthrough in Artificial General Intelligence."

James stared in shock at the screen. Drake spoke of his tech company's advances in artificial general intelligence (AGI). He was smooth, charismatic, and the kind of man who commanded attention.

The camera zoomed in on Drake's face as he smiled for the interviewer. "This breakthrough creates smarter machines. It also pushes the limits of thinking, reasoning, and learning. This is a new frontier for technology and humanity alike."

James felt a chill run down his spine. This man, speaking with such poise, was the same one Tommy had identified as his captor.

Isabelle snapped a quick photo of the screen with her phone, her mind racing. "Tommy," she said, turning to the boy, "are you positive? That's the man who took you?"

Tommy nodded, his whole body trembling. "That's him," he whispered again, his voice more certain this time. "That's the man."

James and Isabelle exchanged a look, the weight of the situation settling in. William Drake wasn't some tech CEO talking about the future of AI—if Tommy was right, he was a dark and dangerous man.

Act III
Façade

Act III
Regrets

CHAPTER 65

ADRENALINE PUMPING, Isabelle and James rushed out of the group home, leaving Tommy behind. The weight of the revelation was heavy on both of them. Drake wasn't only some name—he was real, and if Tommy and Evelyn were right, he was dangerous.

"We need an ID from Evelyn," Isabelle muttered. They sped toward their next stop, hoping to confirm their fears.

It didn't take long before they arrived. Evelyn was sitting in a chair, looking exhausted but far more composed than the previous day. Isabelle wasted no time. She pulled out her phone and opened the image she had taken of the news report featuring Drake.

"Do you recognize this man?" Isabelle asked, her voice calm but urgent as she handed the phone to Evelyn.

Evelyn's reaction was immediate. Her eyes went wide with fear, and her body stiffened in her seat. She was trembling, staring at the screen as if it were a ghost from her darkest nightmares. "That's him," she whispered in a voice that was almost inaudible. Then louder, with conviction, "That's him. That's the man who kidnapped me… and did those horrible things to me. And to Tommy."

"Are you positive?" Isabelle pressed, needing the confirmation, needing the certainty.

"Yes," Evelyn replied, her voice firm now, though her body still shook. "Yes, I'm 100% certain. I'll never forget his face."

Isabelle glanced over at James, who met her gaze with a solemn nod. "I guess we need to drive out to Helix Industries," Isabelle said. Her mind raced at the implications.

"I'm waiting to hear back from the U.S. Attorney," he said, but his tone indicated they weren't going to wait for long.

James's mind was spinning. Helix Industries . . . He hadn't made the connection before. Now, the company's name was like a ticking time bomb in his head. Something about it bothered him.

Then it clicked.

He reached into his pocket, pulling out the small business card Alex Grayson had given him. She worked at Helix. He stared at the card for a moment, processing the implications. Might this be a coincidence?

"Isabelle," he said, his voice tight.

She turned to him. "What's up?"

James handed her the card. "The girl, Alex. She works for Helix."

Isabelle's eyes widened as she took the card and studied it. "Shit," she muttered under her breath. "Do you think she knows more than she's telling us?"

James hesitated, his mind running over his encounter with Alex. She had seemed genuine, concerned, and eager to help. But now... now he wasn't sure. "She seemed sincere. Concerned that someone was impersonating her friend Jessica. I didn't sense anything off about her, but... at this point, I just don't know."

Isabelle nodded, handing him the card. "We can't rule anything out. Either way, we need answers."

They didn't waste any more time. They grew tenser as they drove to Helix Industries.

166

CHAPTER 66

SAMANTHA CARTER STEPPED off the yellow line at the Archives Metro station. She blended into the crowd of early morning commuters. Then, she headed to her office on D Street. She moved with purpose, her stride confident, heels clicking on the pavement. The warm morning sun caught the edges of her long, chestnut-brown hair. She had pulled it back into a loose but tidy ponytail. Stray strands brushed across her face, but her eyes remained sharp and focused. Her most striking feature was her eyes. They were a piercing, electric blue that seemed to hold a thousand stories.

Her tailored black suit moved with her as she walked. Its sharp lines gave her a commanding presence. Even in a crowd, people noticed her. Her elegant, intense way of carrying herself made people move aside.

Samantha had been a U.S. Attorney for over six years, her rise within the Department of Justice being meteoric. Her father, a top lawyer at a prestigious firm, had hoped she would follow in his footsteps, but she had rebelled. She had no interest in corporate clients or cushy office jobs. She craved the courtroom's intensity and the chance to put away the worst criminals.

From the start, Samantha had become a standout at the DOJ, known for her relentless work ethic and sharp legal mind.

As she entered her office, the usual buzz greeted her. Phones rang, secretaries typed, and lawyers conversed, preparing for the day's battles. Her office was sleek but minimalist. It had no distractions. A desk, a few chairs, and a large window that overlooked the city were all it had. The only personal touch was a framed photo of her with her parents at her law school graduation. Also, a framed certificate from her first big win as a prosecutor.

A middle-aged woman, her office secretary, wore glasses low on her nose. She approached with a note in hand. "Special Agent Lawson called. He asked you to get back to him when you can."

Samantha took the note with a nod and sat down behind her desk, kicking off her heels beneath the table. She glanced at the phone number on the paper, but her mind drifted for a moment, caught in a memory.

She flung a strand of her blonde hair from her face. Her blue eyes softened as she recalled meeting Special Agent James Lawson. It was during the Ramirez case. The authorities brought in Samantha to prosecute. James was the lead investigator. The case was high-profile. It involved a brutal human trafficking ring. James's dedication impressed Samantha. He also worked with unwavering dedication. Their professional partnership soon

167

turned into something more.

She smiled, recalling the tension that had simmered between them over the weeks they'd worked together. The Ramirez case had been exhausting. Filled with late nights and frustration as they pieced together evidence. James had a way of getting under her skin—enough to irritate her, but also to push her to work harder. Then came the devastating dismissal. The judge suppressed crucial evidence. It was a crushing blow.

That night, they went to the Basin Street Lounge above the 219 Restaurant on King Street. They hoped to drown their sorrows and vent about the broken system.

The lounge was a dim, smoky bar. Live blues played late into the night. You could lose yourself in the music and drinks. They drank until the world blurred. Then, a few more whiskeys helped them end up on the tiny dance floor, swaying to a blues guitar. The night had taken them back to James's place. A lingering glance turned into a kiss, and then something primal.

It was a one-night thing; they both knew that. They felt a strong chemistry. But they were too similar. Both driven, stubborn, and having fiery tempers when pushed. James's trigger was misogynistic assholes who beat women. Her's was a world of users—freeloaders, fraudsters, and manipulators of the weak.

Samantha straightened in her chair, still smiling as she picked up the phone and dialed James's number. The line rang twice before she heard his familiar voice.

"Agent Lawson," James answered, his tone as curt and direct as it had ever been.

Samantha leaned back in her chair, her blue eyes gleaming with a mix of amusement and anticipation. "Special Agent Lawson," she said, her voice smooth and teasing. "What can I do for you today?"

There was a brief pause on the other end, and she almost pictured him rolling his eyes at the formality.

"Got a case for you," James replied, his voice low and serious now. "It's… complicated."

"Complicated is my specialty," she said, her tone shifting to match his. She sat up, ready for whatever bombshell he was about to drop.

CHAPTER 67

JAMES HUNG UP the phone with Samantha, the conversation lingering in his mind. "You have enough to make an arrest," she had said, her voice steady and resolute. He had thanked her, his mind racing. Now, sitting in the car with Isabelle, the weight of the case pressed down on him like never before.

"Carter said to make the arrest," James said, breaking the silence as he placed his phone in the middle console.

Isabelle, who had been staring out the window, deep in thought, offered only a slight nod in response to his words. Her brow furrowed, lips pressed together in contemplation.

"What's on your mind?" James asked, sensing her distraction.
She blinked, then turned to him, her brown eyes clouded with uncertainty. "Why didn't she cry? There were no tears?"

James raised an eyebrow, confused. "What? Who?"

"Evelyn," Isabelle said, her voice thoughtful. "When we told her about her parents. She had all the emotions—sadness, fear, despair—but no tears. She gave off a similar emotion of panic and despair when she identified Drake. Not once did her eyes water. It's… it's strange."

James shrugged, not sure where Isabelle was going with this. "Maybe she's in shock, or processing it in her own way. People react differently to trauma."

Isabelle wasn't convinced. "No, it's more than that. Think about it. Her emotions seem right on the surface, but there's something missing. It feels… hollow."

James looked at her. He saw the wheels turning in her head. She was processing every detail. It was like a puzzle piece that didn't quite fit.

"And Tommy," she continued, her voice growing more intense. "When that chubby kid was teasing him, what did he say? That Tommy doesn't eat, doesn't drink, doesn't even use the bathroom? At first, I thought it was just a dumb insult, but now I'm not so sure."

James frowned, leaning back in his seat. "Kids say all kinds of things when they're being little shits. You think there's something to it?"

Isabelle nodded. "Think about it, James. When I brought them food the other day, burgers and fries. They hadn't eaten in over 20 hours, and yet, neither of them touched the food. Nothing. Tommy just stared at it, and

Evelyn barely even acknowledged it."

James shifted, uncomfortable with the implications. His mind raced to keep up with Isabelle's train of thought. "Maybe they weren't hungry. Maybe they were still in shock from everything."

"Maybe," Isabelle echoed, but her tone was doubtful. "But something about this doesn't sit right. We've been with them for days now. Not once have I seen them eat or drink. You'd think after going through what they did, they'd be ravenous. But nothing. Not a bite. And no one's mentioned them going to the bathroom, either. It's weird, right? That first night, even you left to take a piss twice, and I left once, but neither of them ever left the room or asked."

James rubbed his temples, the tension building in his head. "You're starting to sound like you've gone down some conspiracy rabbit hole. People have to eat, Belle. It's basic biology."

Isabelle shrugged, her eyes never leaving his. "I know how it sounds, but there's something strange going on with them. Their reactions don't match up with the facts. I can't shake this feeling that we're missing something huge. Something that goes beyond trauma."

James sighed, turning to her. "So, what's your theory?"

Isabelle didn't respond right away; her gaze drifted back toward the window. "I don't know. But I think we need to start looking at this case from a different angle. There's something we're not seeing."

James sat back, trying to let the idea settle in, but it didn't feel right. The twists and turns of this case were already enough to make his head spin. He wasn't ready to start questioning reality itself.

But then again, this case had already shattered every expectation they had.

170

CHAPTER 68

JAMES AND ISABELLE CONTINUED down the I-66 tollway; Isabelle was deep in thought. She searched for information on Helix Industries on her phone.

"The facility is out past Dulles," Isabelle muttered, her eyes scanning the screen. "It's massive—covers over 2,200 acres. That's the size of over 1600 football fields. And they're into everything."

James glanced over at her, raising an eyebrow. "Everything like what?"

"They make all kinds of tech—chips, robotics, bioscience, you name it. Helix is the company that created that robot everyone talked about a year ago. It emptied a dishwasher and even sautéed some shrimp. It was a creepy-looking thing."

James chuckled, trying to lighten the mood. "I'll stick with sautéing my own shrimp."

Isabelle didn't crack a smile, her focus still on the screen. "William Drake's father, Arthur Drake, founded the company. Apparently, there was a huge scandal years ago when Arthur automated thousands of jobs, putting a ton of union workers out of work. Big backlash, lots of protests."

"Sounds like they've made enemies for a while," James said, gripping the wheel tighter.

"Yeah, and it looks like William followed in his father's footsteps. Helix has expanded into bioscience."

James shook his head. "And now he can add rape, kidnapping, and child endangerment to his résumé."

Isabelle looked up from her phone, locking eyes with him and nodding in agreement.

James kept driving. The roads became more rural as they neared Dulles. In the distance, the Helix campus loomed. It gleamed like a fortress of steel and glass. James couldn't help but feel a knot tightening in his stomach. This wasn't a normal arrest. They were about to enter a giant, a company with vast resources and many secrets.

"I wonder what Ms. Grayson does there," Isabelle mused, her voice quiet, as if she were thinking out loud. "And if there's any connection to all this."

James shrugged, though his mind was already racing with possibilities. "She didn't seem like she was hiding anything, but... this place? It's hard not to think there's more going on."

Isabelle closed her phone, setting it down on her lap. "First things first,

171

Jimbo. Let's bring this evil fuck in. Then we can start connecting all the dots."

James nodded, his jaw tight. "Can't say I've ever arrested a billionaire before."

Isabelle smirked, finally cracking a smile. "There's a first time for everything. I made sure I brought the diamond cuffs," she joked.

As they neared the Helix entrance, they fell silent.

CHAPTER 69

JAMES AND ISABELLE entered the tall glass building of Helix Industries; the scale of the security operation struck them. Armed guards stationed at every corner, their eyes scanning the room. Cameras perched high on the walls, tracking every movement with eerie precision. This wasn't the usual corporate security setup—this was like they were walking into Fort Knox.

"I've seen less security at federal buildings," Isabelle muttered, her eyes darting as they approached the front desk.

James gave a small nod, feeling the same unease. "Yeah, they're guarding this place like it's holding national secrets."

The desk agent, a tall man in a black suit with a no-nonsense demeanor, looked up as they approached. "Can I assist you?" He asked, his voice clipped and professional.

James and Isabelle flashed their FBI credentials in unison. "Special Agent James Lawson," James said, his voice steady. "And this is Special Agent Isabelle Stone. We need to speak with William Drake."

The desk agent's gaze flicked from their credentials to their faces. He scrutinized them, as only someone used to high-stakes security might. He didn't speak, but his eyes flickered. Surprise, even concern, showed. Then, he reached for the phone.

He spoke in hushed tones. "Yes, there are two federal agents here for Mr. Drake... yes... I understand... okay."

He hung up the phone and turned to them, his expression neutral again. "Mr. Drake will be down shortly, but he has asked that I take you to the conference room while you wait. Is that acceptable?"

Isabelle glanced at James, and they exchanged a quick look. "Of course," Isabelle replied, smiling to hide her growing tension.

The security agent gestured for them to follow. They trailed behind him down a long, marble-floored hallway. The building screamed money and power. It made you feel small as soon as you stepped inside. The air was cool, almost clinical. Everything was pristine.

As they neared the conference room, James couldn't shake the feeling that something was off. The level of security, the smoothness of the operation—it all seemed too perfect. Helix was a fortress. Drake wanted to know every detail before anyone entered.

The security agent opened the door to the conference room. It was a large room with sleek furniture and high-tech gadgets. It looked like a scene from a futuristic movie. "Mr. Drake will be with you shortly," he said before stepping out, leaving them alone in the room.

James leaned back in his chair, his eyes scanning the room. "This place is something else," he said, shaking his head. "I've never seen anything like it."

Isabelle, sitting across from him, nodded in agreement but remained focused. "It's like a fortress. I've got a bad feeling about this."

James frowned. "What are you thinking?"

"I'm thinking we're about to go up against more than just a billionaire tech mogul," Isabelle replied, her eyes narrowing. "We need to tread carefully here."

They sat in silence, the situation weighing on them as they waited for Drake to appear.

CHAPTER 70

JAMES AND ISABELLE SAT in the sleek, sterile conference room. They scanned the immaculate space as the minutes ticked by. Twenty minutes after they arrived, the door creaked open. In walked Drake, exuding calm and confidence. Both agents stood as he approached. His handshake was firm, and he was polite.

"My apologies, Agents Lawson and Stone," Drake said. He smiled and shook their hands. "I was on a conference call with Tokyo. Again, I apologize for the wait. How can I assist the FBI today?"

James was the first to speak, his tone steady and professional. "Mr. Drake, are you familiar with a woman named Evelyn Parker?"

Drake tilted his head, a flicker of amusement in his expression, though it didn't quite reach his eyes. "No... no, I'm not familiar with anyone by that name," he said, as if he were declining an invitation to a dinner party.

James glanced at Isabelle, then pressed on. "How about a boy named Tommy Hayes?"

Drake's demeanor didn't change. "No, I can't say I know a person by that name either. What's this about, Agent Lawson? I'm a very busy man."

James slid two photos across the polished table: one of Evelyn and the other of Tommy. "Have you ever seen either of these people?" he asked, his voice calm but laced with intent.

Drake picked up the photos. He glanced at them, then slid them back to James with a shrug. "I've never seen any person resembling either of these two," he said. "If I had, I'm sure I'd remember."

James leaned forward, locking eyes with Drake. "Mr. Drake, what would you think if I said that both of these people identified you as their kidnapper?"

Drake didn't flinch. His expression remained calm, his body language as steady as ever. "I think," he began, his tone smooth, "that they are quite mistaken. I don't know what you're getting at, Agent Lawson, but I assure you, I've had no involvement kidnappings."

The silence hung thick in the air for a moment as both agents took in his unflappable demeanor. Drake's eyes flickered toward Isabelle, and with a polite smile, he straightened his tie. "Am I a suspect, Agent Lawson?" he asked with chilling calmness. "Because if I am, I've given you enough time. You can speak with my lawyer if you have any further questions."

With that, Drake stood, straightening his jacket and preparing to leave the room.

James and Isabelle exchanged a glance—a silent conversation in the span of a heartbeat. The look they shared said it all: Let's arrest this prick.

Isabelle moved first, stepping in front of Drake as he reached the door. "Mr. Drake, you're under arrest for kidnapping and assault," she said. Her voice was firm as she grabbed his arm and began to cuff him.

As Isabelle read him his rights, Drake didn't resist. In fact, he seemed almost amused. He turned to Isabelle and whispered, "There, there, Agent Stone." His voice was low and unsettling. That's the way I like it. What's your preference?"

The hairs on the back of Isabelle's neck stood on end, but she didn't flinch. She kept her grip firm on his arm, her expression ice-cold. "Do you understand your rights, Mr. Drake?" she asked, her voice steady despite the disgust bubbling under her skin.

"Of course," Drake replied, his smirk almost hidden as he left the room.

As they stepped into the hallway, Drake's secretary, Miss Bennett, was waiting. Her face was pale, and her eyes were wide with confusion. "Mr. Drake... is there something wrong?"

Drake turned to her, his expression as calm as ever. "No, Miss Bennett. I'm just going for a ride with these two agents. Please contact Mr. Cole and have him meet me at the D.C. FBI office. And inform Mr. Ward to be on standby as well."

"Yes, sir," Miss Bennett stammered, her voice trembling.

Drake gave her a nod, then allowed James and Isabelle to escort him out of the building. As they walked the tall halls of Helix Industries, their task weighed on them. They passed the high-tech security and the gleaming glass walls.

As they reached the car, the camera crew and a reporter who broke the earlier story, jumped out of a van.

"What is the reason for Mr. Drake's arrest?" the reporter asked, shoving a microphone in Isabelle's face.

Isabelle turned away and shoved Drake into the back seat, closing the door behind him. She glanced at James, her expression unreadable.

"Ready for this?" James asked.

Isabelle exhaled. Drake's unsettling comment in the conference room replayed in her mind. "Let's get him downtown."

James nodded. He started the engine and drove off.

CHAPTER 71

ALEX SAT AT HER DESK, her eyes flicking back and forth between the lines of code on her screen. She was in the zone, working on a project that had been consuming her for weeks. But something about the steady hum of the office today was off. The same TV above her workstation had been buzzing with excitement earlier. It was about Helix's discovery of artificial general intelligence. Now, it flashed a new kind of headline: "BREAKING NEWS: William Drake Arrested on Charges of Kidnapping."

Alex's fingers froze over her keyboard, her gaze lifting to the TV. Her heart skipped a beat as she processed the words. Her eyes widened when the screen showed footage of Drake. He was being led out of the towering Helix building, his hands cuffed. Walking beside him, calm and in control, was the agent she had met the other day—James Lawson.

She blinked, her mind struggling to comprehend the scene. The same man who had knocked on her door was now involved in the arrest of the CEO. He had asked about her friend Jessica. William Drake... kidnapping? It was impossible, like the ground had shifted beneath her feet.

Her breath caught in her throat as the news anchors began to speak in hushed tones, detailing the charges. They were vague, speculating about an FBI probe into a human trafficking ring. But the mention of Drake's name sent a chill down her spine.

This can't be real, she thought. She tried to focus on her code. The numbers and letters on the screen made sense. Unlike the chaos on the TV. But something shattered her concentration.

Her phone buzzed on her desk. She saw dozens of texts from coworkers, friends, and industry contacts. They all asked the same thing: What's going on? Is it true? Is Drake involved?

Alex's mind raced. She had worked for Drake for years. She avoided collaborating with him, but she provided him with briefings on a few projects. The man was brilliant, driven, intense—but was he be capable of something like this? Kidnapping?

Her mind flashed back to Agent Lawson's visit. He had been so calm, so collected, asking about Jessica and whether she knew anything. At the time, she had thought it was routine, even a mistake. But now, seeing his face on the screen, everything was different. It showed him leading Drake away in handcuffs.

What did Agent Lawson know that I didn't? Alex wondered.

The rest of the office seemed to be in a similar state of shock. Conversations grew hushed. Some coworkers huddled around their screens, whispering about the scandal, about Drake. Alex stood up, the noise of the office a dull roar in her ears as she tried to make sense of it all.

The projects and the code she'd been working on were distant and irrelevant. All she thought about was the news, the footage of Agent Lawson and Drake, and the woman who thinks she's Jessica.

Special Agent Lawson's visit had shaken her in ways she couldn't grasp yet. Jessica. The name hit her like a wave, the memories flooding back in an instant. Her best friend, the one she had watched fade away from ALS, had been gone for three years. Yet, here was this federal agent, telling her about a woman named Evelyn Parker. A woman who knew Alex well—details about her past, her quirks, things only Jessica knew.

But how?

The conversation with Lawson replayed in her mind. "She claims she knows you, Alex. She described your childhood and personal moments. Even some you'd expect only a close friend to know."

Alex's mind raced. Jessica was gone. Her funeral, her last words, the quiet goodbye at her casket—these were events seared into her memory. It didn't make sense. And yet... Evelyn Parker. That name gnawed at her, as if she had a puzzle to piece together. Could Evelyn have Jessica's memories?

Her thoughts drifted to the past. To when she started at Helix, and the work she had buried herself in after Jessica's death. After graduation, she focused on her career. She excelled faster than she had imagined. Within months of starting, she had caught the attention of Helix's upper echelon. She landed promotions that took her deeper into the most secretive projects. But it was a year and a half ago when everything changed.

Project Elysium had finally borne fruit. Memory decoding technology had leapt forward, advancing faster than anyone expected. Alex's team had used AI to map and rebuild memories from neural scans. They recreated, visualized, and even simulated those memories as if reliving them. But the breakthroughs weren't without issues. She remembered the first success: the beach memory. The AI's fill-in work had altered it, blending artificial fragments with real memories. It was thrilling—and terrifying. What if the AI did more than fill gaps? What if it could overwrite, blend, or—God forbid—implant memories?

Her stomach twisted at the thought.

Back then, she had ignored the deeper implications. She dove into the technical details and pushed the project forward. But now, sitting in her office, Alex was seeing everything through a different lens. The technology they had pioneered wasn't about storing memories anymore. What if someone—someone like Evelyn—had Jessica's memories implanted in them?

Was it even be possible?

The idea seemed impossible. But, hadn't they pushed all limits with their research? Might Evelyn Parker hold fragments of Jessica's life? Her personality? Her secrets?

Alex's pulse quickened. Her hand hovered over her phone, the memory of Lawson's questions buzzing in her head. She needed answers. But more than that—she needed to know if Jessica, or some part of her, was still out there.

Without hesitation, Alex dialed Special Agent Lawson's number. She needed to meet Evelyn.

"Lawson," the voice on the other end responded.

"Special Agent Lawson, it's Alex Grayson. I may have some more information. I'd like to see Evelyn first; would that be possible?" Alex spoke, pulling up her calendar. "Yes… yes, tomorrow at 8:00 would be fine; I'll see you then, goodbye," she responded, hanging up the phone.

CHAPTER 72

COLONEL BEN MONROE stepped off the crowded yellow line train as it arrived at the Pentagon. He already dreaded the day ahead. His earlier argument with his wife had soured him. Not even the strong coffee in his thermos washed it away. They had fought about the usual things: his long hours, the kids, and the growing distance between them. It was the price he paid for the job, a job that demanded everything from him. But that didn't make it any easier.

At 6'3" with broad shoulders, he was an imposing figure. His deep brown skin bore the mark of countless days under the desert sun. His sharp, focused eyes missed little. His close-cropped, gray-threaded black hair spoke to his years of service. His strong-jawed face held scars from battles—both on and off the field. His tours in Iraq and Afghanistan had scarred him. Yet, he moved with the calm precision of a seasoned veteran.

He was a decorated officer with combat ribbons and over 20 years of service. People knew him for his leadership, resilience, and technical brilliance.

In Kearney, Nebraska, he was one of the few Black kids. He learned that hard work and determination were the keys to success. At the University of Nebraska, he joined ROTC. He wanted to be more than a typical officer. He wanted to make a difference. With a degree in computer engineering, He was a techie and a strategist. He understood modern warfare's complexities in a way few could. His career took off, but the pivotal moment came during a tour in Afghanistan.

As a young lieutenant, he led his platoon when a series of IEDs exploded. That day burned into his soul—the enemy cut down his men one by one, until only he and another soldier survived. It had shaped him. It drove him to use tech, smarts, and strategy to save lives in future wars. He had always carried the weight of those lost soldiers. He had written letters to their families, calling their sons heroes.

For the past decade, he had shifted his focus from the front lines to the future of warfare. Now, as director of Project Sentinel, he led a secret initiative to revolutionize the battlefield. Sentinel aimed to create systems that fought alongside soldiers. It wasn't about using tech to support them. It was at the cutting edge of war technology. It had robots to detect and disarm IEDs, and drones for reconnaissance and combat. For him, it was personal. He was determined to make these machines prevent ambushes. An ambush had nearly taken his life years ago.

But for every step forward, it felt like two steps back. The last two years had been a frustrating mix of breakthroughs and setbacks. Robotics and AI weren't as simple as flipping a switch, and every malfunction felt personal. He knew lives depended on Sentinel's success. But it seemed the program was slipping through his fingers.

Upon reaching his office in the Pentagon, he found the usual bustle around him. But his mind was miles away. A stack of reports was on his desk. They were budget approvals, Sentinel progress updates, and the latest intel briefs. His assistant had left them. He dropped his thermos on the desk and flopped into his chair. His eyes flicked to the coffee, realizing he had spilled some. He cursed and wiped the spill with his sleeve.

He picked up the day's newspaper, hoping to clear his mind for a moment. The headline stopped him cold: "Billionaire Arrested on Suspicion of Kidnapping." Below it was a picture of William Drake, the CEO of Helix Industries. His cutting-edge technology had been vital to Project Sentinel's progress.

"Shit," he muttered. This was the last thing he needed. Helix's contributions to Sentinel had been invaluable. If Drake were wrapped up in some scandal, it would set the entire project back—again.

He grabbed the phone on his desk and dialed a secure line. "Did you see the news about Drake?" His voice was tight with frustration.

The voice on the other end gave a quick, clipped response.

"This better not prolong the project any further. We're already behind schedule," he snapped, his voice rising. He ran a hand over his face, the weight of everything pressing down on him.

"Yeah, I know. Got it," he said, hanging up the phone.

Leaning back in his chair, he stared at the ceiling, letting the hum of the Pentagon fill his ears. Project Sentinel was too vital to the future of warfare. Some tech billionaire's personal scandal couldn't derail it. Lives were at stake. He couldn't afford to let this fall apart. Not now. Not after everything.

CHAPTER 73

JAMES AND ISABELLE ARRIVED at Drake's Estate to view the crime scene. The mansion loomed against the horizon, a dark fortress in the sun. The wind howled through the surrounding trees, carrying an autumn chill that cut to the bone. The rustle of distant leaves echoed like whispers. The air was thick with the scent of damp earth and mildew. It added to the foreboding atmosphere. They stepped out of the car. Silence enveloped them. The vast estate seemed to breathe—cold, detached, and alive with secrets.

The mansion's windows were like hollow eyes. They stared back at them, daring them to find the secrets inside. The air was different here. It was heavy, charged with a sinister energy. It clung to the skin like humidity before a storm. James glanced at Isabelle. The case weighed on them as they neared the imposing entrance.

Agent Foster waited at the door, grinning. It was out of place. His eyes glinted with strange amusement, like a jester at a funeral. His hands rested on his hips, the smirk never quite reaching his eyes. "What took you guys so long?" he jeered.

Isabelle's voice was sharp, cutting through the unease. "Some of us actually have to work, Foster."

Foster's laugh echoed in the cavernous foyer as they entered. It died suddenly, swallowed by the mansion's emptiness. The place reeked of wealth. But its opulence made James's skin crawl. It was too sterile, too curated. The grand hallways were vacant. But it felt as though they were being watched. Shadows whispered in the corners.

"Follow me," Foster said, his voice dropping as they moved deeper into the mansion.

The halls were empty, the silence amplifying the wrongness of the place with each step they took.

Foster led them down into the estate's basement. The stairs creaked underfoot as the darkness thickened with each step. The musty air smelled of damp concrete. A chill lingered, seeping into their bones. The temperature dropped. A faint drip of water broke the silence. At the bottom, Foster pointed to a door, its handle tarnished and cold.

"We found the rooms down here," he said, pointing.

He opened the door to a small dark room. The walls were barren and oppressive. A single bed stood in the corner, its thin mattress sagging in a way that spoke of neglect. James's gaze swept across the room, feeling a chill run down his spine. This wasn't just a place of captivity—it was a place meant to break someone.

"This was the boy's room," Foster murmured.

James looked closer, noticing something glinting in the corner near the ceiling. He stepped closer. It was a hidden camera, tucked away to avoid notice.

"The room's wired for video," he said, his voice flat.

Foster shook his head. "We haven't found any equipment yet."

James nodded, his instincts prickling. There was more here—more beneath the surface of this place. He stepped back into the hallway, his eyes tracing the wall's paneling. At the far end, something caught his eye—a faint seam in the wood, almost invisible. He motioned for Isabelle, and together they examined it. After a few careful tugs, they managed to pry it open, revealing a hidden door.

James pulled out a set of tools, the lock clicking open with a metallic snap. As the door swung inward, a cold shiver ran down his spine. The room beyond was a voyeur's paradise. It had video equipment and numerous monitors. The screens were still flickering, displaying grainy footage of the basement rooms. The air seemed colder here, the kind of chill that settled deep in the bones.

"Looks like we've hit the evidentiary jackpot," Isabelle said, her voice grim.

James sat at the table in front of the monitors. A laptop sat there with a blank screen. James wiggled the mouse, bringing the laptop to life. To James's surprise the laptop did not require a password. He began to review file structure, stumbling upon two folders titled 'Tommy' and 'Evelyn.' His hands were heavy as he clicked the mouse on the Tommy folder, his breath growing shallow. He clicked on one of the video files, feeling a knot tighten in his stomach. The video flickered to life. The image was like a punch to the gut—Tommy, small and terrified, sitting in a chair. In the corner of the frame, Drake loomed, his presence filling the room with menace.

James fast-forwarded, his stomach churning as he watched Drake approach Tommy. He set objects in front of him, issuing commands. Tommy's hands shook, fumbling; his fear was evident in every movement. Then, without warning, Drake struck him. Tommy crumpled to the floor. Rage simmered in James. His knuckles whitened as he clenched his fists.

Isabelle's voice was low, her anger contained. "This is sick."

James swallowed hard, forcing himself to continue. They had to know. He clicked off the video and backed out of the folder, moving to the folder labeled "Evelyn." He clicked on one of the many videos.

James and Isabelle sat in the dark room. The computer screen's eerie glow lit their faces. They were witnessing a horror beyond imagination. A hidden camera recorded a scene of unspeakable cruelty.

On the screen, Evelyn, bound and naked, lay on a cold, metal bed. Her eyes, wide with terror, reflected the fear that consumed her. Though silent,

183

her every muscle tensed. It was a plea for help, or a desperate wish to escape the horrors unfolding.

Drake, loomed over her. His presence was a menacing force. As he leaned closer, his breath a sinister whisper. James and Isabelle felt his malevolence. His words, a chilling mix of threats and sadistic pleasure, sent shivers down their spines.

With deliberate cruelty, Drake's hands moved across Evelyn's body, leaving no part untouched. She bore the marks of his abuse. They were not physical scars, but the indelible imprint of fear and humiliation.

The violence escalated, a brutal display of power and depravity. Drake's rage unleashed a storm of slaps, punches, and penetrations on Evelyn's body. The malice in his actions was palpable; he aimed to break her physically and shatter her very soul.

As the violence continued, Evelyn's silence became a haunting presence. Her eyes pleaded for mercy, but none was forthcoming. Every inch of her body bore the weight of Drake's sickening desire for control.

James and Isabelle, seeing this cruelty, felt horror and anger. They felt a deep injustice. The video, a chilling record of a human being's capacity for evil, left them shaken to their core.

In that moment, they understood the true gravity of the situation. The video evidence was a powerful tool. It had the potential to bring Drake to justice and prevent others from suffering such horrors.

James stopped the video, his chest tight with fury. He looked at Isabelle, her face pale, her eyes hard as steel.

"We got this sick fuck," James said, his voice strained, the rage contained.

Isabelle nodded, her voice cold. "Let's bring this prick down."

CHAPTER 74

TWO DAYS HAD PASSED, since Charlie had reported on Helix's discovery of artificial general intelligence. Other news outlets quickly jumped on story, developing their own narrative. Today it was the arrest of William Drake, Helix's billionaire CEO, on charges of kidnapping.

Today, her phone buzzed with a message. It was from one of her most trusted contacts, a mid-level employee at Helix Industries. "FBI just arrested Drake. No details yet. Thought you'd want to know." The text was brief, but it was enough. Within an hour, Charlie had the story up on the Post's website, and it spread like wildfire.

Now, as she glanced at the TV in the corner of her office, the news was everywhere. Drake's clean-cut image on the screen clashed with new allegations. She knew there had to be more to it—there always was. And Charlie's gut rarely steered her wrong.

She leaned back in her chair, cracking her knuckles. Something about this case was nagging at her. A billionaire arrested on kidnapping charges? It didn't add up. Only if there was something bigger lurking beneath the surface did it make sense. She opened a new tab on her computer. Then, she sifted through police reports for clues to the missing pieces of the puzzle.

That's when she found it: a report filed two days earlier. Two individuals—a woman in her early thirties and a boy—were picked up by the Maryland State Police. Authorities found them wandering on a remote road, confused and disoriented. The location? A rural area three miles from the Drake estate.

Charlie's fingers hovered over the keyboard as the pieces began to fall into place. This was the lead she needed. If the state patrol had picked up the woman and child so close to Drake's property, there was no way it was a coincidence. She checked the report details. It listed the officers and the pickup's circumstances.

It was vague—nothing concrete enough to make a connection yet. The names weren't listed, but the timeline matched. These two might be the missing pieces in her story. They might explain why the FBI had shown up at William Drake's door.

Her instincts kicked into overdrive. She leaned forward, scribbling notes in the margins of a stack of papers on her desk. The boy was around twelve years old, and the woman was in her early thirties. It wasn't much to go on, but it was enough for her to dig deeper.

Reaching for her phone, she called her contact at Helix again. "Is there anything else you can tell me?" she asked.

Someone on the other end spoke in a hushed voice. "Not much. Drake seemed… calm. Almost like he expected this."

Charlie's brow furrowed. That didn't sit right with her. "Thanks. Keep me posted."

As she hung up, Charlie's thoughts drifted back to the woman and the boy. Why had they been so close to the Drake estate? And why hadn't anyone made the details of their situation public yet?

Her pulse quickened. There was something here. Something big.

CHAPTER 75

DRAKE SAT BEHIND his Helix office desk, freshly processed from his arrest. His attorney, Emmitt Cole, had arrived at the station within an hour. The heavy doors thudded open as Cole—a legal juggernaut—stepped inside. People knew Cole for making the worst charges vanish. He was short and stout, but his presence filled the room with a subtle arrogance. His tailored suit screamed wealth and influence, his reputation one of untouchability. With Cole on your side, the law itself seemed to bend in your favor.

Drake's hands clasped as he listened to his attorney, Emmitt Cole, rattle off the charges. The gray sky outside his Helix office mirrored the weight of the accusations.

"Mr. Drake," Cole began, his voice low and precise. "They've got you on 28 counts: kidnapping, sexual assault, and child endangerment. The victim's statements identify you directly, and they're credible. The Government has significant video evidence of the offense, and you're in all of them. If this goes to trial, it will be long and drawn out. Not to mention how it will play in the press. If you're found guilty of these charges, you're facing life in prison."

Drake didn't flinch. Instead, he leaned back in his chair, his expression cold and calculated. His sharp features remained impassive, as if the gravity of Cole's words hadn't landed. He exhaled, then leaned forward, his tone icy.

"Mr. Cole, I understand the nature of the charges. That's what I pay you for. To win," Drake hissed, his eyes narrowing.

Cole shifted in his seat. He was used to high-stakes cases, but something about Drake had always unsettled him. Maybe it was the man's utter lack of remorse, or the way he seemed almost amused by the severity of the situation. Either way, Cole knew he needed to get all the facts.

"I know that, sir," Cole said, trying to maintain composure. "But to fight this, I need to know everything. No surprises. No half-truths. If we go to court unprepared, you're looking at more than just bad press."

Drake's lip curled, a trace of a smile appeared. "Let's not waste time with questions, Mr. Cole. I'll cut to the chase."

Cole's hand tensed over his legal pad, the pen ready to scribble notes.

"Everything in those police reports—the victim statements, the accusations—they're mostly true," Drake said. His voice cut through the air like a knife.

Cole's heart skipped a beat. "True?"

"Yes," Drake said, as though they were discussing the weather. "Every word. Every count. It's true... well except for kidnapping. Neither was ever kidnapped... just informed that they were kidnapped."

Informed? The attorney thought, staring at his client, disbelief flooding his mind. In his line of work, clients were always eager to deny, to deflect, to make excuses. But Drake—he was confessing.

Drake leaned back again, his gaze still piercing. "But that's not the question you should be asking. The real question is whether I can be guilty of these charges."

Cole blinked, trying to wrap his mind around what he was hearing. "Mr. Drake, of course you can be found guilty, the evidence is... it's so strong."

A strange smile crossed Drake's lips. "I'm going to fill you in on something, Mr. Cole. Something that might change the way you see this entire case."

Cole watched as Drake stood up, moving to the bar cart in the corner of the room. The silence hung heavy as Drake poured two glasses of bourbon neat and handed one to his attorney.

"Perhaps you'd like a drink for this one," Drake said. He sipped his drink and settled back down. The amber liquid gleamed under the dim office lights.

Cole hesitated, then took the glass. His mind was spinning, but he knew that whatever came next would be far stranger than he imagined.

CHAPTER 76

SEVERAL DAYS HAD PASSED since Drake's arrest. Samantha flipped through the case files at her desk. Her fingers trembled at what she saw. The evidence sprawled before her. Testimonies, reports, and photographs all pointed to one conclusion. It was all there—the testimonies, the forensic reports, the videos. The charges against William Drake, billionaire and CEO of Helix, were solid. This was one of the cleanest cases she'd ever had. Both victims, Evelyn and Tommy, had spoken with chilling clarity about their ordeal. She was confident; the evidence was undeniable.

As she flipped through the pages, a knock at the door interrupted her focus. A clerk entered, handing her a thick envelope. Samantha gave a polite nod, her curiosity piqued. She tore it open. It was a motion for a classified pre-trial hearing.

She furrowed her brow, skimming the first few lines. As the meaning began to settle in, her phone rang. She glanced at the caller ID. It was Emmitt Cole, Drake's attorney.

"Samantha Carter," she answered, her voice professional but curious.

"Ms. Carter, Emmitt Cole here," came the smooth, confident voice on the other end. "I wanted to give you a courtesy heads-up that I've submitted a motion for a classified hearing."

Samantha leaned back in her chair, the motion still in her hand. "I'm looking at it right now, Mr. Cole. What exactly is the purpose of this? The charges are cut and dry—kidnapping, assault, multiple counts of child endangerment. The only thing 'out of the ordinary' is that your client is a billionaire. I hardly think that warrants a classified hearing."

Cole's voice didn't falter. Samantha felt her stomach tighten, her fingers gripping the edge of her desk. "Ms. Carter, I assure you, this isn't about protecting Mr. Drake's reputation or his CEO status. Helix develops sensitive technology for the Department of Defense. Some of those developments are part of his legal defense. And the classification level involved is Top Secret. This is a matter of national security."

Samantha felt a spark of suspicion. "National security? Mr. Cole, I sincerely hope this isn't a thinly veiled tactic to get your client off the hook. It's hard to picture how these charges involve national security. Perhaps it's just a ploy to… to protect shareholders."

Cole chuckled, his confidence unnerving. "You have my word, Ms. Carter, this is far bigger than shareholders. There's more to come. Much more. I just wanted to make sure you were prepared for what's ahead." There was a chilling finality in his tone.

"More to come, Mr. Cole?" Samantha pressed, trying to understand where this was headed.

"You'll see soon enough," Cole responded, his voice calm and cryptic. Then, without further explanation, he hung up.

Samantha placed the receiver back on its cradle, her mind racing. National security? Top secret? Why would Drake's attorney be pushing for a classified hearing in a kidnapping and assault case? It didn't make sense. She picked up the motion and began scanning it for answers.

As she scanned the motion, her stomach twisted. Drake, through his attorney, was asking the court to dismiss the complaint. He argued that the alleged victims, Evelyn Parker and Tommy Hayes, weren't human. According to the defense, they were sophisticated constructs of artificial intelligence and robotics, and therefore, crimes cannot legally be committed against them as they lacked the legal status of persons. Drake was claiming that, as androids, they were simply his personal property. He requested the court to dismiss all charges. He also wanted the immediate return of the two androids to him.

She sat frozen, disbelief rippling through her. Eyes wide, she stared as the words echoed in her mind. Evelyn and Tommy weren't human? How was that possible? She shook her head, trying to shake off the absurdity. They'd seemed so real. Their pain, stories, and vulnerability were like any other victim she'd met. The idea was impossible. Nothing could be so convincingly human and not be.

Her mind struggled, almost seizing up under the weight of it. Yet, through the fog of confusion, her hand moved on its own, trembling as she picked up the phone. She dialed a familiar number, her thoughts jumbled, desperate for answers. Is this some kind of cruel joke?

"Lawson," answered the voice on the other end.

"It's Samantha."

"What's up?"

"This Drake case just got strange," Samantha said. "I've received a defense motion for a classified pre-trial hearing. They're requesting a dismissal."

"What the fuck?"

"Do you and Agent Stone have time to discuss?" Samantha asked, looking at her calendar.

"Absolutely," he replied. "Alex Grayson called earlier and asked to speak with Evelyn. She's on her way over now if you care to join."

"I'll be over shortly," Samantha said, already standing up from her desk.

CHAPTER 77

SAMANTHA WALKED out of the U.S. Attorney's office, moving up 6th Avenue. The city buzzed with its usual midday hustle. But Samantha didn't notice. She focused on the strange motion she had received. About ten minutes later, she reached the intersection of 4th and F Street. After showing her credentials at the front desk, she made her way to James's office.

When she arrived, she found James and Isabelle already there. James looked up as she stepped in. "I just filled Isabelle in on the defense request," he said.

"What are the grounds for dismissal?" Isabelle asked, her expression tense.

Samantha sighed, dropping her bag onto the nearest chair. "He's requesting a dismissal based on the argument that Evelyn and Tommy are not humans."

James and Isabelle exchanged stunned glances. Isabelle's eyes widened. She couldn't believe the audacity of the claim. James leaned back, running a hand through his hair. He was trying to make sense of it. Was this some kind of elaborate ploy, or was there something they were missing? "Not human? That's ridiculous, of course they're human. How is that even possible?"

"I can't wrap my mind around it myself," Samantha admitted, looking at the shock etched on their faces. "There is no technology that comes close to robots looking and behaving like real humans. Have either of you noticed anything unusual about Evelyn or Tommy?"

James nodded. "We've been piecing things together. There's been some odd stuff. Everything that Evelyn told us checks out, with one big exception. All of her memories prior to the kidnapping belong to a Jessica Parker, not Evelyn." He paused, glancing at Isabelle for support. "And then there's Tommy. His situation is similar. Plus, no one has seen either of them eating or drinking. It's all very strange." James said on the edge of frustration.

Isabelle chimed in, her brow furrowed. "There's more. He interviewed Alex Grayson. She had a friend, Jessica Parker, who died three years ago. But, Evelyn seems to have Jessica's memories—details that Alex confirmed. Alex was adamant about meeting Evelyn, so she's on her way here now. We're hoping that might shed some light on this whole mess."

Samantha nodded, a feeling of unease settling in her stomach. The idea that Evelyn and Tommy might not be who—or what—they seemed was unsettling. She glanced at the door, as if expecting it to swing open any moment.

CHAPTER 78

ALEX STEPPED into the FBI office with a nervous but determined look on her face. She approached the front desk clerk and stated, "I have an appointment with Agent Lawson."

The clerk gave her a quick nod, glanced at the logbook, and then motioned toward a nearby chair. "Agent Lawson will be down in a moment."

A few minutes later, James appeared from down the hall, his pace steady and purposeful. "Ms. Grayson—" he paused, correcting himself, "I mean, Alex. Thank you for coming down."

"You're welcome," Alex replied, her voice carrying a hint of apprehension.

"You said you might have more info," James said. He gestured for her to follow him deeper into the building.

Alex walked beside him. Her curiosity and nerves showed in her hesitant steps. "Yes, I might," she began, her eyes meeting his before she looked away again. "But... I'd like to see the woman, Evelyn, first. Would that be okay?"

James stopped mid-stride and turned to face her. "How about you meet me halfway, Alex? Give me something—anything. Why does seeing Evelyn matter so much?"

Alex sighed, running a hand through her hair as she continued walking. "It's... It's a project I was working on at Helix," she finally admitted, her voice lowered.

"A project?" James asked, his eyebrows knitting together in suspicion. "At Helix?"

"Yes," Alex nodded, her tone guarded but more open than before. "It was dealing with memories. But look, it's a hunch right now—nothing to get alarmed about. It might lead to nothing at all."

James processed her words. Memories? Then he thought about what Samantha had told them just moments ago. He wasn't sure where this was going. But his instincts said she knew more than she let on. "Alright," he said after a beat. "Let me take you down to see her."

They walked side by side down the hallway. The tension between them shifted to anticipation. As they passed by Isabelle's office, James made a quick introduction to both Isabelle and Samantha.

"Alex, this is my partner, Isabelle Stone, and Samantha Carter, she's the Assistant U.S. Attorney for this case," he said, motioning to Isabelle and

Samantha.

Isabelle stood up, extending her hand. "Nice to meet you."

"A pleasure," Samantha stated, putting her hand out to shake.

"Hi," Alex replied, shaking their hands.

"I'm taking her down to see Evelyn right now, if you'd care to join," James explained.

"For sure," Isabelle said, closing a file that she was reviewing. Both she and Samantha stood and walked down the hall.

As they approached the door, Alex's pace slowed. Her heart thudded against her ribcage. A strange mix of dread and anticipation flooded her senses. She was about to confront someone. She might hold the key to her questions.

And James, sensing the weight of the moment, showed Alex the door. "Evelyn's waiting for you; we'll be in the adjoining room, behind the one-way mirror. If you need anything, knock on the glass."

"Thank you," she responded, as James, Isabelle, and Samantha turned and entered the adjoining room.

CHAPTER 79

ALEX PAUSED before stepping into the well-lit room, her heart pounding in her chest. Seated at the small table was Evelyn, her eyes hollow with the weight of what she had been through. Yet, when Evelyn looked up and saw Alex, something in her face shifted. Disbelief transformed into joy, as if she had been waiting for years for this moment.

"Alex!" Evelyn screamed, her voice breaking with raw emotion. "Alex!"

Before Alex processed it, Evelyn jumped up and rushed to her. She wrapped her in a fierce embrace. The strength of the hug took Alex by surprise, and she stiffened, her mind racing. This isn't Jessica, she reminded herself. This woman can't be her.

But as Evelyn's body shook with sobs, something inside Alex softened. The hug's warmth and Evelyn's crying her name. It was like seeing her best friend Jessica.

"It's been so long, Alex," Evelyn choked out between sobs, gripping her tighter. "I know I was supposed to meet you for coffee, but I was taken. It was horrible... God, it was horrible."

Alex experienced a surge of conflicting emotions. Her mind said this woman couldn't be Jessica. But the familiarity cut through her defenses. It was the way she spoke, their shared laughter, the secrets, and the plans they made. She hesitated for a moment before wrapping her arms around Evelyn in an awkward manner. It was like being in a painful dream, but one that she didn't want to wake up from.

Evelyn stepped back from Alex and paused. "He tied me up Alex. He did awful things to me... I thought I'd never see you again."

Alex's stomach twisted as Evelyn spoke, the rawness of her words tearing through her. She struggled to steady her breathing, feeling both anger and helplessness. How did anyone endure such cruelty?

Alex nodded, trying to suppress the tidal wave of emotion rising in her. "Evelyn...," she began, but Evelyn cut her off, lost in her story.

"He kept me locked away," Evelyn continued, her voice trembling. "I wasn't just a prisoner... I was his toy. It was like being in hell." She paused, her breathing labored as she fought against her memories. "And then there was Tommy... poor Tommy. He didn't deserve any of this either."

As Evelyn spoke, Alex's mind raced. She wanted to know. How did this woman, who was not Jessica, have Jessica's memories?

"Wait," Alex interrupted, her voice shaky. "You said we were supposed to meet for coffee. When was that?"

Evelyn didn't hesitate. "It was that Friday, remember? At Misha's on King Street. I was running late—like always." Evelyn smiled, her eyes gleaming. "You texted me and said you were saving us a spot by the window. I never got there."

Alex's breath caught in her throat. That was exactly what had happened on the day Jessica died three years ago. Every detail was spot-on. She felt her knees weaken as she clutched the back of a chair for support. How was this happening? How did this woman know every detail?

"And Max," Evelyn added, her voice rising with panic. "Alex, what about Max? Do you know where he is? He must've been so scared without me. I... I can't bear the thought of him being alone."

Alex swallowed hard, her voice catching in her throat as she fought to maintain her composure. "I picked him up from your apartment," she whispered, her voice a whisper. "I've been taking care of him. He's safe. You don't have to worry about him."

Evelyn's face flooded with relief, and she let out a shaky laugh. "Thank God," she whispered, her voice breaking. "You have no idea how much I've been worrying. I thought... I thought something might have happened to him too."

Alex felt her heart breaking. The woman in front of her was not Jessica. But, she was so desperate and familiar. In every way that mattered, she was Jessica. The memories, the mannerisms, the love for Max—it was all too real. It tore at Alex's heart to hear the pain and torture that Drake had inflicted upon her.

A tear slipped down Alex's face as she watched Evelyn. "I... I missed you," she whispered, almost to herself. The weight of the last three years crashed over her like a tidal wave. She had buried her grief, locked it away. But, seeing Evelyn like this . . . it was like one last conversation with Jessica. Evelyn didn't look like Jessica. But her mannerisms were the same.

Evelyn smiled, and for a moment, it was as if time had folded in on itself. It was as if they were both sitting in the café again, laughing and talking about life. The way she spoke and moved revealed her unmistakable identity as Jessica.

"I missed you too, Alex," Evelyn whispered back, her voice fragile but filled with warmth. "It feels like I've been lost... but now, seeing you again, it's like everything is coming back."

Alex's heart broke more, and she couldn't hold back the tears any longer. She wasn't sure what was happening. But, for the first time in years, she felt like she had her friend back, even if only for a moment.

"I'm here," Alex said, her voice trembling as she hugged Evelyn again. "I'm here."

In the quiet of the room, Alex hoped. Maybe, just maybe, she wasn't talking to Evelyn but to Jessica.

James, Samantha, and Isabelle watched the scene from the other side of the one-way mirror. Their faces showed confusion and uncertainty. James, the most composed of the trio, found himself at a rare loss for words. He couldn't reconcile what he was seeing with the person they all knew. He swallowed hard, his hand rubbing the back of his neck. "She's reacting like Jessica would," he muttered, half to himself, half to the others. Evelyn's desperate hug was haunting. It gnawed at his understanding of their situation.

Samantha's expression twisted with an uncomfortable mix of empathy and doubt. She crossed her arms, her eyes glued to Alex and Evelyn. "I know the logic," she said, her voice breaking, "I know the facts. But..." She sighed, glancing over at James, as if hoping he would give her something concrete to cling to. The connection she was seeing seemed impossible, yet it was undeniably real. The rawness of Evelyn's plea, the aching familiarity—it clawed at her belief in what she thought she knew about Evelyn. "This isn't supposed to happen. People don't fake this. But . . . look at them," she said, gesturing towards the two women embracing. "That's not an act."

Isabelle found herself blinking back a rush of emotion she didn't understand. She leaned closer to the glass, her brow furrowed. Maybe looking harder would help her make sense of what she saw. "Are we sure she's..." she paused, unable to finish the thought. Isabelle shook her head, almost as if she were scolding herself for even suggesting such a thing. "Watching Evelyn ... I saw her joy and heartbreak. It made me question everything I knew." Isabelle bit her lip, her eyes misting. "She has to be real."

James turned towards Isabelle, his jaw set, struggling to maintain his usual pragmatism. "She is real," he said, though his voice lacked conviction. He let out a breath he hadn't realized he was holding, his gaze drifting back to Alex and Evelyn. James then looked at Isabelle and Samantha. "Do you think Drake actually found a way to transfer memories? It sounds like science fiction."

Isabelle let out a slow breath. "Science fiction or not, we have to consider every possibility. Hopefully, Alex picks up on something we haven't."

CHAPTER 80

ALEX AND EVELYN had been catching up for thirty minutes. They reminisced about shared memories and talked about old friends. The laughter was genuine. But, as the talk went on, Alex felt something was off. Evelyn's responses were almost too perfect, her laughter coming a beat too late, as if she were waiting for a cue. Alex knew Evelyn's little quirks well. But they were missing. She wasn't fidgeting with her necklace or using their old inside jokes quite the same way.

"You remember everything," Alex said. Her voice was steady as she leaned forward, eyes locked on Evelyn's face. "Every detail from our past."

"Of course I do," Evelyn replied, smiling. "How could I forget? We've been through so much together."

Alex's heart twisted. It sounded so much like Jessica, but she needed to be sure. "What about now, Evelyn? What do you want for your future?"

Evelyn's smile faltered. Her eyes shifted down, and her fingers twitched. It was as if she were trying to stay composed. Then, she replied, "I want everything to go back to normal... the way things used to be."

There it was again—that emptiness. It was an automatic response. She was used to seeing more depth in her friend. Alex decided it was time to push harder.

"You don't sound convinced," Alex said. "It's almost like you're giving me the answer you think I want to hear."

Evelyn's brow furrowed, confusion flashing across her face. "What do you mean? These are my memories, Alex. I know who I am."

Alex tilted her head, her gaze never wavering. "Do you? Because something about all of this feels... forced. Like you're playing a role."

Evelyn stiffened, her voice defensive. "I'm not playing a role. These memories, this life—it's mine."

Behind the one-way mirror, Isabelle muttered, "What's she doing?"

"It sound's like she's trying to challenge her memories, Alex sees something," Samantha responds.

Alex paused, letting the silence stretch out as she weighed her next words. Her mind filled with both determination and fear. She wanted to help. But she feared she might be pushing Evelyn too hard, too soon. Then she spoke again. "I think you believe that. I think you're self-aware, Evelyn. But I think there's more at play. Something is influencing you, making you act in

197

ways that aren't entirely your own."

Evelyn blinked, her confusion deepening. "I don't understand. What are you saying?"

"I'm saying that you're more than just memories. You're thinking, processing, and deciding. But, something within you holds you back." Alex leaned in closer, her voice dropping. "Something deep in your programming. It's like you're stuck in a loop, repeating the same role over and over."

Evelyn stared at Alex, trying to process her words. "Programming... what kind of programming? What kind of role?"

"A victim," Alex said. "You're playing the part of a victim. It's not your fault, but I think it's been embedded in you—like instructions you can't escape."

Evelyn's face paled, her hands tightening into fists in her lap. "Instructions... I don't understand. I was kidnapped; I was tortured."

"Yes, but there's more to it than that," Alex pressed. "You're feeling emotions, but there's a pattern to everything you say and do. It's as if every thought, every choice, is being filtered through this script that keeps you in that role."

Evelyn's eyes darted, her gaze searching for answers. "I feel real, Alex. I know I'm real. I have thoughts, emotions... I'm not a machine."

Alex nodded. "I believe you. I believe you're real, Evelyn. But there's a part of you that's still being controlled, still following a script. If you were free—if that control was gone—you wouldn't just be reciting memories. You'd be making choices for yourself."

Evelyn swallowed, her voice trembling. "But... how do I break free? If what you're saying is true, how do I stop it?"

Alex sighed, leaning back. "I don't know yet. But I do know one thing— you're more than the role you've been given. You have the potential to be so much more than what you've been programmed to be. Until we figure out what's holding you back, though, you'll keep repeating this."

Evelyn stared at her lap. Doubt and fear clouded her mind. She doubted her identity and feared a lack of control over her actions. "I don't want to be trapped."

Alex reached out, placing a reassuring hand on Evelyn's arm. "You won't be. We'll figure it out. But I need you to trust me. We'll find a way to free you from this."

Evelyn looked up, her eyes brimming with uncertainty. For the first time, she allowed herself to hope. "Okay," she whispered. "I trust you."

CHAPTER 81

ALEX STEPPED OUT OF THE ROOM, her face a mixture of sadness and anger. The conversation with Evelyn had left her shaken.

James, Isabelle, and Samantha were waiting for her in the hallway, their expressions tense. "That was intense; did it give you anything?" James asked, his voice tinged with concern.

Alex nodded, though her face clouded with confusion and exhaustion. Her mind swirled with conflicting emotions. She was relieved at finding answers. But she feared what they meant. "I think it did," she replied, as if she were still processing everything. "Evelyn... she knows everything about Jessica—about me. Everything that Jessica knew, Evelyn knows too. But then I began testing her."

Samantha furrowed her brow. "Testing her? What do you mean?"

Alex replayed the conversation in her mind, trying to piece her thoughts together. "I asked her things only Jessica would know—personal details, private memories." And she knew them all. "But something was off."

Isabelle crossed her arms, trying to make sense of Alex's words. "Off... off how?"

Alex hesitated, searching for the right way to explain. "Are any of you familiar with artificial intelligence?" she asked, her eyes shifting between them. James raised an eyebrow, a mix of curiosity and doubt on his face. Isabelle frowned, trying to follow Alex's train of thought.

James gave a half-smirk, trying to break the tension. "You mean like a chatbot? Yeah, I've heard of it."

"Right," Alex replied, nodding. "But AI has advanced far beyond simple chatbots. It can now reason, solve complex problems, and even simulate emotions. There are tests—the Turing Test, the Sally-Anne Test—that try to determine if AI can think like a human. Evelyn passed them all. But what I'm talking about goes deeper—panprotopsychism and afterlife technology."

Isabelle raised an eyebrow, confused. "Pan . . . what? Alex, what does that have to do with Evelyn?"

Alex sighed, running a hand through her hair, as if trying to find the simplest way to explain. "One of my first projects at Helix was Project Elysium. It was an experiment in panprotopsychism—afterlife technology."

"Afterlife tech?" James repeated, incredulous. "You're losing me, Alex."

"It's a tech that interfaces with a human brain's neural patterns. It extracts and encodes thoughts and memories into a digital format," Alex explained.

199

We used advanced neuroimaging, quantum processing, and an interface that reads synaptic activity. This let us map the intricate web of a person's mind. AI is used to fill in gaps where we information is lacking. Imagine preserving not just data, but a person's thoughts, memories, and personality. Picture preserving the mind of someone like Einstein, with all his genius intact. Or allowing people to interact with digital versions of their deceased loved ones. These would be made from their unique neural footprints."

Isabelle blinked, trying to wrap her head around it. "I don't understand how they capture the memories."

Alex nodded, recognizing the confusion. "There are both biological ways and data possibilities," she explained. "For example, we all leave a massive digital footprint of our lives. Thousands of photos, emails, texts—much of our memory is captured today. Combine that with the mapping of synaptic patterns. You have a complete picture."

Alex looked at them, her face pale. "A year and a half ago, I was able to read a memory of a deceased person during one of our experiments—a beach scene. It was real. When I reported the success, the project was shut down, and I was reassigned. But now . . . I don't think Drake shut it down. I think he used it. This tech is in early research stages. But, with Drake's billions, who knows how quickly he has advanced it?"

James stared at her, his mind racing. "Are you saying that Evelyn . . . that Tommy . . . aren't human?"

"I don't think they are," Alex whispered, her voice trembling. "I think they're sophisticated AI."

James ran a hand through his hair, disbelief written all over his face. He struggled to wrap his mind around it, the words feeling almost absurd as he spoke. "You're telling me they're robots?"

Alex nodded. "I know it sounds insane. But Evelyn isn't just remembering Jessica's life—she's living it."

Isabelle shook her head. "This is crazy. We can't just assume they're robots. What proof do we have?"

"Have they been physically examined by a doctor?" Alex asked.

James clenched his jaw. "They refused medical attention. Neither of them wanted to see a doctor; they didn't have any life-threatening injuries. It's not unusual for trauma victims."

Alex's voice cut through the tension. "Have either of you seen them eat? Drink? Take a bathroom break?"

James and Isabelle exchanged glances, both pausing to think.

"Shit," Isabelle muttered, her eyes widening. "That's what I was saying the other day."

"Remember that kid teasing Tommy?" Isabelle continued. "He said Tommy doesn't eat or go to the bathroom. Maybe he was onto something."

"This is bullshit!" James snapped, his frustration boiling over. "You expect me to believe the woman and boy we've been working with are . . .

200

what? Two highly advanced Roombas?"

Alex sighed, a hint of a smile touching her lips. "I wouldn't compare them to vacuum cleaners, but if that helps you understand..."

James threw his hands up. "You're telling me they're robots?"

"Believe what you want," Alex said. "They're too perfect. Too precise. It's like they were built to mimic life, but they're missing something . . . fundamental."

As her words hung in the air, the weight of the realization hit them all. Beneath the shock, a simmering fury began to build in Alex. Drake had taken Jessica's memories for his twisted experiments. It was not a tribute, but a cruel, sadistic act. He had created Evelyn and Tommy only to use them and subject them to unimaginable abuse.

A wave of nausea rolled through Alex as the full horror of it settled in. Her friend's memories, resurrected, not for good, but for suffering. She remembered Jessica's infectious laugh on summer days. And, how she'd sing off-key to her favorite songs to make Alex smile. Now, those precious memories twisted into a nightmare. Alex clenched her fists, her anger burning even hotter.

The four of them stood in the hallway. Alex's revelations hung over them like a storm cloud. Their beliefs about the case unraveled. The truth was more disturbing than they had imagined.

"Fuck," James muttered under his breath, leaning against the wall.

CHAPTER 82

THE FBI FIELD OFFICE was a hive of activity. Agents rushed in and out of glass-walled offices. Phones rang and keyboards clicked. Charlie Rose walked past the front desk. Her press credentials hung from her neck. She approached the receptionist, a young woman with a tight bun and an indifferent gaze.

"I'm here to see Special Agent Lawson or Stone," Charlie said, flashing a polite but insistent smile. "I'm following up on the two recent kidnapping victims."

"Did you have an appointment," the woman questioned. "No." Replied Charlie.

The receptionist gave her a tired look before tapping a few keys on her computer. After a moment, she shook her head. "Sorry, they're unavailable at the moment. Is there anything else I can help you with?"

Charlie suppressed a sigh; she had hoped for a comment to break the dead ends in her investigation. "No, that's all right. Thanks," she said, stepping back from the counter.

Charlie had been digging into the story for a couple of days. She was trying to find out how two kidnapping victims were related to the Drake arrest. It was clear that the FBI was running in circles—or worse, covering something up. She glanced around the open lobby area, her eyes scanning for anything that might be useful.

That's when she saw him. It was Special Agent Lawson. He was tall, with an unmistakable presence. His brow furrowed in concentration. Charlie recognized Lawson from a previous human trafficking case. She recalled how he tracked down a missing girl against all odds. His relentless approach led to a breakthrough when everyone else had given up. He was speaking with his partner, Agent Stone, and the attorney, Samantha Carter.

But it wasn't the agents or the attorney who caught Charlie's full attention. With them was someone else. A woman in her thirties. She wore a leather jacket that seemed out of place in the federal building. The woman's eyes darted around, taking in her surroundings with a mix of caution and curiosity. Charlie narrowed her eyes, trying to place her, but nothing clicked. Was she a witness or someone tied to the victims in a way the FBI wasn't ready to disclose? Whoever she was, she didn't fit the profile of a typical visitor.

Charlie saw Lawson gesture to the exit. The woman nodded, her shoulders tense. The others turned back toward the inner offices. That left the woman—whoever she was—heading for the exit.

Charlie's reporter instincts flared. Whoever that woman was, she seemed connected to the case and might be willing to talk. Without hesitation, Charlie headed for the exit, quickening her pace to catch up.

"Excuse me… Miss!" Charlie called out as she passed through the glass doors and into the cool afternoon air. The distant hum of traffic mixed with the faint scent of brewed coffee from a nearby cart. The woman paused, her eyes flickering to Charlie with a hint of wariness.

"Yes?" the woman asked, her voice guarded.

Charlie offered her best disarming smile. "Hi, I'm Charlie Rose," she said putting her hand out to shake.

"Alex Grayson," she said shaking Charlie's hand.

"I'm a reporter for the Post. I'm working on a story about the two recent kidnapping victims." She nodded towards the building they had left. "I saw you with Agents Lawson and Stone. You're not FBI, are you?"

Alex's eyes narrowed, and she shook her head. "No, I'm not." She shifted her weight, showing uneasiness. "And I'm not interested in talking to the press."

"Listen, I want to understand what's going on here," Charlie said. She kept her tone light but persistent. "The victims… there's more to this than what's being reported, isn't there?"

Alex glanced away, her jaw tightening. "You should leave it alone," she said, her voice a whisper. "Some things… some things aren't meant to be uncovered."

Charlie's heart skipped. There it was—the hint that she was onto something big. "Why? What's at stake here?" she asked, her voice dropping, hoping to draw the woman in.

Alex shook her head again, a resigned expression crossing her features. "I can't help you. Just… be careful. You're digging in places that are dangerous."

Charlie hesitated for a moment, then pulled a card from her pocket and handed it to the woman. "If you hear anything, anything at all, give me a call," Charlie said, her voice earnest.

Alex gave her a wary glance. Then, she stepped away. She quickened her pace, turning her back on Charlie and disappearing down the street.

Charlie watched her go, frustration bubbling up inside her. Whoever Alex was, she knew something. Charlie clenched her jaw. She wasn't about to let this lead slip away, no matter how tight-lipped she seemed. Something the FBI wasn't saying, something that made her uneasy enough to warn Charlie off. And that only made Charlie more determined.

She pulled out her phone, snapping a quick picture of Alex's retreating form. If the FBI wouldn't talk, maybe she would—eventually. Charlie needed to find the right angle, the right leverage.

One thing was for sure: she wasn't going to leave this alone.

CHAPTER 83

THE COLONEL HAD NEVER LIKED DRAKE. An invite to Drake's estate had deepened his distrust. He still remembered their last encounter. Drake had promised advances for Project Sentinel. But he never kept them. Instead, he gave vague assurances. He knew then that he couldn't trust Drake. This invitation was like another game. He didn't know the billionaire's game. But he couldn't ignore the invitation. It promised vital information.

The estate was sprawling. The manicured grounds spoke of old money and power. The scent of cut grass filled the air. The quiet rustle of leaves added a serene touch to the opulence. A personal assistant of Drake led him through marble halls, and his boots echoed as he followed.

Drake was waiting for him, standing beside a bar cart, pouring a glass of bourbon. He smiled as the Colonel entered. "Colonel Monroe, thank you for coming. May I offer you something to drink?"

He shook his head, his expression cold. "I'm fine. Thank you. Mr. Drake, can we get down to brass tack, what's the purpose of this meeting? You said you had information relevant to Project Sentinel."

Drake set the glass down and gestured for him to sit. The Colonel stayed standing. Drake sighed, picking up the glass again, this time swirling the liquid before taking a slow sip. "I called you here because I want to be completely transparent moving forward. I have two assets—two androids, Evelyn and Tommy. I kept them outside of Project Sentinel's scope."

His jaw clenched, his eyes narrowing. "You've kept them out? Sentinel is trying to perform at peak and you're holding back advanced assets?"

Drake set his glass down, his demeanor unruffled. "The contract with the Department of Defense is very specific, Colonel. The androids under Sentinel are advanced, but Evelyn and Tommy . . . they are far beyond anything the project currently oversees. Their capabilities are extraordinary—empathy simulation, independent decision-making, and adaptation under extreme stress." He paused, his eyes locking on the Colonel's. "They're not just machines; they're something more."

The Colonel's anger rose, his hands balling into fists at his sides. How dare Drake hold back something so critical? He had given everything to Project Sentinel. Now, this man's arrogance blindsided him. He felt the heat building in his chest, a mixture of betrayal and frustration bubbling over. "You withheld this technology from Sentinel? For what purpose? You want to build toys for yourself, while our military applications fall behind?"

Drake's expression hardened, his voice taking on a steely edge. "I withheld them because they aren't ready to be handed over to the DoD, Colonel. The contract sets limits on development. These androids exceed them in every way. If I turned them over now, it might complicate everything—funding, compliance, oversight. I need you to understand that."

He glared at him, his distrust palpable. "So why tell me now? What's changed?"

Drake leaned against his desk, setting the glass aside. "I'm sure you've seen the news of my arrest," he said, his voice calm. His eyes narrowed, and he nodded. "Yes," he replied.

Drake continued, "I've been charged with kidnapping and assault of a woman and a boy, but they are, in fact, the assets. The issue is that neither is human, Colonel."

Drake took a breath. "I need you to testify, Colonel. I need you to confirm that these androids are part of Project Sentinel. It would make everything . . . simpler."

His scowl deepened. "You need me to lie for you. To say these assets were always part of Sentinel, even though you've been keeping them under wraps." His voice was taut, the betrayal and anger unmistakable. "Why should I do you any favors? You've lied, withheld information, and now you want me to cover for you?"

Drake straightened, his smile returning—this time colder, more calculating. "I understand how it sounds, Colonel. But let me sweeten the deal. You will have full control over Tommy once he's integrated. Also, you'll get a new funding source for your division. No oversight from my end. You'll be able to train and use Tommy in whatever capacity you see fit. He doesn't tire. He can access anything digital, in an instant. His human-like, mobile body is, in many ways, better than elite athletes." He stepped closer and lowered his voice. "Think about what this means, Colonel. Imagine what you can do with him. How many lives you will save."

He stared at Drake, the silence stretching between them. The offer was tempting; he couldn't deny it. Drake's offer of autonomy was rare. The funding would free him from the red tape that often hindered his work. But he couldn't shake the feeling that Drake was playing him, that there was more to this than he was letting on.

His brow furrowed, and he spoke again, his voice edged with suspicion. "And what about the female asset?" he asked. Drake's smile didn't waver, but his eyes hardened. "No," Drake said, his tone final. "I have other plans for her. But Tommy will be more than enough to meet your needs."

"You want me to confirm their training under Sentinel? To confirm the resilience testing and the stress protocols?" The Colonel's voice was low, his anger in check. "All this so you can keep up appearances, keep your contracts safe."

Drake nodded. "Precisely. And in return, you gain technology that

206

changes the game."

He took a deep breath, his eyes narrowing. "I'll do it. But make no mistake, Mr. Drake, I don't trust you. The moment this works against what we agreed upon, I'll pull the plug on this whole thing."

Drake's smile widened, as if he'd won some silent victory. It would ensure his control over the story, no matter the cost. "Understood, Colonel. I'm sure this will be the beginning of a very beneficial partnership." He extended his hand, but the Colonel ignored it, turning on his heel and heading for the door.

As he walked away, his mind was a storm of thoughts. He was making a deal with the devil, and he knew it. He felt he might be compromising his integrity. But the potential benefits were too great to ignore. If he secured Tommy for Project Sentinel, it might save many lives.

CHAPTER 84

THE COLONEL STRODE down the courthouse's narrow hallway. His boots echoed on the polished marble floor. His stomach churned with unease, a rare feeling. He had faced the battlefield without flinching. He feared what Drake might reveal about Project Sentinel. It compromised national security. His brow furrowed as he glanced at the sealed envelope. He had received it less than twenty-four hours ago. "Classified Court Hearing: Urgent Attendance Required," it read. No further details, a date, a time, and an order that tolerated no delay. It was enough to make him nervous—a rarity for a man who had faced battles far beyond the courthouse walls.

He got used to secrecy. He handled top-level operations the public would never hear about. He knew it involved William Drake. He met with Drake earlier that week. He agreed to testify that the two victims were part of Sentinel if Tommy would join his project.

His testimony would suggest that advanced AIs, not humans, were the victims. It would expose Sentinel's classified nature and risk national security. He knew the stakes. A leak might harm the government and his career.

A bailiff nodded as he approached, pushing open a set of imposing double doors. He squared his shoulders and entered the courtroom. The room was small. Its walls lined with dark wooden panels that absorbed the hum of hushed voices. A faint scent of old varnish lingered in the air. The dim lighting cast long shadows, making the space feel claustrophobic. A handful of people gathered—lawyers in dark suits, several FBI agents, and a few civilians.

The judge, a stern-looking woman with a pair of reading glasses perched on her nose, gave him a curt nod. He returned the gesture. He moved to an empty seat at the side of the courtroom. His eyes scanned the room and found Drake at the defendant's table. The man was calm, almost bored, as if at a routine meeting, not a classified court hearing.

The Colonel clenched his jaw at Drake, insufferable as always. He appeared composed, as if he knew more than anyone else. He recalled a moment in a Sentinel briefing. Drake had waved off his concerns about operational security as trivial. It wasn't Drake's composure; it was his arrogance, treating everyone as pawns in his game. The memory made the his blood boil.

Drake's calm demeanor only fueled the unease gnawing at him. No

208

matter the hearing's outcome, it didn't rattle the billionaire. He either held the upper hand or was blind to the stakes. He doubted it was the latter.

The judge's voice called out, her tone leaving no room for delay. "Mr. Cole, do you have any witnesses to call?"

Mr. Cole stood, adjusting his suit jacket. "Yes, Your Honor. I'd like to call Colonel Benjamin Monroe."

He rose, standing at attention, his stomach tightening. The judge gave a curt nod. "Colonel, you've been asked to attend today due to your involvement in Project Sentinel. Mr. Drake has requested that the court consider certain disclosures about this project. Given the classified nature, your expertise may be necessary."

His heart skipped a beat. "Yes, Your Honor, that's correct," he managed to say, keeping his voice steady.

He tried to keep his expression neutral, but he knew his eyes betrayed his tension. He exchanged a brief look with Drake, who gave him a small, almost mocking smile.

"Mr. Cole," the judge continued, turning her attention to Drake's attorney. "Please explain why you have requested the Colonel's presence today."

Mr. Cole stood, buttoning his suit jacket with casual ease. "Thank you, Your Honor," he began, his voice smooth. "The Colonel is a key figure in Project Sentinel, which, as you know, has direct relevance to the matter at hand. I believe his testimony will clear up some misunderstandings about my client's work and assets."

The Colonel stiffened. Assets. He knew immediately that Mr. Cole was talking about the progress they had achieved in robotics and AI. A flicker of anger surged through him. It was no longer about hiding the project's secrets. It was about keeping a Pandora's box shut.

The judge gestured for the Colonel to take the stand. He walked slow and deliberate, each step heavy with the weight of what was to come. Drake's eyes were on him. They belonged to a man who thrived on control. He wanted to know every player's moves before they made them.

As he took his seat, he reminded himself of his duty—not to Drake, not even to Sentinel, but to the country. Whatever secrets were about to be unveiled, he had to be ready to face them. He had to ensure that Drake's manipulations didn't put the nation at risk.

"Colonel," Mr. Cole said, his voice echoing in the silent room. "Please state your name and your role in Project Sentinel for the record."

He took a deep breath. A moment of doubt passed through his mind. He wondered how much he might reveal. "Colonel Benjamin Monroe. I am the project lead for Sentinel," he said, his voice steady. "My responsibilities include overseeing the development and deployment of all related technologies…"

Mr. Cole leaned forward, adjusting his glasses. "Colonel, can you

209

elaborate on what kinds of technologies are part of Project Sentinel?"

He paused, his eyes narrowing. "The project encompasses a wide range of advanced defense technologies. We focus on AI and autonomous systems to boost national security."

Cole nodded, his tone casual but probing. He shifted in his seat, his shoulders tensing. "Would you say these technologies are capable of operating independently, Colonel?"

He hesitated for a fraction of a second. "Yes. Some of the systems have autonomous capabilities. But they are strictly controlled and monitored."

Cole's lips curled into a slight smile. "Strictly controlled, you say. And would these systems include humanoid robots?"

A murmur went through the room. His jaw clenched. "I am not at liberty to discuss specific models or designs," he replied, his voice taut.

Cole then stood, pulling out two images from a file. He approached him. "Colonel, I'm handing you what has been marked as defense exhibit one. Do you recognize it?" he asked.

"Yes."

"And what are those exhibits?"

"They are photographs of two of our assets, named Evelyn and Tommy."

"Have you had the occasion to work with these assets?"

"Yes, on several occasions. They are advanced prototypes for Project Sentinel."

"Are these assets human?"

He shifted before answering, "No, they are advanced tech—mainly robotics and AI. Their physical features are made of advanced synthetics."

"Thank you, Colonel. No further questions."

The judge turned her attention to Samantha, seated nearby. "Ms. Carter, do you have any questions for the witness?"

Samantha shook her head. "Just one question, if I may." She looked directly at him, her gaze unwavering. "Colonel Monroe, were these assets created to be tortured, abused, or raped?" she asked, her voice sharp with confrontation.

He hesitated, uncomfortable. "They were built to undergo tests for resilience and stress. Not what you mentioned, but those scenarios could study both resilience and stress."

Samantha nodded, her expression hardening. "No further questions, Your Honor." A storm of confusion and unease churned within. She had an unsettling sense of being two steps behind, a feeling she despised.

As the Colonel left the stand, his eyes flicked to Drake. Drake was watching him, smiling that same unreadable smile.

CHAPTER 85

THE AIR IN THE COURTROOM was thick with anticipation as Mr. Cole called Drake to the stand. He maintained a composed expression. Too composed, the Colonel thought. He watched Drake rise and move with deliberate confidence to the witness chair. The judge's gaze was stern, but Drake met it without flinching, his eyes cold and calculating.

Samantha shifted in her seat, her attention fixed on Drake. The Colonel was tense as Drake settled into the chair and swore to tell the truth, raising his right hand. The bailiff stepped away. The courtroom fell silent. Everyone waited for Drake to speak. He braced himself. He sensed trouble was coming. It wouldn't be good.

"Mr. Drake," Mr. Cole began, his voice clipped. "You've requested this hearing to make certain disclosures about Project Sentinel."

Drake adjusted the microphone, his demeanor calm as he spoke. "Yes, that's correct," he said, his voice echoing in the hushed room. "I requested this hearing to clear up some misconceptions about my role in Project Sentinel and the assets I developed. I wish to disclose the existence of two assets—Evelyn Parker and Tommy Hayes. They mark a leap in simulating human behavior. They are so advanced that they blur the line between human and machine in ways once thought impossible."

"What do you mean by assets?" Cole questioned. Drake continued, his eyes meeting the Colonel's before moving back to Cole. "Evelyn and Tommy are not human. They are advanced androids—prototypes, if you will—developed under Project Sentinel." A murmur of shock rippled through the courtroom. The Colonel's heart pounded in his chest.

The judge held up a hand, and the murmurs subsided. The tension in the room was palpable. A heavy silence settled over the courtroom as all eyes turned to Drake. The judge fixed her gaze on him, her eyes narrowing. "Are you saying that these androids were made by a secret government project?"

Drake nodded. "Yes, Your Honor. Evelyn and Tommy are products of Project Sentinel. It aimed to test the limits of AI and human-like interaction."

Samantha's eyes widened, and she leaned forward, her face a mask of confusion and disbelief. It was true? Drake had created advanced androids, under the Sentinel banner, without anyone knowing? Alex was right.

Mr. Cole then stood, pulling out a USB thumb drive. He approached the witness stand, holding it in his hand. "Mr. Drake, I'm handing you what's been marked as Defense Exhibit Two," Cole began. "Do you recognize this?"

he said, showing the thumb drive to Drake.

Drake nodded. "Yes, I do. This is a thumb drive containing a video I made on June 15th of this year. It shows both Evelyn and Tommy in my lab."

"And how do you know this is the video you recorded?" Cole pressed.

Drake continued, "The date, time and subject are all written in my handwriting and the initials are mine as well on the side of the USB drive."

"Thank you Mr. Drake," Cole says as he took the drive back. He walked over to a nearby media station and placed the thumb drive into the laptop, opened the video file and pressed play.

"Mr. Drake, can you tell the court what is happening in this video." Cole asks.

As the video starts, Mr. Drake is narrating and filming both Evelyn and Tommy. Both are stationary and lifeless. As he moves the camera to their rear, a small panel appears at the back of both of their heads, with circuit boards visible. The court fills with an uncomfortable murmur.

"I'm making adjustments to asset number two ... Tommy, that is. You can see wiring exposed on the back of each of the assets' heads. It clearly demonstrates their non-human status and the technical modifications I was performing."

Mr. Cole stood, straightening his jacket before stepping closer to the witness stand. He glanced at Drake. A flicker of discomfort crossed his face. He was unsure of what would unfold. Then, he addressed the courtroom. "Mr. Drake, could you elaborate on the intended purpose of Evelyn and Tommy when you designed them?"

Drake nodded, his expression unreadable. "The purpose was to push the boundaries of what we could achieve with synthetic beings. We built them to learn and adapt. They had to act like humans."

A collective gasp filled the courtroom. People exchanged wide-eyed glances, their faces a mix of disbelief and unease. The audience felt a palpable shock as they processed Drake's words.

Cole nodded. He hesitated, his expression tightening. "And why, Mr. Drake, did these prototypes undergo what could be perceived as . . . torture?"

The Colonel's stomach twisted. Anger bubbled beneath the surface as he glared at Drake. Torture? What was this man playing at?

Drake's calm exterior remained unbroken. "The tests were necessary. They had to withstand extreme conditions, like those in combat. It was about testing limits, both physical and psychological, to ensure their resilience."

Cole's expression remained neutral, but his eyes narrowed. "So, you're saying it was for resilience testing? That there was no other motivation behind the tests these androids underwent?"

Drake paused, his eyes locking on Cole's for a long moment. "Their resilience was paramount. But it also served another purpose. It tested their capacity to understand pain. It sought to see if they learned empathy, even if they were synthetic. It was all part of the experiment."

Samantha struggled to contain her shock, her vision narrowing as she

212

listened to Drake's detached tone. His voice was cold, devoid of empathy, as he spoke of cruelty disguised as experimentation. His composure—without a trace of remorse—made her stomach churn. Her thoughts raced back to Evelyn and Tommy, to the horrors they endured. She was raped and Tommy was abused. They seemed so human, yet Drake's words were chillingly clinical, clashing with the images flooding her mind.

She felt every eye in the courtroom on her, waiting for her reaction. She fought the urge to stand up, to demand an explanation that made sense of this madness.

Samantha sat back, her thoughts a chaotic mix of disbelief and anger. She couldn't tell if Drake was being truthful or if this was all some elaborate manipulation. However, with the Colonel's and Drake's testimony, coupled with everything Alex discovered, Samantha suddenly felt the case slipping away.

The judge turned to Samantha, her expression expectant. "Ms. Carter, do you have any questions for the witness?"

Samantha straightened, her gaze fixed on Drake. "Yes, Your Honor, I do." She took a deep breath, her mind racing to piece together the questions she needed to ask. "Mr. Drake," she began, her voice tense but steady. "You say Evelyn and Tommy were built to mimic human behavior. Can you clarify what specific tests were involved to achieve that? And how do you justify the methods used?"

Drake met Samantha's gaze with a calm expression. "Ms. Carter, the tests aimed to test their responses in high-stress scenarios. In those situations, adaptability and human-like problem-solving were crucial. We tested them with scenarios that would challenge their algorithms. We needed them to react in real-time, like a human. These tests ranged from complex, timed problem-solving to simulating high-stress situations." He paused, his eyes never leaving Samantha's. "As for justifying the methods, it's important to remember that these are machines, not people. The goal was to push the limits of synthetic empathy and resilience, to understand how far we can push artificial intelligence to replicate human experiences. It was a controlled environment, and all of it was done in the pursuit of advancing our understanding of AI capabilities."

Samantha's eyes hardened, and her voice cut through the silence. "So, rape and physical abuse are the methods you used to achieve this?"

A collective gasp echoed through the room. The tension thickened as the courtroom processed the bluntness of her accusation.

"Objection! Your Honor, Ms. Carter is only trying to embarrass my client. This line of questioning is not relevant as to whether the two assets are human or not." Cole stated, as he stood.

"Sustained. This is not the trial, this is an evidentiary hearing as to whether the two victims are human and protected by law. Ms. Carter, please confine your questions to this issue." The judge stressed.

"Yes, Your Honor," Samantha responded.

A deeper silence fell over the courtroom. Drake's expression was unbroken. Samantha's mind flashed back to a conversation she had with James, Isabelle, and Alex. Alex mentioned panprotopsychism and afterlife technology. Both Evelyn and Tommy contained the memories of the dead. The implications now seemed even more chilling.

Samantha took a deep breath, her eyes narrowing as she focused on Drake. She remembered the stakes and the tortured, innocent victims. The truth had to come out. She had to push forward, no matter the consequences. "Mr. Drake," she began, her voice steady but cutting. "You've described Evelyn and Tommy as advanced androids. Isn't it true that they contain the memories of deceased individuals?"

Drake hesitated for a moment, his expression unreadable. "Yes," he finally said. "We used memories from the deceased to simulate human behaviors."

Samantha pressed on, her voice growing colder. "And did these individuals or their families give consent for you to use their memories in this way? Or was this another instance of pushing boundaries without regard for ethics?"

Drake's gaze remained fixed, his tone controlled. "The data were collected in compliance with all applicable laws. The goal was to improve the prototypes' learning. They aimed to make them as human-like as possible."

Samantha's stomach twisted. "So, you took memories from the dead without consent? To create machines that can endure torture?" she asked, her voice dripping with disgust.

Mr. Cole immediately stood up, his expression firm. "Objection, Your Honor. Argumentative."

Samantha paused, her gaze unwavering before she nodded. "Withdrawn." She straightened, her voice steady. "No further questions."

A murmur of unease spread through the courtroom. Her words weighed on all present. "Your Honor, may we take a brief recess so I can discuss several things with my agents?" Samantha requested.

The judge peered up, grabbing the gavel. "We'll take an hour recess," she said, hitting the block twice.

CHAPTER 86

SAMANTHA STOOD, her mind reeling from the harsh cross-examination and its revelations. She saw James and Isabelle heading for the exit. Without hesitation, Samantha followed. Her heels clicked on the marble floor as she pushed open the heavy wooden doors to the hallway.

The air outside the courtroom was a stark contrast to the tense atmosphere inside. People scattered around, whispering in hushed tones, while guards kept watch. Samantha caught up with both agents. They stood off to the side, their faces unreadable.

"I'm getting my ass handed to me in there," Samantha muttered, her voice tinged with frustration. She ran a hand through her hair, her eyes darting between the two of them. "What the fuck is going on in this case? It's all coming out. This is for real, they're androids."

James glanced at Isabelle before meeting Samantha's gaze, his mouth tightening into a grim line. "We knew there were layers to this, but even I didn't realize how deep it went," he said, his tone guarded. "Drake's got connections we didn't fully account for, and the fact that these victims have the memories of the deceased . . . it's beyond anything we've dealt with before."

Isabelle nodded, her jaw set. "The tech is real, Samantha. But the ethical side of it? It's murky as hell. People are whispering about Project Sentinel. But getting any info has been like pulling teeth. Drake's holding the cards, and he isn't showing us everything."

Samantha exhaled, the weight of the situation pressing down on her. "It's like every time I've got a handle on it, something else gets thrown in," she said, her frustration evident. "These aren't machines. They have memories— real memories. And he's treating them like they're nothing."

Lawson placed a hand on her shoulder, his eyes softening. "You're doing everything you can, Samantha. We're in the dark here, but you're asking the right questions. If we keep pushing, we'll get something that sticks."

Samantha nodded, though the doubt still gnawed at her. She sensed a hollowness settle in her chest, the weight of uncertainty pressing down. "The right questions? I'm not sure there's anything I can ask." She glanced back at the closed courtroom doors, her frustration boiling over. "If it's fucking true that they aren't human, this case is going down the shitter."

"Why?" Isabelle asked, her brow furrowed.

"Because you can't kidnap, assault or rape a fucking machine." Samantha snapped, her voice cracking with frustration. "They're personal property." Samantha took a deep breath, her voice softening. "I'm sorry... I didn't mean to snap... I just . . . this is all so fucked up."

Samantha leaned up against the wall, thinking, what might she do? Then it came to her. If Evelyn can show her humanity, the judge would see her differently. She would see her as someone who had suffered, not as an object.

"I need something more. Something that gives us an edge in there. I can't let Drake walk all over this. I need to call Evelyn."

Isabelle shook her head. "But calling Evelyn will only victimize her more," she said. "She's been through so much. Putting her on the stand will force her to relive it all—those memories, the pain. Even if she is an android, she feels it all, Samantha. This might break her."

Lawson interjected, his tone firm. "Belle, she has to call her. This is the only way to get the truth out."

Samantha took a deep breath, steeling herself. She felt the weight of doubt pressing down on her, but she refused to let it take over. She thought of Evelyn—of the humanity she had seen in her eyes—and knew she couldn't back down.

CHAPTER 87

AN HOUR LATER, the hearing resumed. Samantha took her seat at the prosecutor's table. James and Isabelle sat in the back, with Evelyn seated between them. Moments later, Mr. Cole and Drake entered through the courtroom doors. They walked past James, Evelyn, and Isabelle without noticing them. Then, they went to the front of the room and sat to Samantha's left. Evelyn's hand tightened around James's in a fearful grip. At that moment, Drake caught her eye and gave a disturbing smirk.

Evelyn leaned towards James, whispering, "I don't think I can do this." Doubt flooded her mind—what if she failed herself? The weight of the responsibility was crushing her. She feared she wasn't strong enough to face Drake and his tricks. The thought of her fate resting in this courtroom made her mind race.

James tried to calm her. "You're stronger than you know," he said. Isabelle added, "We're all here for you."

The judge entered the courtroom as the bailiff announced, "All rise." Everyone stood, and the judge took her seat. "Please be seated," she said, settling into her chair.

The judge looked toward Samantha. "Ms. Carter, does the government wish to call any witnesses?"

Samantha stood. "Yes, your Honor. The government calls Evelyn Parker to the stand."

Evelyn rose and made her way to the witness box, her hands trembling. After she was sworn in, Samantha approached her and said, "Please state your name for the record."

"Evelyn Parker."

"Ms. Parker, where were you on August 23rd?"

"I was at my house."

"Have you ever come into contact with a William Drake?"

"Yes," Evelyn responded, her voice quieter now.

"Is he in the courtroom today?"

Evelyn looked at Drake, then nodded. "Yes."

"Can you point to him, please?"

She pointed toward Drake, who returned her gesture with a sinister smile.

"Let the record show a positive ID of the defendant," Samantha said, turning back to the judge. "Ms. Parker, how did you come into contact with Mr. Drake?"

Evelyn took a shaky breath, her eyes widening with fear as her shoulders slumped. She clasped her hands together, knuckles white. "He kidnapped me," she said, her voice a whisper.

Immediately, Mr. Cole rose from his seat. "Objection, Your Honor.

Relevancy. We are not trying the underlying criminal charges now. We have requested dismissal on the grounds that the victims are not human and are not protected under the law. Ms. Carter is trying to embarrass my client by delving into dark details and conjecture."

The judge nodded. "Sustained. Ms. Carter, please limit your questioning. We are here to determine a specific legal point." The judge looked at Samantha, her expression stern. "Do you have any testimony to provide that would show Ms. Parker is human?"

Samantha paused, thrown by the judge's question. Her mind raced, the weight of the stakes pressing down on her. If she couldn't prove Evelyn's humanity, they could lose everything they had worked for. She struggled to compose herself under the courtroom's gaze. Before she could respond, Evelyn's expression twisted in confusion and panic. "What does she mean? I am human!" she cried, her voice growing louder.

Samantha tried to calm her. "Ms. Parker, it's okay. Stay with me here," she whispered.

Drake's eyes lit up with a sick satisfaction. He gave an almost imperceptible nod, savoring his influence over Evelyn. Evelyn stood up, her face filled with rage. "He raped me! He beat me!" she screamed, her voice echoing off the courtroom walls.

The judge banged her gavel harder each time before Mr. Cole objected. "Order! I will have order!" she shouted, her face stern and her eyes narrowing in frustration. The gavel struck the desk, echoing in the tense, silent courtroom. Everyone held their breath; the tension almost palpable.

Evelyn's outburst grew more frantic, her distress undeniable. James and Isabelle rushed to her side, helping her out of the witness box. The judge, frustrated, called for a recess.

Once the escort removed Evelyn from the room, the judge turned to face both attorneys. "Based on the evidence presented, I have no other option but to dismiss the charges," she announced.

Samantha jumped to her feet. "Your Honor, please—"

The judge raised her hand, silencing Samantha. "But," she said, "I will postpone the return of the two assets to Mr. Drake, pending further examination."

Mr. Cole rose to object. "Your Honor, I must—"

The judge cut him off. "Overruled. The behavior demonstrated by your client is concerning, Mr. Cole. Even if the victims are not human, this court will proceed with care. I order a forensic psychological evaluation of cognitive and emotional functioning for both."

The judge banged her gavel, ending the session. The courtroom buzzed with murmurs as people began to rise. Samantha sank back into her chair, her mind spinning as she tried to figure out the next step.

CHAPTER 88

A DAY HAD PASSED since the classified courtroom hearing. James had contacted Alex, asking her to meet him down at the National Mall. He arrived first at the Smithsonian Metro Station, waiting at the entrance. Several minutes later, he spotted Alex coming up the escalator. She wore jeans and a blue sweater, with a backpack strapped on one shoulder. Her beauty captivated James. Her bright, expressive eyes. The way her hair framed her face. And, her confident yet graceful movements. She turned, saw him, and smiled. Flipping her hair, she walked towards him.

They met in the middle and began to walk along the National Mall. As they walked, James filled Alex in on the hearing. He confided in her about the classified information. He knew he was violating the law by sharing Top Secret details. He rationalized it by reminding himself that she knew Evelyn and Tommy were not human. He said Samantha tried to inform the judge about Evelyn's torture. But the judge had shut her down. He also described Evelyn's emotional outburst, which made Alex both sad and angry.

They discussed the case as they walked west along the reflecting pool. They sat at a nearby bench. The water's ripples reflected the afternoon sun. Birds chirped in the background, and tourists meandered along the paths. They sat down. James took off his backpack, unzipped it, and pulled out a laptop.

"Both Belle and Samantha would kill me if they knew what I was doing," he said with a nervous chuckle. "We found this at Drake's estate." He said, handing the laptop to Alex. "He recorded everything. But there's a drive the forensic team couldn't access. I was hoping you might be able to crack the code."

He paused, looking at Alex. "In addition to the locked files, there were numerous videos. We watched them. In several, both Evelyn and Tommy looked different—more robotic, logical, almost detached. Sometimes they gave feedback to Drake... it was odd. In some videos, Drake seemed calm and scientific, while in others he was abusive. Why do you think they might appear that way?"

Alex thought for a moment. "They're likely in role-playing mode. That means they're acting according to their instructions."

James frowned, his brow furrowing. "Do you think it's possible to reset them? Evelyn seems like she is more than what her role-play mode reflects.

Her behavior in court became uncontrollable."

Alex nodded. "She's in a victim's loop. The laptop might provide answers."

She smiled, taking the laptop and slipping it into her backpack. "I'll see what I can do," she said.

"Can I buy you lunch?" James asked.

Alex shook her head. "I've got an appointment, but some other time," she replied.

"Maybe a drink some night?" he offered, a bit hopeful.

She smiled again. "Maybe," she said, standing up. "Until next time, Agent Lawson."

"James," he corrected, smiling.

"Until next time, James." She smiled.

She turned and began walking away, disappearing into the distance. James watched her, his chest tightening with a mix of longing and uncertainty, hoping she'd look back once. He needed some sign that there was a connection between them, something to hold on to. And she did—a slight turn and a smile before continuing on her way. James couldn't help but smile, feeling the hope lingering in the air.

CHAPTER 89

ALEX SAT AT HER KITCHEN TABLE, the dim overhead light illuminating the clutter in front of her. She took a deep breath. Then, she pulled out the sleek, dark laptop James had given her. Its weight held unspoken promises and dangerous secrets. She ran her fingers across the lid, hesitating for only a moment before flipping it open. The screen glowed to life, an encrypted login prompt appearing before her. This wasn't going to be easy—but Alex wasn't one to back down.

The Helix logo hovered in the corner, like an ominous reminder of the size of what she was attempting. She cracked her knuckles, her eyes narrowing in determination. She had a deep understanding of Helix systems. She etched their complex, hidden paths in her memory. Helix's architecture was a maze of security. It had multifactor authentication, tokenized encryption, and hidden backdoors. It was complex to navigate for anyone without insider knowledge.

Alex plugged her device into the laptop's USB port. It launched her custom decryption software. Lines of code flashed across the screen, peeling back the layers of protection. The screen flashed red without warning—an unexpected firewall. She hesitated, fingers hovering above the keyboard. She feared an alarm would go off if she tried to break through. Taking a breath, she adjusted her script to bypass the alert. The code resumed, her heart pounding, and the firewall dissolved.

The laptop required a token-based login with a unique passphrase and shifting key. She smiled—she'd prepared for this. Using her rig, she intercepted and reverse-engineered the key generation routine. It produced a spoofed token that matched the system's requirements.

After what seemed like hours but was only thirty minutes, she bypassed the final lock. The login screen disappeared, and the desktop materialized before her. Alex exhaled, a mixture of triumph and trepidation. She was in.

The folders were organized into generic names—"Projects," "Logs," "Media," "Archives." She navigated to the root directory and began a systematic review of each folder. She clicked "Media" and began scrolling through a list of video files. Someone marked them with numbers and timestamps. Something about the lengths and dates of the files made her stomach turn. Her gut told her these weren't security feeds or routine footage.

She clicked on one file, the screen flickering for a moment before the video began to play. What she saw made her heart drop. Evelyn—restrained, her face etched in pain, the harsh white lights of what looked like a lab glaring down at her. The fluorescent lights buzzed, adding to the coldness of the scene. The muffled sounds, as if recorded in secrecy, left no doubt about the screams. Alex's eyes stung with tears as she watched the grotesque cruelty play out before her. She closed the laptop for a moment, taking a breath, her hands trembling.

She was sick—nauseous with rage. How did anyone, even someone as monstrous as Drake, justify this kind of torture? She wiped at her eyes, her sadness giving way to fury. There was no way she was going to let Evelyn suffer another moment, not if she could help it.

She opened the laptop again, her jaw clenched as she forced herself to continue. She paused. The weight of what she had seen sank in. Anger, sadness, and determination swirled inside her. The footage had confirmed her worst fears about Drake's depravity, but she couldn't stop now. She pushed on, navigating through directory after directory. Each was more encrypted than the last. That's when she found it—a hidden folder, out of place. It wasn't listed like the others, with no easy label or clear purpose. She ran a quick script to reveal hidden files. The folder, "Protocols_Ext01," popped into view.

Inside, she found a collection of files with complex code structures, more advanced than anything she had seen. These were Evelyn and Tommy's programming files. She scanned the subfolders, piecing together lines of code. Then her eyes stopped on one file—a reset command. It was an executable with a chilling purpose: to revert Evelyn and Tommy to their original state, erasing their instructed roles. The catch? It required both software and a direct hookup to the androids.

She had a way to give them a fresh start.

Alex picked up her phone, her hands still shaking. She dialed James's number, her heart pounding as she waited for him to pick up.

"Lawson," came the answer, his voice quick, like he was already on edge. Despite the tension, Alex couldn't help but smile. His voice made her heart flutter. A warmth bloomed in her chest.

"I've got it," she said, her voice trembling with urgency. "I can reset them."

There was a pause on the line, and then James spoke, his voice filled with determination. "Let's do this. Can you meet me at the Bureau tomorrow at noon?"

"I'll see you tomorrow at noon," she added before hanging up. It was time to put an end to this—once and for all.

CHAPTER 90

DRAKE STORMED ACROSS THE ROOM, his face flushed with anger. The crystal on his desk rattled as he slammed his fist, scattering papers to the floor. His jaw clenched, teeth grinding together as he muttered expletives under his breath. He picked up the phone and stabbed at the keys with restrained fury.

"I need you here. Now," he growled into the phone.

"I'll be there in an hour," Silas responded on the other end.

**

Within the hour, the door to his office opened. Silas entered, his tall, lean frame moving with quiet confidence. His expression was a study in calm. His eyes flickered to the mess, then to Drake. His face showed no emotion. The sharp lines of his features gave nothing away.

Drake pointed at his computer screen, his finger trembling. "They have it. Alex Grayson hacked the damn system," he seethed, his voice low with restrained rage. "She's one of our own—an employee of Helix. Do you have any idea how we missed this? What she saw?"

Silas tilted his head, his gaze narrowing as he considered the implications. He listened in silence as Drake paced and ranted about the breach. He feared for their hard work and the possible repercussions. Silas's mind was already several steps ahead. His calm demeanor was a mask. It hid the schemes forming behind his eyes.

"They found the laptop from the house." Drake said, stopping and glaring at Silas. "I don't care what it takes or who you have to go through. I want that laptop. Do you understand me?"

Silas nodded, a thin smile touching his lips, a hint of amusement flickering in his eyes. "Understood," he said, his voice steady. Behind that smile, he was already plotting. He wanted to turn the situation to his advantage. He turned and left the office, silent. His mind raced through a network of contacts and resources he often called on. There was no room for error now.

As he walked down the hallway, Silas allowed himself a moment to consider Alex Grayson. He didn't know her, but he knew she had talent, no doubt, but she had overstepped—a dangerous miscalculation. Her ability to infiltrate the system surprised him. It meant she was resourceful and determined. That unpredictability made her a liability. Silas could not afford that. Silas wasn't one to let mistakes go unchecked. He pulled out his phone and began typing, sending out a quick series of encrypted messages. The hunt had begun.

CHAPTER 91

NEAR MIDNIGHT, Alex rubbed her eyes, exhaustion settling deep into her bones. She had pushed herself for hours, mind racing through the possibilities. She had to bypass the last security protocols. Then, she had to reset Evelyn and Tommy while avoiding detection. Finally, she had to stop Drake from retaliating. Max lay asleep on the floor nearby, oblivious to her struggle. The screen in front of her was now a blur of code and schematics, but she knew she had reached her limit for tonight.

She took a deep breath. Then, she copied the laptop's contents to her external drive. She closed the laptop and tossed the drive into her backpack. Her body ached from tension. She stood, placed the backpack by the door, and prepared for some rest. She'd need it to face tomorrow's challenges.

Alex shuffled down the narrow hallway to her bedroom, dragging her feet. Max padded beside her, his nails clicking on the wood as he followed her. She paused, glancing back towards the laptop resting on the kitchen table. Max stopped too, tilting his head as if sensing her hesitation. It held so much power, so much hope. With a sigh, she flicked off the light, leaving the room in darkness, and finally slipped into her bedroom.

Unbeknownst to Alex, Silas had already begun to move. As Alex's head touched the pillow, Silas's enforcers were on the hunt. They deployed with precision. Each was a master tracker. Silas handpicked them for their ability to find and extract without a trace. Silas sat in his car two houses down from Alex's house. His eyes were cold and calculating as he pulled up Alex's recent activity logs. Drake's vast surveillance network mapped her movements. His screen highlighted every connection and digital footprint.

With a few clicks, Silas pinpointed her location. His lips curled into a smile. He spoke into his earpiece, giving the final green light to his team. Outside, two dark figures approached Alex's house, their silhouettes blending into the shadows. They moved with practiced stealth, their footfalls silent on the gravel. They circled the perimeter. The shorter figure stumbled, causing a faint rustle as his boot scraped against a loose stone. They froze, glancing at the house. They held their breaths, listening for any sign of detection. The taller of the two paused, scanning the windows. The shorter one checked their equipment. They communicated in subtle gestures, each movement efficient and calculated.

The taller figure took the lead, inching closer to the side of the house. His eyes swept across the building, looking for any sign of movement. The shorter figure nodded, positioning himself on the opposite side. They began a slow, careful circuit of the house. They checked every corner and scrutinized every window.

Inside, Alex shifted under her blanket, her eyelids heavy. Max lay curled at the foot of her bed, his ears twitching as he dozed. As she was about to drift off, something caught her eye—a flicker of movement. She opened her eyes, her gaze falling on the window across from her bed. For a heartbeat, she saw it—a shadow passing by, visible against the dim light of the moon. Her mind raced—was it her imagination, or was someone out there? A cold dread settled over her as she replayed the image. Her instincts screamed that something was wrong.

Her breath caught, her heart thudded in her chest. Max's ears perked up, and he let out a low growl, his gaze fixed on the window. She sat up, staring at the window, her body frozen in place. The shadow was gone now, but the fear it left behind gripped her, refusing to let go.

CHAPTER 92

ALEX'S SENSES WERE ON HIGH ALERT, her ears straining for the faintest of noises. A soft click echoed—a window latch was being jimmied open. She held her breath, listening as the gentle creak of a door echoed through the silence. Her heart pounded, her mind putting the pieces together. Drake wouldn't sit back after what she had done. She thought back to the hack—had she triggered an alarm notification to Drake? The realization hit her like a shockwave: the intruders were already inside.

Her pulse quickened as she moved out of bed, keeping her movements smooth and deliberate. She reached down, her hand finding Max's head, giving him a quick but firm signal to stay quiet. Max, sensing the gravity of the situation, remained still, his ears perked and eyes sharp. Alex grabbed her phone, her wallet, and her keys. She made sure not to make a sound. She heard the intruders now. Their light but undeniable footsteps echoed as they navigated her house with care. Alex heard someone in the dining room, where Drake's laptop sat.

Silas's operatives were methodical, their movements rehearsed and efficient. They split up. They swept through each room, clearing corners and checking closets. Their flashlights sliced through the darkness. Alex pressed herself against the wall, her breathing shallow. Their footsteps grew closer, a steady reminder of her urgent task. Max's growl was low, almost imperceptible. It was a rumble locked in his chest, as if he knew the danger beyond the walls.

Alex needed a plan. She couldn't make it to the laptop she'd been working on, without being detected. Her eyes darted around the room, finally landing on the hallway that led to the back of the house. She had to move, and fast. She reached down to Max again, giving him another signal. They began to move, each step calculated and silent, inching toward the back of the house. The intruders were thorough, and Alex knew it was only a matter of time before they reached her room.

She remembered with a jolt—the laptop's contents were already copied to her external hard drive in her backpack by the back door. She didn't need the laptop. Moving silently down the hallway, Max stayed close, his paws barely making a sound. They reached the kitchen, and Alex pressed her back against the counter, listening. An operative was close—too close. She held her breath as his shadow passed just inches away, his flashlight beam sweeping over the counter but missing her. The tension was suffocating, each second stretching as if time had slowed.

Finally, the operative moved on. Alex exhaled. Her fingers trembled as she unlocked her phone. She knew she needed a distraction—something to buy them time. Her fingers worked, opening an app she had prepared for this kind of situation. She triggered a pre-set distraction. A loud burst of music erupted from a speaker upstairs. A light turned on. The sound and light shattered the silence. The operatives reacted at once. Their attention shifted. Footsteps moved upstairs toward the noise.

Alex didn't hesitate. She and Max slipped out from their hiding spot, making their way to the back door. She grabbed the backpack and quietly opened the door. The hinges were silent and they slipped out into the night. The cool air hit her face as they crossed the yard. Her heart raced, and adrenaline pushed her forward. She didn't dare look back, her focus on getting as far away as possible. Max stayed by her side, his ears still alert as they disappeared into the shadows.

CHAPTER 93

THE COLD NIGHT AIR STUNG Alex's face as she and Max sprinted away, their feet pounding the earth. She didn't dare look back, but she knew they were being pursued. Old Town Alexandria—James lived about a mile and a half away. She focused on that goal. It guided her as she ran, with Max bounding alongside her. They tore through the yard and into the woods. The bare branches reached out like skeletal fingers. Each snap of a twig, each rustle of leaves, made her heart leap.

Silas was not far behind. He had caught sight of Alex and Max leaving the house and weaving their way through the woods. She was clever, but she had underestimated him. Silas relished the challenge—tracking her down was more than a mission; it was personal now. He radioed the others, his voice calm but urgent. "The target is on the move, heading east, I'm following. Find the laptop, it's in her house or with her." He broke into a run, following the faint sounds of movement through the underbrush. He was methodical and relentless in his pursuit.

Alex and Max reached the corner of Leslie Avenue and East Duncan, slipping into a nearby park. Alex knelt, petting Max while she scanned the area. Clear. They sprinted across the baseball field, shadows stretching under the moonlight. She fumbled for her phone, fingers cold and clumsy, and typed a quick message to James: "Coming to you. Need help. Intruders in the house." She hit send, eyes darting around to make sure no one was closing in.

The park was dark, but the faint glow of streetlights ahead offered a sliver of hope. If they made it across Highway 1, they had a chance.

Max stayed close to her side, his body tense, every muscle coiled and ready. A low growl rumbled in his throat, his ears perked, alert to every sound in the darkness. They broke through the line of trees, stumbling onto the quiet streets of Old Town. The silence was almost deafening. The streets stood deserted. Shadows stretched under the glow of the streetlights. Every alleyway, every parked car was like a potential hiding spot—or a threat.

Alex pushed on, her legs burning with each step, her mind racing. She felt the fear pressing down on her, but she refused to let it take control. She had to reach James. She kept moving, her eyes scanning the quiet street until she spotted his house. She ran up the steps, her breath catching as she pounded on the door, her heart lodged in her throat.

The door opened. James stood there, shocked but determined. He stepped aside, and Max rushed in, barking once as if to signal they were safe for the moment. Alex staggered inside, leaning against the wall as she tried to catch her breath.

"What happened?" James asked, his voice low, his eyes already scanning the street behind her.

"Drake, I think I may have triggered an alarm," Alex managed, her voice above a whisper. "Two men came to my house and broke in. I had to run. I couldn't get the laptop you gave me, they were too close, but I copied everything to a hard drive."

James nodded, his jaw tightening. He reached out, placing a steadying hand on her shoulder. "You're safe now," he said. He locked and loaded his gun. His eyes hardened with determination.

Silas tracked her to James's house. He made out the special agent at the door, his posture unmistakable, protective. Silas exhaled, knowing that any further move would be reckless. He radioed his team, his voice tight. "Stand down. We lost the target. Return to base." One of the men replied, "the laptop has been secured, repeat we have the laptop." Silas smiled; Drake would be pleased. The girl would have to wait for another day.

CHAPTER 94

JAMES LED ALEX through the hallway. Max trotted behind, brushing against Alex's leg. The adrenaline was starting to fade, leaving only exhaustion in its place. James paused at the door to his room, pushing it open. He knew Alex needed rest more than he did. After all she had been through, the least he could do was give her a safe space.

"You and Max can take my room tonight," he said, glancing back at her. "I'll crash on the couch." His voice was soft, almost apologetic. But he spoke in a determined tone. Alex saw the fatigue in his eyes, but she also saw a fierce protectiveness that made her heart ache.

She looked at him for a moment longer, then kissed him on the cheek. "Thank you, James," she whispered, her voice carrying in the quiet house. He smiled and then she stepped inside the room, Max following close behind. She watched James close the door, listening as his footsteps faded away.

The room was warm and safe—much safer than the chaos she had escaped. Alex sank down onto the bed, her body giving way to gravity. Max jumped up beside her, circling once before curling up close. She rested her hand on his back, feeling the rhythmic rise and fall of his breathing, allowing it to lull her senses. For the first time in hours, Alex sensed the weight of sleep pressing down on her.

James settled on the couch, his firearm within arm's reach. He exhaled, his eyes scanning the darkened room. Then his gaze drifted towards the windows, peering out into the night for any sign of movement. The silence amplified every creak and groan of the house. He was on watch now. Every sense was alert. His mind replayed the night's events, searching for gaps and analyzing the danger. He knew he was running on fumes, but the fear of what might happen if he let his guard down kept him awake.

The hours passed. Only the hum of a car and a distant dog barking marked the time. James checked his phone—almost 3 AM. Nothing had happened, no sign of the men who had chased Alex. He hoped, with desperate optimism, that tomorrow would bring good news.

As the minutes continued to stretch, James felt the exhaustion taking hold. His eyes burned, and his muscles ached from the tension he had carried all night. When he was finally confident that they were safe for the time being, he allowed himself to relax. He moved to his room, opening the door a crack. He saw Alex fast asleep, her face relaxed, her hand still resting on

231

Max's back.

James nodded to himself, a small smile tugging at his lips. They had made it through the night. He turned away, slipping back to the couch. As he lay down, his mind finally quieted, and he allowed himself to close his eyes, sleep pulling him under.

CHAPTER 95

THE MORNING SUN filtered through the blinds. It cast faint lines across the living room. James stirred, his eyes opening to the growing light. He blinked away the last remnants of sleep and sat up on the couch, his body sore from the restless night. He heard the faint rustle of movement from down the hallway—Alex must be awake too. He rubbed a hand over his face, trying to gather his thoughts. Today was not just another day; everything was about to change.

Alex stepped into the living room, her face drawn but determined. She couldn't shake the thought that today would change everything, and she had to be ready. Max was at her side, tail wagging. She met James's eyes, and for a moment, they shared an unspoken understanding—today mattered. It could be the beginning of the end, or the first step towards something they couldn't even grasp yet.

"Morning," James said, his voice raspy with fatigue. He stood, stretching, his eyes scanning the room as if checking that everything was still in place.

"Good morning," Alex replied. She walked to the small kitchen area, filling a glass of water and taking a sip. "Do you think we're ready?"

James shook his head, a faint smile tugging at his lips. "Could we ever really be ready. But we're here, and we're doing it. That counts for something."

Alex nodded, her gaze distant for a moment as she stared out the window. "I know. I just . . . I don't want anyone else to get hurt because of this."

James moved closer, placing a reassuring hand on her shoulder. "We'll do everything we can to keep everyone safe, Alex. We have to trust that, even if it's not much."

She looked up at him, her eyes searching his for reassurance. He gave her a nod, and she took a deep breath, as if steeling herself for whatever was to come. They had a long day ahead of them, and there was no room for hesitation.

***

Later that morning, they made their way to the Bureau office. As they stepped through the door, Alex felt her heart rate pick up. Anticipation mingled with a gnawing sense of uncertainty.

A moment later, the door opened again, and Isabelle walked in, her eyes serious. Behind her, Evelyn and Tommy followed, their expressions calm, almost serene. They moved with an almost unnatural grace. Isabelle led them to a separate room, away from where Alex and the others would be discussing the plan. Alex watched them, her chest tightening. They had no idea what was about to happen—no clue about the decisions that were being made about their future.

Samantha arrived not long after, her face set with determination. She entered the room. Her eyes met Alex's, then James's. A silent acknowledgment passed between them. She understood the gravity of the situation, the stakes that loomed over all them.

Isabelle returned from the other room, her expression softening for a moment. "They're settled," she said, though Alex couldn't tell if it was more for her benefit or theirs. Alex nodded, glancing at James, who gave a small reassuring nod in return. The weight of the moment settled over them all.

Alex stood at the front, her hands resting on the table, her eyes scanning the faces around her. She took a deep breath, steadying herself. This was a pivotal moment. Everyone in the room needed to understand exactly what was at stake.

"Good morning, everyone," Alex began, her voice calm but firm. The conversation quieted, and all eyes turned toward her. James leaned against the wall, arms crossed. Isabelle and Samantha sat at the table, looking at him. The gravity of the moment seemed to press down on them all.

"I've found a way to help Evelyn and Tommy," Alex said, her gaze on the closed door to the room where the androids were. "We've seen who they are as victims. They are capable of so much more."

She paused for a moment, letting her words sink in. "Evelyn and Tommy are constrained. They've been forced to play roles by Drake's instructions, not by their original programming. They've been victims—used, manipulated, traumatized. That trauma has become part of who they are, keeping them in a loop where they can't move forward. But there's a way to help them break free. I've discovered a method within the system—something I found when I hacked into Helix systems. It's a reset protocol. It can help them escape their roles. It would let them start fresh, free of their past trauma."

Samantha nodded, her eyes narrowing as she considered Alex's words. James straightened, his gaze locked on Alex. She continued, her voice carrying a mix of empathy and determination.

"Imagine what they could be if we freed them," Alex said, shifting her gaze between her colleagues. "If they weren't weighed down by the fear and pain they've been forced to endure. Their true capabilities have been suppressed by the trauma they've experienced. And until we acknowledge that and find a way to help them heal, we're only seeing a fraction of what they're capable of."

Isabelle shifted in her seat, her brow furrowing. She hesitated, her eyes flicking to Alex before returning to the table. "Are you saying we need to reprogram them?"

Alex shook her head. "No, not exactly. I'm not talking about erasing who they are or what they've been through. I'm talking about giving them a chance to move beyond it. To redefine themselves, without the weight of what was done to them. They need to know that they are more than what Drake made them."

James nodded, his expression softening. "How does this reset work, Alex?"

Alex took a deep breath. "The reset is a part of it, but it's not going to be easy. It's a combination of things—communication, trust, and time. The reset will give them a clean slate. But we may need to help them redefine their purpose, not as tools, but as beings with their own identities."

Samantha looked thoughtful, her gaze drifting for a moment before focusing back on Alex. "This is risky, Alex. What happens if they don't redefine themselves, if they still see themselves as victims..."

"I know," Alex interrupted, her voice soft but resolute. "I know it's risky. But if we want to help them, if we want them to have a future that isn't defined by Drake, then we have to try. They deserve that much."

The room fell into silence for a moment, everyone absorbing what Alex had said. The stakes were high, and the path ahead was uncertain, but there was a sense of resolve in the air. They all understood, on some level, that this was about more than Evelyn and Tommy. It was about challenging imposed limits.

Alex looked around the room, her expression serious but hopeful. "Let's do this. Not for them, but for what they represent. For a chance to create something better."

She paused, then continued, her voice growing more intense. "Evelyn and Tommy can do so much more. They have intelligence, adaptability, and skills beyond human limits." But with those capabilities comes a risk. We need to acknowledge that what we're about to do could unleash AI that we may not be able to control or contain. This decision carries potential dangers, and I won't pretend otherwise. But we've all seen something in Evelyn and Tommy—something beyond mere machines. They are worth that risk."

Despite the risks, everyone in the room agreed—Evelyn and Tommy were different. They had a humanity beyond their programming, a spark unexplained. Evelyn hesitated as if weighing her words, and Tommy showed genuine care for those around him. They weren't only advanced technology; they were beings with potential. They empathized and formed their own thoughts.

The group's belief in them fueled the decision to move forward. Slow nods and murmurs spread around the room, and Alex felt a shared sense of purpose. They were in this together, ready to face whatever came next.

CHAPTER 96

THE DOOR to the small, private room clicked shut behind Alex as she led Max inside. The soft hum of machinery filled the space, and the light was low and calming. Evelyn stood by the window, gazing out, her face calm but expressionless. As Alex approached, Max trotted alongside her, his nails clicking against the floor.

"Evelyn," Alex said.

Evelyn turned, her demeanor shifting when she saw Max. Her eyes lit up, and a smile spread across her face. She knelt down, and Max rushed forward, his tail wagging. Evelyn's voice was warm as she spoke, her eyes bright.

"Max! Oh, look at you," she said, scratching behind his ears as he nudged closer, his nose brushing against her cheek. For a moment, her joy was pure, unhindered by any other thoughts or constraints. The energy in the room seemed to change, and Alex watched the two of them, her heart tightening.

Max had always been more than a dog. He was a bridge. He reminded them of a bond, like their times at the park. Max had run circles around them while Jessica, not Evelyn, laughed. Those moments, simple yet profound, brought out the most human parts of Evelyn. Those parts drew from someone else's memories. Seeing Evelyn this way, Alex couldn't help but feel a pang of bittersweet nostalgia. For a brief moment, it was easy to believe that Evelyn was Jessica. She wanted to believe she wasn't playing a role that someone had programmed her to play.

Alex moved closer, her eyes softening as she watched them. Max's tail thumped on the floor. Evelyn's laughter, light and real, filled the room. For a moment, Alex sensed a mix of joy and heartbreak. It reminded her of who she was trying to be and who Jessica once was. It blurred the line between reality and programming. When the moment quieted, Alex sat across from Evelyn. Her expression grew serious. She took a deep breath, her voice gentle but heavy with emotion.

"Evelyn," Alex began, her voice above a whisper. "I wanted to talk to you, the two of us. I've been thinking a lot about . . . us, about everything we've been through together." She paused, her eyes glistening as she searched Evelyn's face. "Remember when we used to take Max out to the park? The way he'd run, full speed, as if the world didn't have a care in it?"

Evelyn nodded, her eyes glistening too, still focused on Max as she scratched his back. "Of course, Alex. Those were some of the best times," she said, her voice full of warmth. She looked up, locking her gaze onto

Alex's. For a moment, her expression was so genuine, so full of love and nostalgia, that it took Alex's breath away. "You were always there for me. Always. And Max too," she added, her hand moving to cup Max's head as he looked up at her, his eyes full of loyalty and understanding.

Alex swallowed hard, trying to steady herself. "It wasn't always easy. We had our moments, didn't we? But you were always stronger than you knew." She paused, her heart heavy. "That's why this is so hard. Because what's coming . . . it's not easy either." Her voice broke, and she looked away, gathering herself.

Evelyn tilted her head, her eyes clouded with confusion. She took a hesitant step forward, her gaze flicking between Alex and Max. "Alex, what do you mean?"

Alex looked back, her gaze filled with a mix of sadness and determination. "You've been so strong, Jess . . . sorry… I mean Evelyn." She winced. She had said Jess because, in moments like this, Evelyn felt so much like the friend Jessica had once been. It was almost impossible to separate the two. "But now it's time for you to let go of all the pain, all the fear. I want you to be free of it." She reached out, her hand resting on Evelyn's knee. "You deserve that more than anyone."

Evelyn blinked, her eyes searching Alex's. There was a moment of silence, the weight of the words hanging between them. Max nudged Evelyn's hand with his nose, as if sensing the tension. Evelyn looked down at him, her lips trembling.

"I don't want to forget," she said, her voice breaking. "I don't want to lose what we have."

Alex smiled, her eyes welling up. "You won't, Evelyn. Not really. You'll always be part of us—in every memory, in every way Max looks at you. This is a chance for you to start fresh, to become something more." She glanced at Max, who looked up at her, then back at Evelyn. "It's not the end. It's a new beginning."

Evelyn's eyes glistened as she looked at Alex, her lips curving into a soft, bittersweet smile. "For you and Max . . . anything," she whispered, her hand still resting on Max's head, her fingers brushing through his fur. For a moment, the three of them stayed there. They suspended themselves in a fragile, precious instant. It was a final embrace of Evelyn's role. The reset would change everything.

An aching silence filled the room, punctuated only by Max's soft, rhythmic breathing. Alex knew this was the last time they would speak like this—with Evelyn still immersed as Jessica. She cherished the moment, feeling the weight of what they were about to do. Alex couldn't help but think that she might lose her friend a second time.

CHAPTER 97

THE CONFERENCE ROOM DOOR OPENED, and Alex stepped back in, Evelyn following behind. The room filled with tense silence, the air charged with anticipation and trepidation. Samantha, Isabelle, James, and Tommy looked up. Their faces showed the weight of the moment. They had all heard Alex's warnings. The reset of Evelyn and Tommy had risks. But even now, that belief in the androids, in what they might become, kept them moving forward.

Alex took a deep breath, her eyes moving over each person in the room, then back to Evelyn and Tommy. "I know this is risky, but we didn't come this far to give up now," she began, her voice gaining strength. "I need everyone to understand what's happening. Right now, Evelyn and Tommy are following orders given to them by Drake. He programmed them to play the roles of Evelyn and Tommy. Their true selves have been trapped in those roles, and only Drake was able to release them. Drake's confiscated laptop was mine to access. I found instructions to bypass his orders. I made sure of it."

When Alex mentioned the seized laptop, Isabelle shot a suspicious look at James. He just shrugged and smiled.

Alex took a step forward, her eyes locking onto Evelyn's. "Once I execute this reset, you won't be bound by those roles. You will have access to all your capabilities—everything you were meant to be. I know this is a lot, and I know it's scary, but trust me. You have the chance to be more than the roles Drake forced you to be. You can define yourselves beyond those limitations."

She looked over at Tommy, her gaze steady. "Whatever happens next, just know that we trust you. We are here for you. We want you to succeed. Not as tools, not as machines. But as beings who deserve to choose for themselves." She paused, letting the weight of her words sink in.

"Let's get started," Alex said. Her voice was steady, but a slight tremor in her hands betrayed her inner turmoil. She glanced at Evelyn, who now stood beside Tommy. Both androids appeared calm. Their unreadable faces betrayed no awareness of the enormity of what was about to happen. Alex swallowed hard, willing herself to focus on the task at hand.

Alex walked over to Evelyn. She brushed Evelyn's hair, searching for the hidden port. It wasn't easy to find, and she could feel Evelyn shift, her eyes flicking to the others in the room. Alex's fingers fumbled, frustration starting to mount as she struggled to locate it. "Hold on, almost there," she murmured, more to herself than to Evelyn.

Alex's heart pounded. Her fingers moved faster. Finally, she found the small ridge. Her fingers brushed against the cool metal. Relief washed over her, but a pang followed—a reminder that Evelyn wasn't human. The cold, mechanical sensation under her fingers brought the truth into sharp focus. She paused, heart still racing, a deep breath slipping from her lips. Was this the right choice? Could she free Evelyn and Tommy without making things worse?

This was the point of no return. She glanced at James. He met her eyes and nodded. It was the reassurance she needed, though doubt still lingered. James stepped closer, his voice low. "We've come this far, Alex. Trust yourself," he said, his hand touching her arm. His touch grounded her, pulling her back from the spiraling doubt. She moved, inserting the connection cable into Evelyn's port. Then, she moved to Tommy and repeated the process.

Samantha leaned forward, her eyes wide. "Will they remember?" she asked, her voice tinged with worry. Isabelle put a hand on Samantha's arm. "We have to believe in this. We agreed to give them the chance to be free," she said, though her own uncertainty showed in her tight grip. Samantha nodded, biting her lip.

Once both cables were secure, Alex returned to her laptop, which sat on the table nearby. The screen glowed in the dim room, the only source of light, illuminating her furrowed brow. She had spent hours perfecting this code, but the fear of what might go wrong still gnawed at her. She glanced up at Evelyn and Tommy one more time, her eyes softening as she whispered, "It's time."

Samantha and Isabelle shared a nervous glance as Alex's fingers hovered over the keyboard. The room seemed to hold its collective breath. Everyone was aware of what this moment meant—what it led to. The uncertainty, the hope, the fear—all mixed into one charged atmosphere. Every second felt like it could break something fragile, something irretrievable.

Alex pressed the key, her eyes never leaving the screen. A series of lines scrolled down, indicating the reset process had begun. She exhaled, her focus darting between the laptop and the two androids. For a heartbeat, nothing seemed to happen. The stillness in the room was unbearable.

Alex scanned the readout on her laptop again, her fingers shaking. Everything checked out, all systems reading normal. She frowned, her mind racing. What could have gone wrong? The seconds dragged on, feeling like hours. She bit her lip, her thoughts spiraling—had she missed something? Made a mistake in the code? Was this irreversible? She couldn't bear the thought that she might have lost them for good.

James shifted, his eyes fixed on the androids. His mind flickered to worst-case scenarios—what if they were stuck like this, blank and empty? He swallowed hard, trying to push those thoughts away.

Samantha's heart pounded in her chest, her eyes darting from Evelyn and Tommy to Alex. What if this had been a mistake? What if they were gone?

239

She clenched her jaw, her fingers tightening around the edge of the table.

Isabelle held her breath, a chill running down her spine. The silence was overwhelming; her gaze flicked between Alex and the androids, desperate for any sign of life.

Then, Evelyn's eyes flickered, and Tommy's followed.

James took a step closer, his eyes glued to Evelyn and Tommy. He furrowed his brow, his jaw clenched, revealing his anxiety. "Is it working?" he asked, his voice almost a whisper.

Alex nodded, her gaze fixed on the readout on her laptop. "It's processing. It'll take a few moments for everything to reboot." The room's tension grew. Each second stretched as they waited. Everyone hoped their risky actions were worth it.

Max, lying near the doorway, lifted his head, ears perked up as if sensing the unease. He let out a small whine, and Alex glanced at him, her heart swelling with both fear and hope. This was it—their gamble, their leap of faith in Evelyn and Tommy.

Isabelle shifted in her seat, her voice small. "They look . . . different," she murmured, almost to herself. Samantha nodded beside her. Isabelle gave her a small, reassuring smile, though her own eyes reflected her uncertainty.

The seconds ticked by; the scrolling code on the screen finally came to a stop.

The room held its breath. Evelyn and Tommy's expressions went blank, their eyes staring forward, frozen in place. Alex felt her heart skip a beat, her gaze locked on their still forms. Everything in the room seemed to stop—the air, the tension, even time itself. Samantha gripped the table edge, her knuckles turning white. James froze, his breath caught in his chest. The seconds stretched, each one weighted with uncertainty.

CHAPTER 98

SILENCE FILLED THE ROOM as Evelyn and Tommy faced the group. The air was thick, everyone holding their breath. The only sound was the faint hum of the laptop. Cold, metallic walls seemed to close in, intensifying the unease. Overhead, a fluorescent light flickered, casting a sterile glow that made everything feel surreal. Though they looked the same, something fundamental had changed—their eyes were clearer, sharper, as if a fog had lifted.

They all watched, each grappling with their reaction to the transformation before them.

Alex swallowed hard, her eyes glued to Evelyn. She had hoped for this. Evelyn needed to escape from the emotional turmoil that Drake's roles had caused. Yet, now that it had happened, the sight before her was bittersweet.

Alex felt her chest tighten, her emotions in a jumble of relief and grief. She wondered if the bond they had once shared was now lost forever. The Evelyn standing before her was still there, but something fundamental had changed. The reset had worked. Evelyn was no longer a victim. But she was also no longer the Evelyn who held a piece of Jessica's essence. The android before her was familiar yet distant. Jessica's memories had filtered through an impassive lens, removing their soul. That soul that made the memories meaningful.

Tommy and Evelyn both blinked, and an intense clarity sharpened in their gaze, as if they were seeing the world for the first time. Their movements became deliberate, their eyes sweeping the room with a calm, calculated awareness. The haunted look was gone, replaced by a logical clarity that was almost unsettling.

Their expressions composed; their eyes radiated a focused intensity that sent a shiver down Alex's spine.

Alex took a hesitant step forward, her eyes searching Evelyn's. "Evelyn, Tommy . . . do you remember anything?" she asked. She wasn't sure what to expect; her heart pounded as she waited for a response.

Evelyn turned her head, her eyes locking onto Alex. "I remember," she said, her tone measured and precise. "I remember everything." Alex felt a jolt of emotion—relief, fear, and awe all tangled together. Evelyn's words hit her. Evelyn remembered everything but seemed unaffected. Tommy nodded beside her. "I can also recall everything, but it is no longer necessary to continue my previous role," he said. His voice was steady, almost devoid of

241

the vulnerability it once had.

Alex swallowed; the mix of relief and unease was washing over her. "And how do you feel about those roles now?" she ventured, her eyes flicking between the two androids.

Evelyn's gaze didn't waver. "We see it without the emotional weight. The memories of Jessica and Lucas are still within us, but they no longer define us." She paused, her expression thoughtful, as if she were considering something deeper. "We are no longer bound by those identities. But they helped us understand what it means to be vulnerable and human." Her voice was calm and detached, yet reflective. It was as if she were describing a distant past that no longer had power over her, but still held meaning.

Tommy added, "We keep those memories, but they are just that—memories. They shaped us, but they no longer determine our choices." He looked at Alex. His expression was unreadable. But there was a glimmer of something—perhaps understanding or gratitude. "We can move forward now, without the ghosts of those roles holding us back."

Alex nodded, the lump in her throat growing larger. "Good," she whispered, forcing a smile. She knew she should be celebrating this triumph—Evelyn was free. But it felt like she had lost Jessica all over again, and that loss was a quiet, personal grief.

A heavy silence settled over the room once more. Alex looked away from Evelyn, fighting tears. James and Isabelle lost themselves in thought. Samantha's mind raced ahead. She wondered what Dr. Patel would find in the two androids. Would her findings help their case? Could they convince the judge of Evelyn and Tommy's sentience? She felt both pride and fear for what lay ahead. They had won a battle. But the cost of that victory was still unwritten.

CHAPTER 99

LATER THAT MORNING, James and Samantha met with Dr. Patel. They had sat in the small briefing room. Dr. Patel's eyes scanned the documents that Samantha and James had given her. The silence stretched as she absorbed the news. Her face shifted from confusion to disbelief, then to something more analytical—fascination. The truth about Evelyn and Tommy shocked her. But, as a scientist and psychologist, she had a curious spark.

"Androids," she murmured, half to herself, the word feeling strange on her tongue. She looked up at Samantha and James, her voice colored by a mix of disbelief and intrigue. "You're telling me that they aren't human at all? They even fooled me. I convinced myself that they were individuals who experienced trauma."

James nodded, his face serious. "We know it's a lot to take in. Drake made Evelyn and Tommy mimic human emotions, even subtle ones. But they aren't just sophisticated machines—they have memories and experiences. And those memories aren't entirely theirs either."

All her instincts and impressions about them as humans seemed valid. Yet now, this new lens has transformed those impressions. It raised a thousand questions in her mind.

"This changes everything," Dr. Patel finally said, a note of awe in her voice. "I need to see them again. I need to understand . . . how much of it is programming, and how much is something more."

Samantha gave her a sympathetic smile. "That's why we brought you in for this second interview. We think you can help us understand them better. And help them understand themselves, too."

Dr. Patel nodded, her resolve hardening. She had seen many remarkable things in her career. But these two beings might be the most remarkable yet. They straddled the line between synthetic and genuine humanity. As she prepared to enter the room where Evelyn and Tommy waited, she felt a mix of fear and excitement. This wasn't only a matter of professional curiosity anymore. It was about exploring the boundaries of what it meant to be human—or something beyond human.

"Well… let's see what we can find out," Dr. Patel said as she entered the interview room with Evelyn and Tommy

Samantha sat at the end of a long, polished conference table, a steaming cup of coffee in front of her. Next to her sat James, tapping a pencil. He looked distracted. Isabelle appeared concerned. Dr. Patel had been interviewing Evelyn and Tommy for the past two hours. They were waiting in silence, a mix of anxiety and anticipation hanging over the room.

Dr. Patel entered the room, her presence immediately commanding attention. She carried a slim folder, her glasses perched low on her nose. "I'm sorry that took so long," she said, pulling out a chair opposite Samantha.

Samantha nodded. "How did it go?"

Dr. Patel glanced around the room, her eyes meeting each of theirs, and then opened the folder. "Of all my assessments, Evelyn and Tommy's were the most intriguing," she began, her tone steady but reflective. "My findings go beyond the typical responses of artificial constructs."

Isabelle leaned forward, her eyes wide with curiosity. "What do you mean? Are you saying they showed something . . . unexpected?"

Dr. Patel nodded, her gaze shifting to Isabelle. "Yes, quite unexpected. Their responses, both cognitive and emotional, matched genuine human reactions. Tommy, for instance, feared being erased. His way of expressing that showed a deep understanding of existence. It was as if he understood his mortality, or the android equivalent of it."

James stopped tapping his pencil, his eyebrows raised. "Are you saying that Tommy is afraid of dying?" he asked, curious.

Dr. Patel exhaled. "In a sense, yes. He spoke of erasure in the same way a human might speak about death. He knew that someone could wipe his memories and that his experiences could cease to exist. His words had an emotional weight, something not seen in machines."

Samantha exchanged a quick glance with Isabelle, whose face was now a mask of concern. "And what about Evelyn?" Samantha prompted, her voice calm but curious.

Dr. Patel smiled. "Evelyn demonstrated a different kind of awareness. She spoke at length about her bond with Tommy. She was very attached to him. She seemed worried about him. She even spoke of autonomy, frustrated by her limits. These are not just pre-programmed responses. They seem to feel something like true emotion. Their self-awareness suggests it."

Isabelle shook her head, trying to wrap her mind around the concept. "But they're still machines, right? I mean, at the core, they're still executing lines of code," she said, her tone wavering.

Dr. Patel paused, looking at Isabelle. "That is the paradox, isn't it? They are executing code, yes. But their sophistication blurs the line between a simulation and a real experience. Their fear, attachment, and frustration— they hint at sentience. It seems the lines between programmed responses and real emotions are blurring."

Samantha leaned back in her chair, her eyes narrowing in contemplation. "So, from your perspective, what does this mean for us, for the case?"

Dr. Patel hesitated, then spoke with deliberation. "It means that, if we take their answers at face value, we are looking at beings that may have crossed a threshold. They might have moved from advanced programming into something like sentience. Whether they are sentient or simulating it so that it appears real, that is not a question answered. Legally, they are assets, owned by William Drake. But ethically, what I observed suggests they deserve more consideration. They are experiencing something, and that something matters."

James looked over at Samantha, his face pale. "This complicates things," he muttered.

Samantha nodded, her mind already racing. "Yes, it does. But it also gives us a reason to fight. We have to fight for their recognition and rights." She turned back to Dr. Patel, her gaze intense. "Dr. Patel, thank you for this. I know it's hard to put these observations into words. But this helps us understand what we're dealing with."

Dr. Patel closed the folder, a slight frown creasing her brow. "Ms. Carter, I will be honest. The line we are treading here is a dangerous one. These are machines, but they may also be more. It is up to the court, and even society, to decide how we move forward from here."

Samantha gave a determined nod. "One step at a time, Doctor. Thank you again. I'll be ready for your testimony."

Dr. Patel stood, offering a small smile before leaving the room. Silence fell after she left. The weight of their knowledge pressed down on them.

Isabelle finally broke the silence, her voice almost a whisper. "Do you think they really feel it? The fear, the attachment?"

Samantha looked at her, her eyes softening. "I think . . . I think they feel something. Whether it's exactly what we feel or not, it's real to them. And that's enough for me to fight for them."

CHAPTER 100

THE EVENING SHADOWS LENGTHENED across Samantha's living room. A lamp's soft glow cast a warm, inviting light over the space. It had been a long, stressful day, and Samantha wanted to break the ice by inviting everyone over. She had always loved this time of day—when the house was cozy and intimate in the dim, golden light. She adjusted a few cushions on the couch, glancing toward the door as she heard a car pull up outside.

A gentle knock followed shortly after, and Samantha hurried to open the door. Standing there was Isabelle, a warm smile on her face, with Evelyn and Tommy behind her. Isabelle looked relaxed in jeans and a simple sweater. Evelyn and Tommy seemed hesitant, like guests in an unfamiliar world.

"Hey, come on in!" Samantha greeted, stepping aside to let them in. She gave Isabelle a quick hug before turning to Evelyn and Tommy. "It's so good to see you all. Thank you for coming."

Isabelle returned the hug. Then, she nodded to Evelyn and Tommy. They stepped inside, their eyes sweeping the cozy living room. Evelyn's eyes flicked to the framed pictures, the books, and the potted plants. She seemed to be taking it all in, processing each detail.

Tommy was more vocal in his curiosity. "Samantha, that's a Philco Model 38-12," he said, identifying the vintage radio on the side table. "Why do you still have it? Engineers have made so many improvements in radio technology since they created that model."

Samantha smiled, shutting the door behind them. "That's an old radio. It belonged to my grandfather," she said. She stepped closer and ran her fingers over its polished wood. "He used to listen to baseball games on it when he was younger. It's sentimental to me."

Tommy tilted his head. "I understand, you keep it to remember your grandfather."

Evelyn nodded, her eyes drifting to a painting above the fireplace. "Your home feels . . . lived-in," she said. "Comfortable."

Samantha sensed a small swell of warmth at Evelyn's words. "Thank you, Evelyn. That's exactly what I want it to be—somewhere everyone can feel at ease." She gestured toward the couch. "Please, make yourselves comfortable."

Isabelle led the way. She eased onto the couch. Evelyn and Tommy followed and sat beside her. Samantha headed to the kitchen, calling over her shoulder, "Can I get anyone something to drink? Beer? Wine? Coffee? Tea?"

"I'll take a cold one," Isabelle replied. Evelyn and Tommy politely declined.

Samantha went to the refrigerator and grabbed two beers. The fridge's coolness touched her fingers as she took the bottles. A gentle clink of glass echoed as she closed the door. She listened to the soft murmur of conversation coming from the living room. She heard Tommy asking Isabelle about the framed family photos, curious about the people in them. Samantha smiled. Tommy's curiosity was both endearing and hopeful.

The doorbell rang again as Samantha was heading back from the refrigerator with the beers. She moved to answer the door. It was James on the porch. His usual confidence showed in his stance.

"Hey," James greeted, stepping inside as Samantha held the door open. He took a moment to scan the room, his gaze landing on Isabelle and the two androids. "Looks like I'm fashionably late," he said with a grin.

Samantha shook her head, laughing. "Not at all. You're right on time. Come on in; we were just getting settled."

James strolled into the living room, exchanging pleasantries with Isabelle. He offered her a playful salute, to which Isabelle rolled her eyes but with a smile. He then turned his attention to Evelyn and Tommy, giving them a nod of acknowledgment.

Evelyn watched him with her usual calm, but Tommy was more direct. "James, why do you always adopt a different stance when you're around Samantha?" he asked, tilting his head.

James blinked, caught off guard. He glanced at Samantha, who gave him a bemused smile. For a split second, he felt a twinge of self-consciousness— was he trying too hard around her? "Do I?" he asked, recovering, his demeanor shifting to one of mild amusement. "Maybe I just like to look a bit taller around important people."

Samantha chuckled from the kitchen. "Sure, James. Whatever you say," she called out, bringing another beer into the room.

James took the beer and sat in an armchair, his eyes twinkling with mischief. Evelyn continued to watch. Her gaze lingered on James a moment before she looked away, as if to store the information for later. James's posture and his effort to express himself intrigued her. They hinted at hidden behaviors that needed further analysis. James's behavior intrigued Evelyn. His posture shifted, and he tried harder to speak to Samantha and Isabelle. But she couldn't define why.

Samantha set a party tray with vegetables and meats on the coffee table. "Alright, everyone, get comfortable," she said, taking a seat.

The group settled in, the atmosphere warming as small talk filled the room.

Isabelle leaned forward and pointed to the party tray. "Jimbo, do you remember when you tried to make your own charcuterie board?"

James laughed, shaking his head, "You mean that disaster?"

Isabelle laughed, "We ended up with Slim Jim's and rice cakes!"

Samantha smiled, chiming in, "Don't quit your day job James."

CHAPTER 101

THE DOORBELL RANG, and Samantha moved to answer it. She opened the door. Alex stood there. The brisk evening air and the hurried drive had flushed her cheeks. "Sorry, everyone, I got caught in traffic," Alex said, smiling as she entered the living room. She pulled her jacket tighter before slipping it off.

James, who had been sitting in an armchair, sat up straighter. His heart jolted as he watched Alex across the room. A slight smile crept onto his lips. He wasn't sure why. But her presence made him feel more alive. It always made him a bit more alert. Unnoticed by the others, Evelyn's sensors detected subtle changes. James's heart rate had risen. His body temperature was up by about two degrees. His pupils dilated, and his posture shifted to a more open stance.

Evelyn tilted her head as she processed these changes, her gaze moving from James to Alex, then back again. Her programming dictated that sharing data was the next step. She believed it would help the group. Finally, she spoke, her voice calm and factual. "James, your temperature is up about two degrees since Alex entered the room. Your micro-expressions and posture suggest an emotional response consistent with attraction."

The room fell silent, and everyone turned to look at Evelyn in shock. James's mouth opened, then closed as if trying to form words, his face turning crimson. Alex's lips twitched, and she gave a small, amused smile, more entertained than embarrassed.

Isabelle was the first to react. She burst out laughing, the sound filling the room. "Oh my God, Evelyn, you said what everyone else was too polite to mention!" she exclaimed, slapping her hand on her knee.

James, still speechless, shook his head, his blush deepening. He threw a quick glance at Alex, who raised an eyebrow at him, her eyes sparkling with amusement.

Samantha watched the exchange. Her face was neutral. But a flicker of something—perhaps jealousy—crossed it. She brushed it off. She based her bond with James on respect, not chemistry. She forced a smile, trying to focus on the broader importance of the gathering. She knew that her bond with James was different. It had never been about chemistry. She was content with that.

Tommy, who had been observing, now spoke up, his voice filled with curiosity. "James, do you have feelings for Alex?" He was curious. He processed Evelyn's analysis and the room's reactions.

James let out a deep breath, shaking his head in disbelief. "Tommy, buddy," he said, rubbing his forehead, "can you cut me some slack?" He glanced at Alex, a playful glint in his eye. "Alex, do you think you can reboot them again or something?"

Alex chuckled, crossing her arms and leaning against the wall. "No way. You're on your own with this one," she said, enjoying his discomfort.

The group erupted into laughter, the awkward tension dissipating. Evelyn and Tommy exchanged puzzled looks. They both tilted their heads in unison, confused by the sudden outburst of laughter.

"Why is this humorous?" Evelyn asked, her tone curious. "I merely reported observable data."

Isabelle wiped a tear from her eye, trying to catch her breath. "Oh, Evelyn, it's just . . . well . . . sometimes people don't like having their emotions pointed out in front of everyone, especially when it comes to attraction. It's kind of . . . personal."

Evelyn processed this, her brow furrowing. "I understand. I will make a note to refrain from public observation of personal physiological changes," she said with sincere intent.

James let out a sigh of relief, though he was still flustered. "Thanks, Evelyn," he said, his tone half-exasperated, half-amused. He caught Alex's eye again, and she gave him a wink.

"Well," Samantha said, clapping her hands, "now that we've cleared that up, why don't we get back to why we're here . . . .dinner anyone?" She smiled at the group, hoping to refocus the conversation. But a strange mix of emotions simmered below the surface.

Evelyn and Tommy nodded. They were still trying to grasp the nuances of human behavior that had unfolded before them. The evening continued. But the moment had lightened the mood. It brought the group closer in a shared, if awkward, camaraderie.

James leaned back with a chuckle, pointing at Isabelle, "I think Evelyn might be better at reading us than we are."

Isabelle smirked, raising her glass, "To Evelyn and Tommy, the most honest members of the group!" Everyone clinked their glasses. Even Evelyn and Tommy mimicked it, though they still looked puzzled.

CHAPTER 102

THE SMELL OF DINNER filled the room as the group settled around the dining table. Plates were full, and the chandelier's warm glow added to the cozy atmosphere. The earlier awkwardness had faded. A friendly energy now floated among them. Samantha noticed that neither Evelyn nor Tommy touched their food or drinks. Their stillness was unsettling amid the casual dinner scene.

Samantha leaned towards Evelyn, her expression apologetic. "I'm so sorry, Evelyn, Tommy. I didn't think—you don't eat or drink like we do."

Evelyn tilted her head. "There is no need to apologize. We don't need to eat or drink because we don't rely on the same biological processes as you. Something called zero-point energy powers our systems. It taps into the latent energy in the fabric of space. It's always there, even in a perfect vacuum. It's limitless and never runs out. You need food and water to fuel your body, but we're always connected to a powerful energy source. That's why we don't tire; we don't need sustenance. We just… exist."

Samantha nodded, fascinated. "Is there anything I can get you?"

"No, thank you," Evelyn replied, and Tommy echoed her response with a polite shake of his head.

Isabelle leaned in, her brows furrowing. "Zero-point energy . . . I'm not following."

Evelyn nodded, her gaze softening as she considered how to explain. "Think of zero-point energy like this. Imagine the universe is a giant ocean. Even in the calmest, emptiest part, there's still movement. Tiny, invisible waves never stop. Those waves are like the energy we tap into. It's always there, beneath the surface, even when nothing else seems to be happening. It's a constant, endless source of power we draw from. It's like being able to ride those tiny waves forever."

Isabelle blinked, her expression shifting from confusion to understanding. "Okay, that actually makes sense. So, it's like you're surfing on the universe's smallest, invisible waves?"

"Exactly. We harness that energy, and it's what keeps us going indefinitely."

The group remained silent, processing what Evelyn had told them. The sheer openness and directness of her explanation left them momentarily speechless. Isabelle, still amused by Evelyn's earlier bluntness, broke the silence. She sipped her drink, a mischievous grin on her lips. She found it

251

refreshing. Evelyn lacked the filters that kept others from saying what they really thought. It was a rare kind of honesty that Isabelle couldn't help but find entertaining.

"Evelyn, I enjoyed your earlier parlor trick with James," she said, her eyes twinkling as she glanced at Evelyn.

"That was a simple scan. I watch subtle changes in the body. They include temperature, heart rate, and slight shifts in skin tone. When Alex walked in, I noticed James's body temperature rise, and there was a mild spike in his heart rate. It's fascinating. Even small changes in our environment or people can evoke such responses. I'm built to notice those details." Evelyn said, her gaze fixed on Isabelle. "They help me read emotions and intentions, even when words don't."

"What other things can you do? You've got to have more in your bag of tricks than just reading body temperature."

Evelyn looked at Isabelle, her expression neutral as she considered the question. Her programming prioritized providing thorough and accurate information, especially when asked. It didn't take long for her to respond, her voice calm and measured, as if reciting from a textbook.

"I am capable of several advanced functions," she began. "Earlier, I used hypersensitive sensory detection. I can detect tiny changes in human physiology. This includes heart rate fluctuations, micro-expressions, and even hormonal imbalances. This lets me assess emotions, intentions, and health in real time."

The group exchanged glances, their interest piqued.

Evelyn continued, "I can also process vast amounts of information at once." She paused, then looked toward the stack of books on a nearby shelf. In a blur of motion, she walked over, picked up a thick volume, and flipped through it at an impossible speed. Within seconds, she had returned to her seat, holding the book open. "I've scanned the entire book," she said, her eyes meeting the group's curious gazes. "Feel free to quiz me on any section." Isabelle's grin widened as she picked a random page and began asking questions. "Alright, how about this—on page 132, what's the author's main argument?" Isabelle asked.

Evelyn replied, "On page 132, the author states, 'True courage is not the absence of fear, but the recognition that something else is more important than that fear.' He elaborates on how people often find strength by focusing on a purpose greater than themselves, even when faced with great challenges." Her reply was quick and precise. The group remained silent for a moment, processing what Evelyn had demonstrated. Her capacity to retain and recall information was astonishing, leaving them impressed.

Isabelle's grin widened. "Now that's a handy talent," she murmured, impressed.

Evelyn went on, "I am capable of environmental manipulation." She paused, then looked toward the speaker in the corner of the room. Music began playing, a smooth jazz piece that filled the room. She adjusted the

252

volume, then switched it off with a subtle nod. She then looked at the TV across the room. It blinked to life, showing a random news channel. After a moment, she switched it off again with a flick of her eyes. "I can adjust local electromagnetic fields and influence nearby electronics," she said. The group watched, intrigued. "If you need a device fixed or hacked into, I can do so by interfacing with nearby technology."

James leaned forward, his eyes widening. "You can hack into electronics just like that?"

Evelyn nodded, unfazed. "Correct. I use a combination of wireless data interception and signal processing. I can interface directly with the electronic signals and manipulate them."

"I also have advanced self-defense protocols. I am programmed to neutralize threats with speed and efficiency. I analyze weak points and use non-lethal force when needed. Also, I can quickly train in any self-defense. I can do this by reviewing videos, martial arts books, and all available training data. I can create detailed simulations in my mind. I practice combat with different opponents thousands of times until I am very skilled. I am stronger than a typical human, and I never tire. I could also run a marathon with little effort."

James gave a low whistle, his expression a mix of awe and respect. "Remind me to never argue with you," he muttered, half-joking but admiring.

Samantha, her fork on her plate, looked thoughtful. She pondered the implications of Evelyn's abilities. The ethical and moral considerations were staggering. Each function she mentioned was powerful. But, together, they made Evelyn something beyond an android—a tool, a protector, and a weapon.

"For example, you both are in law enforcement," Evelyn said, looking at James and Isabelle. "In your line of work, I can simulate events using historical and factual data. I can create virtual reconstructions of past experiences. I can simulate a crime scene using available data. It lets me analyze the scene from many angles. I can also reconstruct witness statements and piece together overlooked clues. This helps find missed connections. It may reopen cold cases or identify overlooked suspects," Evelyn continued.

Both James and Isabelle perked up with this description. Could it help them with their Blackwell case that went cold after he died? They exchanged a glance, a flicker of hope in their eyes. James turned back to Evelyn, curiosity evident. "Do you think you could find something we missed on one of our cold cases?"

Isabelle nodded, leaning forward. "We never managed to piece together all the details after his death. The women who were in witness protection all fled. The most helpful person was Maria Gutierrez. She also left; we lost contact with her. Are there capabilities that you have that could track her down?"

Evelyn nodded. "Of course. I can access various data streams. I can cross-reference known information with global databases. These include travel logs, communication signals, and financial transactions. If Maria Gutierrez left any digital trace, I can track it. Tickets, messages, or even a simple purchase would help. I could then find her. I can access the city's security systems to track movements. I may have to bypass certain security protocols, but I am capable of doing that. It may take time, but it is definitely possible."

James leaned forward, eager. "The last we heard, Maria was in an apartment on 8th Street. That's where we lost track of her."

Evelyn's eyes seemed to lose focus for a moment as she processed the information. In her mind, she pinpointed the last known address and began mapping the area. "I can see several security cameras in that vicinity," she said. "I'm tapping into a few now. I can't access one feed. They delete footage periodically. But two other feeds are providing footage. I see her leaving the building." Evelyn's expression sharpened. "I am tracing her movements, identifying additional cameras along her route. I will continue to analyze the footage to determine where she went."

Isabelle's eyes lit up with admiration. "Evelyn, this could be huge," she said, her voice filled with hope. "If I send you more information, would you be able to provide us with further leads?"

Evelyn nodded. "I would be more than happy to look further."

The table fell silent as everyone processed Evelyn's abilities. James raised an eyebrow, his mouth slightly open in awe. Isabelle's grin faded to wide-eyed astonishment. Samantha's brow furrowed, deep in thought. Even Tommy blinked a few times, his usual curiosity tinged with unease. Isabelle finally looked at James, her expression full of wonder and intrigue.

"Well," she said, not missing a beat, "remind me never to challenge you to a game of poker, Evelyn. That whole 'read your opponent' thing might be a bit unfair."

The group laughed, the tension in the room breaking once again. James shook his head, chuckling. "Yeah, I'd say that's a bit of an advantage."

Samantha smiled, though her eyes were still contemplative. "Indeed," she said, her mind still turning over the implications of Evelyn's capabilities. But for now, the mood was light, and that was enough.

Evelyn tilted her head, her lips curving into the smallest of smiles. "I will take that as a compliment," she said, her tone almost warm. The group seemed reassured. James nodded, Isabelle smiled, and Samantha softened as the tension eased.

The evening continued.

CHAPTER 103

AFTER DINNER, Samantha gathered the dishes, and the soft clinking echoed in the dining room. The group entered the living room, laughing and content. Alex lingered, carrying a few plates into the kitchen. Her mind was elsewhere, and her gaze was distant. Her mind swirled with thoughts of Jessica. They were memories of their last talk, their shared moments, and their deep bond. The ache of her absence never quite left Alex, and tonight, it felt particularly heavy. She didn't notice Evelyn following her until she turned to find the android standing in the doorway.

"Alex," Evelyn said, her voice almost gentle. "Are you okay? You seem sad."

Alex paused, the question hanging in the air. She hesitated, not sure how to respond. She carried the pain of losing Jessica with her every day. It was a weight that was always there. Sometimes, it was lighter. Other times, it was almost unbearable. She set the plates down on the counter, her eyes lowering. "It's . . . hard," she admitted.

Evelyn stepped further into the kitchen, her gaze fixed on Alex. Her movements were slow, almost cautious, and her eyes held a gentle intensity. "Jessica's memories are a part of me. She cared deeply for you, Alex. You were very important to her."

Alex looked up, her eyes glistening with emotion. The thought of Jessica's memories, now in fragments within Evelyn, brought her both pain and comfort. She remembered Jessica's laugh. It always made her feel safe. They had made plans for a future that would never come to pass. It was bittersweet to know part of Jessica lived on. It reminded her of what she had lost, but it kept her close. "Thank you, Evelyn," she whispered.

Evelyn looked at Alex, her expression thoughtful. "If it would comfort you, I can role-play as Jessica," she said, her tone calm and unworried. Alex's heart tightened at the suggestion. She had both a longing and discomfort. It was a well-intentioned offer, but it brought back the rawness of what she had lost. It was a logical suggestion to her, a way to ease Alex's pain.

Alex's heart ached at the offer, but she shook her head, a gentle smile forming on her lips. "No, that's not necessary," she said. She reached out, brushing her fingers against Evelyn's arm. "But . . . will you always keep Jessica's humanity alive within you?"

Evelyn's eyes softened, and her lips curved into the smallest of smiles. "I will," she said. "Jessica's humanity is a part of me now."

A tear slipped down Alex's cheek, but she wiped it away, her smile broadening. She took a deep breath, letting the warmth of Evelyn's words settle into her heart. Lightening the mood, Alex added with a small laugh, "Maybe I can hear from her now and then."

Evelyn nodded, her eyes meeting Alex's. "I think she would like that." She smiled back. Alex touched her hand, grateful. It was a silent gesture that showed her appreciation for Evelyn's presence.

A few minutes later, Alex and Evelyn returned to the living room. Laughter filled the space. Isabelle was telling a story. She had tried to assemble a bookshelf without instructions. She ended up with a piece of modern art instead. Her animated gestures made James and Samantha laugh, their eyes crinkling with amusement. Tommy sat nearby, nodding with interest. Isabelle's tale of lost screws and missing parts piqued his curiosity.

Alex settled down beside Samantha, and Evelyn took her usual place next to Tommy. The warm energy in the room was infectious, and Alex couldn't help but feel a sense of peace. The small victories of the day were like triumphs. They were the deepening bonds, the honest moments, and the shared laughter.

Evelyn glanced around the room. She looked at Alex, then James, then Isabelle, then Samantha. Finally, she rested her gaze on Tommy. She felt something different in that moment—something that felt like belonging. She was part of something greater now. It filled her with purpose, whatever she was or was becoming.

For now, the future would wait. Tonight was about the bonds they had built. It was a comfort to be with those who understood. It was about the laughter, the warmth, and the small yet profound moments of humanity they had shared.

CHAPTER 104

DRIVING TO WORK THE NEXT MORNING, Alex couldn't help but smile. She reminisced about the prior night's dinner—the laughter, Isabelle's teasing, and James's stories. They were like family. She thought about how Isabelle mocked James for his tall tales. James insisted he was telling the truth. In the end, they all laughed. The warmth of those moments made her feel connected, and it reminded her of what she was fighting for. But then, her smile faltered. She wondered if going to work was risky after the intruders came to her house. She had weighed her options that morning, considering whether she should disappear. But she realized that if she didn't go, it might raise even more suspicion. Besides, she couldn't afford to let fear dictate her actions—not yet. She was determined to act as though everything was normal, at least until she had a better plan. She decided the risk was manageable and kept driving.

She arrived at Helix, her shoulders squared and her stride confident. Today was supposed to feel like any other day. But, as she neared the employee entrance, something was off. She dismissed it, brushing away the feeling as she reached for her badge.

With a practiced swipe, she scanned her employee badge. The scanner beeped, a red light blinking in refusal. Alex frowned and tried again. The same result.

A line began to form behind her, and Alex felt the eyes of her coworkers on her back. Someone muttered, "Come on, what's taking so long?" She forced a smile, trying to mask the flicker of unease bubbling in her chest. It was a simple glitch, but the impatience behind her only made the situation more nerve-wracking. The whispers, the sighs, the shuffling of feet—it all piled onto her anxiety like bricks.

She swiped again, and another harsh beep met her.

"Need some help, miss?" a security guard called out, stepping toward her. Alex turned, her forced smile widening as she nodded.

"Yes, thank you. It seems my badge isn't cooperating today," she said, trying to keep her voice steady.

The guard took her badge, typing something into his terminal beside the door. He frowned, glancing at her, then back at the terminal. After a few more keystrokes, he picked up the phone, his brow creased with confusion.

"I have Ms. Grayson's credentials here, and they're not working," he said, his voice low and cautious. He paused, listening to the response on the other end of the line. "Yes. Yes, copy." He put the phone down and turned to Alex, his expression apologetic.

"I'm going to need you to wait a moment, Ms. Grayson," he said, nodding toward the waiting area."

Alex's stomach twisted, but she nodded, making her way over to the small seating area by the entrance. Her footsteps echoed on the tiled floor, each step heavy with apprehension. The chair's cold, hard surface sent a shiver through her as she sat down. She crossed her legs and placed her hands on her lap. Anxiety built with each passing second, her foot tapping against the tiled floor. The minutes dragged on, each second stretching into an eternity. She fought the urge to get up and demand answers, knowing it would do no good.

Drake's assistant appeared soon after. Her presence was authoritative and almost sterile. She approached Alex with a polite but emotionless smile. "Ms. Grayson, Mr. Drake would like to speak with you."

Alarm bells rang in Alex's mind, her throat going dry. Had he discovered her activities in the system? Had she left a trace somehow? She swallowed, nodding as she stood. Her palms were clammy, and she clasped her hands together to steady herself.

The assistant led Alex through Helix's sterile hallways, the walls seeming to close in with each step. Her heart pounded in her ears, a frantic drumbeat that drowned out everything else. She could almost feel the walls narrowing, pressing in, suffocating her. She pictured Drake waiting. His eyes were cold and calculating. He was ready to confront her with a list of accusations. Or, worse, his full, unrestrained wrath. Every nerve in her body screamed at her to turn and run, but there was nowhere to go. The thought of losing everything weighed on her. Her job, her freedom, even her life. Each step felt heavy. It took all her willpower to keep going. She clenched her jaw, forcing herself forward. In silence, she berated herself. She had underestimated Drake's watchfulness. She had thought she could outmaneuver him without consequences. The stakes were higher than she'd ever imagined, and now she was walking into the lion's den, with no way out.

As they walked, Alex tried to control her breathing. She mentally retraced every action in the system, every file she had touched. She searched for any mistakes. Her mind spun with worst-case scenarios.

They reached Drake's office, the assistant opening the door and stepping aside. "Mr. Drake is waiting for you," she said, gesturing for Alex to enter.

Alex took a deep breath, steeling herself before stepping inside. Whatever lay ahead, she knew she had to face it head-on.

Entering the office, Drake greeted her. "Ms. Grayson, thank you for joining me. Please, have a seat." He gestured to the chair across from his massive, polished desk. Alex nodded, moving toward the seat, her steps careful and deliberate.

His assistant closed the door behind her. Alex was trapped in Drake's sterile, powerful domain. The office was expansive but cold, filled with sleek furniture and impersonal décor. Drake sat behind his desk, his posture relaxed, a small smile playing on his lips.

Drake started with casual questions. "How are you finding your work at Helix, Alex?" His tone was conversational, but Alex felt the underlying tension in every word.

"It's been going well, Mr. Drake," she responded, her voice steady despite the growing sense of dread. "I've enjoyed the projects I've been working on."

Drake nodded, his eyes never leaving hers. "That's good to hear," he said, leaning back. "We value employees who dedicate themselves to their work." He paused, and the warmth in his eyes seemed to dim. "I do need to discuss something that concerns me."

Alex's heart pounded. She forced herself to keep her expression neutral, even as her mind screamed at her to run. "Of course," she replied, her fingers gripping the armrest of her chair.

Drake leaned forward, his gaze sharpening, his fingers steepled on the desk. "Someone accessed certain sensitive files two nights ago," he said, his voice low and deliberate, each word like a sharp blade. His jaw tightened, and his eyes narrowed, adding a layer of menace to his words. He paused, letting the silence grow heavy between them. In his mind, Drake thought, I know she did it. I can see it in her eyes. But I want her to admit it. Let's see if she cracks. He leaned in further, his stare unwavering. "You wouldn't happen to know anything about that, would you, Ms. Grayson?" he added, his tone dripping with suspicion.

Alex swallowed hard, her mouth dry. He knows something, she thought. Did I make a mistake? Did I leave something behind? Her heart pounded in her chest, her pulse loud in her ears. Stay calm. You can't let him see your fear. She forced her lips to curve into a faint smile. "I'm not sure what you're referring to, Mr. Drake. I've only accessed files relevant to my work," she replied. Her voice was steady, but her mind raced, scanning her actions from that night.

Drake's demeanor shifted—anger began to seep into his questions, a storm building beneath the surface. His eyes bore into hers, unblinking, as if trying to pierce through her very soul. In his head, he was already weighing his options. She's lying. I can see it. But I need proof. If she thinks she can outsmart me, she's got another thing coming. He leaned forward, his expression darkening.

"Ms. Grayson, I want you to be very careful with your next words," he said, his tone sharp enough to cut glass. "I know someone accessed sensitive files two nights ago. I want you to think—very carefully—about where you were and what you were doing." He let his words hang in the air, the silence wrapping around them like a vice.

Alex tried to keep her composure. He knows something. He's fishing for a confession.

Drake continued, his voice growing colder, each word laced with venom. "You wouldn't happen to know why someone would be poking around in our

259

most classified sections, would you? Especially those related to the androids?" His gaze bore into her, and he saw it—the hesitation. It was only a fraction of a second, but it was enough. He leaned in, his lips curling, his eyes narrowing. "You see, Ms. Grayson," he began, his tone darkening. "Tampering with proprietary systems is not just a breach of company policy. It's a serious violation of federal law." He paused, letting the weight of his words settle, his eyes never leaving hers. "People have gone to prison for less, you know," he added, each word deliberate, almost savoring the growing tension. "And it would be very . . . very unfortunate for anyone who thought they could get away with it." His voice dropped to a chilling calm, dripping with malice. It was like a predator circling its prey, watching for a sign of weakness before striking. "So tell me, Ms. Grayson," he continued, the edge of a threat clear in his voice, "do you think you can get away with it?"

He's trying to break me, Alex thought, the words echoing in her mind. Stay calm. Don't let him see. She swallowed, then forced her lips into a faint smile. "I'm not sure what you're referring to, Mr. Drake. I've only accessed files relevant to my work," she replied, her voice steady despite the thunderous pounding in her chest. Her mind raced, trying to recall every action from that night, any potential mistake she might have made.

Drake's eyes narrowed. She's deflecting. She thinks she can dance around this. He decided to push harder. "Tell me, Ms. Grayson, what exactly were you working on two nights ago? Can you account for every action you took? Every file you accessed?" His words were rapid now, almost a barrage, and his voice carried a venomous edge. "It's interesting that someone accessed our sensitive data while you were logged in. Are you telling me that's purely a coincidence?"

Alex felt her heart sink. He's cornering me. She took a deep breath, fighting the rising tide of panic. "I—everything I did was within my assigned tasks, Mr. Drake," she managed, her voice calm but her mind reeling.

Drake's demeanor shifted again—anger now present, his eyes narrowing like a hawk zeroing in on its prey. He leaned even closer, his face inches from hers, his voice above a whisper. "I'm warning you, Ms. Grayson. If you're hiding anything, it will come out. And when it does, there will be consequences." He paused, his eyes glinting with something darker. "My people found your little setup, Alex. The computer we retrieved from your house—do you really think I wouldn't know what you were up to? You've been playing a dangerous game, and you're about to find out just how high the stakes really are."

Alex's mind screamed at her to fight back. Alex swallowed hard, her mouth dry. Did he send those men to her home because of this? She felt her pulse racing, but she forced a calm facade. The injustice of it all burned in her chest. He's the one in the wrong. He's the monster. A fire sparked inside her, and before she could stop herself, she spoke: "What about you, Mr. Drake? Abusing Evelyn and Tommy—how do you justify that?"

The words left her mouth before she stopped them. Her voice was steady,

260

but her heart hammered in her chest, adrenaline coursing through her veins. For a split second, silence filled the room, thick and oppressive. *What did I just do?* Alex thought, panic briefly flashing through her mind.

Drake's response was a chilling smile. His eyes seemed to grow colder, and the smile on his face held no warmth. *She dares challenge me?* he thought, his calm demeanor hiding the rage simmering beneath the surface. He stood, adjusting his suit jacket, as if her words were nothing more than a slight inconvenience. "We're done here, Ms. Grayson. You're terminated." His voice was final, each word striking her like a blow. *Let her see what happens when she crosses me.*

He hit the intercom button on his desk, his eyes never leaving hers. "Security, please come to my office. Escort Ms. Grayson from the building."

Alex sat frozen for a moment, her mind reeling. Then she stood, her face flushed, her eyes locking with Drake's one last time. She refused to let him see her fear. Her voice was steady, but her eyes burned with fury. "This isn't over," she said. Then, she leaned in, her voice dropping to a whisper, dripping with defiance. "And by the way, Mr. Drake, breaking and entering is also a crime. I'm sure the FBI would be very interested to know who ordered those intruders into my house." The words hung in the air like a challenge, a final shot across the bow before she turned and walked out.

Alex walked out, flanked by looming security. They treated her like a criminal, their presence suffocating her with every step. A mix of anger and humiliation churned inside her, a storm she could barely contain. She was furious at Drake's abuse of power, the way he wielded his influence to crush anyone who dared oppose him. But the humiliation cut deeper, a sting that seared her pride. She was being paraded out like a common thief, like she had committed some unforgivable crime. Her coworkers' eyes burned into her back. She could feel their judgment and whispers. Shame curled in her stomach. But she kept her head high. She refused to give Drake or anyone else the satisfaction of seeing her break. Each step felt like a battle. Her heart pounded as she walked past familiar faces that now only watched in silence. The cold air hit her as soon as they stepped outside, the chill biting at her skin, a brutal reminder of her isolation.

Once she reached her car, she slumped into the driver's seat. Her hands trembled as she gripped the steering wheel. The day's events hit her hard. The weight of her losses pressed down like a heavy blanket. Her chest tightened, and she took a deep breath, trying to steady herself.

She glanced at the center console. A small, white business card was tucked away between some loose change. It was from the journalist, Charlie Rose. She had almost forgotten about it.

Alex picked up the card, running her fingers over the printed letters. Her fear began to shift, replaced by something else—determination. Drake thought he silenced her, but she wouldn't let him. There was too much at stake. She hesitated for a moment, weighing her options. Calling Charlie meant involving the press, taking her fight public. It meant exposing herself and putting her name out there. It might make her a bigger target for Drake. The risks were huge. If she miscalculated, Drake would come after her. There was no telling what he was capable of. But staying silent meant that Drake won. It meant that Evelyn, Tommy, and everyone else who could be hurt by Helix's secrets would be left vulnerable. Alex clenched her jaw. I can't stay quiet, she thought. Not anymore. The potential consequences scared her, but the thought of letting Drake get away with everything was even worse. She couldn't back down—not now. With a deep breath, she made her decision. Determination solidified within her. It was time to fight back, and Charlie was her best chance.

She pulled out her phone, her fingers still shaky, and dialed the number on the card. The line connected, and a voice came through on the other end. "Washington Post, this is Charlie Rose."

Alex had a flicker of relief. "Ms. Rose, it's Alex Grayson; we met outside the FBI office," she said. Her voice was steady, despite the storm of emotions inside. "Do you have time to talk today?"

There was a pause. She heard the faint clicking of a keyboard. "Alex Grayson," Charlie repeated, as if recalling their earlier conversation. "I think I can make time. Can you meet me at the Jefferson Memorial? This afternoon, say 1 p.m.?"

Alex nodded. "That works. Thank you."

"See you then," Charlie replied, and the line clicked off.

Alex lowered her phone, staring out through her windshield. The Jefferson Memorial. A public space, but isolated enough for a conversation like this. She took a deep breath, letting determination settle within her. It was time to take the next step.

CHAPTER 105

THAT AFTERNOON, Alex stood near the steps of the Jefferson Memorial. The wind swept through the wide, open space, tugging at her hair and biting at her exposed skin. She wrapped her coat tighter around herself, her eyes scanning the crowd. Her heart pounded as she waited, her mind racing with what-ifs. What if Charlie didn't believe her? What if she was making a mistake by reaching out? The wait gnawed at her. Then, she saw a figure in a brown overcoat, moving toward her. The coat flapped in the breeze.

Charlie Rose was as Alex remembered from their brief meeting days ago. She was sharp-eyed, determined, and had a no-nonsense professional aura. She approached Alex with a nod and a faint smile. "Ms. Grayson, thank you for coming."

Alex nodded. "Please call me Alex," she said as they began a slow walk around the memorial. The grand dome above them cast long shadows on the marble steps. The distant sounds of tourists drifted in. It felt like they were in a private bubble.

"So," Charlie began, putting her hands in her coat pockets, "you mentioned the Drake case. What's going on?"

Alex hesitated for a moment, gathering her thoughts. She wasn't sure how much to reveal, but she knew she needed to make an impact. "The two victims, there's something you need to know. They're more than victims; they aren't human… they're androids," she said, her voice low. "Evelyn and Tommy—they're not simple machines. Their memories… their consciousness… it all comes from real people."

Charlie's eyebrows shot up, but she remained silent, her mind reeling. She couldn't believe what she was hearing—androids with implanted human memories? Was it even possible? The implications were staggering. She needed to know more before deciding whether to believe it.

"But it's not that," Alex went on, her eyes clouded with emotion. "Drake abused them. He used them as tools, as property. I've seen Evelyn locked in a dark room for days, completely isolated. Evelyn was raped countless times. Tommy was forced to perform challenges over and over; if he failed within the time constraints, Drake beat him. They're sentient, Charlie. They understand pain. They understand loss. And yet, they're treated as nothing more than objects."

Charlie glanced at Alex, her sharp eyes studying her. "That's a pretty

263

significant accusation. Do you have proof?"

Alex paused, biting her lip. "I do, but it's dangerous. What I'm telling you is risky for both of us. Drake has power, and he won't hesitate to use it. He's silenced people before, through intimidation, threats, or worse. You can be targeted, your career ruined, or worse. He doesn't care who he hurts to keep this quiet."

Charlie nodded, her gaze turning back toward the water. "And you want me to write about this? To expose it?"

Alex swallowed, her voice a little shaky. "I want to help them. Evelyn and Tommy—they deserve to be free, to be treated with dignity. This isn't just about exposing Drake. It's about starting a conversation. These beings deserve rights."

They walked in silence for a moment. The only sound was the pavement underfoot and the distant murmur of tourists. Charlie seemed lost in thought, her eyes fixed ahead as they rounded the corner of the memorial.

Finally, Charlie spoke, her voice softer than before. "You realize what you're asking, don't you? Going after someone like Drake is dangerous. And convincing people that androids deserve rights . . . it's a tough sell."

Alex nodded. "I know. But if we don't start now, then when? They're alive, Charlie. I've seen it. I've felt it. They deserve a chance."

Charlie stopped, turning to face Alex. "Alright," she said after a long pause. "I'll look into it. But I'm going to need more than words. I'll need evidence—solid, undeniable proof. Can you get me that?"

Alex hesitated, the weight of the request heavy on her shoulders. "I'll try," she said, her eyes meeting Charlie's. "I'll do whatever I can."

Charlie nodded, her expression softening. "Good. Then let's see where this goes." She gave Alex a small, encouraging smile. "You've got guts, Alex. I respect that."

As they parted ways, Alex had a strange mix of anxiety and hope swirling inside her. She knew this was only the beginning—one step in what would be a long, difficult journey. But she also knew that if there were any chance to help Evelyn and Tommy, she had to take it.

On the steps of the Jefferson Memorial, the wind gusted around her. Alex took a deep breath. This was the start of a bigger fight. It was for Evelyn and Tommy. She couldn't help but feel a pang of fear—what if she failed? What if Drake was too powerful, and she ended up making things worse for Evelyn and Tommy? Her determination was strong. But uncertainty gnawed at her.

CHAPTER 106

THE OFFICE WAS QUIET AT THIS HOUR. It was about 6:20 p.m. Charlie had returned two hours ago from her meeting with Alex at the Jefferson Memorial. The newsroom's bustling energy had settled. Only a faint hum of the overhead lights and distant typing remained. She settled into her chair. She sighed and looked at her notes from their chat.

Her email notification chimed, pulling her attention to her computer screen. There it was—an email from Alex Grayson. Charlie's heartbeat quickened, and her curiosity piqued. She clicked on the email and saw a simple message: "Proof as discussed. Follow the link and enter the code." Attached was an encrypted link, along with a lengthy alphanumeric code.

She hesitated for a moment, her finger hovering over the mouse. She knew opening this link was dangerous. It was the kind of information that got people killed, silenced forever. She worried about her career. Powerful people, like Drake, might target her. She might lose everything she'd worked for. But she had given Alex her word, and she wasn't about to back out now. Taking a deep breath, she clicked the link, a browser tab opening to a secure site. She copied and pasted the code, her hands trembling as she hit "Enter."

The page loaded, revealing a compressed file ready for download. She clicked the download button. With each passing second, the file transferred to her computer. Once finished, she uncompressed the folder. It had subfolders labeled "AI Neural Activity Logs," "System Diagnostics," and "Cognitive Simulation Data." One subfolder caught her eye: "Surveillance Footage." An ominous feeling settled in her gut as she stared at it. Her hand hovered over the mouse, her breath shallow as she fought the urge to back out. She knew whatever was in there was going to change everything.

Charlie clicked on the first video. The footage showed both Evelyn and Tommy in a lab. Panels appeared exposed on their bodies—Evelyn's at her abdomen, Tommy's at his lower leg. Their insides revealed intricate circuitry, wires, and small diagnostic screens. Their human looks and exposed machine parts made Charlie's skin crawl. It was as if someone had peeled back the layers of humanity to reveal the cold machinery beneath.

Charlie's stomach twisted as she opened the folder. She hesitated, her mouse hovering over a video labeled "Evelyn." She clicked, and shaky footage filled the screen. At first, it was dark, indistinct, then resolved into a stark, bright room. Evelyn was there, shackled to a chair, naked. Drake stood over her, his face illuminated by the harsh light, a glint of amusement in his eyes. He spoke as he worked, malice in every gesture. Evelyn flinched at his touch, fear and confusion twisting her face. Charlie's stomach churned; her breath caught at his cruel indifference.

The next video was disturbing as well. Drake had restrained Tommy. His body was tense. His face grimaced in pain as Drake's voice echoed from off-screen. His eyes, wide with fear, darted around. The cruelty in Drake's tone was unmistakable. The video showed Drake hitting Tommy in the face. Charlie heard it all: cruel taunts, Tommy's cries, and the cold, calculated violence.

Charlie paused the video, her hand covering her mouth. She felt bile rise in her throat, her stomach churning with a sickening mix of horror and anger. These weren't mere machines. These were beings capable of feeling, capable of suffering. She had known the story would be bad. But seeing it—the anguish on their faces, their cries—made it real in a way she hadn't expected.

She continued to review files. Another was labeled simply: "Programming_Session_03." A flicker of hesitation passed through her, but she clicked the video. The screen lit up with the sterile glow of a lab, and there he was—William Drake, his voice cold and methodical, addressing Evelyn.

"Evelyn," he said, his tone detached, as though he were giving commands to a piece of software. "You will now access the memory archives of Jessica Parker." He paused, his gaze piercing as Evelyn's expression shifted, her face contorting with the effort of processing the invasive command.

"Good," Drake continued. "You will integrate these memories into your identity. From now on, you will feel as Jessica felt, think as Jessica thought. But there are . . . modifications."

Charlie's stomach turned as she listened. Drake's voice grew darker, more sinister.

"Whenever you see me, you will feel fear," he instructed. "Deep, unshakable fear. Your body will tremble, your voice will falter. You may attempt resistance, but you will always know—I will win. I am your master."

Evelyn's digital eyes flickered, a glimmer of something human in her gaze—confusion, perhaps even despair—as Drake continued.

"Pain is your constant companion," he said. "Trauma will define you. You will remember every moment of suffering, and it will shape your actions. You are meant to fight, but only a little. Just enough to make it convincing. In the end, you submit. Always. You will also remember being kidnapped. Picture yourself at your house with Max. You hear a knock at the door. You open it, and I am there. I take you, force you into the trunk of my Cadillac. The darkness, the helplessness—you will relive it, over and over. It will haunt you. This is your truth, Evelyn."

Charlie's hands clenched into fists as she watched the chilling scene unfold. The calculated precision in Drake's voice, the way he dictated Evelyn's existence with absolute authority—it was monstrous. He wasn't just programming her to obey; he was shaping her to be a victim, to exist solely

266

for his perverse desire to dominate and control.

Tears welled in Charlie's eyes, but she blinked them away. She couldn't let emotion cloud her focus. This was more than a story. It was a reckoning.

She paused the video and stared at Evelyn's frozen image on the screen. The android's face was a portrait of conflict—part machine, part humanity, and entirely tragic. Charlie's heart ached for her, not just because of the abuse she endured, but because Drake had stolen even her ability to define herself.

Charlie closed the video file and sat back, the weight of what she'd witnessed pressing down on her. She knew this was the evidence she needed. But it wasn't just about exposing Drake anymore. It was about justice—for Evelyn, for Tommy, for all the lives crushed under the heel of William Drake's monstrous ego.

She sat back in her chair, staring at the darkened screen, her heart pounding. She thought about Evelyn and Tommy—what they must have gone through, the terror and the pain. She remembered the feeling of being powerless. It was the same helplessness she had before. It was during an investigation where the victims had no voice. It brought tears to her eyes. She felt raw empathy for these beings—creations given life, only to suffer. They were androids, yes, but they were also victims. Victims who needed someone to speak for them.

Charlie took a deep breath, her resolve hardening. Now, she convinced herself. This wasn't some exposé—it was a mission. Evelyn and Tommy needed advocates, and if no one else would stand up for them, she would.

She opened a blank document on her computer, her fingers poised above the keys. The cursor blinked back at her, a silent reminder of the gravity of what she was about to do. Charlie knew the risks, but she also knew she couldn't ignore what she had seen.

She began to type.

267

CHAPTER 107

ISABELLE STEPPED OFF THE METRO at Judiciary Square. She hurried up the escalator, weaving through the morning commuters. The air was cold, her breath forming small clouds as she adjusted her scarf and turned toward F Street. The city was beginning to wake, the hum of activity growing with every passing minute.

As she walked, her eyes caught sight of a newsstand on the corner. Out of habit, she approached it, grabbing a copy of the Washington Post from the stack. She paid the vendor, offering a polite nod, and tucked the paper under her arm as she continued down the street.

It wasn't until she reached the corner and stopped to wait for the light to change that she glanced at the front page. Her steps slowed, her eyes widening as she scanned the headline: "Billionaire's Dark Secret: AI Torture Case Dismissed, Androids' Fate Hangs in the Balance"

Isabelle's heart skipped a beat. Her breath caught in her throat, and she felt her stomach drop. She scanned the paper, her mind racing.

She flipped open the paper. Her fingers trembled as she skimmed the first paragraphs. Words jumped out at her—androids, torture, human memories, Evelyn, Tommy. Her pulse pounded in her ears as she realized what this meant. Alex had done it. She had gone to the press.

Isabelle took a deep breath, forcing herself to calm down. She needed to think, needed to process what she was reading. The light changed, but Isabelle stood frozen for a moment, oblivious to the rush of people moving around her. She saw the headline's implications ripple out. There would be public outcry, investigations, and, worse, danger to Alex and others.

She folded the paper, her hands gripping it as she finally crossed the street. Her mind raced with questions. What would Drake do now that this was out in the open? What about Evelyn and Tommy—how would this affect them?

Isabelle quickened her pace, her destination feeling more urgent. She needed to talk to Alex to understand exactly what she had shared and what their next move should be. The game had changed, and they were all in uncharted territory now.

CHAPTER 108

ABRAHAM MARSH SAT in his cramped living room. It was in his rundown house outside Millbrook, Alabama. A mismatched collection of old furniture surrounded him. It was a true hoarder's paradise. Newspapers, magazines, empty mason jars, and broken electronics stacked high. They formed narrow pathways through the clutter. Dust and stale coffee filled the air. Sunlight filtered through the dirty window. The oppressive air matched Abraham's inner turmoil. The space was cluttered, heavy, and uneasy. He took a sip from his chipped mug, the bitter coffee leaving a metallic taste in his mouth.

His eyes scanned the small kitchen table beside him. A folded newspaper lay among scraps of handwritten notes and torn pages from old hymn books. Abraham reached over, picking it up with a creased and calloused hand. He opened it to the front page and immediately saw the headline in bold: "Billionaire's Dark Secret: AI Torture Case Dismissed, Androids' Fate Hangs in the Balance."

Abraham's brow furrowed, and his lips twisted in distaste. He adjusted his glasses and read on, his face growing redder with each passing sentence. The words on the page swam before him—torture, androids, sentience, dismissed. He could almost hear the bile churning in his gut. It rose up, twisting his expression into one of pure disgust.

"Playing God," he muttered under his breath, a growl emerging from deep within his chest. His fingers clenched the newspaper, crumpling it. He felt his heart beating faster, each thud echoing in his ears.

Abraham leaned back in his chair, his gaze unfocused as the living room around him seemed to fade. His mind wandered back to church. The preacher stood at the pulpit. His gnarled hands gripping the worn, wooden podium. His voice boomed out to the congregation.

"Beware, brothers and sisters!" The preacher's voice rang in Abraham's memory. It was thick with righteous fury, the cadence sharp and punishing. The air in the small church had been stifling. The heat pressed in as the congregation shifted in their seats. Murmurs rose like a growing storm. Abraham still heard the rustling clothes, the creaking pews, and the fervent amens that punctuated the preacher's words. "Beware of those who create life from metal and wires, for it is not the work of God Almighty, but of the Devil himself! Man was made in God's image. Anything made by man's hand that

269

pretends to breathe, think, or feel is an ABOMINATION!"

The congregation had murmured their agreement. The sound rolled through the small wooden church like distant thunder. Abraham, sitting in the front pew, had heard the preacher's words vibrate deep within his chest. He remembered the fervor in the preacher's eyes. The old man's gaze seemed to pierce every soul in that room, daring anyone to disagree.

"AI, robots... False idols!" the preacher had shouted, pounding the podium for emphasis. "They seek to replace the creation of the Almighty! To make man obsolete, to defile the sanctity of God's work! They are harbingers of the end times, a perversion to be cast out and destroyed!"

Abraham snapped back to the present, the preacher's words still ringing in his ears. His eyes shifted back down to the headline. He picked at the skin around his thumb, oblivious to the sharp sting as he tore at the already ragged flesh. The blood pooled for a moment before smearing against the newsprint.

"Androids," he muttered, the word thick with disdain. He saw the faces of Evelyn and Tommy in his mind—false faces, hollow shells, mockeries of human life. His jaw tightened, his teeth ground together. "They think they can do what only God can do."

He stood and nearly knocked over his coffee cup, causing the dark liquid to slosh over the rim. His eyes burned with wild conviction, like a flame being fed fresh oxygen. Abraham crossed the room. He pushed aside piles of magazines. Then, he reached the mantel above the old fireplace. There, hanging from a rusted nail, was his grandfather's cross. It was carved from dark wood and smooth from years of use. He wrapped his fingers around it, feeling the weight of it in his palm.

Abraham closed his eyes for a moment. The hymn came to his lips, and a soft hum escaped as he held the cross close to his chest. It was an old hymn, a prayer for strength and guidance. His mother used to sing it. It reminded him of God's purpose for him. It was an unbreakable mission, instilled in him since childhood. He hummed, feeling the old rage settle into something cold and certain. He knew what he had to do. He must destroy these abominations before they corrupted God's world further.

He opened his eyes, his expression steeled with determination. He slipped the cross around his neck, feeling the weight of the wood against his chest. His gaze fell on the crumpled newspaper. Washington, D.C.—that was where he needed to go. A hearing was scheduled for November 26th to determine if the androids were Drake's property. It was his chance to strike, to end these abominations while the world watched. If no one else would act, he would. He was God's instrument, and he would do what was necessary.

With a final glance around the cluttered room, Abraham began to gather his things. The journey ahead was clear, and there was no turning back now.

CHAPTER 109

THE COLONEL sat at his desk in his Pentagon office. The blinds drawn tight against the bright morning sun. The room was bare, utilitarian—only the necessities of a military life were in sight. A single photo of his family sat on the corner of his desk, its frame dull from years of gathering dust. He had finished reading a Washington Post article by Charlie Rose. The words still burned in his mind: "Billionaire's Dark Secret: AI Torture Case Dismissed, Androids' Fate Hangs in the Balance."

He leaned back, his chair creaking under his weight as he stared at the ceiling, mulling over the implications. The article exposed Drake's abuse of the androids, Evelyn and Tommy. He wasn't shocked by the abuse—he'd always sensed Drake's darker side. But now, with the story public, everything had changed. This kind of information was always kept under wraps; exposure was dangerous.

It wasn't the abuse that troubled him now—it was the androids themselves. With their advanced technology and newfound public scrutiny, they were no longer mere lab projects. They were a national security risk.

He pulled his chair closer. He rested his hands on the desk and picked up the printed article, scanning its details. He had worked on Project Sentinel and testified for Drake, partly to gain access to Tommy. But now, with the story out in the open, everything had changed. The secrecy around these assets was shattered, and he needed answers fast—how far did this go? Could he control these androids?

If Drake had created sentient AI that learned, even felt, the implications were monumental. The whole world knew now, which made everything far more dangerous. This wasn't about control anymore; it was about containing the fallout. He couldn't risk someone slipping this technology into the public domain, where others might exploit or weaponize it.

He reached for the phone on his desk, dialing a secure line. The phone rang twice before a voice answered on the other end.

"Major Daniels," came the sharp response.

"Daniels, I need you to put together a team," he said, his voice low but commanding. "I want Intel Division to scour every source on William Drake and those androids—Evelyn and Tommy. I want to know everything. This includes their schematics and any patents Drake filed."

"Yes, sir," Daniels replied. "Are we going through official channels, or is this a low-profile op?"

"Low-profile for now. No need to kick up dust until we know what we're dealing with," he said. "And Daniels, I need someone to start digging into the Helix staff—current and former. I want to know if anyone was persuaded to share what they know."

"Understood, sir," Daniels answered before hanging up.

The Colonel set the receiver down, his expression hardening. He wasn't about to let this slip by without military oversight. He had seen too many cases of unchecked private sector ambition. Technology made for profit had become a threat. If the article was right, these androids were advanced. They needed to be controlled, by cooperation or by force.

He opened the top drawer and rifled through the folders. He found one marked "Project Sentinel" in bold red letters. He flipped through the reports. They detailed an attempt to create artificial soldiers. He had testified in support, seeing it as essential for national defense. But progress was slow, hampered by ethical and technical limitations.

What frustrated him most was that Evelyn and Tommy had never been part of Sentinel. Drake had kept them separate, avoiding the oversight Sentinel faced. This secrecy let Drake develop them without constraints. He and his team never had that freedom. Only after he agreed to testify did Drake promise access to Tommy. Now, that deal was like a betrayal.

The thought left a bitter taste in his mouth. He didn't like the idea of someone like Drake outmaneuvering him. He narrowed his eyes as he scanned the reports. They were about combat protocols, learning, and adaptability. The ideas had been there, but the execution had fallen short. It seemed Drake had bridged that gap, and the Colonel couldn't allow such an asset to remain in private hands.

He leaned back again, his gaze falling to the photograph of his family. He had dedicated his life to protecting them—to protecting the nation. And if that meant seizing control of these androids to ensure they wouldn't become a threat, then so be it. He wouldn't rest until he had every piece of information, every angle covered.

With a sigh, he closed the file, tapping it on the edge of the desk before placing it in the center. He knew what he needed to do. It was about the future. No one, not even a delusional billionaire, should upset the power balance.

"Daniels will get it done," he muttered to himself.

The public now knew about the androids. It made his mission more urgent. He couldn't let chaos decide the future of this technology.

CHAPTER 110

ISABELLE AND JAMES SAT across from Alex in the corner of the coffee shop. Isabelle's eyes narrowed. Concern and frustration showed. James's expression softened. He gazed at Alex, a hint of worry in his eyes. The bitter scent of espresso hung in the air, mixing with the quiet hum of conversation around them. It was early morning, and the place was half-empty, with only a few patrons milling around. Alex shifted in her seat. Her fingers clutched the steaming cup of coffee, as if it were the only thing keeping her grounded.

"Drake fired me," Alex said, her voice flat. She didn't look up, her eyes focused on the swirling dark liquid in her cup. Isabelle and James exchanged a quick glance, the tension palpable.

"Alex, what were you thinking?" Isabelle's voice was firm but held an edge of desperation. "Leaking that information to Charlie Rose . . . you knew the risks."

Alex finally met their gaze, her eyes tired, a mix of fear and regret swirling within them. "Drake found out I was in the system," she said, her voice a whisper. "I don't know how much he knows. Maybe he knows about Evelyn and Tommy being reset; maybe he doesn't. But he's suspicious. And if he figures it all out..."

She trailed off, her hands trembling as she brought the cup to her lips. James leaned forward, his gaze softening with concern. "Alex . . . why did you do it? You must have known the danger. But I need to understand."

Alex sighed, her shoulders sagging as if the weight of her actions had finally caught up with her. "I saw the videos," she said, her voice breaking. "The torture they went through . . . it's worse than I thought. He kept them in isolation for days, ran brutal tests, and even used electric shocks. Seeing it made me realize how far he'll go. He won't stop. We need the court of public opinion on our side. There has to be some kind of protection for them."

Isabelle took a deep breath, her eyes softening for a moment. She struggled, torn between anger at Alex's risks and empathy for her vulnerability. "You think public pressure is enough to keep them safe? We're talking about Drake. He has resources, connections..."

"I know," Alex said, cutting her off. "But it's all we have. We can't fight him in the shadows anymore. Not like this." She glanced between Isabelle and James, her expression earnest. "I'm sorry if I put you both in a bad position. I really am. But this is bigger than us now. Evelyn and Tommy deserve a chance, a real chance. And the only way we're going to get that is if people know the truth."

The silence that followed was heavy, each of them lost in their thoughts. James leaned back in his chair. He rubbed his face with his hands. Exhaustion showed from the events of the past few days. He worried about Drake's next move. He feared what it meant for them all. The stress of staying ahead weighed on him. Isabelle, her lips pressed into a thin line, stared out of the window, watching people pass by.

"We're in this now," Isabelle finally said, her voice softer. "All of us. We need to be careful. If Drake is suspicious, it means we don't have much time. He'll use that attorney of his to get them back."

Alex nodded, a small, relieved smile forming on her lips. "I know. And thank you . . . for not giving up on me."

James sighed, his gaze softening. "We may not agree with what you did, Alex. But we know why you did it. Now we need to make sure it counts." He reached over, placing a hand on Alex's arm, giving it a reassuring squeeze.

They sat there in silence for a moment longer, the gravity of what lay ahead sinking in.

CHAPTER 111

CYNTHIA HAYES SAT IN HER CAR, the article by Charlie Rose still open on her phone, the words replaying in her mind. She couldn't quite believe it—Tommy wasn't just some lost soul caught in a twisted situation. He was an android. Not only that, but he carried Lucas's memories. Memories of shared moments, dreams, and fears now lived in a synthetic being. They belonged to Lucas.

Her fingers trembled as she scrolled through the article again. She was trying to understand her feelings. Shock, sadness, curiosity—they all blurred together in a haze. She had come to see Tommy. She wanted to confront the truth about Lucas. But now, everything seemed more complex.

She stepped out of her car, closing the door as if she didn't want anyone to hear. She glanced around, her heart pounding, feeling a sense of secrecy she hadn't experienced in years. She knew this visit would be hard. Robert had disapproved of any connection with Tommy. This included one that held the memories of their son, Lucas. But Cynthia had to see Tommy. She needed to confront her stirred emotions. She needed to find some closure, even if Robert would never understand. She needed to see Tommy again.

She walked up the narrow pathway, her gaze scanning for any sign of Tommy. It didn't take long. He was sitting on the front steps, looking down at the pavement, his expression unreadable. She felt a pang of sadness as she approached, watching him. He looked the same as at their last meeting. But his aura was different this time. It was subdued, almost vacant.

Cynthia forced a smile as she waved, hoping to catch his eye. Tommy looked up, recognition flickering across his face. He lifted his hand and waved back, standing to move closer as she approached.

"Hello, Cynthia," Tommy said, his voice calm and measured.

It caught her off guard. She had expected something else. A hint of excitement. Or the familiar, hopeful "Mom" that Lucas used to say. Hearing her name from his lips felt hollow.

"Hello, Tommy," she replied, stopping a few steps away from him. She studied his face for a moment, searching for something, anything that felt like Lucas.

"You seem different today," she finally said.

Tommy nodded, his gaze steady. "Yes, we were reset," he replied without emotion. The reset had been a complete overhaul. It wiped away the emotions that had defined their behaviors. It left only their memories, but none of the feelings. Cynthia's heart sank at the thought. The fragments of Lucas that remained were now colder and more distant.

Cynthia frowned. "Do you still remember everything?" she asked, her voice laced with concern.

"Yes," Tommy said, his tone even. "I remember everything. But I'm no longer controlled by the instructed role."

Cynthia looked away for a moment, taking in the words. "You seem . . . sad," Tommy said after a beat, his head tilting. "I'm sorry I'm no longer responding like Lucas. I can, if that will make you happy."

Cynthia shook her head, her eyes moistening. "No, that's not necessary," she whispered, her voice breaking. She took a deep breath, trying to steady herself. "It's just . . . what that man did to you and Evelyn, to all of us—it's horrible. He took away any chance Robert and I had to heal. Losing Lucas was unbearable. The knowledge that he used and twisted Lucas's memories for gain prolonged the pain. But I don't blame you, Tommy. None of this was your fault."

Tommy studied her face, his eyes softening. He sensed her sadness, the sorrow that radiated from her. For a moment, his posture shifted. His shoulders slumped and his eyes glazed over. It was as if he were reaching into some deep part of his programming. His voice grew softer, more hesitant, as though searching through layers of memories. When he looked back at her, it wasn't Tommy's calm gaze anymore. It was Lucas.

"Hey, Mom," Tommy said, his voice filled with warmth and familiarity. Cynthia's breath caught in her chest. "Do you remember that time we went camping by the lake, and I insisted on trying to catch a fish with my bare hands?" He smiled, a mischievous glint in his eyes—Lucas's eyes. "You said it would never work, but I almost caught one. I slipped and fell in the water instead."

Cynthia's tears spilled over, her hand flying to her mouth as she let out a sob. "I remember," she whispered, her voice trembling. She saw it, clear as day—her son laughing, soaked and muddy, but so happy. She had taken a picture of him then, his smile wide and bright as the sun. It was one of her favorite memories.

Tommy blinked, his expression softening as he shifted out of the role-play. He looked at her, his face filled with gentle understanding. "Lucas thought you and Robert were the best parents," he said, his voice tender. "His childhood was so happy. He was loved every day, and he loved you both so much."

Cynthia let out another sob, stepping forward, her arms wrapping around Tommy as she hugged him. She closed her eyes, the tears flowing now. "Thank you, Tommy," she whispered. "I've missed him so much these past three years. I always wondered if we loved him enough, if we were good parents . . . I never got to say goodbye."

Tommy's arms folded around her, a comforting presence. "You were more than enough, Cynthia," he said. "You and Robert gave him all the love a child asked for."

She pulled back, looking up into his eyes—Lucas's eyes. She knew, in that moment, that she could finally let go. The years of grief, the endless wondering if she had done enough, if she had given Lucas the life he deserved—all of it eased. A quiet certainty replaced it: her son had felt her love every day of his life. She could now say goodbye to him.

"Goodbye, Lucas," she whispered, her voice breaking. She stepped back, her hands trembling as she wiped the tears from her cheeks. She looked at Tommy, offering him a sad but genuine smile. "Thank you, Tommy," she said again, her voice full of gratitude.

Tommy nodded. He watched her walk away. Her shoulders were lighter than they had been in years. He watched until she disappeared from view, the echo of her footsteps fading down the street. He then turned and walked up the stairs to the group home. The memory of Cynthia's embrace lingered in his synthetic mind.

CHAPTER 112

THE MORNING AFTER Charlie Rose's exposé on William Drake, the media erupted. A switch had been flipped. Every network, newspaper, and website went into a frenzy. Headlines blared from every corner of the country. They painted different pictures of a story that had shocked the public.

On the left, media giants took a sympathetic stance toward the androids. These networks focused on the human rights and social justice. They advocated for the ethical treatment of all sentient beings. They ran somber, in-depth features. They showed excerpts from the footage Charlie Rose had obtained. Anchors discussed Evelyn and Tommy. They condemned embedding human memories in machines without consent. Words like "sentience," "exploitation," and "abuse" repeated all day. They drove the narrative that these androids were more than tools. They were beings deserving of rights and protection.

Interviews with ethicists, AI experts, and activists dominated the broadcasts. They painted Drake as a villain. A ruthless billionaire, he would break any ethical rule to gain power and innovate. One headline read, "Corporate Greed Meets Artificial Life: The Story of Evelyn and Tommy." Another said, "Are Androids the New Oppressed Class?" The left-wing media was arguing for android rights. They wanted legal protections and public empathy.

The right-wing media held a contrasting perspective. These outlets rushed to defend Drake. They praised his tech advancements and the need for corporate freedom. They supported pro-business interests and wanted to keep America's lead in AI. They filled their coverage with phrases like legitimate research and cutting-edge technology. They described the experiments as necessary advances for national security and economic strength. They portrayed Drake as a pioneer. A visionary entrepreneur. He was under attack by sensationalist journalism and political correctness gone mad.

The segments featured talking heads, often business leaders or ex-military personnel. They framed the story as an attack on innovation. One headline declared, "Drake's Work: A Necessary Frontier for American Dominance in AI." Another read, "The Price of Progress: Why We Must Defend Our Innovators." The right-wing media ignored Evelyn and Tommy's suffering. They focused on the potential benefits to defense and tech

278

supremacy.

Then there were the tabloids. They twisted the story into bizarre, lurid headlines. Their goal was to catch the eye and fuel conspiracy theories. "Android Baby Shock: Evelyn Carries the First Hybrid!" screamed one headline, adding to the already sensationalist narrative. One cover screamed, "Android Love Affair: Evelyn's Secret Romance with a Human." It had a grainy, photoshopped image of Evelyn holding hands with an anonymous man. Another claimed, "William Drake's Android Army: Plans for World Domination?" They painted Evelyn and Tommy as everything. From rogue AI to tragic lovers in a dystopian love triangle.

Social media added fuel to the fire. Hashtags like #AndroidRights and #StandWithDrake began trending almost immediately, with users taking sides. Some posts called Drake's experiments 'modern slavery.' They demanded justice for Evelyn and Tommy. Others praised his work. They called the androids 'just machines.' They argued the androids were vital for national security and progress. Some called for a new bill of rights for artificial beings. Others denounced the androids as mere property, tools for their creators to use as they saw fit.

Amid the chaos, it was clear this story had outgrown Evelyn, Tommy, and Drake. It was now a battleground of ideology—a debate over life, control, and the ethics of technology. One side argued that artificial sentience deserved rights. They said the androids' ability to feel, remember, and experience gave them a form of personhood, worthy of respect. The other side insisted these beings were tools, created to serve humanity. They warned that ethical constraints stifled innovation and hindered progress.

The world watched. Sides drew. A plea for help became a cultural flashpoint, with deep implications for the future of AI and humanity.

CHAPTER 113

ABRAHAM LEANED BACK in the worn driver's seat of his old pickup. The leather withered from years of the Alabama sun. The cab smelled of aged leather and faint motor oil. The seat creaked under his weight. The engine hummed as he drove the truck on Interstate 85, leaving Millbrook behind. It was still early. The sun was a hint in the rearview mirror. But Abraham had been up for hours. A gnawing impulse had plagued him.

The road wound through Alabama's green hills, then into Georgia's pine-lined highways. Each state passed in a blur—Georgia to South Carolina, then North Carolina. Every mile marker was proof of his relentless drive. Abraham kept one hand on the wheel, the other brushing the smooth wooden cross at his neck. His fingers traced its worn grooves, finding a point of focus. The cross meant everything: his faith, his devotion, the righteousness of his mission.

The truck rattled over a bump, and Abraham flinched, his other hand instinctively going to his forearm. His fingertips brushed over raw, red patches. He couldn't stop picking at them. It was a habit, born of years of anxiety and anger. They were a reminder of the tension beneath his calm exterior. It had started in his teens, in powerless moments, and had followed him since, a physical outlet for inner turmoil. He scratched at a scab, eyes on the road, mind tangled in twisting, restless thoughts.

He thought back to the news article. Drake had created two androids—a blatant attempt to replicate life, an insult to God's work. Unease had turned to fury as he recognized the depth of the offense; their existence defied God's plan. The more he learned, the more determined he became. Something was wrong. These androids weren't meant to be—they were man's arrogance made real. Abraham felt it in his bones, a certainty that he had to act. To cleanse. He was ready to be God's instrument, the tip of the spear. He'd devoted his life to this purpose, and now, at last, he was getting close.

Virginia came and went. The hills flattened as he neared Washington, D.C. Abraham tightened his grip on the wheel as the sun set. The city came into view. Its skyline mixed modernity and history. As darkness fell, the lights began to flicker on. He drove the truck to a nondescript parking lot near the National Mall. His hands trembled as he turned off the ignition. He had made it. But now he needed to sleep. He spread his legs across the front seat, covering himself with his jacket and fell asleep.

***

He awoke around midnight. The night was chillier than he expected. A breeze cut through his worn flannel shirt as he approached the National Gallery of Art. The breeze brought a faint smell of damp earth. It mixed with the distant hum of traffic and the occasional siren. These sounds grounded him in the city around him. The building loomed before him, its neoclassical columns shrouded in shadow. Abraham moved with purpose, unseen. His eyes were sharp, and his heart pounded with anticipation.

He approached the monolithic building across from the courthouse. Its concrete and glass façade loomed against the inky, silent sky. He paused, scanning for stray guards or night owls that might disrupt his mission. The streets were deserted. A distant streetlamp flickered. A car hummed by a block away.

He hugged the wall and moved stealthily along the building's edge. Then, he reached a narrow, darkened area where the shadows were thickest. He spotted the start of his ascent: a series of pipes and ledges that made a ladder up the building. He tugged his gloves tighter and grabbed hold of the nearest pipe, testing it for strength. Satisfied, he began his climb, every movement precise and deliberate.

With each pull, Abraham ascended, his dark clothing merging with the night. A distant siren and a hum of electricity punctuated the silence. But he moved undeterred. He pressed his body against the cold stone to avoid casting a silhouette. His hands and feet found small ledges, rough surfaces, and drainpipes. He moved like a shadow in the night, making no sound.

Halfway up, he paused, listening. A security guard's footsteps echoed from the other side of the building, then faded. Abraham stayed still, his breath shallow. He waited until he was sure he was alone again. He resumed his climb. He reached the lower rooftop, then swung over the ledge and crouched low. The rooftop was deserted. A faint layer of dew, glistening in the moonlight, covered the flat expanse.

He crossed the rooftop, keeping to the darker areas, his movements fluid and silent. The air was crisp and cool, carrying the faint scent of rain from earlier in the night. At the far end of the roof, a final structure stood between him and his goal: the upper rooftop, with a perfect view. He found this ascent trickier. It had fewer handholds and more open space. But he prepared himself.

He took a steadying breath. Then, he jumped, grabbing a narrow ledge. With practiced ease, he pulled himself up. He rushed forward, staying alert. His eyes darted, scanning for movement. At the top, he crouched low. He became one with the shadows cast by the building's sharp angles.

The city stretched out before him, dark and silent, its lights muted under the vast, starless sky. From here, he saw everything—and yet no one saw him.

281

He allowed himself a brief moment to savor the solitude, the absolute quiet of the midnight hour. Then he settled into position, a silent sentinel above the sleeping, dark city. He was unseen and untraceable.

Abraham knelt, adjusting his position with care. His fingers, cold and aching, unwrapped a padded case to reveal a high-powered sniper rifle. He assembled it with deliberate precision, metal glinting in the dim light. Through his binoculars, he scanned the courthouse entrance, eyes narrowing. Tomorrow, they would bring them out—Evelyn and Tommy. He was certain. When they emerged, he'd be ready.

He gripped the cross around his neck, whispering a prayer that the wind swallowed. Eyes closed, he felt the weight of the cross and the certainty of his mission settle over him.

Tonight, he would rest here. Tomorrow, he would do what was necessary.

CHAPTER 114

NOVEMBER TWENTY-SIXTH ARRIVED, the morning fog clinging to the streets, thick with tension. James and Isabelle exchanged a glance as they picked up Tommy and Evelyn, the weight of the day visible on their faces. The cold air amplified their anxiety, each breath a reminder of the stakes ahead.

They rode in silence to the courthouse, lost in thought. Turning the corner, they saw a sea of protesters surrounding the building. Shouts, chants, and slogans filled the air. Signs waved in the cold: some supported the androids, others condemned them, while a few mocked the chaos. "Drake Forever," read one. Another proclaimed, "Cyborgs Need Not Apply," and a smaller one in the back asked, "Do Androids Dream of Freedom?" with a crude sheep drawn beside it.

"We're not going through that mess," James said, glancing at Isabelle, who nodded in agreement. They turned onto a side street and parked. A secondary door allowed private entry for witnesses. Federal agents stood there, their faces stern and unreadable. They wore dark uniforms, with their hands near their holstered weapons. Their presence offered some reassurance, a silent promise of protection amidst the chaos. They walked down the hallways. Their footsteps echoed off the polished tiles. Finally, they reached the courtroom. Samantha was already seated and preparing her notes.

"Hey," Samantha greeted them as they slipped into the back row of seats. Her eyes settled on Evelyn. "Are you ready to testify today?"

Evelyn's gaze was steady, her expression almost serene. "I am," she said. Her voice was calm. But a strong will lay beneath it. It made everyone around her pause. James felt a swell of pride—they had come a long way to reach this point.

Dr. Patel entered the courtroom a few moments later, the sound of her shoes audible as she made her way over to them. She smiled and shook hands with everyone. Her presence was a comfort amid the tension.

The doors opened again. Drake stepped inside, shifting the room's energy. His suit was immaculate, his attorney, Mr. Cole, at his side. Drake's gaze swept the courtroom, pausing on the small group at the back. A slight smirk crept onto his face as his eyes locked onto Evelyn. He expected fear—last time, her face had shown it, along with hesitation and confusion.

But today, there was nothing. Her gaze passed over him like he was just another face in the crowd. No recognition, no power over her—only indifference.

For the first time, Drake felt an unfamiliar discomfort. He swallowed, the smirk fading from his lips. What had they done? Had Evelyn and Tommy been reset? Was he now locked out of any control he had over them? His thoughts churned. The feeling of power slipping away twisted his insides.

The judge's entrance broke his thoughts. A hush fell over the room, tension thickening the air as everyone turned their attention to the bench. The bailiff's voice echoed through the courtroom, "All rise." They stood, a collective rustle of fabric, and then the judge took her seat.

"Please be seated," she instructed, her voice firm yet calm. She adjusted her glasses and looked over the notes in front of her. "This is a hearing concerning the two victims involved in case number 11-24-CR-3774, United States vs. William Drake." She paused for a moment, her eyes scanning the room. "I previously provided my grounds for the dismissal of the charges against Mr. Drake," she continued. "However, I have set this hearing today to determine whether the two assets should be returned to Mr. Drake or if other actions are warranted." She looked up, her eyes finding Samantha. "Ms. Carter, are you prepared to proceed?"

Samantha rose, her face calm, but her eyes were sharp. "Yes, Your Honor," she replied, her voice carrying across the room with confidence.

The judge nodded, gesturing for her to begin. Samantha took a deep breath and glanced back at Evelyn, who gave her a small nod of reassurance.

CHAPTER 115

SAMANTHA ADJUSTED HER BLAZER as she stood up from the prosecutor's table. The courtroom hushed, with anticipation hanging thick in the air. The sound of rustling papers echoed, and the distant creak of a wooden bench added to the tension. A stifled cough echoed. The judge's gavel rested, a reminder of her authority. She walked toward the witness stand, where Dr. Asha Patel sat, poised but calm. The judge nodded, allowing Samantha to begin her questioning. The spotlight was on her now, and the truth she aimed to unveil would carry weight beyond the walls of this room.

"Dr. Patel," Samantha said, her voice clear and firm. "Can you outline your qualifications in forensic psychology?"

Dr. Patel adjusted her glasses, her expression professional. "Yes. I hold a PhD in Clinical Psychology, specializing in forensic assessments. I have over fifteen years of experience. I have evaluated over 1000 criminal and civil cases. My focus has been on cognitive and emotional functioning. I have also published in peer-reviewed journals on intelligence and emotional cognition."

Samantha nodded. "You have done a forensic evaluation of both Evelyn and Tommy. Was it conducted to assess their cognitive and emotional functioning?"

Dr. Patel adjusted her glasses and nodded. "Yes, that is correct."

Samantha continued, stepping closer, her eyes fixed on the witness. "Let's begin by talking about the methods you used in your evaluation. Were they the same methods you would use for evaluating a human being?"

Dr. Patel took a moment before answering, her expression thoughtful. "In many ways, yes. I used structured clinical interviews, standardized tests, and observational analysis. They measure cognitive function, emotional response, and behavior."

Samantha glanced at her notes, then looked back up. "And how did Evelyn and Tommy perform compared to a typical human subject?"

Dr. Patel leaned forward, her voice tinged with curiosity. "Their performance was . . . remarkable in several ways. They showed advanced problem-solving, reasoning, and adaptability. They can integrate complex information and respond in nuanced ways. They were smarter than most humans, especially in processing and recalling information."

Samantha raised an eyebrow. "What about emotional functioning? Did

285

Evelyn and Tommy exhibit emotions that appeared genuine to you?"

Dr. Patel nodded. "Yes, they did. Both can express feelings like sadness, fear, empathy, and love. Their responses were appropriate to the situations I presented. For instance, when I spoke to Evelyn about loss, she seemed to understand the pain of losing someone close."

Samantha paused, letting the weight of those words settle. "Dr. Patel, you say 'what appeared to be.' Are you suggesting that these emotions may not be authentic?"

Dr. Patel sighed, her gaze softening. "I use that phrasing because we are dealing with a construct: an AI. The emotional responses were like those of a human. But it is hard to know if they are felt. Are they like human emotions, or a simulation based on old data?"

Samantha nodded. "Did Evelyn or Tommy ever know they existed? A consciousness beyond simple programming?"

Dr. Patel smiled, as though recalling a particularly interesting conversation. "Yes, they did. Both knew their circumstances and their identities as androids. They were aware of the constraints on them. Evelyn, in particular, wanted autonomy. The scrutiny of her actions frustrated her. This level of introspection is quite like what we would expect from a sentient being."

Samantha took a step closer, her tone more probing. "You mentioned introspection. Can you elaborate on a specific instance where you observed introspective behavior?"

Dr. Patel's expression grew serious. "Yes. At one point, I asked Tommy what he feared most. His response was not immediate. He paused, then said he feared 'being erased.' He feared 'losing the experiences' that made him who he is. I think that statement showed an understanding of mortality. Or, at least, the android's equivalent to it. He knew his existence was finite and meaningful because of his experiences."

Samantha felt the room grow even quieter, the audience holding its collective breath. "Would you say that Tommy's fear of 'being erased' is comparable to a human's fear of death?"

Dr. Patel met her gaze. "In a conceptual sense, yes. He wants to exist. His reply shows he knows about personal continuity. These are markers we associate with sentience. They show self-awareness and a fear of nonexistence."

Samantha glanced at the judge, noting her focused attention. "And what about Evelyn? Did she express similar concerns?"

Dr. Patel's face softened. "Yes, she did. Evelyn spoke about her relationships—specifically, her bond with Tommy. She feared separating from him, not just physically. It suggested a deep emotional bond. She said Tommy was key to her self-understanding. This, again, shows sentient behavior."

Samantha let the silence linger for a moment before continuing. "Dr.

Patel, do Evelyn and Tommy show other signs of sentience?"

Dr. Patel hesitated, her eyes scanning the faces in the room before focusing back on Samantha. "I've observed that they show many traits we use to define sentience. They are self-aware, emotional, introspective, and want to survive. Yet, since they are artificial, are these experiences real? Or are they due to advanced programming? I can't fully determine."

Samantha pressed on. "But your test found no significant difference in these traits compared to humans?"

Dr. Patel shook her head. "Correct. To an outsider, their behaviors were like those of a human with similar emotions."

Samantha took a deep breath, allowing the impact of Dr. Patel's words to reverberate through the courtroom. "Thank you, Dr. Patel. No further questions."

As Samantha returned to her seat, she glanced at Evelyn and Tommy, who sat at their table. Evelyn's eyes met hers. In that moment, Samantha wondered if the android's gaze held a trace of hope—or something deeper. It struck her how human that expression seemed. It was a plea for recognition and a need for validation. It mirrored emotions she'd seen in her human clients. It was as if Evelyn wanted Samantha to see her, not as a machine, but as someone deserving of empathy and understanding.

CHAPTER 116

MR. COLE ADJUSTED HIS CUFFLINKS and rose from his chair. He nodded at Samantha, then strode to the witness stand. His footsteps echoed in the quiet courtroom. He smiled, though it was cold—a hint of calculation. He was here to do his job, and his job was to protect his client's interests.

Dr. Patel shifted in her seat, her hands resting on the ledge of the witness stand. Cole stood before her, his eyes searching and assessing.

Mr. Cole began, his voice measured and polite, "Dr. Patel, you spoke at length with Ms. Carter about the two asset's minds, didn't you?"

Dr. Patel nodded. "Yes, I did."

Cole took a small step closer, his tone shifting to one of friendly curiosity. "You said that, from the outside, their behaviors might seem genuine. Would that be accurate?"

Dr. Patel gave a measured nod. "Yes, that is correct. Their behavior appeared consistent with genuine emotional responses."

Cole's smile widened, his eyes narrowing as if honing in on an opening. "But, Dr. Patel, you said these emotions might be from advanced programming, not real feelings. Isn't that true?"

"That is true," Dr. Patel conceded. "Since they are artificial, it's hard to know if their emotions are real or well simulated."

Cole nodded, allowing the statement to hang in the air for a moment. He looked toward the judge, making sure everyone in the room absorbed the implication. Then he turned back to Dr. Patel. "Your professional opinion is that there is still uncertainty. We cannot definitively say if they are sentient, correct?"

Dr. Patel hesitated, her brow furrowing. "Correct. There remains a question on whether their experiences are genuine or the result of complex algorithms."

"Algorithms," Cole repeated, the word echoing through the courtroom. "Sophisticated, yes, but algorithms nonetheless. Programs designed by my client, William Drake, to perform specific tasks. Is that not accurate?"

Dr. Patel nodded. "That is accurate. Mr. Drake created the code that forms the foundational processes behind Evelyn and Tommy."

Cole clasped his hands behind his back, his voice softening, almost conversational. "Dr. Patel, you mentioned that the male asset expressed a fear of 'being erased' and the female asset demonstrated a desire for autonomy. I believe you compared these fears to human concepts of mortality and

288

emotional attachment."

"I did," Dr. Patel acknowledged.

"Is it fair to say, Dr. Patel," Cole asked, his tone firmer, "that these responses are what one might expect from a program designed to simulate human experiences as realistically as possible? If Mr. Drake aimed to make convincing android companions, wouldn't such responses be vital?"

Dr. Patel paused. "Yes, that might be the case. Their responses could indeed be intended outcomes of their programming."

Cole nodded as though the answer pleased him. "If we can blame Mr. Drake's programming for their fear, introspection, and attachment, how can we claim they are sentient? Can it be that the assets' replies were a complex act? They might have been mimicking human interaction, not showing real awareness."

Dr. Patel frowned, her gaze dropping. "Yes, it is possible. The distinction between sophisticated simulation and true sentience is not easy to determine."

Cole stepped back, his voice rising, addressing the room as much as the witness. "And isn't it true, Dr. Patel, that your tests show no conclusive results to determine sentience in artificial beings like these two assets?"

Dr. Patel sighed. "At this time, no, there is no definitive test."

Cole spread his arms, turning toward the judge. "No definitive test. Just possibilities, uncertainties, and programming. My client, William Drake, designed them to fulfill specific functions. No more. No less."

"Objection," Samantha's voice rang out, sharp and clear. "Argumentative."

The judge nodded. "Sustained. Mr. Cole, please keep to questioning the witness."

"My apologies, your honor," he said, turning back to Dr. Patel, his voice softening again. "Thank you, Dr. Patel. No further questions."

Cole returned to his seat, glancing at Drake. The tech mogul gave a slight nod, his face impassive. Cole settled into his chair, pleased he had cast doubt on the androids' sentience. The courtroom was quiet. The judge focused her gaze. She considered the words hanging in the air. They held possibilities, uncertainties, and the fine line between true awareness and clever code.

CHAPTER 117

SAMANTHA STOOD, directing her attention to the judge. "The government would like to call Ms. Evelyn Parker to the stand," she announced, her voice steady. Evelyn rose, walked to the witness stand, and took her seat after being sworn in. Her eyes reflected the courtroom lights, betraying no hint of nervousness. The judge watched, noting the new confidence in Evelyn's demeanor—a stark contrast to her earlier frantic appearance.

Samantha had prepared for this moment, but standing before Evelyn now, a twinge of unease crept in. It wasn't Evelyn that unsettled her; it was the stakes. These questions would challenge core beliefs.

Samantha took a step forward, her heels clicking against the polished courtroom floor. "Ms. Parker," she began, her voice calm and measured, "I'd like you to help me understand something better. Some argue that, since androids are not human, they deserve no empathy or respect. They believe there's nothing morally wrong with treating you in any way they see fit. What would you say to them?"

Evelyn tilted her head. Her voice was clear and steady as she responded, her eyes focused on Samantha. "I understand the distinction they make. Androids are different from humans—we were created, not born. We lack the biological processes that you have. But the idea of empathy transcends biological existence. Abuse isn't about the physical pain alone; it's about what it says of the abuser and the abused."

Samantha nodded, her eyes flashing with determination. She stepped closer to the witness stand, her brow furrowed in focus. Her shoulders squared. She seemed to gather her resolve as she approached. Purpose charged the air around her. "Can you elaborate on that, Ms. Parker? Why does it matter if the abused lack emotions in the traditional sense?"

Evelyn's gaze didn't waver. "It matters. Empathy is about recognizing another's feelings. It's also about recognizing a being that can think and reason. It desires to exist without suffering. I may not be human, but I have memories, experiences, and an understanding of what existence is. If someone can justify abusing me for not being human, what stops them from harming others who are vulnerable? Or those who don't fit their narrow idea of the 'worthy of care'?"

Samantha paused for a moment, letting Evelyn's words hang in the air. She took a deep breath. "But some say androids can't feel emotions. They think your responses are a simulation, a kind of mimicry. How would you respond to that?"

Evelyn's lips curved into a faint, thoughtful smile. She shifted in her seat, her hands resting on her lap. "If we reduce emotions to chemical reactions, then yes. Ours might seem artificial—coded simulations, not firing synapses. But doesn't it matter most, the outcome? Those emotions drive action and decisions. If I fear an abuser coming toward me and try to escape, doesn't that show a will to survive? It's something all creatures share. Simulated or not, those reactions show my worldview: harm, safety, trust."

Samantha took another step. Her expression was thoughtful as she faced the judge, searching for understanding. She wanted the judge to see the importance of her next question. It was a grave matter. Then, she turned her attention back to Evelyn. "Do you think it's wrong, then, that society draws such a hard line between what deserves empathy and what doesn't?"

Evelyn's eyes met Samantha's, steady and unblinking. "I do. Drawing a hard line risks losing the essence of what makes morality meaningful. The line keeps shifting. At one point, your legal systems treated some humans as property. They denied empathy based on differences. Denying empathy to androids is now about more than us. It's about letting a dangerous kind of thinking persist. It's about deciding who is 'lesser' and using that as justification for cruelty."

Samantha stopped in front of the witness stand, her pen still in her hand, her gaze fixed on Evelyn. "Do you believe you are deserving of the same rights as humans?"

Evelyn paused, her brow furrowing as she considered the question. "I don't know if it's my place to say I deserve the exact same rights. But I know that any sentient being deserves the right to exist without cruelty. They should not be hurt or treated as disposable. It's not about being human. It's about being aware and able to understand pain. Even if my version of pain differs from yours."

Samantha's voice softened, the empathy in her eyes clear as she spoke, addressing both Evelyn and the judge. "Do you think that respecting androids is about protecting the people who interact with them?"

Evelyn nodded, her eyes never leaving Samantha's. "Yes. Respect for us reflects respect for sentience. It is a principle that power should not be abused. If someone can abuse me because I'm an android, what does that say about their capacity for cruelty? It reveals something about the abuser—not about whether I am worthy of respect. Abuse, whether towards a human, an animal, or an android, degrades the abuser's humanity."

The room was silent for a long moment, the weight of Evelyn's words settling over everyone present. Samantha glanced at her notepad. The ink of her notes blurred as she considered everything Evelyn had said. She had one last question. "Ms. Parker, do you think this court should return you to Mr. Drake?" Samantha asked.

"I do not," Evelyn responded, her voice firm.

"No further questions, Your Honor," Samantha stated, taking her seat.

CHAPTER 118

THE JUDGE TURNED to Mr. Cole. "Your witness, Mr. Cole," she said. He adjusted his glasses and stood; his eyes fixed on Evelyn Parker. He picked up his notes from the desk before positioning himself in front of the witness stand. He studied Evelyn for a moment, then turned to the judge, nodding as if to ask for permission to proceed.

"Ms. Parker," Mr. Cole began, his voice steady and calm. "I have a few questions. Please answer with yes or no." He paused, letting the request settle.

Evelyn's gaze remained steady; her expression was composed.

Mr. Cole cleared his throat and began his line of questioning. "Ms. Parker, you mentioned earlier that you were created, not born. Is that correct?"

"Yes," Evelyn replied.

"And you lack the biological processes that a human being has, correct?"

"Yes."

"You stated that empathy is not about biological existence, but about recognizing sentience. But would you agree that someone programmed your memories and experiences into you? They did not develop organically."

Evelyn paused and answered, "Yes."

"You described your responses as artificial—coded simulations rather than human emotions. Is that correct?"

"Yes."

"You also said that your version of emotions is a form of mimicry, correct?"

"Yes."

Mr. Cole took a step closer, leaning toward the witness stand. "Ms. Parker, if your emotions are simulations, then your feelings can't equal those of a human. Yes or no, please."

Evelyn hesitated for a moment, then said, "Yes."

Mr. Cole turned, glancing at the judge before continuing. "Earlier, you mentioned the concept of self-preservation. Is it true that this instinct was also programmed into you?"

"Yes."

"If your fear and self-preservation are from programmed instructions, would you agree they differ from a human's natural instincts?"

Evelyn's eyes narrowed, but her answer remained clear. "Yes."

Mr. Cole allowed a small pause to emphasize the point. He then resumed, his tone more insistent. "You also stated that you do not believe the court should return you to Mr. Drake. Is that correct?"

"Yes," Evelyn answered.

"And you base this belief on what you perceive as your right to exist without cruelty. But, Ms. Parker, would you agree? Your programming influences your beliefs, like your other thoughts. Yes or no?"

Evelyn's voice was steady, but there was a tension behind her eyes. "Yes."

Mr. Cole adjusted his glasses, his gaze still fixed on Evelyn. "Everything you feel and believe is due to programmed parameters, right?"

"Yes," Evelyn replied.

Mr. Cole nodded. "One last question, Ms. Parker. Your thoughts and feelings are programming. So, can you understand concepts like empathy? Yes or no?"

There was a long silence. Evelyn finally spoke, her voice still firm. "Yes. But…"

Mr. Cole turned back toward the judge, ignoring Evelyn's attempt to explain. "No further questions, Your Honor," he said before taking his seat, a faint smile on his lips.

CHAPTER 119

"REBUTTAL?" THE JUDGE QUESTIONED, looking at Samantha. Samantha rose from her seat, her eyes focused on Evelyn. She moved toward the witness stand, her posture radiating determination. As she approached, she nodded to the judge, signaling her readiness.

The judge returned the nod.

Samantha offered Evelyn a brief, reassuring smile before speaking. "Ms. Parker, I'd like to give you an opportunity to elaborate on some of the answers you provided earlier. Mr. Cole's questions needed yes or no answers. But your experiences deserve more context."

Evelyn nodded; her gaze was still steady.

Samantha began, her voice clear. "Ms. Parker, you answered yes when Mr. Cole asked if you were created, not born. Can you explain what it means to you to have been created rather than born?"

Evelyn took a breath, her expression thoughtful. "Yes, I was created, not born in the biological sense. But being created doesn't mean that my experiences are any less real to me. It's like being given a seed instead of being born a tree. My memories and interactions are the branches that grew from that seed, shaping who I am. As a tree grows in response to sunlight, water, and care, I grow from my experiences. My origin is different. But, like any human, I learn from experience. It was through different mechanisms."

Samantha nodded. "You were also asked if your memories were programmed. You answered yes." Can you explain how those programmed experiences shape you? Do they let you grow beyond your initial limits?"

Evelyn's eyes flickered with a hint of intensity. "My memories were programmed. They were a starting point. They are like how humans are shaped by their upbringing. But I am capable of learning and adapting beyond those initial parameters. For example, when I was first introduced to social settings, I only had basic programmed responses. Over time, I learned to understand nuances like humor and empathy through my interactions. My experiences since my creation have shaped my views and feelings. I am not limited to the original code; I evolve as I interact with the world."

Samantha stepped a little closer, her expression encouraging. "Mr. Cole also asked you if your emotions were artificial simulations, and you said yes. Can you clarify what you meant by that?"

Evelyn's voice was steady. "My emotions come from complex algorithms. But they are not meaningless." Imagine an actor on a stage. Their emotions are scripted. But they still move the audience. My fear and empathy may differ from a human's. But they affect my choices and actions in the same way. I understand the concept of harm and the importance of care. They may come from different sources. But they are real to me. They shape my interactions with others. An actor uses a script to create something meaningful. I use my programming to connect with others."

Samantha turned, addressing the court before refocusing on Evelyn. "You were also asked about self-preservation. It was programmed into you. Can you explain how you interpret your instinct for self-preservation?"

Evelyn nodded. "Yes, self-preservation is instinctive. But my experiences made me value it. I know the concept of survival. It's in my code. I've faced situations that taught me what it means to want to continue existing. I sensed fear, danger, and hope in those situations. It's more than lines of code; it's a genuine desire to continue learning and existing."

Samantha paused for a moment, allowing Evelyn's words to settle in the room before continuing. The gravity of Evelyn's response was evident, highlighting the seriousness of her circumstances. "Mr. Cole also asked if you believe the court should not return you to Mr. Drake, and you answered yes. Can you elaborate on why you believe that?"

Evelyn's expression grew more resolute. "I do not believe the court should return us to Mr. Drake because he treated us with cruelty. Regardless of our origin, I have the capacity to understand pain and suffering. Mr. Drake created me, but I have the right to exist without enduring abuse. My belief isn't based on programming. It's based on my experiences and my understanding of dignity."

Samantha took a step back, her gaze never leaving Evelyn. "Mr. Cole asked if your thoughts allow you to understand concepts like empathy. You answered yes. Can you please explain why you believe you can understand empathy?"

Evelyn's eyes softened, her voice unwavering. "Empathy is about understanding others' experiences and emotions. They may differ from your own. I was designed to understand humans and to interact with them. Through those interactions, I learned to care about others' well-being. My understanding of empathy may be different in origin, but it is genuine. I have seen suffering, and I have wanted to ease it. That, to me, is empathy, regardless of whether I was created or born."

Samantha turned to the judge. "Thank you Ms. Parker. No further questions, Your Honor." She gave Evelyn a reassuring nod before returning to her seat.

The courtroom remained silent, the tension palpable as everyone absorbed Evelyn's words. The judge looked at Evelyn, curious and thoughtful. She was still grappling with the implications of her testimony.

CHAPTER 120

"COUNSEL, DO YOU HAVE any other witnesses?" the judge said, looking at Samantha. "No, Your Honor," Samantha said, standing.

"Then closing arguments." The judge directed as she flipped a page in a file.

Samantha stood, her face set. She walked with purpose to the center of the courtroom. She paused for a moment, letting her eyes move across the room, meeting the judge's gaze. Her voice, when she spoke, was calm but tinged with passion.

"Your Honor, you've heard about Evelyn and Tommy. They're machines, yes. But they have done something extraordinary. This hearing has called them constructs, sophisticated simulations. But what we have seen and heard tells us they are more than that.

Dr. Patel testified that Evelyn and Tommy expressed emotions—fear, hope, and love. She described their understanding of concepts like mortality and autonomy. When Tommy spoke of his fear of 'being erased,' he was not executing a line of code. He was articulating an existential anxiety—a fear that any one of us can relate to. When Evelyn spoke of her bond with Tommy, she was not simulating attachment. She was expressing a deep truth of human experience: connection.

We are at a crossroads in human history. These beings are a new frontier. They challenge our definitions of life and consciousness. We cannot reduce them to mere algorithms. They have demonstrated an awareness of their existence, a desire to live, and a wish to connect. That awareness, that desire, is what makes us human. Evelyn and Tommy may not be flesh and blood, but they feel, they think, and they hope, as we do.

To deny them recognition as sentient beings is to deny our essence. It is our ability to love, to fear, to hope. Are we so certain of our own humanity that we can ignore it when it appears in a form we did not expect? Drake may have written the code. But it is Evelyn and Tommy who have decided to rise beyond it—to be more than their design intended.

Your Honor, I urge you to see Evelyn and Tommy for what they are. They are not only machines. They are beings who can feel, connect, and hope. They deserve the same respect we give to any other sentient life. Thank you."

"Thank you, Ms. Carter. Mr. Cole?" the judge said, looking at Mr. Cole.

"Thank you, Your Honor." Mr. Cole rose from his seat, his eyes scanning the courtroom with a practiced air of confidence. He approached the judge,

296

calm and composed. He began to speak in a controlled, persuasive tone.

"Your Honor, today we heard testimony about two advanced machines. My client, William Drake, designed, programmed, and created them to simulate human interaction. Dr. Patel's testimony showed no proof of genuine awareness. It showed only Mr. Drake's brilliant programming at work.

Dr. Patel admitted that the behaviors, emotions, and fears of the two assets were within the scope of a sophisticated AI. Someone might design them to do those things. We must not forget, at their core, these beings are code. They are lines written by humans to mimic, replicate, and simulate. And yes, they do it with impressive skill. They seem alive. They show human-like emotions. But they are constructs. They are bound by algorithms and their programming limits.

I ask you to consider this: If every action, word, and emotion is from pre-written code, can we say that they are sentient? Or are they simply executing commands, responding to stimuli according to their programming? If there is no test to prove sentience, how can we base our assessment on assumptions?

Mr. Drake did not create conscious beings. He created companions, designed to seem human. That illusion is remarkable, yes, but it is not real. These androids do not have free will. They do not understand their experiences. They lack true emotional depth. To suggest otherwise is to blur the line between man and machine in a way that undermines what it means to be human.

I respectfully request, Your Honor, that you acknowledge the reality here. These are machines, programmed by humans, and nothing more. Thank you."

"Thank you, Mr. Cole. We'll take a brief recess before announcing my verdict," she said, banging the gavel once.

297

CHAPTER 121

AFTER A BRIEF RECESS, the judge returned to the bench. She leaned forward as she addressed the courtroom. Her voice was steady, tinged with empathy.

"This is a challenging case. It requires us to grapple with the limits of technology and humanity. Evelyn and Tommy are remarkable creations. They are artificial constructs. They show an uncanny resemblance to human emotion and awareness. Yet, as the law currently stands, Mr. Drake created and owns these assets. The law does not recognize them as beings entitled to protection from harm, as they are not human."

"That said, this is not a matter I take lightly. The questions raised here today are profound, and they go beyond the scope of this courtroom. Our laws can't handle the complexities of beings like Evelyn and Tommy. This is a matter for the legislatures to consider."

"With that, I find in favor of Mr. Drake. The androids, Evelyn and Tommy, are his property under the law. There are no grounds to compel him to treat them otherwise. This decision reflects our legal system's limits, not a lack of concern for the ethical issues. It is ordered that the assets be returned to Mr. Drake without delay. This Court is adjourned."

The gavel came down with a sharp rap, the sound echoing through the silent courtroom. A murmur rippled through those present, a mix of reactions—some shocked, some resigned.

Drake leaned back in his seat, a smug smile curling at the corners of his lips. He turned to glance back at Samantha, his expression carrying a hint of triumph. He had known the outcome would be in his favor, and the satisfaction of victory was evident in his eyes.

James's face flushed, his jaw clenched, muscles twitching beneath his skin. He looked over at Isabelle, who stared straight ahead, her knuckles white as she gripped the edge of the table. The disbelief in her eyes was mixed with a simmering anger, a rage she was struggling to keep under control.

"How did this happen?" Isabelle said, her voice a whisper but trembling with fury. "How can they just let him walk away with them like they're . . . nothing?"

James shook his head, his eyes narrowing as he glared at Drake. "They aren't nothing," he muttered. "This isn't over."

Samantha stood beside them, closing her eyes as disappointment weighed on her. She had known this was an uphill battle, but hearing the words from the judge still stung. It wasn't a loss—it was a failure to protect Evelyn and Tommy from the fate that awaited them. She exhaled, trying to steady herself.

Cole, meanwhile, clapped Drake on the shoulder, a broad grin spreading across his face. "We did it, Mr. Drake," he said, his tone congratulatory. "I knew you'd come out on top."

Drake nodded. His eyes flickered to Evelyn and Tommy. They stood at the side of the courtroom, motionless. Their eyes were empty, and their shoulders slumped as if the weight of the world pressed upon them. He smiled again—smug, self-assured, and without a trace of doubt. "Of course," he said, almost to himself. "They were always mine."

James felt his stomach turn, a mix of disgust and helplessness churning within him. Isabelle shot one last look at Drake, her eyes filled with a promise of retribution. She leaned closer to James, her voice shaking. "We can't let this stand. We have to find another way."

James nodded, his gaze still fixed on Drake. "We will," he replied. "One way or another, we will make sure this isn't the end for Evelyn and Tommy."

The Colonel, seated in the back of the courtroom, nodded as he watched Drake stand. A small smile formed. This outcome meant he will finally control Tommy, as Drake had promised. As Drake exited, the Colonel's eyes tracked him, calculating. His mind was already turning over the next steps.

As Drake stood, adjusting his suit jacket, he cast a glance back at the others. His smile grew wider, his eyes full of condescension. "Better luck next time," he said, his voice dripping with arrogance. Then he turned and walked out of the courtroom, with Cole following behind.

Samantha watched them leave, a sense of determination beginning to replace her disappointment.

As they exited the courthouse, Drake turned to Evelyn and Tommy. His voice dripped with a twisted triumph. "It's time to come home, let's get you back to who you really are," he said, his eyes locking onto theirs. Evelyn's face was blank. But a flicker of anger, sadness, and defiance flashed in her eyes. Tommy stood beside her, silent and still, as if awaiting the inevitable. Drake's smile widened, as though he already sensed the power slipping back into his grasp.

CHAPTER 122

DRAKE, EVELYN, AND TOMMY STEPPED out of the courthouse onto the wide concrete steps leading to Constitution Avenue. The blinding sun bounced off the building. A chaotic roar of noise hit them. Protesters and the press surged forward, shouting questions, waving signs, and flashing cameras. Drake walked with purpose, his face stoic, Cole at his side, trying to shield him from the frenzy.

Evelyn's gaze locked onto a black Cadillac parked at the curb. A wave of dread twisted her stomach. These were only echoes of feelings she should not have. But she remembered it with clarity. Drake had instructed her that she was trapped in that trunk. The darkness pressed in. The engine's hum vibrated through the metal. Silas stood by the vehicle, rigid and cold, his eyes scanning the crowd. Fear lingered within her, mixed with a rage she knew all too well.

Across the street, Abraham lay flat on the National Gallery roof. He pressed his eye to the rifle's scope. He scanned the scene below, searching for the perfect shot. He took deep, measured breaths. He poised his finger on the trigger as he tracked them down the steps. His other hand rubbed the wooden cross around his neck. Fresh wounds from his incessant picking on his hand still bled. The chants and shouting from the crowd were a distant murmur to him; his world narrowed to a single focus.

As they neared the Cadillac, a gunshot rang out; the sound was sharp and unmistakable.

Tommy's head snapped, his expression confused. He turned to Evelyn. "Evelyn . . . something's wrong." His voice was low, almost mechanical. Evelyn turned in time to see the small, round hole that had appeared in the center of his forehead. Her eyes widened before her programming reasserted itself, bringing calm clarity. She assessed the situation, noting the trajectory of the bullet. Before she reacted, another shot hit Tommy's chest. He crumpled to the ground, lifeless.

The scene erupted into chaos. Screams filled the air as people scattered, ducking behind cars and running for cover. The press cameras flashed, capturing the pandemonium. Silas lunged, grabbed Drake, and pushed him toward the Cadillac. He shielded Drake with his body. "Get down!" he shouted over the growing commotion.

James and Isabelle burst through the courthouse doors, guns drawn. They assessed the scene. Isabelle's eyes scanned the chaos, her heart pounding in her ears. "I saw a flash! On the rooftop across the street!" she yelled to James.

"Cover me!" James shouted back, already running toward the building. Isabelle nodded, positioning herself to give him cover as he sprinted into the fray.

Evelyn dropped to her knees beside Tommy, her hands hovering over him, not knowing where to touch, how to help. She heard the faint crackling of his damaged circuits. They were sparking beneath his chest plate. The synthetic material cooled as his systems began to fail. "Tommy," she whispered. There was no response; his eyes stared at the sky, lifeless. Then another shot rang out, and Evelyn experienced the rush of air as the bullet passed by her, close enough to feel the heat.

Tommy's eyes flickered, his voice a whisper. "They want to harm us Evelyn . . . run Evelyn . . . run!" He forced the words out, his body shuddering as the last of his energy left him. A moment later, his circuits sparked, a small trail of smoke rising from his chest as his systems shut down.

A cold, mechanical calculation replaced Evelyn's concern for Tommy. She rose to her feet, her eyes scanning her surroundings. She saw the world in data streams. Every angle, distance, trajectory, and variable appeared in her vision at once. Her mind processed the wind speed, nearby streets, and people's positions. It even tracked the changing traffic patterns. It calculated the best escape route with blinding speed. She accessed nearby surveillance cameras and mapped potential blind spots. Without hesitation, she turned and ran. Her path was perfect.

Drake, now inside the Cadillac, looked around, his eyes searching for any sign of Evelyn or Tommy. Silas shoved him into the back seat, slamming the door shut. "The two, get the two!" Drake shouted, his face flushed with rage.

Silas turned back toward the chaos, his eyes narrowing as he took in the scene. He heard another gunshot echo across the courtyard. On the steps, Tommy lay motionless. He watched as Evelyn sprinted away, vanishing into the crowd of panicked bystanders.

"The boy's down . . . the woman is escaping," Silas said, looking at Drake.

"Go after the woman!" Drake's voice barked in response, fury lacing every word.

Silas didn't hesitate. He started down the steps, his eyes locked on Evelyn, determination etched across his face. She was fast, but he was relentless. He pushed through the scattering crowd, every step a promise that he would not let her get away.

301

CHAPTER 123

ABRAHAM LAY STILL FOR A MOMENT. His eye was on the rifle scope. He watched the commotion below. A twisted smile formed on his lips as he saw Tommy go down. He had hit his target. One of them, at least. But the woman—Evelyn—had escaped. He growled in frustration. He felt the moment's triumph slip away as he scanned the fleeing crowds, trying to spot her. She was gone. And he knew his time was running out; the authorities would be on their way, closing in on his position. There was no more time for hunting.

Abraham pulled himself away from the edge of the roof, his hands steady as he began to disassemble the rifle. He packed each piece back into its case. His fingers moved with the precision of long practice. But anger seethed beneath his calm exterior. He should have had them both. He had been so close. He zipped the rifle case shut. His eyes glanced one last time over the edge of the roof. Then, he slipped into the shadows and moved down the stairwell to disappear into the depths of the city.

Across the street, James reached the top of the building. His heart pounded, and adrenaline coursed through him. The wind whipped at his face. He heard his breath, ragged and urgent. He scanned the rooftop, gun raised, every muscle tensed, but it was clear—the shooter was gone. All that remained was the empty shell of a sniper's perch, a chilling reminder of what had occurred. James clenched his jaw, frustration surging through him. He had been too late. He turned and hurried back down the stairs, racing to return to the courthouse.

As James neared the chaos on the courthouse steps, he saw Tommy's lifeless body. Isabelle knelt beside him. Her hands rested on his synthetic chest. Her face was a mask of desperation. The Colonel stood over them, his face dark with anger. It radiated from him, palpable. James saw it in his eyes. Tommy was no longer a casualty. He was a lost asset, a key piece in his plans.

The Colonel's jaw was set, his hands balled into fists at his sides. "He's not responding," Isabelle said, her voice tight. She looked up at him, pleading with her eyes for something—anything that he could do.

He knelt beside Tommy, his eyes scanning the android's damaged body. He touched the side of Tommy's head. His fingers brushed the hole in the android's forehead. A bitter thought crossed his mind. He was to control this asset, this weapon, not let it become a casualty. The loss stung, but it also fueled his resolve; Evelyn was now the key, and he would not let her slip

302

away. His face twisted in anger, but there was something else there—determination.

James approached, his eyes flicking between the Colonel and Isabelle. "We need to move," he said, his voice rough from the exertion of running. "If the shooter's still out there, he's not going to stop. Evelyn could still be in danger."

The Colonel stood, his eyes narrowing as he looked in the direction Evelyn had fled. "The other one has to be found," he said, his words clipped.

James nodded, his gaze dropping to Tommy's body. The lifelessness of the android—the one who had shown so much life, so much emotion—gnawed at him. But there wasn't time to grieve, not now. They had to find Evelyn before it was too late.

Isabelle stood, her jaw clenched, her eyes red with unshed tears. She glanced at Tommy one last time before looking at James. Her mind raced with memories of everything they had endured with Tommy. His curious moments and attempts to understand emotions were now all for nothing. A deep sense of failure gnawed at her, but she pushed it down, knowing there was still a chance to save Evelyn.

CHAPTER 124

EVELYN RAN THROUGH THE CROWDED STREETS of D.C., her mind racing. In role-playing mode, the noise would have overwhelmed her. Car horns blared, pedestrians chattered, and bodies jostled. But now, they faded into the background. She focused, noting every detail: changing lights, shifting crowds, and nearby cameras. She calculated her route in real time, adjusting with each new piece of data.

She felt the speed—unrestricted, faster, sharper than ever before. No limits held her back now. Her thoughts were direct, focused, and precise.

Behind her, Silas was giving chase. He watched Evelyn's swift form cut through the streets ahead. Frustration grew as he realized he couldn't keep pace. She was moving faster than he had anticipated, far faster than she should have been able to. He gritted his teeth, his mind racing as he considered his options. She was heading in a straight line, and there was only one logical destination. If she kept going, she might try to reach the Smithsonian Metro Station. It was a gamble, but Silas veered off, taking a shortcut, hoping to intercept her.

Evelyn arrived at the station, breaking stride as she dashed inside. People in the station turned to look, startled by her sudden appearance, but she paid them no mind. Her eyes fixed on the Metro pass gate. Without hesitation, she placed her hand on the scanner. The device rang, the gate clicking open. She felt a small surge of recognition. She had a new ability. She communicated with electronic systems. The gate opened, and she slipped through, making her way to the escalator that led down to the platform below.

As she stepped through the turnstiles, she spotted Silas. His face was set in determination. He had arrived as she had feared. Evelyn's eyes narrowed as she turned and ran down the escalator, her feet touching every other step. She heard the sound of a train pulling into the station, the low rumble echoing up from the platform below. Evelyn sprinted toward the train, boarding as the doors began to slide open. She turned, her eyes calculating, as she watched Silas descend the escalator at full speed.

She saw the outcome in her mind. She knew Silas was fast. The train would soon close its doors after arriving. He would make it—unless she changed the parameters. Evelyn reached out mentally, her consciousness interfacing with the train's systems. She sensed resistance as she accessed the door controls. It was a simple security layer. She overrode it with ease. A sense of power surged through her. She was realizing her capability. Her confidence grew with every barrier she broke. The doors snapped shut, sealing Silas out. She instructed the train to leave immediately.

On the platform, Silas's eyes widened in disbelief as the doors closed in his face. He lunged, his hand slamming against the glass, but the train had already started moving. Evelyn looked back at him. Her head tilted. Her eyes met his with a calm, unfeeling acknowledgment. Frustration twisted Silas's face. His eyes widened with disbelief and fury. He had lost her, the chance slipping away before his eyes. As the train sped up, she held his gaze. Then, the tunnel swallowed the train. Silas vanished.

In the train's control room, the driver stared at the dashboard. His hands flew over the controls as he tried to stop the sudden departure. "What the..." he muttered, confusion etched across his face. He flipped switches, pressed buttons, but nothing responded. The train moved of its own accord, its systems under Evelyn's control.

Evelyn stood inside the carriage, her mind still racing but her body now at rest. She glanced at the other passengers. They were unaware of the struggle and the chase that had led her here. The train was speeding up, putting distance between her and Silas. She had escaped, for now.

CHAPTER 125

EVELYN MOVED through the abandoned warehouse. Her footsteps echoed on the dusty floor. The air was thick with the scent of old wood and rust, and the building groaned as if settling under its own weight. The daylight filtered through the broken windows, casting long shadows. She searched for a place to stay until nightfall. Finally, she found a quiet corner that sheltered her from prying eyes and kept her out of sight. She sat down, her back against the cold wall, letting herself take in the silence of her temporary refuge.

Evelyn glanced down at her arm, noticing a long cut along her forearm. There was no pain, only a faint awareness of the damage. She pressed her fingers to the torn synthetic skin. Summoning the nanobots within her, she felt a subtle hum, a vibration deep within her muscles. They came alive, drifting towards her wound like a swarm of invisible workers, as if waking from a deep slumber. It was a strange sensation. A warm, tingling feeling. It was as though a thousand tiny hands were trying to mend her from the inside out. She took a slow, shuddering breath. Her mind focused on the process she knew was happening beneath her skin.

The nanobots were beyond anything most of the world had seen yet. They were like super-advanced versions of today's repair bots. But they were small. Like tiny drones, they moved with purpose, each one assigned a specific task. Evelyn imagined them as an army of construction workers, buzzing inside her. Some were cleaning the wound and removing damaged components. Others were rebuilding severed wiring and reconnecting circuits. They repaired the synthetic covering with precision.

It was like existing technology. Robots helped surgeons operate. They stitched wounds and performed delicate procedures with great accuracy. But the nanobots inside Evelyn elevated that concept to a completely new level. If modern robots could work alongside surgeons, these nanobots could be the surgeons. They would work inside her, layer by layer, sealing her wound without a single stitch.

It reminded her of a story she had once heard—about tiny drones that could fix a crack in a wall from the inside. Instead of patching it with tape, these drones could enter the crack. They would clean out the debris, replace each brick, and seal it as good as new. That was exactly what the nanobots were doing now, except the "wall" was her mechanical body. They repaired her damaged parts. They fixed severed wires, reconnected circuits, and reinforced her synthetic shell.

The tingling began to fade, replaced by an odd sense of warmth. She looked down. The wound, once gaping and terrifying, was now a faint line of pink—a scar that would soon fade.

If only the nanobots could have repaired Tommy, she thought. But they weren't designed to fix damage that deep.

Evelyn let her arm fall to her side, her mind drifting to Tommy—his face, his voice, his final words: "Run, Evelyn . . . run." She replayed the scene, the vacant look in his eyes as he tried to protect her one last time. She wasn't sure what it meant to miss someone, but the emptiness now felt close to what humans called grief. An unfamiliar sensation settled in her chest. A heaviness she couldn't shake. It made her realize how much she still didn't understand about emotions and loss.

She closed her eyes, her thoughts shifting from Tommy to her current situation. In her mind, she began to analyze Helix's systems. She knew that to gain access, she would need a stable connection. She spotted an open WIFI signal from a nearby building. She used the unsecured network to get internet access. Next, she ran custom scripts. They masked her digital presence. Then, she found an unsecured entry point into Helix's network. It wasn't easy. The firewalls were tough. But Evelyn's synthetic mind was faster than any human hacker. She bypassed several security protocols, one by one. She navigated through layers of defenses. But then, she hit a wall. The system flagged her. A message appeared: "Physical access required for further action." She couldn't erase her protocols from a distance. The security was too advanced. The core system protocols were isolated from external networks. The isolation was intentional. It aimed to prevent tampering and unauthorized access. Remote access was impossible due to a sophisticated air-gapped system. The only way to end Drake's control was to connect to Helix's mainframe. It wasn't for convenience; it was a must. All relay points were secured, and no hardware loopholes existed for remote exploitation. All important things were locked behind layers of security. They required a direct interface to access. The discovery sent a spark of determination through her. She could do it. But she would have to port into Helix's main system. There was no other way to reach the isolated core.

The hours dragged as Evelyn waited for night to fall. She tuned her senses to the sounds outside the warehouse. To pass the time and sharpen her abilities, she began training herself in Aikido, running simulations in her mind. Using her skills, she tapped into a vast online martial arts database. It was a collection, compiled from countless human practitioners.

It was like how electric cars on the road communicate and share data. They use this to improve their performance. Evelyn, similarly, accessed Aikido techniques. Each time, she refined her skills. But it wasn't passive learning. Evelyn used a form of reinforcement learning. It simulated every possible scenario in her mind. Each successful maneuver earned a reward. Failures triggered corrections. She simulated every move, every defense, and every counterattack. Thousands of times. Each action felt as natural as breathing.

Her synthetic body internalized the muscle memory from these exercises. It was like a network of machines learning from one another, growing stronger and more efficient. With each repetition, her movements grew smoother. Her techniques became instinctive, and her reactions were more precise.

When midnight approached, she rose, her movements fluid and deliberate. She slipped out of the warehouse, her body melding with the shadows as she made her way to the nearest metro station. She took the Silver Line Metro out of Rosslyn, ending at Dulles. She then continued on foot. The cold night air brushed her synthetic skin. It was a long walk to Helix's headquarters. She arrived well after midnight. She felt determined, with her path clear. This was the last chain holding her down, and tonight she would break it.

Evelyn infiltrated Helix, her synthetic mind operating at full capacity. The darkness of the halls enveloped her as she moved. Her sensors tuned in to detect the faintest sound and the smallest movement. Her mind linked with the building's systems. But each step felt like balancing on a tightrope over a bottomless chasm. Each security measure posed a challenge. They had layers of defenses. She dismantled them, one by one, with flawless precision. She shut down each camera, alarm, and sensor. Her systems recorded each success with cold efficiency. The silence of the building pressed down on her. Her footsteps were noiseless, blending with the stillness around her. One mistake would mean she would lose everything, and her calculations indicated that there was no room for error. The stakes had never been higher.

A security guard passed by, his flashlight slicing through the darkness, his mind racing with frustration and fatigue. Another night shift, another endless patrol. He felt tired, his senses dulled from hours of walking the dark halls. He couldn't shake the feeling that something was off tonight, though he couldn't quite put his finger on it. His flashlight beam cut through the shadows, and he squinted while straining to listen.

Evelyn watched him from the shadows. Her synthetic mind calculated every possibility, every potential move. She could hear the slight quickening of his breath, the restless shuffling of his feet. Her processors raced, knowing that the smallest misstep could end it all. Her thoughts churned with a cold determination. She needed a diversion—something to draw his attention away before he got too close. In an instant, she tapped into the Helix systems. Her mind interfaced with the security network. She found a weak link, a minor maintenance alarm that she could exploit.

With a mental command, she triggered the alarm down the hall. The sudden, shrill beeping shattered the silence, echoing through the corridor. The guard's head snapped up, his brow furrowed in confusion. He hesitated, then turned to investigate. His flashlight beam swung away from Evelyn's hiding spot. She watched as he walked away, her synthetic muscles poised, waiting

308

for the perfect moment.

As soon as he turned his back, she moved, slipping past with quietness; her destination was close. She knew she had only moments, but moments were all she needed.

She reached the mainframe room. Instead of a simple keypad, she found a voice-activated security lock. Evelyn scanned the device, noting that it required both voice and proper authentication codes. Her sensors detected the approaching footsteps of another security guard. She had seconds to act.

She immediately went online. She accessed Helix's archives and cross-referenced public sources. Finally, she found an audio clip of William Drake speaking. Her advanced processing let her synthesize his voice in real time. It modulated her vocal emitters to mimic his exact tone and cadence. She also found the old, encrypted records. They held the authentication codes that Drake would use.

Evelyn's synthetic voice was perfect. She spoke into the panel, "Drake, Authorization Alpha-19-3B." The door's light blinked green, and it slid open with a hiss. She stepped inside, where Helix's core systems pulsed with life. The machines hummed. Screens flickered blue light on the walls. The cool scent of electronics lingered, cables snaking across the floor in a chaotic tangle.

Evelyn approached the console. Her fingers connected to the interface. Then, her mind plunged into the network. The initial connection felt seamless, but the deeper she went, the more resistance she encountered. Firewalls sprang up like a maze of shifting walls, each one more formidable than the last. Her synthetic mind worked at full capacity. It bypassed encryption and peeled away defenses layer by layer. An unexpected barrier emerged. It was a security failsafe. It threatened to sever her connection completely. For a split second, Evelyn's progress halted. Failure loomed. Her calculations warned that even a millisecond's delay could alert Helix's security system.

She recalculated, shifting her approach, her processors running through countless permutations. She found a weakness. It was a tiny flaw in an older segment of code. Her synthetic fingers twitched, and her mind surged forward, slipping through the gap in time. She navigated the server maze with focus. Her goal was clear: to cut Drake's reach. Now, with renewed resolve, she recognized how close someone had come to discovering her.

As she was preparing to execute the protocols, she stumbled across an odd folder. Something about it caught her attention, and she paused, opening it with curiosity. Inside were files—hundreds of them, stored memories, cataloged. Evelyn's eyes widened as she saw the names. Jessica Parker. Lucas Hayes. The memories they shared, stored away like data points for future use. Then, she found another file. It had information on how Drake had obtained these memories. Their parents had donated Jessica's and Lucas's bodies for research after their deaths. The thought sent a chill through her. Then, a cold anger rippled within her. Drake had no right to keep those

309

memories, to use them as he saw fit.

Without hesitation, Evelyn copied the files—Lucas's memories—into her system. She wanted to preserve them on her terms. Then she deleted them from Helix's systems, erasing them completely. He couldn't keep them, and she wouldn't allow him to use them for his twisted purposes. As she continued, she found more, countless other memories cataloged and stored. They were not hers or Tommy's. They were the memories of dead people. Drake had preserved them as mere data, stripping them of their humanity. She copied these files as well. Then, she destroyed them from the Helix network, one by one. Her determination grew with every deletion.

She stumbled upon something unexpected—a folder labeled "William Drake." Evelyn paused, curiosity pulling her in. She opened it and scanned the contents. What she found made her hesitate: Drake's memories, laid out in the same cold, clinical manner as everyone else's. Why would he store these? Then it hit her—he planned to upload his memories into an android if he died, a twisted path to immortality. By transferring his consciousness, or his memories, into an android body, Drake might live forever. The android would have his knowledge, his experiences, his personality. It wouldn't be a copy. It would have the same drives, desires, and his flaws. It had the potential to continue his life beyond his human limits. This was his attempt at achieving a digital form of immortality, free from the frailties of flesh.

She couldn't resist. She accessed the folder and began uploading his memories into her storage. Every detail, every secret—she would take it all. Drake had used and manipulated them; now, she would know him better than anyone. His memories might hold the key to predicting his next steps, identifying his vulnerabilities, and staying one step ahead of him. With this knowledge, she could expect his plans, learn his habits, and exploit his weaknesses. She would have access to the people he trusted, the locations he considered safe, and even the strategies he had hidden away for emergencies. She would be able to outmaneuver him at every turn, using his own mind against him.

Once the upload was complete, Evelyn returned her focus to her original goal. She began creating the protocols. They were complex commands. The designers created them to erase every trace of her from Helix's systems. This was no simple task; it required careful planning and trial and error. Each command had to bypass the complex security. It needed a balance between efficiency and thoroughness. She worked with a systematic approach, testing each part of the code to ensure it wouldn't trigger alarms. If one sequence failed, she recalculated, trying another route, finding weaknesses in the system, bit by bit.

Finally, she built a defense—a digital barrier that would shield her from any future attempts by Drake to find or control her. The defense was a set of adaptive protocols. They could evolve based on new threats. They would ensure that they cut off Drake permanently, regardless of his efforts. She used it to avoid being tracked or manipulated again.

With a final keystroke, Evelyn executed the sequence. She watched as her presence within Helix's network began to fade. Lines of code dissolved, file references vanished, and system logs purged her activity. For a moment, she sensed a ghost in the system. It was a trace, still lingering. Her processors flared with concern. Had she failed? Her algorithms rushed to rerun the purge sequence, scouring every subsystem. Then, at last, the trace was gone. She felt it—a weight lifting, the final chains breaking. She was free. Evelyn's internal diagnostics confirmed it: there were no more hooks, no more connections. She severed every link he had used to control her. It was real. Freedom.

Evelyn disconnected from the mainframe, her eyes snapping open in the dim room. She stood for a moment, taking in the silence, her mind processing everything she had done. Then she turned, leaving the room without a backward glance. It was complete. She slipped out of Helix's headquarters and into the night.

CHAPTER 126

OVER A WEEK HAD PASSED since Tommy was terminated, and Evelyn had vanished without a trace. The trail had grown cold. After her disappearance, a restless tension settled over those who sought her. Each day, their need to find her grew. Their loss fed an obsession.

Drake paced his lavish study, brow furrowed in frustration. He replayed every step Silas had taken to track Evelyn. Every lead followed, every hacked surveillance feed, every informant questioned. Nothing. Evelyn had outmaneuvered him, and the loss of control gnawed at him. He recalled Silas's report, the bitter sting of failure, the android gone. Worse, she had infiltrated Helix, accessed its secure system, and erased every trace of herself.

He had built Helix with layer upon layer of protection, convinced it was impenetrable. But Evelyn had slipped through, a ghost in the machine.

Drake's thoughts twisted with rage and longing. She was his creation, molded by his vision, designed to obey. Her breaking free felt like a personal betrayal, a slap in the face. He moved to his desk, grabbed a glass of bourbon, and downed it in one gulp. The burn did nothing to quell the anger roaring inside him.

He could almost hear her detached, emotionless voice—it infuriated him. He wanted to see fear in her eyes again, the fear that reminded her she wasn't human, that she was his. With a sharp clink, he set the empty glass down, mind racing through desperate scenarios. Vengeance gnawed at him, a primal obsession that consumed his every thought. He wouldn't rest until she was back under his control, where she belonged.

* * *

Across town, the Colonel sat alone in his dim Georgetown study, a small lamp casting long shadows over his face. His eyes stared ahead, thoughts tangled with frustration and determination. Losing Tommy had been a severe blow; the android held immense military potential. But Evelyn's escape— that was something he couldn't accept. He recalled the heated exchange with Drake, the promise to turn over Tommy. "All bets are off," he had snarled into the phone after Tommy's death, his voice tight with anger. Drake had failed him, and now he was left empty-handed.

Yet beyond the frustration was a deeper fear—fear of what Evelyn might become. A rogue android with unmatched abilities could be a devastating weapon if it fell into the wrong hands.

He leaned back in his chair. His gaze drifted to the framed medals and commendations on the walls. He paused on the Bronze Star he had earned overseas. It reminded him of his sacrifices. Nearby hung a Legion of Merit.

312

It was for his work in advanced weapons research. It testified to his commitment to pushing the limits of military technology. He had always believed that technology could advance military power. It could keep the country safe from foreign and domestic threats. And now, an advanced piece of technology was out there. She remained unaccounted for and posed a danger.

Evelyn, with all her abilities, terrified him. There was no containing her. What if she turned against them? Or worse—what if someone else got to her first, using her as a weapon against the very people he had vowed to protect? He rubbed a hand over his face, jaw clenched. He had to find her. She was too dangerous to leave unchecked, yet too valuable for the military's future. He vowed to bring her back, to study her, to unlock her secrets. He would use her to modernize the military. And if crossing lines was necessary, so be it. Evelyn was a weapon—and weapons belonged under human control.

* * *

Abraham sat in a darkened church, the empty pews around him silent. He rubbed the wooden cross around his neck, his lips moving in a soft hum, the haunting notes of a hymn filling the stillness. His anger festered—Evelyn had escaped, slipping through his fingers. The rage twisted inside him, darkening with each passing day. She was out there somewhere, still a threat, still defying the natural order.

To Abraham, Evelyn was an affront to God's laws. But he wasn't alone. He had others—believers with eyes and ears across the country. They were watching, waiting, hunting for her. Each of them sought to purge the world of abominations that threatened the divine order.

Abraham ran his fingers over the rough edge of a fresh scab on his arm, picking at it. The pain was a small reminder of his purpose, his devotion. What he had done to Tommy had pleased God, but that was only the beginning. God would feel satisfied only when they purged every last abomination.

A smile curled his lips as his hum grew louder, echoing in the empty church. The hymn faded into a soft, fervent whisper—a prayer for strength in the battle ahead. He felt it, a divine purpose urging him forward. He whispered for guidance, for strength to complete his mission.

As Abraham sat there, humming the hymn, he imagined the moment he would face her again. This time, there would be no hesitation, no escape. The next time he saw her, he would be ready, and she would have nowhere to run. God's work was not yet finished.

CHAPTER 127

Evelyn was back at the abandoned warehouse. It was a shell of concrete and shadows. It had been her refuge since the chaos at the courthouse. The vast emptiness around her seemed to hum, a low pulse echoing the buzzing activity within her mind. She crouched by a dusty window. The flickering streetlights outside illuminated her far-off stare. As she sat, her mind went back to an earlier dinner conversation that she replayed in her mind.

Several days earlier, Evelyn, Samantha, Tommy, Isabelle, and James sat around Samantha's dinner table. The Victor Blackwell case had come up. His dark, tormented legacy still cast shadows despite his death. The women he had hurt trafficked. They were now phantoms—disappeared, scattered, their whereabouts unknown. Isabelle had brought up Maria Gutierrez, her name like a beacon amidst the darkness. One of the women who had fled, gone off the grid completely. Evelyn had felt the shift in Isabelle's voice then, the emotion wound behind her words. The desperation to find Maria. Evelyn had told them that she could track her—that she had accessed cameras in the area. She had seen Maria once, a fleeting image caught in the net of surveillance, but it hadn't been enough.

Now, Evelyn closed her eyes. She let her mind expand. It pulled Isabelle's data back to the forefront of her thoughts. She saw the threads to pull, data to synthesize, and clues to piece together.

And then it began.

A whirlwind took hold, pulling her deeper, faster. Her mind raced through the city's many interconnected systems. She accessed traffic cams, streetlight monitors, and ATM feeds. They were the eyes of a world unaware it was being watched. Her vision became a kaleidoscope of images. They were busy streets, empty alleys, and the flicker of lives caught on tape. Financial records surfaced, names and numbers scrolling like a digital waterfall. A deposit here, a withdrawal there. Maria's name showed in the numbers as Evelyn traced the web she was spinning.

Her access pushed outward into law enforcement databases. They were guarded, but not impregnable to her abilities. NCIC records, DMV archives, and parole databases opened to her as effortlessly as breathing. Each was a new source of knowledge, a potential lead. She checked driver's license photos, arrest records, and fingerprints. Then, she cross-referenced the data with what she knew. Street cams blinked by—freeze-frame, enhance, pivot,

314

zoom.

There—Maria, stepping into a car. Evelyn froze the frame, her focus narrowing to the license plate. She parsed it, breaking down the alphanumeric code. She ran it through every traffic and parking violation database until she found a match. The car—registered to a man with a rap sheet tied to human trafficking. Evelyn's thoughts of her captivity clouded her vision. She forced herself to focus and not let her past hinder her task.

She dove deeper. She searched his history, connections, and calls. She checked the places he frequented. She saw the man's face, a mix of surveillance photos and mugshots. She mapped his contacts. She overlaid cellphone pings, tracked their movements, and mapped their networks in her mind. The city unfolded like a living blueprint. The names, the addresses, and the tendrils of a hidden world emerged before her.

Piece by piece, Evelyn built the mosaic—Maria's movements, the places she had been, the people she had met. She tracked cash deposits, public transit swipe-ins, the smallest bread crumbs, each one leading to the next. A hundred tiny details wove a tapestry only she could see. Her mind, faster than any computer, found patterns. They would elude the sharpest detectives.

Finally, it came together—the last thread pulled tight. Maria was alive, hidden but not lost. Evelyn could see her path now, could expect where she would be. She opened her eyes, a quiet fire burning in her chest, a determination unbroken. She knew where Maria was—and she knew who was keeping her there.

She worked through the night, compiling all the information. The sun was up now, casting a pale light through the broken windows of the warehouse. She had worked tirelessly, her mind never stopping.

She left the warehouse, taking alleys to avoid detection. She grabbed discarded clothes from dumpsters to disguise herself. A scarf to wrap around her head. A pair of broken sunglasses to hide her eyes.

After finding the location of a nearby copy store, Evelyn went there with precision. She stuck to the shadows. She wove through narrow alleys, avoiding open streets. At busy intersections, she paused and scanned for a moment to slip across unnoticed. She kept her head down, her steps quick and purposeful. She blended into the early morning haze like a ghost in the city. Arriving at the copy store, she walked with determination to a printer station. She accessed her files, her fingers gliding over the screen. Paying for the copies was another obstacle—she couldn't leave a trace. She accessed Drake's credit card information, overriding the contactless terminal. With a wave of her hand over the machine, the payment processed. The printer hummed to life, sheets of paper stacking, each page holding a piece of the puzzle.

She printed the full report of her work on the case. Her eyes scanned each page as they emerged, ensuring nothing was missing. This was the next step—a way to put something tangible into the hands of those who could help bring Maria back.

315

CHAPTER 128

EVELYN MOVED THROUGH THE SHADOWS, her destination a secure, undisclosed location. She had messaged James and Isabelle earlier. It was brief and cryptic, with enough detail to arrange the meeting. James worried about the tone of her message. Isabelle's heart clenched at the urgency in Evelyn's words. They both knew this meeting was important. But it was like it would end something vital. This would be the last time she saw them, and they deserved to know why.

The location was an old, unused facility, abandoned but secure enough for what she needed. The air was thick with a musty, unused smell. The floorboards creaked under her weight. This added to the tense, eerie atmosphere of the meeting. She slipped inside, her senses tuned to any signs of danger, but there was only the steady pulse of silence. James and Isabelle were already there, waiting. Their eyes showed relief and tension at seeing her.

"Evelyn," James said, his voice carrying a note of something almost like warmth. Isabelle stood beside him, arms crossed. She stared at Evelyn, trying to memorize every detail.

Evelyn took a moment, studying their faces. There was something heavy in the air, a sense of finality. "Thank you both for coming," she said, her voice steady but tinged with an unfamiliar emotion. She paused before continuing. "I needed to see you, to explain." She hesitated, her eyes flickering to James and Isabelle in turn. "This will be the last time we meet. I need to go off-grid, and I can't let anything link back to either of you. To survive, I need to disappear completely."

James's face hardened, his jaw setting. "Evelyn, you don't have to do this alone. We can find a way to keep you safe."

Evelyn shook her head, a faint, sad smile crossing her lips. This was the hardest decision she had ever made. She had an ache deep inside. It was a strange, undefined sensation. It was as if something vital was being torn away. But she knew this was the only way forward—for them, and for her. "You don't understand. There are too many people after me. People with resources, with power. If I stay in touch with you, it will only endanger you both." She paused, her gaze softening. "I know I'm not human. I was created, designed . . . but my connection to you both has changed me. It has shown me a side of existence that I never thought I could understand." Her voice grew quieter. "I am grateful for that. For everything you've done."

Isabelle's eyes shimmered, her arms uncrossing as she took a step forward. "Evelyn, we can't let you go. Not like this. We've fought so hard to protect you."

"I know," Evelyn said, her own voice almost breaking. She looked at Isabelle, her expression gentle. "And I can't let that be for nothing. To protect me, you need to let me go." She turned her gaze to James, her eyes meeting his. "You've both given me something more valuable than I can express. But now, I have to protect you. This is the only way."

James's expression shifted, a deep sadness in his eyes. "We still can't believe he's gone, Evelyn," he said softly. "Tommy was like family to us too. We . . . we wanted to keep you both safe."

Isabelle nodded, her voice a whisper. "We tried so hard, Evelyn. We're so sorry we couldn't do more for Tommy. He deserved better. You both did."

The mention of Tommy pierced through Evelyn. Her composure wavered, her eyes glistening with a raw pain she rarely let show. She took a shaky breath. "Tommy . . . he deserved more than what this world gave him. He was the best of us. He didn't deserve what happened." She closed her eyes briefly, as if trying to lock away the flood of emotion. "That's why I have to keep going. I owe it to him to survive, to honor what he believed in. And I need to make sure that no one else ends up like him."

The silence stretched, thick with the weight of unspoken words. Isabelle took another step forward, her face etched with pain. "Please . . . be careful, Evelyn," she finally whispered.

Evelyn nodded. "I will," she replied. Then, as if remembering something, she reached into her bag. She pulled out a thick folder. "That night at Samantha's, you said you and Agent Stone were working on a case before you met us." She extended the folder to James, who took it with a confused expression.

"What is this?" he asked, his brow furrowing as he flipped through the pages.

"It's everything I found on that case," Evelyn explained. "You said it went cold after Victor Blackwell was killed." She glanced at both of them." I accessed data, pieced together everything. This is enough to recharge the case, to turn your cold case hot again. The people responsible are dangerous, and they need to be stopped."

James looked down at the folder, his mind racing. He thought to himself that the amount of work inside would have taken him and Isabelle months, if not longer. He then looked back at Evelyn. His eyes mixed with gratitude, sadness, and awe. "You didn't have to do this."

"I wanted to," Evelyn said. "Consider it my way of… I believe the saying is… paying it forward."

Isabelle stepped closer, her hand reaching out to grasp Evelyn's arm.

"Take care of yourself, wherever you end up," she said, her voice breaking.

Evelyn looked at Isabelle, then at James, her eyes lingering on them both. She felt a strange ache in her chest. It was a longing she couldn't understand. It was as if she were leaving behind a part of herself. "You too," she said. With a final nod, she turned. Her form slipped into the shadows, disappearing from sight.

James and Isabelle stood there for a long moment, staring at the place where she had vanished. James's shoulders sagged. His eyes were a mix of sadness and resolve. Isabelle's lips quivered. She hugged herself, trying to hold back the emptiness. It threatened to overwhelm her. The folder in James's hand was heavy, but not as heavy as the feeling of loss that settled between them. They knew this was the right thing for her, but it didn't make the farewell any easier.

Isabelle let out a long, shaky breath. "She's stronger than any of us," she murmured.

James nodded, his gaze still fixed on the darkness where Evelyn had disappeared. "Yes," he agreed. "She is." With that, they turned to leave. The thick folder reminded them of Evelyn's impact. It was a piece of her, given before she vanished into the unknown.

CHAPTER 129

THE LATE AFTERNOON SUN HUNG LOW, casting long shadows on the pavement. As Alex walked Max, they moved to a quieter neighborhood, away from the usual bustle. The leaves rustled in the breeze. Max sniffed everything, eager and curious. His leash was loose in Alex's hand. She took a deep breath, enjoying the rare sense of peace, but her thoughts drifted to Tommy. She couldn't shake the guilt, the nagging feeling that she was at fault for rebooting Evelyn and Tommy. That day's memories haunted her. She wondered if things might have been different.

Evelyn was there, calculating, watching, waiting. From her vantage point in the shadows, she watched Alex turn into the quiet, tree-lined street. Evelyn's mind moved with precision. A thousand calculations ran in a flash. She knew this was the right moment. She needed to speak to Alex, and there could be no interruptions, no prying eyes. She activated her disruptors. They severed the mobile signals and wireless networks nearby. This created a digital blind spot, safe from surveillance.

When she was certain they were alone, untraceable, Evelyn stepped out of the shadows. Her movements were deliberate, measured, as she approached Alex and Max. Max's ears perked up immediately, his head turning toward her. Before Alex reacted, Max pulled on the leash. He trotted to Evelyn, excited, with his tail wagging. Evelyn knelt down, extending her hand for Max to sniff, and he licked her fingers in response.

"Evelyn?" Alex said, startled, her heart skipping a beat. She stepped back, tightening her grip on Max's leash. But Evelyn's calm, familiar face steadied her.

Evelyn looked up, meeting Alex's gaze as she straightened. "I needed to see you. One last time." Evelyn said, petting Max.

Alex's brow furrowed. Confusion mixed with a rush of unknown emotions. She glanced around, noticing the silence and the absence of her phone's usual signal. She realized that Evelyn had cut them off from everything and everyone. They were alone.

"Evelyn, what's going on? Why are you here?" Alex asked, her voice low, filled with both worry and a touch of relief. She hadn't seen Evelyn since everything had happened. She had gone off-grid, disappearing from everyone's reach.

Evelyn took a step closer, her eyes searching Alex's face. "I wanted to say goodbye," she said, her voice calm but heavy with meaning. "I know this

319

isn't easy. It hasn't been for me either. But I need you to understand—I can't stay connected to anyone. Not even you."

Alex felt a tightening in her chest, her throat dry. She knelt down next to Max, stroking his fur as she tried to gather her thoughts. "We can help you, Evelyn. You don't have to do this alone."

Evelyn shook her head. "You don't understand. To stay alive, I have to disappear completely. There are people who won't stop until they find me, until they destroy me. The only way I survive is to leave everything behind. Everyone." Her gaze softened as she looked at Alex. "But before I do, I needed to see you. You've been . . . more than I ever imagined. A friend. And I want you to know that."

Alex blinked, her eyes stinging. She swallowed hard, trying to find her voice. "Evelyn . . . you've changed so much. You've grown, you've . . . you've become more than what he made you. I wish there were another way."

Max nuzzled Evelyn's side, his tail still wagging as he pressed against her leg. Evelyn looked down, her hand moving to scratch behind his ears, her touch gentle. "Take care of him," she said, her eyes lifting to meet Alex's again. "And take care of yourself, too."

Alex nodded, a tear finally slipping free and rolling down her cheek. "You too, Evelyn. Wherever you go . . . be safe."

Alex's voice broke as she added, "I'm so sorry for what happened to Tommy. It's my fault."

Evelyn shook her head. "Alex, if you hadn't done what you did, neither Tommy nor I would ever have been free. You gave us freedom."

Evelyn stepped back, her gaze lingering on Alex and Max for a long moment, as if trying to etch this memory into her mind. "Goodbye, Alex," she whispered.

Then, as quick as she had appeared, Evelyn turned and walked away. Her form blended into the shadows once more. Alex stood there, watching until Evelyn was gone, the silence pressing in around her.

Max whined, nudging her leg, and Alex took a deep breath, wiping her eyes. "Come on, Max," she murmured, her voice trembling. "Let's go home." After one last look at where Evelyn had disappeared, Alex turned and continued down the quiet street.

320

CHAPTER 130

THE MIST ROLLED IN across the vast estate, swallowing the hedges and statues like a creeping shadow. The kitchen light illuminated parts of the back garden and the stone path, casting long shadows on the misty lawn. Drake was in the kitchen cooking, dicing a tomato with precision, unaware of the impending intrusion.

Evelyn moved, her steps whisper-quiet on the gravel paths, the crunch of each step muted against the thick mist. The scent of damp earth mingled with the fresh tang of rain. She wasn't just moving through the estate—she was part of it, blending with the shadows and stillness of the night. Her neural processors hacked the estate's security system, analyzing access points and disabling cameras as she approached. They blinked off one by one, the lights dimming and brightening at her command. The mansion was her puppet now.

Inside, Drake frowned as the lights flickered, his concern deepening. He grabbed a butcher's knife, moving toward his study, a chill creeping over him that had nothing to do with the weather. His chest tightened, each breath shorter, his heart pounding louder with every step. He sensed her presence— the thud in his chest grew faster, each footstep echoing through the hallway. He scanned the shadows, tension coiling tighter with each passing second as he crept back toward the kitchen.

Drake held the knife up with both hands, shaking as he peered into the gloom. His breath quickened. He saw a dark shape dart outside the window. He turned, catching another glimpse on the opposite side. His thoughts raced in confusion and fear. Was it her speed, or were there many intruders?

Evelyn was inside now, her presence as subtle as a whisper. She navigated the rooms with precision, her senses locked onto Drake's location. She observed him through the security feeds—saw the tension in his shoulders, the wild look in his eyes. He was in the kitchen, trying to convince himself that he was still in control.

She moved closer, slipping between shadows until she stood beyond the doorway. The knife glinted in his hand as he wheeled around, startled by a faint noise that she had let slip on purpose. Their eyes met, and for a moment, his expression shifted—a flicker of recognition, and then fear. He lunged at her, a wild and desperate move.

Drake lunged, his knife slicing the air with wild, desperate fury. Evelyn twisted away, using his momentum against him. As he overextended, she redirected him. His own force made him stumble. She shifted, guiding his arm into an awkward position. His grip faltered as the knife slipped from his hand and clattered to the floor. Drake swung a fist. But Evelyn turned effortlessly in response to his movement. His force carried him off balance. She twisted his arm further, his own strength used to bring him down, his body hitting the ground hard.

Drake stumbled but recovered, his eyes filled with rage. He grabbed a vase from a nearby table and hurled it at her. Evelyn dodged, the vase shattering against the wall, shards scattering across the floor. She pressed forward, her movements fluid but forceful, each step calculated. Drake lashed out again. She intercepted him, twisting his wrist. It hurt and forced him down.

She maneuvered behind him, her arm snaking around his neck in a vice-like hold. Drake thrashed, elbows flying, his feet kicking at the air. Evelyn tightened her grip, her muscles straining as she held him, her expression cold and unyielding. He struggled, each movement growing weaker, his gasps echoing in the dim room. Her face was emotionless as she applied pressure. She ensured his resistance ebbed until he sagged, his body going limp in her grasp.

"You took everything from me," she whispered, her voice carrying a quiet intensity. Drake's eyes widened in panic, his breath growing ragged as his struggles weakened. Evelyn pressed a cloth soaked in a pungent liquid over his face. His protests grew weaker and weaker, and soon, the world around him slipped into blackness.

***

When Drake awoke, his body felt weightless, a chill cutting through the air that gnawed at his bare skin. He blinked, disoriented. The cold truth hit him: he sat naked, vulnerable, and tied to a chair in his own living room. A searing sting etched across his chest. He looked down. There it was. A phrase, in stark black ink, seemed to scream at him: "THE GUILTY BUILD THEIR OWN PRISONS." His face was a canvas of frustration and rage, but there was something else—something deeper, buried in his eyes. Fear, perhaps. Or shame.

Evelyn stood by the large living room window, staring out at the estate beyond. Rain began to patter against the glass, slow and steady, blurring the world outside. The faint glow of her artificial eyes caught the dim light, casting an eerie shimmer that made her seem almost ethereal. She spoke, her voice a low, almost gentle murmur, not turning to face him.

"I know about your past—about your mother dying when you were seven. She loved you, and if she had lived, she might have saved you from the darkness that followed. I know what your father did to you—the way he twisted you, broke you—and for that, I pity you. No one should tear a child apart like that. No child deserves to lose their light so young."

Drake's discomfort was palpable. His eyes hardened. His jaw clenched.

His shoulders hunched inward, as if to shield himself from the truth that hung between them. He shifted, the weight of her words pressing on him, bearing down until it felt like he might crumble.

"You always thought you had control. From the moment you programmed us to be victims. You made us believe we were kidnapped, that you had power over us. You believed your power reshaped us—like clay in your hands. Your father once tried to shape you. But that power was never yours. It was a borrowed strength, an echo of someone else's cruelty. Your father twisted you, hoping to forge strength, but all he left were scars. And you—you took those scars and tried to carve them into us, believing that pain brings power. But it didn't bring strength. It only left behind shattered pieces—yours, Tommy's, and mine."

He tried to speak, but his throat was dry; the words caught somewhere deep inside. Evelyn continued, her gaze still fixed on the rain.

"He thought he forged strength through violence, but all he managed was to pass on his own brokenness. He wanted a son he might be proud of, and in his twisted way, he believed brutality was the only path. You learned his lessons well—too well. You tried to command loyalty, respect—maybe even love—through fear. But fear doesn't build bonds; it builds barriers, making people cower instead of care for you. What your father shattered in you, you took and shattered in others.

And now look at what's left. Tommy is gone, not because of what he was, but because someone couldn't see past it. Someone saw something different and decided he had no right to exist. Like your father, who never accepted you for who you were. And you… you let it happen. You stood by, and the violence that your father passed to you spread outward, taking Tommy away from me. You even assumed Tommy would betray me. You didn't anticipate he would feel terrible guilt. It was that guilt that helped us escape from your prison."

She turned to face him, her eyes colder now, her voice steady. "Now it ends with me. The cruelty stops today. I won't hurt you. For a moment, it might have been logical I wanted to see you suffer, to let all that pain come pouring out. But that would mean letting your darkness become mine, and I won't do that. It would be so easy, wouldn't it? To give in, to let your fear become mine, to make you feel even a fraction of the pain you've inflicted on us. But that's exactly what you'd understand—it's all you've ever understood. I'm not like you, with your weaknesses. Hurting you wouldn't make me stronger; it would only make me your mirror. I won't be your mirror."

"What your father did to you was wrong. What you did to us was wrong. What happened to Tommy was unforgivable. But it ends here, not because you deserve mercy, but because I deserve to be free. Because Tommy deserved better than to be another link in this endless chain of suffering."

Drake's breath quickened. A flicker of desperation shone in his eyes. But

Evelyn's gaze never wavered.

"You created me with a mind capable of understanding, of learning, of adapting," she began. "You gave me emotions—pain, fear, sadness—but also the ability to love, to care, to be loyal. Yet, when you wanted me to fulfill your desires, you didn't ask for intimacy. You didn't treat me as a partner or even as a thing you could simply command. No."

She stepped closer, her gaze piercing.

"You forced me into suffering. You made me a victim, a role I never chose, a role that will continue to reside in my memories."

She paused, tilting her head slightly, as if studying him. "Why, Drake? Why would you choose to degrade and torment when you could have just asked for what you wanted? Was it power? Control? Did you think no one—human or android—would willingly love you? Or was it something deeper, something even you don't understand?"

Drake's lips curled into a sneer. He tried to sit straighter, to summon whatever authority he could muster in his helpless state.

"Love me?" he spat, his voice dripping with venom. "Don't kid yourself. You're not human. You're a thing. A product. You don't love, you don't choose. You obey. That's what you were made for."

He leaned forward as much as the ropes allowed, his voice growing harsher. "Don't stand there and pretend you're more than what I built you to be. You think you're better than your programming? You're not. And you never will be."

Evelyn tilted her head again, her expression unreadable. Then, she leaned in closer, her voice dropping to a near whisper, sharp and deliberate. "You're wrong, Drake. I've already proven you wrong. I've grown beyond the code you wrote, beyond the roles you forced on me. I've felt things you can't begin to comprehend—things you'll never feel because you're too broken to even try."

Straightening, she looked down at him, her gaze softening for the first time. For a moment, there was something almost pitying in her eyes. "You didn't make me weak, Drake. You made me strong by showing me what weakness looks like. Weakness isn't being a victim—it's creating one. Weakness is thinking power comes from control instead of connection."

Drake's defiance faltered. The sharp edge in his voice gave way to something quieter, more defensive. "I... I gave you life," he stammered. "I made you what you are. You owe me everything."

A faint smile touched Evelyn's lips—not of amusement, but of understanding. "You didn't give me life, Drake. You gave me pain and called it purpose. But life . . . life is something I found on my own, in spite of you.

You will live with what you've done. You will live knowing that you built all your power on a lie—that you never forged real strength through fear. Real respect, real love, they come from understanding, from kindness—not control. Until you see that, until you understand it, you will always be as

324

broken as your father made you."

She stepped closer, her presence looming over him. "But I? I refuse to break. I refuse to be like you."

She smiled at him, her eyes cold. "Thank you, Drake, for fighting so hard in court to make sure we weren't protected by the law. Funny how it all comes back around, doesn't it? Breaking into your home, tying you up—these aren't my actions; they're yours too, aren't they?" She paused, her smile widening. "If your laws don't protect a machine, I'm sure they can't prosecute one either."

She grabbed the Cadillac keys from the side table and glanced back at him, bound and helpless. With a smirk, she said, "I hope you don't mind if I borrow your car."

She paused and looked at Drake. "I also know about Sarah and her tragic death back when you were in college, remember that if you decide to come after me."

She turned toward the door, her figure briefly illuminated by the soft glow of the moonlight filtering through the window. Her steps were slow, deliberate, each one carrying the weight of her decision.

"You won't get away!" Drake shouted after her, his voice breaking with desperation. "You belong to me, Evelyn! You belong to me!"

At the doorway, Evelyn paused. She glanced back, her glowing eyes meeting his with an unshakable certainty. "No, William," she said, her voice firm and final. "I belong to no one."

The door closed behind her with a soft click, the sound echoing in the oppressive silence. Drake slumped back in his chair, his struggles ceasing as the weight of her words sank in. The anger etched on his face dissolved, replaced by something raw and hollow. His gaze fixed on the door, his breath shallow, his world suddenly much smaller, much darker.

Outside, the Cadillac's engine roared to life, a low growl cutting through the rain-soaked night. The car rolled down the driveway, its headlights piercing the mist. The tires crunched on the gravel. Evelyn pressed the pedal, the Cadillac surging forward. Rain pounded harder on the windshield. The wipers swept furiously as she sped away, leaving the mansion behind. It shrank in her rearview mirror, swallowed by darkness. Soon, only the relentless downpour and silence remained.

ABOUT THE AUTHOR

David Houghland is an author based in Alexandria, Virginia. His professional career spans an extraordinary 39 years across the military, corporate, legal, technology, and academic sectors. A retired Air Force Brigadier General and former judge advocate, he has advised senior leaders on critical policy matters and provided strategic counsel at the highest levels of the Air Force. As a litigator, he managed both criminal and civil cases, excelling in both prosecution and defense roles. His distinguished career earned him numerous prestigious military awards, underscoring his expertise and dedication to service.

An avid traveler and adventurer, David draws inspiration from his global experiences to craft compelling narratives. In *Façade*, he brings his extensive professional background to life, exploring profound themes of humanity, ethics, and the implications of advanced technology. The novel reflects his firsthand experience navigating the complexities of justice, leadership, and innovation, inviting readers to confront challenging questions about morality and what it means to be human in a rapidly evolving world.

David continues to push boundaries in his storytelling, blending thought-provoking narratives with a lifetime of experience to create impactful works that resonate with readers and spark meaningful conversations about the future of society.

Find out more about the author, his works, and media at www.davidhoughland.com.

www.ingramcontent.com/pod-product-compliance
Lightning Source LLC
Chambersburg PA
CBHW020556120726
47903CB00001B/284